MW01147097

THE SANIA DIMENSION

THE SANIA DIMENSION

Transformation and Human Evolution

Deborah Amelia

THE SANIA DIMENSION
TRANSFORMATION AND HUMAN EVOLUTION

iUniverse books may be ordered through booksellers or by contacting:

iUniverse
1663 Liberty Drive
Bloomington, IN 47403
www.iuniverse.com
1-800-Authors (1-800-288-4677)

ISBN: 978-1-4917-9964-2 (sc)
ISBN: 978-1-4917-9965-9 (e)

Library of Congress Control Number: 2016911636

Print information available on the last page.

iUniverse rev. date: 07/21/2016

Dedication

This book is dedicated to my niece, Kristen Semon-Lynch. Her unwavering, dedicated support cannot be expressed with mere words. The hundreds of hours of phone conversations that had us laughing and crying will be impressed in my memory forever. It takes a very special soul to give as she has given to me.

Kristen is raising a special needs son who also contributed to my understanding of his world by making his presence known on several occasions in my dreams. He has been a source of guidance and direction for this book.

Kristen's husband also deserves much credit since I monopolized much his wife's time seeking support while exploring the ideas to create and record existential and metaphysical experiences brought to you in this book. I thank you nephew-in-law.

With sincere gratitude and love, I couldn't have done it without the love and support of the Lynch Family. Together we explored and created The Sania Dimension and I wish to extend to you my everlasting thanks.

CHAPTER 1

Beyond The Seven Sisters

Far into the universe is a dimension of existence called Sania, just slightly beyond The Pleiades Star Cluster. The highly evolved Light Beings that exist there know they have evolved into their existence after many incarnations of many different life forms and know their present state of being in Sania to be bliss.

Their nature is of pure vibration and energy but indeed posses individual frequencies which gives them separate identities. There is no nature of sexuality. All are one and one are all. They do not require a governing body. It is understood at their level of evolution that the need to be governed is pedestrian. They live by the laws of universal physics. It is understood that the acts of kindness or harm can only be towards themselves because all are one.

Frequently, they will visit other planes of existence. One of these places is the planet Earth. The Sanian Light Beings are responsible for inspiring, guiding, and assisting the lower level conscious beings with insight and elevated thought processes. Their inspiration may come in a form as happenstance - such as a book becoming available to someone who may need its contents; a musical melody to finish a brilliant song; enabling a subtle difference in a brush stroke to enhance or create a new form of artistry; and even inspire breakthroughs in the sciences and metaphysics. The Sanian's influence is to help inspire those on Earth who exhibit a greater than average sense of wonder and purpose and feel the frustrations of not being understood or not receiving what is needed but feel the intuitive sense that there is more.

Ava is one of the Light Beings joyfully living in Sania. She is a very highly evolved being who continues to blossom in all aspects of existence in Sania and is a delight of energy to all she meets. Ava refers to herself as female because of her many lifetimes as a female that have allowed her to experience the wonders of enlightenment albeit there is no nature of sexuality in Sania. She is one of the chosen ones to be a guiding light to inquisitive minds on the planet Earth. She enjoys her influence and takes great pride in her abilities to sweetly encourage and promote the attributes of special minds on Earth.

Because of Ava's own inquisitive nature and the many lifetimes she has used to elevate her consciousness, she was a natural in empathizing and participating in this special task of honor.

On hundreds of occasions, Ava has left her mark and proudly. Her reward is the sense of good doing which provides her with joy and pleasure. However, there was a time that she was tempted by the beauty of two people making love. Ava could not recall her mission because she was captivated by the memory of the ecstasy of that sensation. Her memories of being in a physical body and enjoying the pleasure of sex clouded her mission and she attempted to meld with the female body who was on top of her lover. While that female was enjoying her male partner in the act of love making, Ava began to meld into her and began to feel her arms and legs were that of the female. Ava delighted in the energy that began to pulsate through her limps as she began to feel the memory of her human female body once again. Before long, the male noticed her presence which caught the attention of his female partner who glanced behind also seeing Ava. Ava disappeared in shame over her discretion. She understood that her actions would be dealt with but she could not foresee how harshly. She certainly regretted her temptation and could not believe she could be so tempted. After all, there was no real good reason for her doing so. She was full of remorse for the first time in centuries!

In a non-governing reality, Ava knew exactly what she needed to do to make amends for her fall from grace. She understood fully that she would be leveled to the plane of Earth yet one more time! She would need to exist among less evolved beings retaining the knowledge of her evolution and state of existential wisdom. This was indeed going to be a frustrating existence and she could only hope that her Sanian counterparts would come to guide and assist her whenever she needed their support and love.

CHAPTER 2

Earthbound

As Ava begins to gracefully and slowly open her eyes waking from a deep sleep, she sees a lovely single swan buoyantly swimming in a delicious blue lake. She began to tell herself in her ethereal voice I AM INFINITE and I AM LIGHT from the fabric of the Universe. I AM holding my consciousness, my Being and I will bring my consciousness to Earth with me. I will remember who I really am. Ava realized she was returning to a human existence feeling the sensation of being within a field of gravity adding heaviness to her now human body. She knew that the Swam was not really there but an alchemical representation of her knowledge being used as the conduit for transforming into this new reality. In the most effortless way, the Swam spirit animal signified spiritual devotion and exudes the presence of angels. In the moment of first seeing the Swan, Ava's breath entered her body. A message from an angel was awaiting her offering the wisdom and guidance she needed at that very moment, her first moment of becoming human again. She knew to let go and just allow and know all would be well even if it didn't seem so. Her eyes fully open now and quite alert, Ava found herself in bed in her apartment and what she thought she was looking at, in reality, began to transform itself into a double wide fan secured to the bedroom window. Amazed, and somewhat dismayed, Ava now knew she was Earthbound and would begin a life of advanced intelligence and ethereal gifts among a civilization that would be difficult to navigate but she would have angelic help.

She could feel the sensation of living within a field of gravity adding heaviness to her now human body. With the feeling of texture to the air, she began experimenting by deliberately making objects fall. She got a kick out of this regardless of having to maneuver through gravity suspecting that in a short time this would become the norm. She was now observing air from the framework of a different perception. She could no longer think and be somewhere. Now she had to abide by the rules of this physical reality understanding the root assumptions that governed it. This dimension of experience and consciousness must now be a deliberate coexistence with what was her "normal" reality and she believed she could exercise her abilities to do so without jeopardizing her true identity. She knew her wisdom was with her but the "magic" would be gone.

Ava looked at her surroundings and was pleased with her one bedroom apartment. It was cozy and nicely furnished. "Well, thank God for that" she told herself. Then immediately wondered "what do I look like"? She ran to the bedroom again to the full length mirror. Immediately she smiled from ear to ear. "Well, I certainly gave myself a very attractive appearance!" She was very pleased with her height, weight, attractive features and was excited to begin showering and dressing hoping she had a high degree of fashion sense for her lovely new body. As she opened her closet doors, its contents appealed to her sense of fashion. She began touching the garments and was especially drawn to silks and chiffon. She selected a dress and brushed the fabric across her arms and torso delighting in its sensual nature across her skin. Before dressing, Ava needed to know what day it was and what year it was. Happily she turned on the television and discovered it was April 1985, a Saturday. She dressed and decided her curiosity of the neighboring outside world was beckoning her. It was a sunny day and the temperature was perfect. Ava checked the key ring on a small table next to the front door. It looked like many keys and she wondered what they unlocked. Quickly surmising one must be a car key she began to wonder what type of car she owned. Upon leaving her front porch, a nearby neighbor greeted Ava and said he left something by her car and pointed in the direction where it was parked. "Well, thank God again for that support" she said to herself. She began walking in the direction the fellow pointed and realized with glee and excitement that she would be driving a sports car! A Camero Z-28 with T-tops! Wow, I do have great taste! Positioned on top of the car was a giant Hersey's Kiss. Well, I guess this guy likes me she thought. The note on the candy Kiss said for you Ava, Robert. OK, I know his name, she sighed.

Ava unlocked the door to this beautiful vehicle and entered the driver's seat. She took a moment to look around and admire its beauty. She could not believe this was hers! Noticing a leather strap on the floor sticking out from under the passenger seat she reached down and lifted it to her lap. It was a purse! She rightfully concluded it was hers and hoped it contained forms of identification and helpful hints of who she decided she would be in her form of repentance.

Ava searched the contents of the purse and found a driver's license. Of course she murmured to herself. I can't drive without a license! The photo displayed on the ID was certainly her and she discovered her last name to be St. Claire. How fitting and clever she told herself. I've always been so fascinated with the supposed royal bloodline stemming from the Merovingians associated with the descendants of Jesus Christ and Mary Magdalene. What a clever girl I am she acknowledged! Upon further investigation she discovered she was 36 years old and lived at this address. Things were beginning to feel comfortable for Ava as she felt more grounded and more "identified". It was beginning to feel less like she fell from the sky! She laughed to herself at her amusing joke and it made her wonder what sense of humor she might have if any at all. As Ava continued to search the wallet and purse she discovered an unusual identification badge, again with her picture on it. It displayed the words Computer Enterprise, Inc. and contained a bar code of sorts. Ava could only conclude that she must have a job at this place. Before deciding to take a test run in her fabulous new sports car, she remembered there was a computer in her apartment and knew she could search this company to find more information about the company and her connection to it.

She ran up the stairs and opened the computer to begin her investigation. Her mind flashed back to her true identity and was grateful for her high degree of intelligence and insight knowing that without her "future" she would not be able to comprehend any of this supposed new existence.

She began her search and found the company with an address and a listing of high level employees with a description of the function of the organization along with a picture of what the building looked like. She was listed as the Inventory Control Manager. She quickly summoned her knowledge of parallel universes and knew that alongside her lifetime in Sania and anywhere else in the span of eternity, this was one of her realities, living alongside her many parallel lives. She was grateful for her elevated consciousness which of course was the reason she had, after all, risen to a Light Being living in Sania. The consciousness and knowledge that she achieved came along with her as she understood it would. She also understood that her repentance was to integrate into a society that was not yet at her level and therein was her challenge.

Ava told herself she was up to the task. She really had no choice. This was her decision because of her indiscretion. It did not matter whatever parallel lives she was living in, in however many parallel universes, Sania was her true home and if she did her time here with an attitude of excellence and patience, she would return. Here on Earth there was still the idea of time which she needed to deal with which led her to wonder, how fast will time go for her; how long would it take her to return home.

CHAPTER 3

Ava Explores Ava

Ava decided to give that sleek powerful engine in her sports car a spin and go exploring. It was a powerful machine with an engine that roared and gripped the roads like a tiger. At one point she decided to pull over and take the T-tops off so that the sunlight and spring breeze could be enjoyed as well. There was a radio and a cassette player. Ava was curious what kind of music she enjoyed.

Very much to her surprise, the radio dial was set to heavy metal! Really? Wow, who am I here on this planet? She figured she would listen and see what the fuss was about and why she would have selected such a rudimentary musical genre. However, as Alice Cooper screamed out the song Poison blaring through those magnificent speakers, she found herself bopping in her seat and enjoying the vibration of her physical body along with the music. Oh, I really like this, she thought to herself, wondering if she owned the cassette. Continuing on her quest to find the location of where she worked and not familiar with the area, Ava leaned toward the side of caution and decided she would look through her cassettes when she came to a stop.

She had the address of the company she supposedly worked at

and with map in hand, she began to look for the building where she was the Inventory Control Manager. She found it easily and it looked like the picture on the computer. Slightly concerned that there may be people working today, she was careful not to be seen but quickly realized the building was closed and not a single vehicle was in the parking lot. She considered it to be a well kept building with a spacious parking lot and decided Monday might be an exciting albeit scary day. Ava truly had no idea what to expect but felt an assurance of aptitude and confidence considering she still possessed the existential consciousness of the Ava from Sania. Nevertheless, she sensed the conflict within herself wondering what her coworkers' experience of her was and if there would be a significant, obvious difference in their perception of her now?

Ava would have to appear familiar but there was no way of turning back time and evolutionary progress to be exactly who she had been in 1985. This was going to be interesting, a tight rope walk so to speak. She could feel anxiety bubbling up over the prospect and began talking to herself but I am who I am. I cannot be lesser than who I am. If I appear different in my level of knowing, people would begin to wonder and certainly criticize. Wait, I know better than to be concerned with how others perceive me. More important is how I know myself to be and to be true to that. How do I integrate my learning and my true source of being when an identity has already been established of me by my "peers"? Oh heck. I'm oscillating back and forth on this issue. This is the decision I made to make amends. I knew this would be a dilemma and I must focus on seeking the guidance and support from my counterparts from Sania and especially my own inner voice. I can see I will be talking to myself a lot!

Ava quickly concluded that the physicality of her future experiences was not going to be the big issue here. It was going to be her intellectual and emotional navigation and the understanding and integration of these two aspects that would affect any physical manifestation that may come. She has discovered, and quickly, what it feels like to be human.

Ava needed to find her place of centering, a place to balance the fountain of emotions that were flowing up from her heart to her brain and causing a sensation that could be considered mild anxiety, loneliness and confusion. She decided to go back home and explore her apartment filled with the things that identified her. Somehow she instinctively knew that it would provide a sense of comfort.

As she walked into her home, she felt the peacefulness. Indeed it was comforting to be there and after a couple of hardboiled eggs, toast and tea, she sat down on the couch and looked around. Excitement began to fill her again as she began to notice her personal treasures around the house. She loved her curtains and her color scheme. Her furniture was pleasing to the eye and she began to fall in love with her surroundings. She knew without a doubt it provided a sense of refuge and solace and could predict that it would become a place of great insight and learning which would assist her in her journey.

She checked out her books; music; jewelry; art work and the special and unique way she organized things. She could tell she possessed the mind of a very logical, insightful and passionate inner explorer. She told herself, no wonder I had advanced to such a high level of consciousness. It was my purpose all along. It was my need, it was what mattered to me the most. I wonder what conflicts I dealt with in this life to evolve to being so inquisitive and dedicated to the inner and outer worlds of myself and the Universe? What experiences and responses to those experiences propelled me toward the fulfillment of my nature. How did I shape my intensities, what influenced my nature to blossom or was it simply a natural process all humans aspire to? This most certainly was not the only lifetime that led to my evolution to Sania but I felt a deep sense of knowing that this twentieth century experience was a culmination of many lifetimes toward that evolution.

Well, I still had Sunday to relax into knowing who I was supposed to be now and I would call upon my inner knowing to guide me in fulfilling that goal. That goal being integration with a level of knowing beyond those that I was to interact with allowing myself, in a sense, to go undetected.

With that Ava began to select soothing background music while seeking books from her well organized collection. Apparently she enjoyed Native American Music as well as the greats like Mozart, Beethoven and Debussy but decided on the Native American Music instinctively. She found a collection of Jane Roberts' books on Seth and started the first one, "The Nature of Personal Reality". She felt an immediate connection and recognition and was curious about her choice. As she began to read, she felt at home.

CHAPTER 4

Seth Speaks

Seth is a nonphysical entity who would speak through the author of the Seth Books, Jane Roberts while she was in a trance. Jane had no knowledge of what was being said while her husband took dictation. She was put into an altered state of consciousness and provided with ideas of how we create our personal reality through our conscious beliefs about ourselves, others, and the world. Following this is the idea that the "point of power" is in the present, not in the past of this life or any other. Seth stresses the individual's capacity for conscious action, and provides excellent exercises designed to show each person how to apply these theories to any life situation.

Ava could tell she made the right first choice of reading material. She sensed she was being guided on how to integrate into this society by not focusing on what her future had been. She would be able to set her future intellect and intuitions aside if her "point of power" was focused in the present. Well, at least it gave her hope, however, she needed to read on because she began to feel an immediate contradiction. How does one forget what they've known? Here comes that doubt again and the tightrope walk. Is it possible in this lifetime that I had little self-confidence? I find that hard to believe but it could have been a probability. Ava continued to read and read and read. Before long, she noticed it was dark outside. She had become so immersed in the Seth book that she completely lost track of time and felt an unfamiliar sensation of hunger. Before seeing what was in the kitchen to make a meal, she walked over to the window and looked up into the night sky. She nostalgically wanted to see the stars and locate the Pleiades. However, with such a narrow view and trees in the way, she could not find the Seven Sisters and her home hiding behind them. Ava decided that the next day she would locate an observatory or a viewing site where she could satisfy her desire to look at the stars. As she walked to the kitchen, the telephone rang! It startled her but it made sense that someone would have her number. After all, she just popped back into this reality which has been going on for at least 35 years. "Hello," said Robert. "Oh hi, Robert, I'm so sorry I did not thank you for the gift of chocolate! It was very thoughtful of you." He said, "I'm glad you liked it, I thought it was a perfect gift for you since you are a chocoholic" and he laughed. Ava didn't know she was one but agreed and laughed as well. He said, "Are you ready for dinner?" Ava couldn't have known she had a dinner date but told Robert, "I am almost ready. I need 10 minutes!" Ha, who knew I had a date she said to herself. Ava quickly showered and dressed looking more than presentable when the door bell rang, right on time. It was Robert. He looked very casual but presentable. "Where are we going?" She asked. "That new Italian place down on Boulevard I told you about. Let's see what they have to offer," Robert replied and then asked, "are you okay?" I told him "I am fine, why?" "Because I told you last night we were going to check out that place." "Oh, I'm sorry Robert, I guess I got caught up in stuff and I forgot." Yikes, here goes nothing I said to myself. He looked at me strangely but didn't press for any more information. Thank God. Ava had so many questions but didn't want to sound like she had suffered a head injury causing amnesia! Questions like, how long had she known this guy, what was the nature of our relationship, had they been intimate, and so on and so on. She figured she would receive clues from him. What else could she do. As they approached a white Ford pick up truck, Ava was astonished. This is what we are going out in? She quickly noticed he hadn't even opened the door for her.

The restaurant was pleasant and Italian music was playing softly from overhead speakers. They were seated quickly and Ava selected Lasagna from the menu. Orders taken, Robert immediately asked for a beer. Robert asked Ava, "Why don't you ever drink alcohol?" "I don't really know, I guess I don't like how it makes me feel" was the best answer Ava could come up with. He said, "But it is so relaxing and takes your mind away from the craziness that goes on in the world." Ava was very turned off by his response. She told him, "It certainly would never satisfy my curiosity about the world and it would inhibit actions and reactions combining direction to my conscious mind which relies upon the interpretation of the reality which my outer, physically focused self perceives." Ava immediately realized she had said too much.

Robert raised his eyebrows and said, "What the hell are you talking about?" Ava simply laughed and lied that she was yanking his chain. She took a deep breath and vowed that she was going to keep her mouth shut the rest of the evening. She hated lying!

After dinner Robert asked Ava if she would like to shoot some pool. "Yes," she said. "I love billiards" and had a brief memory of someone having taught her at an early age in this lifetime. She was excited to play again. They got back into that Ford pick up and Robert drove to what Ava would call a "dive" of a bar! Upon entering, she realized she was clearly too well dressed and refined for such a joint. Everyone had tattoos and cutoff shirts and holes in their jeans. She could do nothing but laugh to herself. Ava felt a suspicion that she was in a dangerous place but tried to keep it together. Immediately Robert ordered a beer. It had to have been his seventh of the evening. She grew concerned because he was driving and her sensibilities told her she was in the hands of a driving drunk and how could she possibly have had anything in common with this guy. She still had no idea about their relationship. In the meantime, she enjoyed a couple of games of pool and they were headed home. A quick stop for a six-pack (Oh dear) and back to my place. Ava grew concerned. She didn't know where this was going, having more concern for his feelings than her own instincts. She asked him if he wanted to go home since he looked tired but he said he was fine. Ava was not going to take this any further. She told Robert that she had a pleasant evening and that she would be able to walk herself to her door. Robert looked surprised. Ava was relieved she had the guts to speak her mind and be done with the evening. She could not understand ever having made a date with this type of man and was no longer interested in what their history was about. He looked somewhat dismayed but simply asked if I had everything packed for tomorrow. Not knowing what plans were made I decided I would simply tell him that I don't think we are right for each other. I did not want to date him any longer. He looked surprised and just left. I got the feeling that he was just too inebriated to argue.

Guilt began to overtake her emotions and it didn't feel good. She felt sorry for him but at the same time, she had her own agenda. She wondered if she was being selfish. Her inner drive was stronger however and she really wanted to shift her focus toward what made her excited and anticipated a great adventure for her Sunday. It did not stop her emotional shift to and from, however. She didn't like this feeling. She wanted to reach out to Robert and explain what her goals were but also did not want to lecture him on his frailties which would seem like judgement. She could not be sure how he would receive it. He didn't seem to have a receptive nature to this type of conversation. Besides, right now she was sure he was passed out in his bed snoring away.

Ava picked up the Seth book again, "The Nature of Personal Reality" as she prepared for bed. She felt comfortable but could not shake the disturbance going on in her emotional energy. She began questioning herself. Why was I punishing myself for someone else's personality traits that I disliked? After all, didn't I have a right to express my needs and desires and fulfill them? The emotional state that humans need to navigate is truly a labyrinth of knowing that I could foresee would take a human lifetime or possibly even more lifetimes to understand. I'd like to speed it up, however.

Ava read more of the wonderful Seth book and gradually fell into a sleep. Upon awakening, she realized the Seth book was still in her bed and she looked at the last paragraph that she had read: ***"At once" does not imply a finished state of perfection nor a cosmic situation in which all things have been done, for all things are still happening. You are still happening - both present and future selves; and your past self is still undergoing what you think is done. Moreover, it is experiencing events that you do not recall, that your linear-attuned consciousness cannot perceive on that level." (Seth: The Nature of Personal Reality, Jane Roberts copyright 1978)***

Ava realized from that last paragraph read that she was receiving extremely insightful guidance to the emotions she fell to sleep with. It made great sense to her and again began talking to herself. It only feels like I'm back in time, however, I am still living all my lives simultaneously. It is a hard concept for a human to wrap her head around but, it certainly answered the emotional conflict I was experiencing the evening before. I began to see my redemption less like a "punishment" and more like an "experiment" if I was choosing to experience linear time all at once. This ought to be interesting I suggested to myself. I felt less angst about Monday morning being at work. Well, at least for now.

CHAPTER 5

Observatory

I showered and dressed for my excursion to find an observatory yet somehow it didn't feel so pressing after reading that paragraph from Seth. I decided to stick with my original plan anyway.

After doing some research I came across the William D. McDowell Observatory located in DeKorte Park in "The Meadowlands". I called and got my driving directions and I was excited about my adventure in my Z-28.

The drive proved to be pleasant and I was taken back by the beauty of The Meadowlands, a wet marshy area filled with wildlife and tall grasses. Such an open space was quite the perfect location for an observatory, however the trees and grasslands were conscious beings and they were living alongside a congested intrastate highway creating a perpetual challenge for them. Ava conveyed her appreciation to them through her vibration and she felt they responded likewise. As I approached the visitor parking I became even more impressed and excited. I was happy that I made the right decision. The observatory contained a 20" research grade telescope right in the middle of The Meadowlands Environment Center free of charge on viewing nights, and a visit is incorporated in all learning series sessions and special events. I felt like I died and went to Heaven. Laughing to myself, I thought how silly that sounds. There was so much to see and do. I wanted to also visit the Gift Shop with the hope that I could buy a book on the constellations. I not only found a book to my liking, a geode caught my eye and I had a brief momentary flashback that I studied geology at some point. I just had to have it. I knew the perfect place I would place it in my bedroom on top of the armoire. I felt delight in my new possessions and decided to explore the grounds a little more. Beginning to feel hungry, I found a cafeteria on the premises and had something to eat. Quite expensive I thought. Going forward I would pack a lunch. I also couldn't help but notice that everyone was with someone. Either two people holding hands or a family together enjoying their experience and I felt odd. I concluded that this was a "pack" society. People seemed more comfortable being with others. No one was alone except for me. That had me wondering what was wrong with me. Why had I not felt the need for company? I concluded that I would probably find my answer soon enough.

After spending so much money at my outing, I began to think about my bank account. It never occurred to me to look. It never occurred to me to go through any financial files I might have in the apartment. What was my rent? What were my expenses? Have I filed income tax returns? All these mundane chores of a human existence that had to be addressed. Maybe I needed to head back home and check into these crucial items which would clarify my identity even more. With that, I headed to my Z-28 with observation viewing schedule, book and geode in hand.

Pulling up to the apartment complex I realized I lived in a very lovely place that was quite and beautifully kept. There were flowers planted and plenty of trees. I noticed a sign on a door that said Laundry Room. Oh, of course, laundry would need to be done. I never spotted any neighbors. Maybe everyone was out enjoying the beautiful spring air in "packs" and I wondered if I had developed friendships with any of them?

As I entered my home, that feeling of comfort and high frequency energy came over me again. It was a familiar feeling and I felt completely at peace here. It was a safe haven. I placed my packages down and hung up my jacket in the hall closet.

I began to prepare a meal and felt bothered by the idea that food was running low and I would have to attend to the mundane task of grocery shopping. Well, later in the week I suggested to myself. It reminded me that chores like laundry and cleaning would have to be done by me as well. How interfering this felt to my true mission of grabbing as much knowledge and transcendence that I instinctively knew would create joy for me.

I certainly was no longer bothered by Robert and what might be his issues or mine for that matter regarding how he would perceive my behavior towards him. It was inconsequential to me and my happiness. I was surprised by my insensitivity but I just wanted to down some nourishment and begin reading my books again, especially Seth. I had a clear focused point of attention and it had nothing to do with other's perceptions. I was hoping that would serve me well on what would be considered my "first" day at work tomorrow. Then I remembered I needed to find where I kept my financial papers to get an idea of where I stood in the monetary realm! Disappointed I could not get to Seth.

I rummaged around and found a neat file cabinet in the hall closet. I sure am organized and instinctively knew it stemmed from a desire to not have interference from my preferred goals by dealing with such mundane, rudimentary activities. I quickly recognized what appeared to be a budget that listed incoming and outgoing finances. I was living quite well. I was able to maintain a happy existence and apparently enjoyed investing and maintaining a large monetary cushion. My review of my financial documents brought relief that I was on time with all bills and nothing was pressing at this moment that would require me to postpone my evening reading. I wondered for a moment, if that could be the reason I was apparently not married or had any children or even a pet at the time. It seemed I structured a life with a specific goal or maybe I just didn't know how to integrate into the world around me in this lifetime. Who knows? It didn't seem important enough to think about. Nevertheless, I was simply happy to have time for my reading.

I snuggled up in bed in my comfy PJs and figured I would need to set the alarm for work the next morning. I had no idea when start time was but I would err on the safe side and set it for 5:00 a.m. I began insatiably soaking in my book. As always, I awoke after a delightful sleep with my Seth book next to me to the alarm going off. What an awful sound. I knew I had had a dream but was so startled by the sound of the alarm, I lost all memory of the dream. I wanted to see the last paragraph I read and possibly it would assist in remembering the dream.

"Because beliefs form reality - the structure of experience - any change in beliefs altering that structure initiates change to some extent, of course. The status quo which served a certain purpose is gone, another creative process begins. Because your private beliefs are shared with others, because there is interaction, then any determined change of direction on your part is felt by others, and they will react in their own fashion." (Seth: The Nature of Personal Reality, Jane Roberts copyright 1978)

There it was! The answer to my dilemma and anxiety of how I would handle my perceived difference in behavior, if any, at work today! I understood that change was a natural, creative process and it was natural for other's to feel that difference in their own way. Oh, I was surely beginning to suspect that I was receiving Divine Intervention through the Seth book and exactly at each moment I needed it. I sensed that my fellow beings from Sania must certainly be around and assisting!

CHAPTER 6

New Life

No more time for reflection now, I must shower, eat breakfast and prepare for my "first" day of work in this new reality. I now possessed a higher degree of confidence which kind of led me to a feeling of excitement. That was something I didn't expect to own going into work today. I understood that behavior does change based on one's experiences and it was the responsibility of the witness to that change to react however they wished, if they wished to change at all. Yes, I felt I was in charge.

I drove to work and arrived at 7:00 a.m. I found the scanning device that allowed me to swipe my ID badge and heard the click of entry. I opened the door and immediately could smell the scent of papers; office furniture; moreover, I realized I was alone. In a sense, that was a good thing. I noticed that there were name plaques on the offices and desks and I felt reassured I would know where the heck I belonged! Walking through the building which was only one level, I found my name plaque "Ava St. Claire". How gratifying that looked! I walked into my office which had a very familiar feeling of peace and tranquility. I placed my belongings down and began exploring every nook and cranny of my office. The computer looked different from the one I had at home. I found the On button and clicked it. There were piles of printouts on my desk that looked like inventory reports all well organized with labelled file folders and summaries of rebates owed Computer Enterprise by various vendors. I instinctively knew this responsibility was something I was good at because at first glance, it represented a very analytical, organized and structured mind, right up my alley. I did not have a fear of numbers and enjoyed the prospect of organizing and tracking the company's inventory. I tried to search for an annual report in my desk drawers and of course I found one. It gave me a quick review to determine its assets; and future prospect of survival. This was a healthy business and growing. I searched through the desk calendar and noticed I had an 11:00 a.m. meeting today with the V.P. of Finance along with one of our vendors from Hewlett Packard. I checked my file folder for HP and sure enough, my report was ready for discussion.

I checked to see what the computer had to offer. I discovered it was a specific program designed to track the incoming vendor orders as well as outgoing sales and provided bin locations, ID numbers and quantities of all the inventory we contained. This computer was specifically designed for this function alone. I surely was the inventory control manager.

As time neared 9:00 a.m. employees began entering the building. Some passing my office said, "Morning Ava; How was your weekend Ava [ha, they should only know], and there were those who said, 'Ugh, Monday again'. Well, of course, there would be a wide variety of individuals with all different beliefs and experiences shaping their attitudes and their realities. Apparently, one of my staff a young girl of about twenty-three arrived and said, "Why do you insist on always arriving so early to work?" I simply smiled and said, "The early bird catches the worm" and it quickly reminded me of how gross it would be to do that. Poor worms!

Next person who popped his head into my office was my boss, the VP of Finance, Paul DeMato. "Ava, our 11:00 am meeting got pushed up to 10:00 am. Can you be ready?" "Of course Paul," I stated. "No problem." I knew I had my HP folder from my earlier review and it looked perfectly ready but I opened it again and made especially sure.

Doug Rice, the Warehouse Manager now entered my office. He was a handsome guy in his early 30s, married with two children. He had an issue about some laptops not being available that should be according to inventory records. I turned to my computer and asked him for the part number; did a search and gave him the count from our last physical inventory and he agreed that's what we should have on hand. I then checked the computer for incoming orders and outgoing shipments for that part number and determined how many we should have on hand presently. Doug agreed with my findings and we both agreed that there were three missing. I quickly reminded him that there was a massive shipment on the loading dock for our Michigan location, "Please double check, never mind.

"I've got forty-five minutes until my next meeting. Let's go to the warehouse together and look." I thought maybe they are in the staging area for added value, but I secretly knew if that was the case, they would have appeared on the inventory screen as an outgoing order. Doug and I searched and could not find them. These were the first ever Compaq laptops to be made and certainly quite desirable as well as expensive. As much as I couldn't believe they would be stolen, I had a very intuitive feeling they may have been smuggled onto the massive shrunk-wrapped order bound for Michigan awaiting its trailer at the shipping dock. I had great respect for our Shipping Manager and felt a sinking feeling in my stomach. I reviewed the printout of that order attached to the pallets just to be sure that it did not contain laptops but I already knew my answer. I made my request to the Shipping Manager, that he unwrap the order. He looked at me exasperated but I also detected a hint of fear in his expression. He did as I requested, he had no choice. Doug and I lifted boxes from the sides after the shrink wrap had been removed and I said to Doug, "No need to remove all the boxes. If they're hidden, they would be located at the very center to go undetected."

I could see the Shipping Manager slumped over in the corner. He was caught! Sure enough, there were the 3 laptops. Doug looked at me in amazement and asked me "how the hell did I know?" "I just knew" I told him, not caring how I would be perceived. I went to the Controller's office and reported my findings and he said thank you, I'll deal with this. I proceeded back to my office. Doug followed me and I simply told him that now we know why monthly we are never able to reconcile the inventory. He was probably making deals with truckers who could so easily remove items in transit and re-shrink at point of destination. Doug was amazed by how I put the whole picture together for him. "You've got to believe the street value of those computers is more than pocket change for all those involved," I told him.

Ava quickly realized that she had no patience for the elementary thinking process of these individuals. She resented the stares of amazement and was annoyed by their inability to figure these things out. Ava needed to control her abilities to mesh into their vision or at the very least, control what might be her ego taking over. She continued to feel on edge about the "perspective" they would have of her, again loosing her sense of confidence that it was up to them to deal with their perceptions and not her.

She tried to remember the last paragraph of the Seth book she was reading so that she could ground herself into her surrounding environment and go undetected but the conflict popped into her head again, she could change to a higher level of consciousness and anyone who was willing to join her could change along with her if they wished. If not, their vision of her would change and the possibility of alienation would take place. Oh what a juggling act. She had to find her center and wondered what vehicle for centering she might have used for this lifetime. She seemed to possess the ability to compartmentalize many different thoughts in her mind simultaneously and questioned if all humans could do this. Anxiety began to flood her persona and she wondered if others could detect that. At this moment, she sat in her office and moved on to thoughts of her meeting. She reviewed her paperwork again and could see that she had three minutes until her meeting.

The phone rang and it was the VP's admin who said they were ready for her in Conference Room A. Recalling the plaques on the doors, Ava knew where to go.

As she entered the room the vendor from Hewlett Packard stood up and greeted Ava with a beautiful smile and extended his hand for a soft, gentle handshake. Ava reciprocated in like manner. She could sense the gentleness of this soul and a higher degree of intellect unlike those she had been dealing with. He also seemed familiar to her. They all sat down and opened their paperwork to discuss the topic at hand. She allowed the VP to facilitate the meeting and considered her presence as backup support for any inquiries he may have. He frequently looked over to her asking for confirmation of his facts and numbers to support his findings. Ava gladly and knowledgeably concurred. The meeting concluded within fifteen minutes with an agreed upon figure for rebate to Computer Enterprise and the necessary inventory required for CE's next quarter. After leaving the conference room, Ava's boss gave her a smile as if to say well done, well prepared, and Gary from HP asked Ava for a few more minutes of her time in her office. She complied.

Ava entered her office and quickly took her position of control behind her desk and noticed a look of content come over Gary's face as he entered. She smiled and Gary quickly commented how tranquil and serene her surroundings always were. He loved being in her office. She couldn't help but ask him why he felt that way. Gary stated that he could always feel an energy shift and a peacefulness when he was in her office. Ava thought to herself, I guess there was an enlightenment to me in this lifetime and wondered what existential tools I may have used to achieve that level of energy and what Gary was all about that enabled him to detect that energy.

The more time that passed the more Ava realized that she may have brought back with her the wisdom and knowledge from Sania but unfortunately and knowingly, had no memory of this lifetime.

Gary spoke in a familiar manner to her and she surmised that they must have formed a friendship but did not know to what level. After a brief discussion, Gary asked if they could lunch the following day since he was going to be in the area at another client. Ava checked her calendar and agreed with apprehension because she truly didn't know the extent of their relationship.

"Great," Gary said, "I'll meet you at the Steak House on Route 22 at Noon." Ava smiled in agreement and wished Gary a great day. It was simply 11:30 a.m. and instinctively knew she needed support in putting all this "stuff" into perspective. She decided her evening would be focused on seeking guidance and how she did this "act" when she really was living in 1985.

Before more time had passed, Ava wanted an impromptu staff meeting and asked her staff to gather in the conference room with a summary of their current projects. It was a clever way of her knowing where she herself stood regarding her daily/weekly/monthly activities and who these people were. Three young women piled into the conference room all young and all smiling. They liked Ava and she could tell they had great respect for her. What a good start she thought. Carol, a single mother of a small son, was very attractive and in her late twenties. She was well spoken but insisted on an old fashioned hair style and old fashion clothes giving a complete contradiction to her beautiful face and makeup. She worked on the reconciliation process for our biggest vendor and was stuck and needed my support. I could fully understand this. IBM was a complicated account and I would offer my assistance so I suggested that after lunch she should come into my office and we'll work on it together but in the meantime let me have a quick glance. I perused the report and quickly found Carol's dilemma. She smiled and said, "You are amazing." I smiled back and thanked her. Liz, a very young 20 year old, very short and stocky in build and very self-conscious of an excessively large bust for such a tiny girl, was working on shipment records and assisting Accounting in verifying the accuracy of their invoicing. Mina was Eastern Indian and a mature woman in her late 30s with a brilliant son who she enjoyed talking about and updating us on his accomplishments. Mina worked on receivable inventory records and had no obstacles to report. Ah, I had a great staff working and supporting me and I was grateful for their dedication. I was pleasantly surprised that they did not respond to me in a confused manner which only confirmed that my integration was easier than I had thought it would be.

The day continued with a steady stream of people in and out of my office with a mountain of questions, mostly from warehouse management and Purchasing. This I surmised was an average day in the life of Ava St. Claire. I had no objections, I felt needed, useful, accomplished and appreciated and I figured that I worked really hard and diligently at achieving this discipline. I was adept at this function and could do it with my eyes closed and one hand tied behind my back. It was not boring however, it was challenging from the perspective of juggling questions, research puzzling predicaments, and sharpening my 'detective' skills. I felt like a detective and it stimulated me. It was one giant puzzle within a puzzle that continuously fascinated me. A little like life I considered.

Before long, I could hear folks passing my office saying, "Goodnight Ava," "See you tomorrow Ava," and realized it was five o'clock and the day was over. Shipments and Receiving were closed down so I thought I'd touch base with the Warehouse Manager, Doug and see how things went. He had a good day and made some suggestions about changing locations of more recent popular inventory items to make it easier to pick and transport to the shipping area. I complimented him on the idea and agreed. We could set up a schedule for tomorrow to accomplish the task. I continued back to my office to complete the days inventory activities and did my printouts. I played with the idea of which bins would require changes suggested by Doug and what staff I could take away from normal daily tasks to achieve the project in the least amount of time and interference to the flow of the day's activities. I thought I came up with a viable plan.

I reviewed my calendar for the following day and realized I had a meeting at 10:00 a.m. with a new IBM representative that I would be meeting for the first time. Her name was Mari Starly. I also knew I had a luncheon with Gary of HP at noon. Considering a new IBM rep was coming onboard, I thought I'd gather the most recent reports to prepare for our introductory meeting and found Carol had placed the reconciliation we worked on earlier in the day in my inbox, completed and signed. I've got a very conscientious staff. I wondered if I had anything to do with that. Did I train these women to be so responsible in their performance? Did I hire these women because of something I saw in them? I didn't know. After more compilation of data for the 10:00 a.m. meeting I realized it was 7:00 PM. Yikes, I think I should call it a day. After all, it has been 12 hours of constant, nonstop interruptions, analyses and investigating. I could tell that this was a fun job and the only thorn in my side was Sales. They seemed to think they had carte blanche to the control of my inventory. "I need samples to provide potential clients" was always their excuse. "I get that but do you really need that many? When will you return them and why do you not document them with me? You are constantly throwing off my inventory levels!" They didn't care. I had to come up with a better method of controlling their uncontrollable excuses.

Upon leaving the office, Ava realized, indeed she could only be who she was. In trying to balance her two selves she would be doomed and jeopardize her human existence on so many levels. She saw in her mind's eye an excerpt from Seth's book. ***Discard those beliefs that are not bringing you those effects you want. In the meantime you will often be in the position of telling yourself that something is true in the face of physical data that seems completely contradictory. You may say, I live amid abundance and am free from want" (Seth: The Nature of Personal Reality, Jane Roberts copyright 1978)***

She thought about that snippet and realized she was living that very paragraph throughout what she considered her very successful "first" day without conscious knowledge of it. She thought the information was coming from somewhere deep within her and wondered where? She knew she brought her wisdom from Sania but she felt a more complex reason for this knowing. Possibly it had something to do with who she was in this lifetime and what drove her to the self-actualization privilege of existing in Sania.

CHAPTER 7

The First Dream

Ava realized that she was starving when she arrived home which was only a ten minute ride from the office. Oh God, I forgot to eat lunch. What was I thinking? There were slim pickings in the kitchen but regardless, she needed nourishment and knew that tomorrow she would be eating lunch with Gary and afterwork she would go grocery shopping. She heated up two cans of soup and ate a peanut butter and jelly sandwich. It was enough to stave off the hunger pangs and provide mental agility for the Seth book she needed to continue to read. She was still hoping for the remembrance in the morning of a dream she might have during the night.

Before relaxing into her Seth book, Ava quickly figured how to change the mechanism on her alarm clock from that shrill buzzing noise in to wake to a symphony music station set very low.

Prepared for bed she began reading Seth: ***According to your energy, power and intensity, you can help change the beliefs of many people, of course. (Seth: The Nature of Personal Reality, Jane Roberts copyright 1978)***

Interesting, why is it that every time I have a question, it always seems Seth is reading my mind and presents me with what is necessary to find the answers to my questioning thoughts. I find this experience "other worldly" to say the least. Again, I must believe I am receiving divine guidance from Light Beings as was my chosen profession in Sania. A pleasant thought with which to drift off into sleep.

Ava awoke at 5:00 a.m. to the melodic sound of Debussy's Claire de Lune on the clock radio. Ah, such sweetness smiling to herself and quickly realized she had had a dream! So excited, she went to her briefcase and found a spiral notebook and began to write the dream down:

> I was at the top of a Christmas tree but placing ornaments at the base of the tree (odd). Why go from the top to the bottom I thought and laughed. The ornaments were royal blue and frosty white, very beautiful and shimmering in appealing shapes. When I was done I noticed someone trying to secure the top of the tree with string to the ceiling so it would not tip over. I checked the security of this string and hook but decided it was never going to keep the tree from falling. I tried to re-hook the string but was unsuccessful. I then decided to check the base of the tree and found all the roots still attached to the base of the trunk. I was trying to balance the tree on its roots but it kept toppling from side to side.

Ava could immediately relate to being "above" the tree. To her it was a representation of Sania. She also realized she was trying to assimilate herself into the Earth plane, clearly representing bringing her knowledge from Sania to the lower realms where she had chosen her redemption. Checking the security of the string and concluding it would never hold the tree, was also confirmation that she had to do her time here. She would not provide herself with an easy pass. The failing attempt to secure the top of the tree brought her to the roots of the tree, clearly signifying that she is well rooted in this reality and because she was unable to balance the tree on its roots, she had forthcoming challenges to face.

Ava felt concerned about the symbolism it contained. She was confident in her interpretation and sadly suspected the dream indicated she was not acclimating well to the situation she had chosen. It made her wonder. What challenges are to come her way that she would have to wrestle with that would disturb her current sense of balance and the great day she had yesterday? She supposed it would be naive to think that everyday would be the same and that she shouldn't expect surprise situations to pop up threatening that balance. Her sense of wonder with mild anxiety began to enter her energy field again and said to herself, "Well, there's one right there!" However, she knew that guidance was always at hand. It seemed she had a connection with Seth and felt that there would be others entering the realm of influence for her betterment. She knew it would be foolish to try to predict anything but began the development of a strong sense of faith and belief not only in herself but in the Universe.

Ava headed to work in her car that she loved so much. She was quite unaware of her physical beauty. She was blonde with light brown, hazel eyes and possessed a slim, tall body type. Driving a Z-28, she was completely unaware of male attention being sent her way. Somehow she was oblivious to this fact. She simply had a different set of priorities. Unbeknownst to Ava, she turned many heads. Men were intimated by her looks but if they were able to drum up the nerve to get a conversation started, they quickly became intimated by her level of intelligence and areas of interest. Ava did not perceive this message clearly and simply blamed herself for some sort of inadequacy that would drive men away. It gave her a sense of insecurity and confusion. Nevertheless, it truly was not a priority for her, at least not at this time.

Ava began her "second" day on the job that she loved arriving sharply at 7:00 a.m. She already knew she had three appointments and was preparing for her first meeting with Mari Starly from IBM. She then began reviewing her inventory reports from yesterday's days-end and perused them for any glaring discrepancies. She sent an e-mail to Doug Rice, the Warehouse Manager asking for a 3:00 PM meeting to discuss the inventory rearrangement he suggested the day before. She sent an email to Gary of HP to confirm their lunch was still on. She opened an email from her boss, the VP of Finance who was requesting a meeting with her at 9:00 a.m. She wondered what he wanted to discuss but certainly replied with her availability.

Soon, she began to hear "morning Ava, how was your evening Ava, it's only Tuesday! Ugh!" She chuckled to herself. You can tell a person's perspective on life simply by what comes out of their mouths. In some cases, that's too bad. She thought to herself, you always have a choice - the choice is simple - either be happy or be miserable. The same amount of energy goes into both. Ha ... there was that slight sense of humor again.

In only a few minutes it would be 9:00 a.m. and Ava walked over to her boss' office to see if he was ready for their meeting. He was sitting in his office with the Comptroller of CE and she could feel slight butterflies in her stomach. As they noticed her they waved her in to take a seat. Ava could only imagine the worst. But what? It was simply her underlying lack of self-confidence which no one could detect she could possibly possess.

The VP began to speak first and presented Ava with an offer of a promotion to Director of Inventory Control. She couldn't believe her ears! She tried to remain professional and only exhibit a small sense of joy. After all, this was a corporate setting and any display of excitement would be looked upon as inappropriate. The VP continued, explaining the responsibility of the position; a larger staff to manage; a new office in the executive wing and of course a brilliant new salary! Ava was looking at a $20,000 per year increase over her current salary along with an annual bonus. She did not need time to think it over. She already knew her capabilities and that she had put in her time managing to make strides for the company in rebates and thefts and integrating functions within the inventory department. Ava felt a tremendous sense of pride and gratitude. She said, "Yes, I would be honored."

Ava wanted to know when the promotion would become effective. Her boss told her that it was confidential for now and they would consider making the announcement in two weeks. There were conditions that Finance needed to work out first. Ava assured him she would comply with their wishes. They shook hands and she walked back to her office. She felt a sense of pride and accomplishment. How do you contain such elation she thought to herself? Ava shook hands on the deal and part of that deal was to keep it confidential.

Noticing Doug Rice had replied to her email, Ava confirmed their 3:00 PM meeting in the warehouse for efficiency sake.

10:00 AM arrived quickly enough and Ava received a call from the receptionist that Mari Starly was in the reception area waiting for her. "Thank you, I'll be right there" she told the receptionist.

Ava walked through the building and as she approached the reception area, noticed a well dress professional woman with blonde hair. She approached her and asked if she was Mari. "Yes," Mari acknowledged and they extended their hands in introduction. "I'm Ava St. Claire, pleased to meet you. Won't you follow me to my office."

As they walked together, Ava asked how long she been with IBM and how familiar was she with Computer Enterprises. Mari assured Ava although she was relatively new to IBM, she had received considerable support from her counterparts who filled her in on our organization.

Entering Ava's office, Mari took one of the guest chairs and

Ava closed the door. Ava could not help noticing Mari's piercing blue eyes. There was an electric energy to them. Ava figured her to be around her own age and noticed she was wearing a wedding band. They began a review of the business relationship between both their companies in terms of volume in sales and inventory levels. They reviewed the rebate system and the added value aspect of CE brought to IBMs customers. They reviewed report timing as well as systemic reporting capabilities hoping to hear an electronic process might be in development from IBM's end. "After all," Ava interjected, "we are in the computer business." They both laughed at the irony. Mari responded that their IT staff were developing a process to accommodate the request.

Ava could not provide a tour of the warehouse however, because of competitive products CE carried but considered it might be productive to introduce her to the Sales Manager and asked if she had met him yet. She had not, so Ava quickly picked up the phone to see if he was available. Unfortunately, he was out in the field at a client. With apologies, Ava told her she might want to contact him directly to introduce herself.

Our meeting had come to a successful conclusion but upon rising, Mari looked Ava straight into her eyes and asked the oddest question. She wanted to know if Ava had ever had anything strange or unusual happen to her? Ava was quite surprised by the question and told Mari she wasn't quite sure what she meant. Mari kept staring into Ava's eyes. Ava instinctively knew on a deeper level Mari's reason for asking and said, "Yes." Mari smiled at Ava and said, "I have a book for you to read. Next time I'm in, I'll bring it by." As she walked Mari to the front door, they shook hands and said goodbye and Ava could still see a glimmer of knowing in Mari's eyes.

Before Ava headed back to her office she asked the sales admin to schedule a meeting with the Sales Manager to meet with new IBM rep. Ava wanted to be sure the book Mari spoke of would make it to the office. She gave her one of Mari's business cards and the admin happily set up a meeting. Strange, Ava thought to herself, that almost felt “other worldly”. That’s the second time I’ve said that phrase. There’s more to this than meets the eye so to speak. She laughed to herself again.

CHAPTER 8

Reaching For The Highest Fruit On The Tree

As the week went by, Ava was consumed with the tasks of managing the company's inventory and worked diligently at answering questions and solving complicated analyses with precision and skill. She loved her job and fell into a comfortable routine. She felt at home with corporate protocol, something that she appreciated without question realizing that it coincided with her own natural structure of relating to life. She was also filled with anticipation and excitement over the upcoming announcement of her promotion.

On Friday, Ava noticed that Mari Starly was in the building, presumably to meet with the Sales Manager. Ava was excited to see Mari again secretly hoping she had remembered the "book." With anticipation, she asked the Sales Manager's admin what time their meeting would be over so she would "accidentally' make herself noticed and available when Mari was finished.

Ava did not have to put herself through the trouble, since Mari, smiling, dropped by her office and said, "I have that book I told you about." Ava was delighted. She looked at the cover of the book "Reach For The Highest Fruit On The Tree". She thanked Mari for remembering and was intrigued by the title of the book and immediately thought of her recent dream, the one with the Christmas tree. She could not read it right away of course, but decided that evening Seth would have to wait, or not, depending on how captivating this book would be. Mari left her office and said, be sure to tell me what you think. I will," Ava said. "Thanks again for remembering. You have peaked my interest."

Ava not only began to fall into a comfortable routine at work but also in her home life. There were plenty of manageable chores, like groceries; laundry; house cleaning and since she lived alone and was well organized, she attended immediately to anything that needed to be accomplished.

As the staff began to leave the office with expressions of "have a good weekend Ava," "thank God it's Friday," "any plans Ava?" "There's a group of us heading to Crackers down the road for some drinks and dancing, want to join us?" Ava politely and appreciatively declined the invitation and said she would be unable. She wondered if she'd ever done that with her coworkers in the past. It felt inappropriate but nevertheless, she was looking forward to going home and beginning her new book.

She also decided she would take a trip to the observatory Saturday evening and try to find Pleiades and enjoy the evening spring air. As Ava prepared a light dinner and turned on MTV to see what videos she could enjoy, she realized how diverse her taste was in music. She loved symphony and she loved rock. She could appreciate both genres. She began reflecting back on her luncheon date with Gary as the "Top Gun" video came on. She discovered they shared a love of flying and war jets. Laughing to herself, she suspected in another lifetime, she may have been a pilot in the Air Force because she could not explain her fascination with these machines in any other way. The thunderous roar of their engines and awesome power thrilled her to the core. She was delighted to have this connection. Gary knew a great deal more about fighter jets but their mutual excitement was evident. They had planned for sometime in the near future to visit the USS Intrepid docked at thirty-fourth Street in NYC and she almost couldn't wait! Her luncheon brought her a better understanding of her relationship with Gary.

He was a very sensitive soul with whom she had a deep connection because of his spirituality and his perceptions about reality. He felt like a good friend and an old soul and someone she could easily connect with on a much deeper more enriching level. It made her very happy. Gary was a corporate man but only in disguise, similar to herself. She looked forward to developing a great relationship with him but as a true kindred spirit nothing more than that, after all Gary was a married man with a young daughter. She felt she could learn from him and suspected they would be engaged in long philosophical discussions that would allow her to freely explore ideas openly with no judgement.

Ava began to prepare for bed and was looking forward to reading Mari's book. She placed the Seth book in her nightstand drawer and said, I'll be back Seth, not to worry and giggled at the prospect of talking to the book.

Opening to the first page of "Reach For The Highest Fruit On The Tree", Ava realized the book was written by a well-known personality who was going to take a leap of faith exposing to the world her real life journey of discovery - that discovery being an existential, spiritual awakening that she initially emphatically resisted but was predicted by the characters she encountered throughout her journey of ten years. Ava's interest was peaked to say the least!

She immediately began to suspect that Mari saw something in her that encouraged her to provide Ava with the treasures in the book. Ava could not have predicted that this book was truly meant for her to read at this very time in her life on Earth in the year 1985. She began to read Chapter One.

Ava saw herself in the author. She understood the author's journey and could relate to the conflicts of exposing her well-known personality to what surely would be negative criticism by the popular masses. Ava related to the gradual, evolutionary courage and conviction the author would experience exposing these spiritual and existential ideas onto the world stage. Ava wondered if she herself had anything to do with providing guidance to this personality to act upon her revelations when she was a Light Being.

Ava was so mesmerized by the journey and the so called "coincidences" that occurred to the author, who upon reading further, encountered a being from Pleiades telling her she would be a teacher - a teacher through a book detailing her evolutionary journey. The book took this writer to Machu Pechu in Peru and the hot baths where she meditated and experienced her first ever astral projection. She was brought to profound experiences of psychic abilities assisting her in the deep, dark jungles of the Peruvian Mountains. It brought her an ability allowing a vehicle to safely drive itself with her in it. It brought her to knowing a "channeler", a concept she had no knowledge of previously. She witnessed UFOs as second nature to the Peruvian Mountains. After this woman's ten year journey, she knew she had to write her book. She knew that the Light Being from Pleiades was guiding her to do this and it would be done no matter how much resistance the writer expressed.

Ava was completely captivated by the story and its spiritual richness. She felt validated by the ideas of how capable humans are and that we truly are spirit beings existing in a human dimension. Ava understood the nature of evolution and the nature of allowing. She began to suspect that her earlier thought of deliberately causing her discretion from what she labelled "her fall from grace" was indeed a created purposeful event to evolve beyond the consciousness of Sania and that there may even be more beyond.

It was an insightful and thought-provoking book which had the effects of opening Ava's mind to many different dimensions simultaneously and the concepts are never-ending! Ava was introduced to a new way of conceptual and linear thinking providing her with insights into different levels of realities. She felt like she was living in a dream within a dream and potentially even another dream wrapped all around that! It reminded her of Shakespeare, "We are all actors on a stage". She laughed at the thought of how these brilliant secrets are tucked away in inauspicious ways but they are truly in plain site. It all depended on the mind of the eyes looking at them.

Ava began to see daylight pouring through the window blinds of her bedroom. Ava realized she had been up all night reading and finished the book! In true Ava style, wanting to be sure that she hadn't missed anything, she began to read it again beginning at page one. This was how powerfully the author's journey affected her. She could not bring herself, on this Saturday, to do anything else. She got out of bed, washed up, made a light breakfast and then headed back to bed to begin again. If she could have, Ava would have eaten the book to absorb all the nuances of its hidden meanings. After her second read, it was dinner time.

Ava now understood how Mari Starly felt her energy and knew she had to read this. Mari knew Ava had the potential. Mari was clearly a guide so to speak in human form as real as any human. She simply had a higher level of understanding and noticed it within Ava. She knew Ava would be receptive and it would answer so many questions for her along with directing her steps forward to develop skills and a gradual evolutionary process.

Ava was feeling quite blessed. Her good friend Gary was a blessing and she knew they would share many enriching talks going forward. She knew Mari was going to be a great source of friendship and inspiration to her. Ava thought, how interesting that these two wonderful people have entered my circle of energy. Like attracts like. They were conscious enough to feel my vibrational field and knew I would be receptive to their energy fields. Here I realize a truth that we don't meet people by accident, they are meant to cross our path for a reason. Even if someone was not to your liking and even irritated you, there was an evolutionary reason for their presence. They are acting as a reflection of something within you that you wish to change.

Ava was so looking forward to exercising some of the ideas

presented in the book and felt confident that she could achieve states of awareness the author came to discover. She was also looking forward to connecting with Mari again to let her know how much she enjoyed the book and was grateful for the gift. Ava did not have Mari's personal phone number so she would have to wait until Monday to reach out to her.

In the meantime, Ava would scratch any plans for the evening at the observatory and seek out books at the book store on meditation; astral projection; and channeling and pretty much anything in the metaphysical realm. She had a new mission for her evening. Oddly, the lack of sleep did not seem to affect her. Ava enjoyed sleep very much but somehow did not feel the need at this time. She took a shower, dressed and started searching for bookstores with excitement in her heart.

CHAPTER 9

The Awakening

Ava found a large two-story massive bookstore. Surely, they will have what I'm searching for here she thought. She quickly asked for assistance to the spiritual, metaphysical, and science sections and was directed to the center of the store on the first level. She certainly had a lot to select from which was a reassuring sign. She didn't know where to begin. There were so many choices. She perused the aisles and decided that she would feel a vibration when she was upon her next reading adventure. She found a collection of Deepak Chopra books; Paulo Collho; Carlos Castanda; and one that really jumped out at her, "Alchemy of Nine Dimensions of Consciousness. She knew that would be the first read mainly because of her recent suspicion of the possibility that Sania was not the end-all which is why she toyed with the idea that her being here was beginning to feel more like an experiment rather than a punishment.

With no more room or strength left in her arms for books to carry, she decided she had enough to satisfy her for the moment. She looked for assistance again at an information booth asking if they had the Video Tape of Chakra meditation created by the author of "Reach for The Highest Fruit On The Tree". The assistant checked his computer and said yes, we do have it and the videos can be found in the back section behind those glass doublewide doors. He offered her a canvas shopping bag so that she could continue shopping more comfortably. Ava was grateful for the loaner and thanked the clerk. Now only her shoulder would hurt but her hands were free to find the video she needed.

Before long, Ava found her treasure. It would be the first thing she would do upon returning home. After checking out, she headed to her car and straight for home.

The introduction of the Chakra Meditation video was extremely informative beginning with an explanation that the Chakras were sacred energy points within the physical body. There were seven of them and each resonated to one of the seven chords on the musical scale. The root Chakra at the base of the tail bone was red; the sacral or sexual Chakra was orange found in the genitalia region; the solar plexus Chakra found between the sacral and heart regions was yellow; the Heart Chakra was Green; the throat Chakra was blue; the third eye Chakra found in the center of the forehead was violet and finally the crown Chakra found atop the head above the pituitary gland was white. Of course by no coincidence, they were the 7 colors contained in the rainbow. Ava thought everything is connected. Everything has a purpose under Heaven ... if you are a seeker, you will find what you are seeking. It was as simple as that. From the "7 Archetypes of Human Consciousness", It is stated:

The Seeker is one who appears to be wandering aimlessly with no real goal, but in actual fact is the most freed up for spiritual transformation. The Seeker is much more secretive, nomadic, keeping to the hills and quietly inquiring about all walks of life. To truly be spontaneous and open to danger is where the real adventure begins, and many a seeker can be found in mythological and psychological wisdom. Like Siddhartha by Hesse and many a seemingly 'lost' soul it can take great bravery to be completely unattached. To be constantly learning with a thirst for knowledge more often than not leads us onto the path

to enlightenment. Questioning everything and searching every corner of this world for answers, the Seeker knows they will not fall into the trap of a charlatan Guru but find a true master or be able to eventually master themselves. Being unattached to earthly desires and distanced from such attachments as family, career and even the pulls of karma, the Seeker often sticks to high places to remain the observer of human nature and steer clear of any obstruction to the divine. (Excerpt from Gary McGee: Fractal Enlightenment Newsletter)

Ava felt complete validation from this inspirational verse which she read on a flyer taped at the end of the Metaphysical aisle of the book store, so much so that she felt compelled to write it down. With that she decided to begin a journal of inspirational thoughts; dreams; and anything that caught the attention of her soul.

She now wanted to begin her first meditation session. She followed the instructions for comfortable clothing, sitting straight with legs crossed on the floor and positioned her arms resting on her legs with index and thumbs touching to close off the energy circulating through her physical body. She was delighted by the prospect of this exercise of meditation and hoped that she would see immediate results.

The meditation was a visual exercise using kaleidoscope designs to represent each of the Chakra with focus on their represented color and the resonation of the musical chord that related to each. After meditation, she prepared for bed and went to sleep.

Ava lazily opened her eyes awakening from a restful and pleasant night's sleep. She began reminiscing a vision of her dream. She immediately reached for her journal placed at her bedside and began writing:

> "I was looking out the back of a house through sliding glass doors and seeing an extremely huge wave of ocean water with its foamed crest. I was feeling

> ecstasy from its power and immensity. It was an overwhelming sensation but very pleasing. She noticed her boss standing next to her, Paul DeMato who turned to her and said, 'what a waste'. I said, 'What do you mean?' He said. 'It leaves no room for a backyard.' I could not focus on the lack of a backyard and only appreciated the immensity of power represented by the ocean wave!

In several attempts to interpret her dream, Ava began to question if her ego was represented by the wave stemming from her upcoming promotion? Possibly, the wave was spiritual symbol that her meditation practice was already showing her the power within herself which would be beneficial to her evolution. Ava could not understand why her boss was there and made such a derogatory comment about something so beautiful and majestic.

She wrote all her thoughts about the dream down and was pleased to have her journal and more than pleased that she had a dream.

For now, Ava knew that she needed to deal with the mundane weekend tasks of every working woman. The vacuuming, dusting, laundry and grocery shopping needed to be done. Boring! Afterwards she would concentrate her efforts on the things that brought her joy; reading, meditation and music. That thought immediately made her turn on MTV, enjoying the sounds of rock music while fixing breakfast and making a list of what groceries were needed. As she sat down at her dining table and opened the window she enjoyed the smell of the spring air and the warmth that could already be felt in the temperature.

She had flashbacks of her dream and continued to hypothesize about its potential significance. She wondered why her boss was in her dream and if his appearance held any significance considering his negative reaction to such a beautiful sight. She realized she really didn't know him well after five years of working with him but suspected she was not part of the "boys club" with frequent lunches and weekend golf outings and was certain it was because she was female. All the other managers, save for the HR manager, were men.

Sunday mid-afternoon proved very rewarding. Ava decided to take her Seth book and journal to a nearby park. There were people walking their dogs, children playing and folks rowing small rented paddle boats enjoying the beginning of spring. Ava loved the smell of the fresh budding Springtime. It was a healthy change from her apartment and the sounds of birds and people was a pleasant diversion from her apartment setting.

She began reading from where she had left off in her Seth book, ***"The nature of your personal beliefs directs the kinds of emotions you will have at any given time. You will feel aggressive, happy, despairing, or determined according to events that happen to you, your beliefs about yourself in relation to them, and your ideas of who and what you are. You will not understand your emotions unless you know your beliefs. It will seem to you that you feel aggressive or upset without reason, or that your feelings sweep down upon you without cause if you do not learn to listen to the beliefs within your own conscious mind, for they generate their own emotions. (Seth: The Nature of Personal Reality, Jane Roberts copyright 1978)***

Ava needed to put the book down and reflect on the material she had just read. She needed to assimilate this information into what her Light Being consciousness already knew with her current human experiences. That passage appeared to be guidance for her integration into the consciousness of her human reality. At least this is how she perceived it. With more introspection, she began to feel drained and before too long, two young guys approached her. She wondered if her energy drop was caused by them or if they approached her, because her energy level had dropped. They were young and casually dressed and seemed to be out for a day of "we've got nothing else to do, let's see if we can pick up some chicks" type of attitude. She felt a little apprehensive at first but decided she needed a diversion. They said hello and she reciprocated with a hesitant smile. They asked her name and began what Ava would consider a nonsensical conversation. Clearly these two young men were just wasting time, hers and theirs, and now she tried to get rid of their attention. Ava politely gathered her things and said I've got to go. I'm running late. "Oh come on, we were just getting started" said one of them. Ava murmured to herself, yeah, I know, but not with me you won't.

Heading to her car she was hoping they would not follow her for fear of them spotting her very noticeable Z-28. You could see that machine coming and going she thought. It was flashy to say the least. Ava could not help but think she brought this on herself. Her human energy field at a vulnerable moment, must have attracted these two boys to her who were wasting their lives. What Ava could not understand was that her underlying self-esteem issues would make her feel this way. This was simply an event out of her control and instead of recognizing it as such, she blamed herself for attracting it.

That was Ava's mission in this lifetime - to search out her strengths and capabilities and understand her self-worth, her true value and not to blame or take ownership of these events. She hadn't fully comprehended the last paragraph of Seth she just read. Had she, she would have known that her conscious beliefs were off the mark and she would be on the road to recognizing what truly just happened. Again, her lack of self-esteem and lack of awareness of her outward beauty was the root cause. Ava would still have plenty of work to do to come to this realization.

Before heading back to the confines of her peaceful, serene home, Ava decided to stop at the bookstore and buy another tool of advancement that had recently caught her attention, a Yoga video. There was a large selection to pick from and it would take some time to make a decision. She wanted one that would include some sort of instruction and background information on the benefits and history of Yoga.

She made her purchase and headed home. She continually obsessed over her isolation and wondered what her cohorts were doing on a day like today. Because of her thirst for knowledge and the desire to foster individualism and tap into the secrets of the Universe, she felt different and non-conforming. She felt loneliness but could not bring herself to divert from her mission. She had a sense of devotion and dedication to consume this knowledge and no desire to "play with the other children". She laughed to herself at the prospect of living like that but not in a snobbish way. Her focus came back and knew her greatest pleasure was in knowledge, seeking and mastering her full potential. She didn't feel she was missing out, if anything, she felt she was finding the magic!

Back home, Ava began to read her Seth book accompanied by Native American music softly resonating in the background. She was better able to absorb the nuances in Seth's writings and could feel a clearer focus. Being at home, she could absorb the wisdom and feel the knowledge effecting every fiber of her being. With each new story she was unknowingly being transformed and changing into a different vibration of energy. She was certain of the value of Seth's teachings and confident it would enhance her experiences in her human world.

When Ava finished reading several chapters, she decided to explore her Yoga book and video just bought. After setting up the video she was on her way to her first Yoga exercise session. She was quite amazed at how easily she took to it. Having a slim body she supposed helped and her flexibility was remarkable but after all she enjoyed skiing and tennis and horseback riding and was obviously fit. However, Ava was seeking the spiritual alignment Yoga provided through the very specific movements designed to achieve that spiritual and mental harmony. She quickly realized a Yoga mat was going to be necessary.

Well, Sunday evening was upon her and she needed a light dinner; organize her wardrobe for Monday; set the alarm clock; prepare for bed and of course the joy of her meditation.

A Visit From Old Friends?

Ava happily began her forty-five minute long meditation and within the practice found herself floating into the night sky. She had no conscious awareness of the event. She was floating out towards the stars in the dark sky and began to feel a softness of air against her cheeks. She slowly drifted further and further into the night sky until she saw a ring of light form. The circle was quite large and she could see stars within it and surrounding it. She felt compelled to continue her journey toward it and suddenly from one area of the circle Light Beings began to appear. She continued moving closer. Eventually there were five Light Beings had entered the circle of light and telepathically told her to stop. Ava would do no such thing. She continued slowly but fervently toward the circle. Again she received a telepathic message to stop. Again, Ava chose to ignore the request.

Finally, one of the Light Beings held up the silhouette of light representing a hand in a stop motion and declared telepathically, "Someday this will be yours, but not now". Ava stopped moving forward. She wanted to communicate, but became disturbed by a sound in the far distance. The sound grew louder and louder and suddenly Ava's eyes popped open. She was dazed and not really present in her living room. She methodically but unknowingly stood up and moved over to the dinning room window, brushed the curtains aside, and looked up into the sky. As she did this, she felt a huge rush of energy flush through her entering the top of her head and traveling to the bottom of her feet. That brought her back to herself! Holy shit she thought. She blurted out oh my God in total amazement. I just had my first out of body experience as a human. I saw my old friends, but I didn't recognize their vibrations as personalities from Sania. The shrill sound she heard in the distance was from her telephone. Her answering machine verified it was a telemarketer, "What pests." She wondered if she would have come back to her body had they not called.

Ava recalled the story from "Reach for the Highest Fruit on the Tree" where the author experienced her first ever astral projection and recognized that in the instant she had a limiting thought, she was thrust back into her physical body with a memory of a silver cord connecting her spirit consciousness with her physical body. Of course I would come back Ava thought to herself. I am supremely guided and safe at all times. I am strength and in keeping with what I have been called to do. She was surprised by that thought. She didn't know where it came from. More than anything, she was filled with excitement and joy realizing she had the most amazing astral projection and congratulated herself on this remarkable achievement!

The following morning, Ava began recalling visions of her dream. It was something that she had never seen before. She reached for her journal to begin recording it. It was a dream confirming her astral projection from the night before had connected her to the Light Beings from Sania. She saw them and they communicated telepathically that going forward, they would communicate with her using a device, showing her a silver metallic rectangular object with round protruding knobs appearing from beneath the surface of the device. The knobs were made of the same metallic material as the device that contained them.

Ava was bewildered by the immediate response of the meditation provoking an astral projection and the appearance of the Light Beings but had no idea what this device was. She had never seen anything like it and wondered where she could find it, or even what to ask for. Nevertheless, first task at hand was getting ready for work. She showered and began her morning routine and wondered if this was the day her promotion would be announced. She thought of all the extra money that she would have to buy books. In a flippant manner she began to think she needed a bigger apartment to accommodate a library, smiling to herself.

First one arriving at work as usual, Ava was satisfied and happy to have such a great job and such fascinating interests. She immediately began reviewing inventory reports and checking for discrepancies against the computer counts. She checked her calendar and it appeared to be a non-committed day and proceeded to check her email. Paul DeMato, her boss had sent an email asking for a 9:00 a.m. meeting with her. She promptly marked her calendar and then began to review documents left in her inbox for her approval. She quickly remembered she needed to work with Doug Rice devising a method of keeping the sales force in check about retrieving inventory from the warehouse for loaner purposes. She would give herself a couple of hours in the morning to think about a fair process and requested a 2:00 p.m. meeting with Doug to review her plan. Well, so much for a non-committed day she thought.

CHAPTER 11

New Revelations

As 9:00 AM approached, Paul DeMato arrived at the office. He passed Ava's office and said, "Follow me in Ava." She picked up her recent reports and some folders and followed her boss into his office. Paul looked glum. There was an uneasiness about him that she had never seen before. She wondered if she had made an error in any of her responsibilities. Paul closed the door behind them and he took his seat. He looked very upset. Ava could not imagine what could be the problem. As Paul began to speak of a change in the promotion plan for Ava, she could feel her heart drop and her anxiety grow. She allowed Paul to continue before speaking. Paul said, "The company's Purchasing Manager is having difficulties in the financial area and an announcement would be made today that he is being made Director and not you."

I was stunned and very disappointed in Paul. I said, "But that is not beneficial to the company. You specifically selected me for this position because of my talents and my history with CE. Is the Purchasing Manager more qualified than I am to oversee the management of the company's inventory? He has been with the company for one and a half years and is a buying expert. I have invested six years in CE's operations and feel my experience is far more beneficial to the company for this task." Ava spoke softly and reasonably but inside she wanted to die. She also felt the need to scream how unfair this was and it appeared to be a "male" thing. Ava did not want to present a tough, aggressive stance for fear that it would potentially damage any future relationship with Paul or her standing in the company. Ava asked Paul if this meant that the Director of Inventory would become her new boss and if so, it would appear as a demotion to her because she would be reporting to a Director rather than a VP. Paul assured Ava that there would be no change in her status as Inventory Manager but she would be reporting to the Director of Inventory. Ava showed Paul her appreciation for the heads up and thanked him for his professional courtesy. She had nothing further to add. Paul shook her hand and thanked her for her understanding. Ava went back to her office, closed her door and began the process of composing herself. Admittedly, some of the wind was taken from her sails but she had to face the reality of her situation.

She tried to rely on the Seth passage she read at the park yesterday because she knew it would inspire her but that book was not with her in the office. Trying to recall Seth's message regarding ***"The nature of your personal beliefs in a large measure directs the kinds of emotions you will have at any given time. You will feel aggressive, happy, despairing, or determined according to events that happen to you, your beliefs about yourself in relation to them, and your ideas of who and what you are.. You will not understand your emotions unless you know your beliefs. It will seem to you that you feel aggressive or upset without reason.***

Ava had felt justified for being so upset and looked upon her judgmental belief that this decision was reversed because one of the boys in the "boys club" needed help. Ava tried so hard to accept this reversal of fortune and maintain an aura of balance and acceptance. As hard as she tried, she could not come to terms with this. It did help that she knew Paul was upset having to make this decision and could only believe in his heart that he didn't want to but was pressured by the powers that be, the owners of the company.

Ava knew it would take some time to sort out her emotions and disappointment and decided to focus on her work instead. She would have time later this evening to process this event and come to terms with it. Her staff had already arrived and were talking about their weekends with happiness and smiling faces. Mina entered Ava's office to share the good news of her son receiving a scholarship and Ava expressed happiness and congratulations towards her. "I'm not surprised, Mina, your son deserves it and you have guided him well." Mina smiled, thanked me and went back to her desk beaming.

I was genuinely happy for her good fortune and secretly within my unconscious awareness, thought, well he's a guy. He already has an enormous advantage but indeed he is brilliant. I really need to get over the disadvantageous attitude of being female in this world. I need to work on determination and foresight that women are equal and desperately need to shift the way of thinking on this planet. It would not become my sole mission but a collective shift stemming from the female population because I knew I was not the only female who felt this way. A movement had already begun in the '70s but I had a sense that it was only the beginning of a long, powerful shift about to take place over the next half century.

An email came through from Paul DeMato to all managers of the company. He wanted all to gather in the conference room at 11:00 a.m. for a corporate announcement. I immediately knew what it was about. Of course I would attend and be in good spirits and a congratulatory mode for Rob Cameron, our new Director of Inventory Control. I knew I would feel the confusion of those there. Why in the world would this promotion not be given to Ava? I would pretend that it never occurred to me and that I was fine with the decision.

At 11:30 AM, Ava received a call from Mari Starly which both surprised and delighted her. She was so excited to speak with her. "Hi Mari" I said. Her initial comment was that from the sound of my voice, I must have started the book! I laughed and said, "I not only started it, I finished it and read it again!" Mari was so surprised. "So what did you think?" I told her that I thought it was uncanny that in our brief introduction she felt the need to bring this book to my attention. Of course, after reading it, I knew why she brought it to my attention and surmised she was of like-minded thinking and frequency and she tuned into that in my presence. We decided that we would make a lunch date for Wednesday and have some fun talking about the concepts. I agreed and was happy at the prospect of seeing her in a more relaxed environment for a non-corporate reason. I knew she and I had so much to talk about.

Shortly after, Gary of HP called to remind Ava that they had a horseback riding date that Saturday. Ava quickly jotted it down on her calendar and was looking forward to it. Great! This is just what I need. Feeling that magnificent, thunderous, beauty of an animal under my control and enjoying every moment of it. Maybe that's why I drive a Z-28! A sense of power and control. Something I did not receive in my professional world. I knew I also enjoyed the thunderous roar of fighter jets and it was probably for the same reason. Ava laughed to herself and thought about the relationship to all three activities. Secretly, she was powerful and strong but given her female existence, felt she could only enjoy that thrill in a private, personal way. Ava did question if her self-esteem issues probably prevented her from expressing that in the corporate world. She was beginning to detect that people were intimated by who she was and they should only know how much she was holding back to control their reactions to her.

Ava began to suspect that her overpowering concern for what others thought of her, put her in a position of literally lying to them about who she was. She felt she needed to control her personality knowing it intimidated others and she would be judged unfairly. Ava could sense a feeling of revelation coming about. By pretending to be something she's not for the sake of not offending someone else, made her feel like a fraud so to speak. In this false persona, she was being perceived as an enigma within a puzzle. She was confusing others trying to relate to her. Ava wondered if it made a difference to anyone but herself and quickly realized it only mattered that she was being true to herself. She decided to cool her jets, relax a bit, meditate some and stop obsessing over it. Her desire was ripe and Source was on it and she was moving in alignment with Source.

She vowed to be completely natural and not twist and turn her personality because of the person she was interacting with. She was a deep thinker and more than likely could think five steps ahead of the next person. She would remain true to who she was no matter what their reaction would be. Let the pieces fall where they may she thought.

Ava still knew that her true Sanian identity and background knowledge could not be revealed. She quickly came to the conclusion that she could still be herself without revealing this and in so doing was unraveling some of that low self-esteem that had been haunting her. Ava couldn't help but give credit to the books she had been reading, opening her mind up to new possibilities as well as new insights into what caused her emotional upheaval. She understood the nature of being human but knew she was more than that. The difficulty in raising her human vibration to the level of Sania without attracting suspicion was indeed a dilemma but she began to suspect from these thoughts that possibly Sania was not the end-all for her. She wondered if she would evolve even further beyond Sania. She'd be okay as long as she continued her steady course of action.

As the announcement was made in the conference room with all managers present, Ava could feel the vibrational rift in the room which stemmed from everyone's surprise that she was not selected for this position. Everyone knew there was an underlying reason. This guy was not qualified to take over directorship of this department and his forte was Purchasing. Ava tried to remain calm and smiling and in a congratulatory mode as if this was not having an impact on her balance. She felt she passed the test but knew her office would be flooded with visitors after the meeting was over. She was right.

She simply replied that it would take a great deal of responsibility off her shoulders and she would have more time to focus on the details of improving the company's inventory operation. She tried so hard to convince her counterparts, but knew she wasn't getting away with it. These were seasoned managers and they could read between the lines.

Ava headed out for her lunch with Mari. Mari entered the restaurant shortly after Ava and she could feel happiness and joy overcome her. She stood up and greeted Mari with a polite hug; a handshake would not do considering the book Mari shared with her.

They selected their lunch from the menus and as the waiter walked away they began to talk over each other and laughed. Ava told Mari, "I'm so excited and grateful for that book. How did you know?" Mari simply replied that there was something about Ava that exuded a sense of being different from most. Mari herself was a seeker and could recognize the energy in a fellow seeker. She also could not believe that Ava stayed up all night reading and then began reading the book for the second time. Ava explained to Mari that she did not want to miss a thing. "Do you think they would ever make a movie of this?" Mari doubted it, stating that it is controversial material in mainstream and predicted that it would not have a large audience. Hollywood was only interested in big money paybacks. Ava thought it was a shame, nevertheless, she was grateful that the author took the chance and presented her journey to whomever was capable of relating to it.

Mari asked Ava if after reading the book, had anything unusual occurred in her life. Ava could respond that many unusual things occurred even before the book but now felt a deeper connection to the topic and sensed that this was a direction she was being led in and must explore. Mari asked her if she would mind helping her in exploring this realm. Ava had no objection.

Ava asked Mari, "How do you propose to start?" Mari revealed that she suspected Ava was capable of psychic activity and could sense, through Ava's energy field that she could tap into another's energy field. Ava was intrigued to say the least. "I'm not sure I can do what you suggest but I am sure you could lead me in the right direction. Recently, I've begun meditation and have immediately noticed a change in my dreams which prompted me to start a dream journal. I have also started Yoga which seems to align my energy properly."

She asked Mari about her personal life. Was she married, did she have children, where did she live? Unfortunately they lived quite a distance apart but she agreed the telephone worked well and they both laughed. Mari was married and had a seven year old son who was quite the little genius. Mari's child rearing philosophy was about providing a minimum amount of direction. She encouraged her son to explore the world around him and to make choices before running those choices past his parents. "What an interesting method of parenting." Mari insisted, "It wouldn't work on most children but my Riley is an exceptional personality."

Mari wanted to know if Ava could come up and meet her family this weekend. Unfortunately, I have a horseback riding date with a friend, Gary this Saturday and Sunday I plan to dedicate to more studying and introspection. Mari was curious about this Gary fellow. "Well, we are really just friends," Ava explained. "He is a delightful soul and we have a lot in common on a spiritual level but he is married with a daughter and besides, I don't feel that chemistry with him. I deeply cherish our friendship and we plan activities together." Mari just smiled and shot those electric blue eyes at Ava. "No, I'm serious," Ava insisted.

Mari asked about planning on something the following weekend. Ava thought about the observatory and asked if her son would be interested in doing something like that just the three of them. Mari thought it was a great idea. Her son would truly enjoy that. So, next weekend it was. Ava asked Mari if she played tennis. Mari said she did but not very well. "You know, we could just rally and enjoy the sunshine and spring air in between lessons and discussions." Mari smiled and liked the idea.

CHAPTER 12

Conscious Transformation

Ava's work went along without a hitch. She didn't feel the effects of Rob Cameron's presence as Director of Inventory Control and wondered what he was doing during his days spent on executive row. She was managing the daily activities and reporting as usual and suspected that Rob would have some plans to change the processes that he would need her for at some point soon. She was not concerned or anxious. When he was ready to fill the role, he would begin to do so.

In the meantime, the work week was at an end and Ava was looking forward to one of her favorite activities along with one of her favorite friends. Friday night would be spent with her Seth material, continued meditation practice and Yoga. Ava began to read from Seth:

Like detectives, we search the world, looking in a completely different way than a physical sleuth. The world is probed with your characteristics in mind, seeking the very characteristics that will best suit your request. And whatever your purpose is, the same procedure on a psychic level is involved.

The organization of your feelings, beliefs, and intents directs

the focus about which your physical reality is built. This follows with impeccable spontaneity and order." (Seth: The Nature of Personal Reality, Jane Roberts copyright 1978)

Ava understood this message from the Seth book and related it directly back to her decision to be who she was rather than holding back her abilities of any kind without revealing her Sanian identity. This time she could see the message came to her in reverse order. She made an observation and based on that observation, she made her decision to be who she was regardless of how she was perceived. Following her decision she was receiving confirmation from Seth rather than the other way around. The next statement by Seth also uncannily reconfirmed her decision.

"As in YOUR terms, the cavemen ventured out into the daylight of the earth, so there is a time for man to venture out into a greater knowledge of his subjective reality, to explore the dimensions of selfhood and go beyond the small areas of himself in which he has thus far found shelter." (Shared from Lynda Madden Dahl Facebook post on the Seth Material.)

Ava was beginning to feel the rewards of reading the Seth books and could not have found greater validation of her convictions. Pleased and satisfied for herself, she began her meditation for the evening hoping for an inspirational dream as a result or, at the very least, heightened awareness to assist her in this Earthly existence.

Saturday morning arrived and Ava did not recall any dreams. She began getting ready for her day of horseback riding with one of her best friends, Gary. Ava was reflecting on some of the discussions and plans she had with Mari Starly. She felt the need to cry and knew it was the emotional upheaval about to take place because of their developing friendship. It almost felt like she could look into the future of what Mari was about to show her about her very own self. She was flooded with visions of their forthcoming discussions and knew she was in for a thunderous ride of visionary expansion. She could envision her abilities of psychic and intuitive knowing sharpen, but could not explain to herself how it would come about and how it would effect her life. She suspected she was about to enter her own personal Rubicon of her soul. Ava could anticipate this without even knowing exactly what would be involved and exactly how it would have an impact on her life. Thoughts flooded her mind which were directly related to her life in Sania. Was this how she achieved her Light Being status in the cosmos?

Ava drove to the riding stables. Gary was pulling into the parking lot just as she was. They greeted each other with smiling faces and a bear hug. "So who do you want to ride today" Ava asked Gary. Gary laughed and said, "I'm looking for a slow, gentle ride today." Ava looked at Gary and said, "Well, I'll be leaving you in the dust then." They both laughed. Ava was determined to have the ride of her life with a golden mare named Big Brave, whom she had ridden in the past. This was the thunderous ride she was hoping for. As they began their gallop Ava had to remind Gary of her intent to take Big Brave to the fullest extent of her capabilities and off she went leaving Gary in the dust.

The sensation of riding and being in control of this massive and gorgeous creature gave Ava an appreciation for the sense of power and strength and exhilaration contained in both her horse and herself. The roaring sound of Big Brave's hooves excited her. She flew through the air in absolute control and knew Big Brave was in sync with her energy in a telepathic sense, they became one with all nature. She could feel the muscular dynamics of her legs wrapped around Big Brave, who understood the ride Ava was looking for. This magnificent creature became one with Ava as Ava became lost in the ecstasy of the wind blowing through her hair and the fast wind against her face. Both were one. There was no difference between horse and rider. Ava lost any sense of reality. She was everything all at once. She was thrilled over the combined experience and knew Big Brave was as well. Possibly the only thing that could make this moment better would be if they were riding along the beach together.

They were headed back to the stables now, exhilarated and

feeling the experience of a natural high, Ava began to realize how hungry she was. She bid Big Brave a fond farewell and thanked her for understanding the ride she needed. Big Brave gave Ava a nod of the head with a sense of 'I understand.' Ava smiled and headed toward Gary. He too was hungry so they decided to take one car to a nearby dinner and ordered food to take out.

They found a relaxing meadow where they could sit on the ground and have their lunch and begin their typical spiritual conversations. Gary found a twig and began drawing what he called the pyramid of life in a sandy patch of the grass. He wanted to explore with me the fundamentals of a happy life. I complied with curiosity because I was confident that Gary always had something fascinating to share. At the base, the widest part of the pyramid were located the fundamentals needed for a safe, happy start. Such as employment providing shelter, food, clothing. The next level up contained interests and activities that were made possible by the lower level, up from there was pursuit of higher learning that was supported by the levels below and at the top was self-actualization - all that we are destined to become.

Ava simply told Gary that I wanted to jump to the top immediately. My respect for the pyramid theory was evident but I questioned that couldn't it be possible to self-actualize and then in that state of being, gain the ability to conquer all the levels below. He looked at me and said, "Ava, that is just like you." I smiled back and said, "I really respect the foundation level theory and I know it to be a typical psychology lesson taught in school." I knew in my consciousness however, I was living the exact opposite because of my history and my life here. I could not tell Gary that, however. I simply wanted to see what he had to say about my perspective. He knew me well but had no suspicions about who I really was. I knew I was being true to myself without revealing my true identity. I vowed that I wouldn't. I also vowed that I would be completely who I should be with or without another's approval. We continued talking about many things through our afternoon and one of those topics was always a curiosity that Gary held about me.

"Why don't you have a boyfriend?" he asked. I simply replied, "I am not completely sure. I date and the beginning of my relationships are always a pleasant and exciting experience. After the relationship finds a comfort zone and I want to continue my involvement in the things that capture my fascination and attention, the guy seems to think that I am being either selfish or no longer interested in him, which is truly not the case. I don't understand why the guy always feels that at this point my life should revolve around him and his interests. It becomes a source of conflict and we usually part ways. I don't see anything wrong with having separate interests that might even evolve into combined interests. The guys I pick want to consume me in every way but I am still my own person." Gary completely understood. He acknowledged that I was not typical, that I was a unique woman who established an identity and had goals and intents of her own. I thanked him for understanding me.

Finally Gary dropped a bomb on me, he said, "My marriage was not going well." I felt simply awful for him and could only offer an ear to listen whenever he wanted to talk. I asked him, "What went wrong, who's decision was this?" He said, "I'm not sure but I suspect that my wife has simply fallen out of love with me but my gravest concern is for my young daughter having to live the pain of divorced parents." I could understand and offered him a sympathetic hug and hoped that he would come through this ordeal unscathed and continue a close father and daughter relationship in the future.

It was beginning to get dark as the sun began to slowly set and we started to feel chilly. He drove me back to my car and in parting I reminded him he could call me any time to discuss whatever was on his mind. I would be a friend for him.

As I drove myself home I couldn't imagine what his predicament must feel like. Divorce is an ugly thing; so many hopes shattered; and there was a child involved. I decided I would seek guidance from my dreams that night for words to console his upcoming challenges or at least be there for him to talk if he needed me.

Arriving home, Ava reflected on her wonderful day riding Big Brave and savored every moment of the joy and exhilaration it brought her. She prepared a light dinner and while eating, was thinking over Gary's situation. It pained her to know that he had to go through this upheaval and what it must feel like.

She began her meditation practice and hoped for guidance through her dreams that night so she could help her friend.

When Ava awoke the following morning, she remembered her dream and began writing it in her dream journal:

> "Gary was in the dream and I was showing him the roots of my hair. He loved them and said they're beautiful.. A woman was in the room making a fire in the fireplace which was really a lit candle in a chair!"

Ava understood her dream to mean that she desperately wanted to tell Gary about who she really was but knew she never could. She would consider it a discretion within a discretion. Lord only knows what the consequences of that would mean! However, if her sense of true identity was revealed to Gary in one of his dreams, well that would be another story. She still could not confirm it for him. In her dream, Gary said he loved her roots affirming for Ava how much he would appreciate the immensity of such a revelation.

Attempting to further understand the context of her dream, Ava tried to figure out why a woman was trying to light a fireplace on a sofa chair which turned into a single lit candle. Ava wondered if the candle was herself and she would be single and on her own. That thought made Ava sad but realistically, how could she tell anyone that she may fall in love with who she really was? Would it be possible to keep that a secret from a spouse and for that matter, from anyone whom she cared deeply about, such as Gary.

She knew she already reconciled within herself that the problem of her full identity and potential no longer existed with her cohorts. They would have to accept her on her terms. But a sincere friend or spouse? That would be an interesting predicament she concluded.

With that written in her journal she got out of bed, showered and prepared breakfast and dressed. It was Sunday and she wanted to do more reading from her Seth book.

Before sinking her teeth into Seth, Ava performed her daily morning Yoga. During her Yoga session, she began to reflect on some of the words she had already read within the Seth book about "***a particular man being a study, a living example, of the effects of conflicting unexamined beliefs, a fierce and yet agonized personification of what can happen when an individual allows his conscious mind to deny its responsibilities - i.e., when an individual becomes afraid of his own consciousness. He was a young man whose beliefs were alive with their own life while he was relatively powerless. No effort had been made to reconcile directly opposing beliefs, until the personality itself was quite literally polarized.***"

Ava could understand why she was seeing these words in her mind during her exercise. There was great poignancy in direct relation to her own conflict. She suspected that most "unconscious" individuals are navigating through their lives like this and must certainly be confused and conflicted very much like herself. Maybe that's why they sought alcohol and drugs to numb the persistent responsibility that continually crept up and sought expression in an attempt to wake them up.

As she looked around her apartment, she decided that the day needed to be focused on cleaning, laundry and grocery shopping. She would consume more of her Seth book tonight after meditation and before bedtime. She felt mentally drained and had less energy than usual. The conflict was getting to her and she needed to shift her focus.

She went about her chores diligently and decided at some point in the afternoon that she needed to take a nap on the living room couch for an hour. The windows were open and the sunshine was still pouring through the light curtains and she decided to rest.

Meeting Zachary

Just as she laid her body on the couch with her face turned toward the back of the couch, she saw a man standing there. He was talking but she could not hear him. She was not the least bit panicked. She felt enveloped in a bubble of protection. He was dressed in a plaid shirt and had a stocky build with a blonde crew cut. He kept talking and gradually Ava began to hear what he was saying.

He introduced himself as Zachary and he was assigned to her as her guide. She knew she was not dreaming. She could hear the sounds of the outside world and she knew she was in her apartment. Gradually he walked down to the foot of the couch at the end where her feet were. Zachary told Ava that she is right in knowing she was not dreaming. He was here for her always and could be summoned at any time she needed him. He would never appear outside the confines of her home however and would only appear when she was alone. Ava felt a heightened sense of concentration and comfort. Zachary lifted his right arm outward to his side level with his shoulder and from it dropped a map of the United States. She could see the map clearly and he pointed his left index finger to a place on the map. She clearly heard him say, "This is where it is." Ava tried to focus on where Zachary was pointing but with such physical effort, she generated a change in her energy field and puff, he was gone. She sat up in amazement from the experience and how no one could possibly believe this really happened. Ava knew differently. She was there and present and witnessed this visual actualization of another dimension and with extreme concentration altering her energy shift, he was gone.

Well, Ava was mesmerized by the event and could only sit and absorb and savor it in all its amazement and considered its implications as well as its rewards and probabilities for her future. She could not do much more of anything the rest of the afternoon. She remained fixed on the experience and analyzed her energy frequency which allowed it to occur realizing that her Yoga and meditation had been fruitful in aligning her energy field allowing the experience to manifest. Ava began to write every detail in her journal. It never occurred to her to get out a map and seek where Zachary was pointing to nor ask, "This is where WHAT is?" She was too bewildered and excited and continued to play the event over and over in her mind.

Never having taken her nap, she decided she would simply begin to prepare for bed and the work week ahead. She made a light dinner for herself and after eating, went to bed along with her Seth book. Feeling too restless to sleep and unable to concentrate on the Seth material, Ava headed back into the living room and turned on MTV.

On the screen was the beginning of a video by a band she did not know. The lead singer was singing "With or Without You". His voice felt like it grabbed her by her shirt and wanted to suck her into the TV. The band was named U2. What? Ava's familiarity with jets brought her to the conclusion that the band was named after the U2 spy plane built by the US for spy missions over Russia. Who are these guys she wondered. What in the world has come over me? She was completely mesmerized by the voice of the lead singer, whom she found out later was named "Bono". What kind of name is Bono? She was fully captivated by his amazing voice, a voice like no other, and by the words of the song along with the black and white visual cinematography of the video. Ava connected to this astonishing performance and knew it held serious spiritual significance for her. She really didn't have a clue why. It resonated within her soul and she knew this band had to be explored in her own unique way! Ava could never accept anything at face value. When she found an interest, she explored every facet of it to the degree that she unknowingly became an expert on it.

For now, Ava needed to get to bed and have the proper rest she needed to perform at an optimum level at work so off to dreamland she went.

Waking with a clear recollection of her dream, she reached for her journal and began writing:

> "Someone had called me while she was sleeping, it was a female voice, saying Hello Ava, I guess you are sleeping, it's 10:15. Okay, maybe you're sleeping, I'll talk to you tomorrow."

Ava went to check the answering machine in the living room. The dream was too real, it must have really happened. She saw the answering machine had no messages on it. Well, Sunday was quite an eventful day for me she thought. A visitor, the U2 song, and now a dream of someone calling me but really not calling me in this physical reality. I sincerely think my compadres in Sania are watching out for me assisting in every way imaginable!

Ava was now ready to begin her work week. When folks started entering the building, she asked a few whom she felt would know, if they had ever heard of the band U2? Of course Ava, where have you been? Ava laughed to herself, you should only know.

"Who are they? What are some of the albums"? Doug Rice from the warehouse told her, "In my opinion, they're the greatest band that ever lived." Okay, Ava thought, I'll take that with a grain of salt, but she sensed they had significance for her. She asked more about them and how she could get cassettes of their music. "Can you recommend some albums for me"? Doug wrote a few titles down beginning with Red Rocks and ending with Joshua Tree their most current. He mentioned that they also had done a live performance movie called "Rattle and Hum" at Sun Devil Stadium in Phoenix, Arizona. I thanked him and made my decision to buy some. He then mentioned, there was a Blockbuster around the corner and I could rent the "Rattle and Hum" video there. I'm sure I know where I'm going after work today, Ava said to herself. My money seems to go towards books and music, for sure I will need a bigger apartment, laughing to herself.

CHAPTER 14

Surprises to Come

During the day, Ava could here a great deal of talking outside her office. Certainly more than usual. Apparently a rumor was going around. Liz from her staff came in and said, "Have you heard? There's talk that Business Land is buying Computer Enterprise!" I looked at her and in my true fashion, I asked "who she had heard this from and how concrete could the information be considered?" Liz could not tell me. She said she heard it from someone in Customer Service and now it's all over the building.

Ava wanted to ignore the possibility that CE was being swallowed up by a corporate giant. We were a privately owned company and the two brothers who owned it couldn't possibly be persuaded to sell out. Maybe they would she supposed if the price was right.

Ava decided she would gently persuade one of the managers to provide insight into this most improbable event. She placed a call to Debbie Jason who headed H.R. and asked if she had a minute to talk. Debbie said, "Sure, come on in." Ava was more blunt than she expected to be. She flatly asked Debbie if she knew anything about this rumor that's flying around the office. Debbie replied, "You mean about a takeover by Business Land?" Ava was surprised, apparently she may have been the only one who didn't know. Ava said, "Yes." Debbie could only say that she heard the rumor but had no information about it. I wondered how true it could be and what the implications were. It might be a simple name change and nothing else affected. Ava was in a wishful thinking mode this day. She did not want to go through a potential change in management; processes; new inventory programs; reporting structure, etc. Whatever transpired, she would consider herself lucky to still have a job. She thought about Rob Cameron and how this would affect his financial situation. Ava looked at the possibility of not receiving the promotion as a good thing after all. She remembered a quote from Shakespeare, "There are greater things in Heaven and Earth Horatio, than can be dreamt in your philosophies" and then gave a nod to the Universe.

As the week ended with continued talk of the take over, Ava could only concentrate on her upcoming visit with Mari Starly and her son Riley the following day at the observatory. She anticipated a fun day and wondered how little of what she had recently experienced she could share with Mari especially considering her seven year old son being present. It should prove an interesting day.

With that thought in mind, she called her friend Gary to see how he was doing. Gary said as well as can be expected and was able to secure two tickets to visit the USS Intrepid for two weeks from then. Ava was elated! She couldn't wait and felt excitement and thanked Gary profusely for the invitation. They planned on an early dinner after the event. She also suggested they take the Port Imperial Ferry across the Hudson which docked only two blocks from the Intrepid and they would not have to deal with driving into the City and paying for parking. "Great idea" Gary said. "That would also be a great photo op experience as well." Ava agreed!

After work, Ava's first stop was the Blockbuster video rental store around the corner. She had never been in one and found it confusing. The store manager asked her if she needed help. "Yes," Ava replied. "I'm looking for the "Rattle and Hum" video by U2."

Craig, the store manager lit up and said, "Oh you will love it!" Obviously he was a fan. Craig was a young, tall, thin, red head and very energetic. He did everything fast. He talked fast, he walked fast, he was a bundle of energy enough for three people. Ava laughed to herself and hoped that the U2 music didn't do this to him. He explained to me the layout of the store and how aisles were categorized by drama, comedy, foreign, etc., and took me to the music video section. He selected the video and walked me to the front counter. He presumed I was not a member of Blockbuster and he was right. He got me started with paperwork and created my membership card. He explained the rules of rental and the costs. I also got the distinct feeling that he was flirting with me. I thought, oh dear, I've got at least 10 years on this kid. In any event, I was happily on my way home and appreciated the great service Craig provided and anticipated a fun evening watching the U2 movie. I picked up a Burger King on the way home because I just didn't feel like cooking.

Well, Ava was completely and thoroughly impressed by the experience of watching the live concert by U2. She was a devout fan now and was moved by the energy and power behind the songs; the words of deep spiritual meaning; the profound performance techniques; the vibrational energy and the sincere message behind their cohesive magic on stage. When they performed "Where The Streets Have No Name" she was completely in love. It felt like Sania. There was an overpowering sense of enlightenment when that song was performed. She considered the meaning of the title of the song and decided it was a physical place they must be talking about that truly existed but surely didn't know where it was. It simply smacked of Sania.

Ava wanted to find the sheet music for their body of work and thought to herself, here I go again, laughing at herself at the space needed for all these books! She had two days to return the rented video and knew they had videos for sale and this was going to be on the top of her video list. She watched the video three times, which brought her well past any reading time with Seth. She didn't mind. There was richness and insight in all things. Tonight for Ava, it was U2 but little did she know for her future as well.

Saturday morning arrived and Ava so loved it when she didn't have to go to work. She did love her work but it was time to play and explore and be with friends. Life was becoming balanced and good, for now.

Mari called while Ava was in the shower and left a message to come by for lunch. Riley was at a friends house until the evening and her husband wasn't returning until dinner time, so they would have time to talk and explore thoughts and ideas. After dinner the three of them would head over the observatory and explore the Heavens. It sounded like a delightful day.

After my Yoga session, I dressed and prepared my directions to get to Mari's and it occurred to me, I hadn't had a dream the night before. Interesting I thought, especially considering how impressed I was with the U2 video. I would have thought something would have been detected in my subconscious that would enlighten me. I quickly stopped by the video store and dropped off my rental only to buy my very own copy. I was excited to own it.

Mari lived about forty-five minutes north of me in Bergen County. I found her house easily enough and arrived at 11:45 AM just in time for lunch. Mari's house was a three-story Cape Cod Tudor, very quaint, old, partially upgraded and it had a large backyard. It was comfy and one could easily feel at home there. We ate in the formal dining room but not in a formal fashion. Mari was very relaxed and laid back, wearing her jeans and a light sweater. We had a delicious lunch of sandwiches and salad in between our constant chattering. I felt like I had known her for years.

After lunch, Mari wanted me to hold a woman's compact in my hand and asked me if I could feel anything about the person who owned it. I knew immediately where our relationship was heading and I had absolutely no objections. Mari felt I had psychic abilities and could sense an energy field about me that was different yet similar to her own. After all, like attracts like.

I concentrated for a bit on the compact and could see an aristocratic woman with wavy black hair of advanced years and possibly of a Spanish background. Mari smiled and her electric blue eyes lit up. I asked her, "Well, am I right?" She said, "Yes, this woman was an aristocrat and she is no longer alive. I don't know if she had a Spanish background but she did have black wavy hair and the compact was from the eighteenth century." I asked her how she came to possess it and she said it belonged to a member of her husband's family and because Mari always admired it they gave it to her.

"Oh, all right then Mari, did I pass your first test?" Mari laughed and said, "I'm not testing you, I just wanted to show you what you don't know you possess." "Oh," I said, "thank you." I was really quite surprised at the images that were coming to me when I held the compact in my hand. "I never would have thought to do that and I thank you for showing me something about myself that I didn't know. You seem to know a lot about me that I do and don't know about myself. How is that?" She said, "I could just sense it. You have something I want. I've worked so intensely for years to develop these types of abilities within me. I have always been fascinated by a higher consciousness and although I have grown in these areas, I'm not quite there yet. Ava, your energy field shot out at me and I could tell you had these gifts." I simply looked at her and said, "Okay, I am a seeker and enjoy explorations in these realms but I feel like I'm a beginner." Mari immediately said, "No you're not. You are seasoned. You simply don't have the awareness of it." I laughed to myself, she should only know! Well, I suspected I was continuing the same work here as I did from Sania for Earthlings. Mari popped into my radar because she sensed something that I could teach her. I was going to go with it. I believe we are all each other's teachers.

Mari began to show me her library! I was overwhelmed with the number of books and albums. A whole room dedicated to their interests! I thought about my tiny apartment and laughed. She began to ask me if I have ever read Edgar Cayce, Carlos Castenade; Elke Tolle; and on and on. Of course, I was familiar with their work and vaguely remembered having influenced one or two of them from the Sania dimension, but I could not admit to that. I said, "No, but I have a feeling your private library is going to become my public library!" We laughed. I asked her, "Would you be willing to lend me a book?" She said, "Take your pick." I asked her what would she suggest. Her response was perfect. "It will come to you." I could sense that Mari was a woman of deep knowing and a deep desire to continue growing and that our collaborative efforts would benefit us both.

Then Mari asked if I had ever done the Ouija Board. I raised my eyebrows in surprise and said, "No, I hadn't." She immediately said, "I know you would be great at this!". I said, "Well, I'll try it but I won't promise anything." I did want to know if she had a specific reason for using this device. Did she have a special need in a special area of her life that she felt she needed the Ouija Board for guidance? Mari wanted information on her son Riley. She felt he had a destiny to fulfill and wanted to be sure that she would provide him with the proper tools to achieve that destiny. I told Mari that Riley knows what he needs to do. You are simply the woman who brought him into this world. His destiny is within himself, he will come to you with questions. Mari was surprised at my answer. "Wow" she said, "See what I mean. No one has ever responded to me like that. I knew you would have a better, more enlightened view of my questions." I asked Mari if she wanted to ask me how you should respond to him when he does come to you with questions? "Yes," Mari said. "Well, I can't tell you that. You as his mother and guardian can only know that." Mari believed if she could contact some of her dead relatives through the Ouija Board, she would be given definitive guidance.

"OK," I said. "Let's give it a whirl." With our knees touching while facing each other, we placed the planchette on the board and our finger tips ever so gently upon it. Mari wanted to contact her grandfather David with a specific request on guiding Riley. The planchette began to move slowly and it spelled "be to Riley as I was to you."

Mari was flabbergasted and confused. She was excited to receive a message and so quickly but didn't understand what the message meant. I asked Mari was David, her grandfather, her main caregiver. She replied "no, but he had a strong influence on my life." "Well, Mari, that is what your grandfather is telling you. He was not your main caregiver, but from a distance was very influential to you." Mari beamed with understanding "yes," she said, "I get it. I've always tried to have a hands off approach with Riley allowing him to come to me for guidance rather than filling him with all kinds of expectations." I replied, "What an interesting way of raising a child. Kudos to you. If you have faith in your son and know if he is in need of something, you allow him the first move rather than imposing on him what you desire for him. Clever, but Riley must be a very special soul to require a partnership with his parents in this manner." Mari said, "Oh yes, he is. There's something about him that boggles my mind and I don't want to deter him in any way from what his heart and soul intuitively tells him." I complimented Mari on her approach and said, "I can't wait to meet Riley. He sounds like an exceptional little guy. Most children need a great deal of direction and discipline while growing up."

"Well, now that you have received a direct communication and affirmation of your suspicions, do you want to continue?" Mari was delighted. We positioned ourselves again and she asked another question. Nothing was happening. I grew impatient and asked Mari to remove connection from me. The Ouija Board was all mine now and the planchette began flying all over the board. Mari's eyes popped open so wide I thought they'd fall out of her head. "Oh my God" she said. "What's happening?" I simply said, "I don't need you for this. Apparently, I can do it on my own" and laughed. Once the planchette calmed down it began to spell the name Zachary. I began asking Zachary questions such as who are you, why are you here. Zachary slowly replied G U I D E and then F O R Y O U.

And continued with F A N O F U2 I started giggling as I looked at Mari and shrugged my shoulders. "I guess no one wants to talk to you Mari." She was okay with that. I explained to Mari that I'd become fascinated with the band U2 and I think there is something in their persona that is important to me. "Apparently, Zachary has been watching too and knows I'm spot on with my observation," I told her.

It was time to put the Ouija board down now and begin dinner preparation. Riley would be home from playing at his friend's house and we would be eating soon.

As I helped her prepare dinner, she wanted to know what I was experiencing while doing the Ouija Board. I told her that I felt a comforting warmth surrounding my physical body. I could sense a slight tingling but it was subtle. I thanked her for introducing this vehicle to me and she quickly said, "Then it's yours!" She was giving it to me! "Are you kidding me?" She said, "No, I want you to have it. You have what it takes to do it on your own. If you don't mind, would it be all right if I call and ask you to read the board for me?" I said, "It's a deal but I meditate at night so I wouldn't want to be disturbed during that time."

"Oh, what type of meditation do you do?" Mari asked. "The one suggested in the book you lent me, Chakra Meditation. I find it balances my energy." Mari replied, "I have a hard time meditating. I can't sit still long enough." I didn't say anything to Mari, I was puzzled by her comment.

Riley entered the house and her husband had come home too. I was meeting them both for the first time. Her husband was quite handsome but reserved. Riley had the same electric blue eyes as his mom. I smiled. He looked like a great kid. During dinner Riley talked about all the things he did at his friends house but Mari's husband didn't say much. He was communicative with his son but not with Mari or myself. He was a pleasant man and polite and after dinner excused himself because he had work to do in his den.

I politely said, "It was a pleasure meeting you." Mari reminded him they were all heading for the observatory. "Have fun" he said.

Being at the observatory was an exciting adventure for me. I know Riley was excited but I was more focused on finding Pleiades and wondering how fascinating it is that I knew Sania existed beyond the star cluster but no one on Earth could detect it since it was a dimensional portal unable to be known by the current physics of the time. Eventually, I'm sure they will discover it.

As I stared at the 7 Sisters, I imagined how I used to look at them from the perspective of the dimension of Sania. They were a magnificent site from that angle too! We headed to the gift shop where Riley wanted to pick up a few things for his school projects. I was growing tired, as we all were.

Mari drove us back to her house and I got into my car for my forty-five minute ride home with a few books from Mari's library, The Teachings of Don Juan; A Separate Reality; Tales of Power by Carlos Castaneda and my Rattle and Hum Video on the front passenger seat. What a lovely day! So many new adventures and new people have come into my life. I am blessed.

I arrived home quite exhausted and decided tonight I did not want to meditate or read. Tonight I was going to take a hot shower and get into bed filled with the blessings of a wonderful day. I quickly drifted off to sleep.

In the middle of the night I awoke. I was still in a dream world and saw Zachary sitting in a sofa chair at the end of my bed, reading a book to me. I sat up and hazily recognizing the plaid shirt. He never looked up at me. He continued to read. I laid back down on my pillow and continued my sleep. I began to dream:

> "A book was floating in mid air. It was too far away from me to make out the words. I asked for the book to be brought closer to me so that I could read it. The book began to float in

midair towards me but I kept prompting it to move closer until the point that I could read it. Within the dream, I realized I was dreaming and making requests within the dream knowing I was having a Lucid Dream. With that realization came the excitement of my achievement and immediately the dream broke up and all I could make out were two words from the book at the tale end of a sentence. 'with fish'."

When Ava awoke Sunday morning, she distinctly remembered everything that happened during the night including the lucid dream. She began writing in her dream journal. At this moment Ava began to suspect that her spirit guide was beginning to work with her. She felt certain Zachary who appeared in her living room and through the Ouija Board and now at the foot of her bed in the middle of the night was a true source of comfort and guidance and if she kept her energy fields aligned and clear, he would be accessible. He was selected as her source of protection and inspiration through this lifetime on Earth. She had no memory of him from this lifetime when she lived it before and no memory of his energy from Sania. She had this connection to Zachary now, however.

Ava knew herself astrologically in this lifetime as a Leo which was a fire element. This work with Spirit Guides was a direct correlation to who was guiding her. It included everything from the flame of a candle to the ethereal flames and light of the sun on a daily basis, thus at this moment gaining insight into the flamed candle on the sofa chair in one of her previous dreams. Somehow everything seemed to be coming together, suddenly and methodically which is how Ava worked. The fire elementals can help awaken in us higher spiritual vision and aspiration. They strengthen and stimulate the entire auric field so that there is an easier alignment and recognition of higher spiritual forces within our lives. Ava felt assured that this was exactly what was happening to her and the reasons for the likely rapport with Zachary. If we do confirm this for ourselves on a conscious level, we can more easily open the doors to inner realm perception. Ava wondered if Mari Starly knew something about this or if she was just magnetized by Ava's energy field.

Ava remembered a book in her living room on "working with spirit guides" which she apparently had read and went to reach for it to review more on the subject. She located the chapter on fire elementals and began reading "salamanders evoke powerful emotional currents in humans. They also stimulate fires of spiritual idealism and perception. Their energy assists in the tearing down of the old and the building up of the new, as fire is both destructive and constructive in its creative expression. The salamander is a mythical animal having the power to endure fire without harm; an elemental being in the theory of Paracelsus inhabiting fire. Ava recognized she had done this in a previous lifetime which elevated her and now here again to achieve an even higher level. This particular lifetime was a strong one for her and one that could again guide her but into an even higher level of consciousness. She no longer wondered about her comment to Gary about skipping the basics of the pyramid of life levels and just begin at the top. Of course her friend did not have the benefit of her future and that she was here again. He did not know her journey of returning.

Ava felt isolated by that idea. She felt alone on this journey that no one could understand - except she wasn't really alone, she had visible guides to assist. It was up to her to communicate with them using any vehicle made available.

It was Sunday and Ava had the entire day to explore more of her favorite books and music. She began with her Yoga practice and then had a light breakfast.

She started going through some of the Seth material in her living room. Looking around she wondered if she would detect any presence there but she did not. She sat on her couch after putting

Wagner on the stereo to a low volume. She began reading and a red blinking light caught her attention out of the corner of her eye. She realized it was her answering machine. A bit surprised because she didn't hear the phone ring. She played back the message. On the tape was playing an Amy Grant verse from her song:

"That's What Love Is For"
Sometimes I see you and you don't know I am there
And I'm washed away by emotions
I hold deep down inside
Getting stronger with time
It's living through the fire and holding on we find
That's what love is for
To help us through it
That's what love is for

Lyrics by: Mark Mueller, Michael Omartian, Amy Grant

Ava again was surprised to receive yet another mysterious message. She couldn't imagine who would have sent it. It was just the one verse of the song. There was no way to determine its origin but Ava began to suspect that the device her Light Beings were showing her in a past dream was a more futuristic answering machine. Only they didn't look like that in 1985 and this was a loving message from them. She knew she was being guided along this journey and it comforted her.

It was becoming increasingly evident that these recordings came from a guiding source. She never heard the phone ring. She even checked the ringer volume on the phone. Hearing the words made her want to cry as she kept repeating the tape. Especially the part that says, "Sometimes I see you and you don't know I'm there". Again she was compelled to repeat to herself her favorite quote from Shakespeare, "There are greater things in Heaven and Earth Horatio than can be dreamt in our philosophies".

CHAPTER 15

Another Hero

Ava felt compelled to put her Seth book down and begin one of the books she borrowed from Mari Starly. It was Joseph Campbell, The Power of Myth. She had a vague memory of this name and with the memory came a strong admiration.

Before beginning the book she looked out her living room window and stared at the trees glistening in the sunlight and could smell the fresh air. She knew she should spend more time in nature and she knew it enriched the soul but she really was torn between both paths. She wanted to read and learn more and she wanted to commune with the green Earth. She decided to sit back down on the couch and conclude that there was time for both. It was just a matter of balancing that time. Always a balancing act she thought to herself. Instinctively she knew she had a mission but also had the need to play. Maybe Wagner was the wrong music to play with. It was beautiful but was bringing on a melancholy mood so she switched to her Native American music. It seemed to filter a sense of nature and spirt into her space at the same time. This was probably a good thing because she felt conflicted about going outdoors or staying in and examining the knowledge she wanted so eagerly.

She began to read from Joseph Campbell's book and for whatever reason, decided to look for another book in her own library. She searched intently and came upon the Fractal Enlightenment Newsletters. They appealed to her. She knew this was necessary to read:

The passage that caught her attention began ... ***One must be willing to stand alone - in the unknown, with no reference to authority or the past or any of one's conditioning. One must stand where no one has stood before. Imagine you're at a crossroads. There are two signs. The one pointing to the right reads: Comfort, security, certainty, and the end of knowledge (blue pill). And the one pointing to the left reads: Discomfort, insecurity, uncertainty, and the pursuit of knowledge (red pill). Which one do you choose?***

This is the ultimate crux of the examined life: if pursued wisely, there is no end to the discomfort and uncertainty. The more you seek, the more cognitive dissonance is experienced, and the more previous knowledge becomes uncouth. The only certainty is perpetual uncertainty. But there is a joy in discovery that trumps the bliss of ignorance. Indeed, there's an ecstasy in new knowledge that utterly eclipses the pleasures of comfort and security.

So if you would be immanent, I beseech you, choose the uncomfortable path of perpetual knowledge over the comfortable path of stagnant knowledge. It's worth any amount of discomfort. And with enough practice, wrestling with your doubt, cognitive dissonance, and insecurity will become an art form and a state of peaceful immanence will be yours." (Fractal Enlightenment Newsletter 2015, Gary McGee)

Ava felt she was being given an answer to her earlier decision about what to do. Go outside in nature or stay indoors and read and gain knowledge. Everything seemed ironic to her now. She switched books, she switched music, she changed her mind about what to do today. She was conflicted and it appeared the answer was just handed to her on a silver plater.

Ava decided she would ride her angst and make decisions based on her emotional reaction to something from now on which alone would be a challenge since she prided herself on her intellect in all areas of life. The newsletter from Fractal Enlightenment reminded her of the story of Alice in Wonderland. She LOVED that story. These passages could so easily be overlaid onto the story of Alice. Life is uncomfortable, but there is no point in remaining stagnant. If you did you would never uncover the riches that are buried deep inside you. You would never discover the many levels of who you are if you did not accept the challenges and question your very existence. Truly, some people reject the challenges and pitifully never grow. Ava did not have that nature. It was her destiny to look deep within and prosper as Machiavelli once said. It assured her of her sense of identity and she was a Red Pill gal. This was who she was. She was on the path of accepting who and why she is Ava.

Her discourse about not having a husband, someone to feel that genuine connection of love and partnership with, had been explained to a degree but she would never give up on the possibility. Her friends often questioned her about it and Ava always felt they wondered what was wrong with her that she didn't have a partner. She suspected they questioned many things about her, such as, what she did in her spare time because she didn't party like an animal, why was she always so focused and why did it seem at times she appeared "spaced out".

These were underlying issues Ava wrestled with but ignored even though they gave her reasons to feel uncomfortable. After all, Ava was living a double life. She had a mission to achieve among a civilization that really did not have her evolutionary success and now finds herself thrust into their reality sticking out like a sore thumb. She would find herself covering up who she really was in one moment and then deciding it only really mattered who she was and witnesses would have to deal with their own confusion about her. This human life gig sure is difficult. She felt that her guiding support; her Yoga; her meditation all assisted in achieving continued growth and less complex internal questioning.

She read another snippet from Fractal Enlightenment:

The deeper you look the more you will see. The more you see, the more you'll see how everything is connected, and the more you'll care. Sure, there are scary things in the Desert of the Real, but so what. There's truth there. There is freedom there. And there can be no immanence without freedom and truth.

This last passage satisfied Ava never receiving clearly the message of the "Desert of the Real". That would coalesce into a purpose of its own later for Ava.

CHAPTER 16

USS Intrepid

As another week went by and Ava was now ready for her Saturday with her good friend Gary. It was their day to explore The USS Intrepid. He stopped by her apartment at 9:30 a.m. and they took her car down River Road meandering along the Hudson River to Port Imperial where they would catch the Ferry. The sun was gleaming over the still river waters almost like glass. Gary, "We couldn't have picked a better day. The sky is so blue and everything is so bright. I'm so happy."

They arrived onto the Ferry and Gary immediately took out his Cannon 360 snapping photos. We were both snapping photos of Manhattan's beautiful and impressive skyline and at each other snapping each other. We could even see a tiny Statue of Liberty way at the end of the Harbor where the Hudson empties into the Atlantic Ocean. It would only take about ten minutes to cross the Hudson and soon we were in Manhattan, the concrete jungle. Always noisy and full of people no matter what time of day or night, it was an exciting place to visit but I did prefer the cozy quiet of the Garden State. We only had two blocks north to walk and I immediately was captivated by the magnificent hull of that monstrous aircraft carrier. The width of the chain that anchors her was literally as wide as three of me. What power, what majesty! I was enthralled by her beauty and magnificence and could only imagine the battles she had witnessed. We entered the visitor gate submitted our tickets to the attendant and found ourselves on her deck. Launched in 1943, the aircraft carrier Intrepid fought in World War II, surviving five kamikaze attacks and one torpedo strike. The ship later served in the Cold War and the Vietnam War. Intrepid also served as a NASA recovery vessel in the 1960s.

The finest fleet of fighter jets imaginable were propped on her deck and I immediately walked over the F-15. It was exciting to see it this close. I could only imagine the roar of her engines and what it would seem like sitting in it's cockpit flying and protecting our country. I asked Gary to take a photo of me from it's front end. I knew the photo would not do it justice. This baby had to be seen in person to appreciate its enormity and power. If only I could fly it, I thought. There were so many jets on top of the deck but there were still levels below to explore. Each jet had a plaque explaining its name and statistics. They were the real thing sitting on top of the real thing. I was like a child in a candy store left all alone to enjoy the sweets until my heart was content. Before heading below deck I had to walk to the end of the carrier to view the water from above. It was a thrilling sensation that I always enjoyed. Of course, for safety sake, a rail was built around the carrier so no visitors would fall off its edge. I could see straight down over the edge into the water. I was amazed at how high off the water we were. It was windy but sunny and I could only imagine what it would feel like out on the open seas. Feeling giddy and sharing such a great experience with such a great friend made us both feel like children.

We headed down to the next deck, the Hangar Deck to visit the museum below. It contained helicopters and older planes as well as original artifacts and historical video footage. Gary and I were snapping our cameras and having the time of our lives. We even explored the insides of some like little children. Gary knew everything about these planes.

The "Captain" or at least the official on duty noticed how excited and captivated we were about our experience and he approached us. He asked if we would like a look at the control tower. Gary and I looked at each other in amazement and surprise and in unison said, "Sure, is it legal?" The official implied no but we seemed to be such enthusiasts he figured we'd get a kick out of it. We traveled up a circular metal staircase that I thought would never end. Perched up high above the carrier was the control room with a full circular view. We were as high as the buildings in NYC. He showed us the controls which of course were no longer in functioning order and he explained what each one did. We were so incredibly honored and amazed. We couldn't take the grins off of our faces! We were like giddy children!

As our adventure ended, we bid farewell to The USS Intrepid and decided we were famished and needed to find food fast. He asked if I would mind getting something from the street vendor and that was fine with me. It would be fast and we could eat along the benches on the Hudson River. Afterwards we would just have a two block walk to the Ferry to return to New Jersey. "What a day!" I told Gary. "This was the best day ever. I'm so thrilled and excited. Please share your photos with me when you get them developed." "Of course," he said, "and make sure you show me yours in case I didn't get some of what you got." "OK friend, it's a deal."

Gary wanted to talk to me about the progress of his divorce proceedings and I listened intently. He said she dropped another bomb on him. Their divorce would be final in a few months and she was planning to move to Colorado where her family lives and she was taking their daughter with her. That was part of the divorce settlement that he agreed to. He was not going to live without his daughter and so decided he would be seeking a transfer through his company to Colorado. My heart dropped! I was about to lose a good friend that I enjoyed doing so many things with. "Oh, Gary, I'm so sorry. I understand that you would want to be part of your daughter's life and I appreciate your honoring your parental responsibilities but I sure would miss you." Ava couldn't imagine not having him around. Gary felt the same but he knew what he had to do. "How soon do you think you'll be leaving, I asked?" Gary didn't have a definitive date but he suspected it would be just before Christmas.

I was beginning to understand the sense of loss and change in the human experience and understood that this was a challenging time for me which would only prove to be a time of growth as well. I knew this much from what I absorbed from my reading material and my guidance. I immediately wondered if I should check out the place on the map that Zachary was pointing to the day he appeared in my living room showing me "this is where it is". I couldn't wait to get back home and figure it out. I also couldn't wait to go home compelled to listen U2's music. I'm sure there was a connection but for now I couldn't figure out what it meant.

We slowly got up and started walking towards the Ferry. I asked Gary if I could go to his house before going home to look at the maps in his den. He looked at me strangely and asked "why"? I said, "I have a reason. You have a large map of the United States on your wall and I need to find something there. Do you mind?" He said, "Not at all, no problem" but he looked at me strangely. I didn't care.

Upon arriving at Gary's home, we walked up to the den. Ava saw the map on the wall. Gary followed her and asked, "If you don't mind, can you please tell me what you are trying to do?" I simply said, "Gary, I can't, just trust me on this one, okay?" He said, "Sure. Do you need privacy?" I said, "Not really." Ava stepped back from the map the approximate distance she was when Zachary displayed the map from his arm. She fixed her vision on the place he had pointed to. She kept a steady eye on the point and began moving closer and closer until she was about five inches from the map and the location read JOSHUA TREE! She was stunned and couldn't talk for a moment. Gary looked at her and said, "What's going on?" Ava asked him if he had ever heard of a place called Joshua Tree.

He had not but knew it was U2's latest album! She said, "Yeah." Ava didn't realize it was a geographic location the band was referring to. She told Gary she didn't want to be rude but she needed to leave. She thanked him again for a great day and for the use of the map. Ava left the house and drove home in great anticipation of what she believed she was about to find, what she was finally looking for. Just a slight twist on one of the band's greatest songs! Ava laughed to herself.

When Ava arrived home, she immediately began playing the Joshua Tree cassette on her stereo. She was staring at the machine absorbing every nuance of sound the instruments produced and Bono's exceptionally unique voice. She felt like a child who sees a Christmas Tree for the first time and is totally captivated by it. All her focus and attention was given to every word sung by Bono's beautiful voice. She was moved to elation. She searched the songs in the songbook while listening and soaked up every feeling of every expressive word. Ava was mesmerized and found herself in another space and time. She made the connection to Joshua Tree being the place they must be referencing in the song, "Where The Streets Have No Name". She was bewildered by the fact that this was the place that Zachary was pointing to on the map, a place she had never heard of and the photo on the cover of the album, "Joshua Tree". She joked with herself "there's gold in them there hills". There was a treasure there for her. She just knew it. Why else would all these synchronisms keep happening. They were all guide posts for her and she knew it deep within herself. She might take a vacation to go there but with the unsettling thought of her job predicament, she might not want to spend the money on a trip just now, at least until she was assured of another job on the horizon. It saddened her but she was confident that it would happen. She would make it to Joshua Tree. There was something there for her, there, where the streets have no name.

As Ava continued enjoying the music of U2 and finding great significance in their words, she decided to summon Zachary who came through immediately. He announced himself and said, FANOFU2. Ava smiled and said, "Hi Zac." Zachary began speaking, "I WILL GO WITH YOU." Ava responded, "I would hope so Zac. How about we go to a concert together too?" Zachary's response was simply WHISTLE. Ava could not understand what he meant. She asked for clarification and he repeated 'T WHISTLE MUSIC'. Ava thought this was strange. "I'd rather sing the songs Zac." He simply replied OFF MUSIC. Ava turned the music off and realized that the tea kettle on top of the stove was whistling! Ava rushed to turn the burner off. She had completely forgotten she put the kettle on to make some green tea. Wow, that could have been a disaster if all the water evaporated and just the kettle was on the flame. She made her tea and rushed back to thank Zachary. "I really appreciate you keeping an eye on things for me. I got so absorbed in the music." Zachary simply replied, 'RING' and again, Ava could not understand, but before she could ask for clarification, the phone rang. Ava laughed out loud and said, "Thanks Zac, talk to you later."

Ava picked up the phone and it was Mari Starly at the other end. Mari asked Ava if she had a minute. Mari wanted to know if Ava would be interested in attending a workshop being conducted by the author of "Reach For The Highest Fruit on the Tree". Ava exclaimed, "Yes of course. Where and when?" Mari informed Ava it was being held at the Commodore Hotel in Manhattan on November 16 and the cost was $55.00. Ava was so excited. She wouldn't have long to wait and she didn't care how expensive this was going to be, she was doing this!

CHAPTER 17

The AX Falls

The persistent rumors flying around the office were becoming louder and louder and finally a decision was made. The rumor was a reality. A deal was struck with Business Land to buy out Computer Enterprises. Ava understood the rumors were a dead giveaway but she chose to ignore them with a hope they were false and simply giving someone a sense of power to talk about something they knew nothing about. Unfortunately Ava realized she had made a mistake. Instead of taking precautions and beginning the process of lining herself up for another position in case there was truth to the rumor, she chose to ignore it and continued to pour all her energies into her job that she was so good at. She felt foolish and wondered why in her divine guidance she was not given a heads up, but considered she had but did not interpret it correctly. She tried to think back on some of her dreams and some of her recent reading material and realized the dream of the enormous ocean wave was probably a clue. She was confused and saddened and could only conclude this was the way of corporate America - basic greed.

Everyone in this company gave their hearts and souls to making a success of the operation only to be betrayed by the almighty dollar. Well, humanity's evolution had not yet reached a level of understanding that your actions can never love or betray another, they can only love or betray yourself. She began again to feel the loss of her existence in Sania and wanted to cry. She remembered the passage from Fractal Enlightenment that conveyed ***perpetual uncertainty and cognitive dissonance is what brought a person to heights unimaginable***. Somehow it was of no comfort to her now simply because she could not see the road ahead and that made her feel uneasy. Well, after all, that is what humans deal with all their lives and mostly in blind faith but sometimes with calculated methodical plans. Ava understood from their level now why so many turned to drugs and alcohol and even formed buddy groups for the sake of either masking the pain or assuring their futures with connections and networking. Interesting predicaments this humanity is experiencing. She felt an empathy and sadness for them and now she was part of them. Her confusion and anger made it difficult for her to concentrate on her work and she feigned busyness so she could deal with the mental pictures of the intellectual meaning of all of this and her emotions toward it. She wondered what would happen to these employees; small severance package; unemployment and the drudgery of finding another job. Worrying about families to feed, clothe, and educate.

Well, on the bright side, it could lead them to a shakeup of their comfort zone and produce a better job and maybe even a startup of new companies. In her wondering, she thought, there is always hope. She was feeling lifted from the pessimistic outlook she was experiencing and began to feel it in her spirit. Maybe this is an opportunity for something even better. Again she reflected back on the Fractal Enlightenment passage **"there is joy in discovery that trumps the bliss of ignorance"**. Well, I have a choice. Expend the energy on sadness or expend the energy on happiness. Ava decided she would look for the positive that stemmed from this predicament. Somewhere within this event, there must be a treasure to be found.

She smiled to herself for her ability to shift her mood and thanked the Universe for its inspiration.

Ava received a call from the V.P of Finance, Paul DeMato, her old boss. He asked if she had a minute to talk. Ava was surprised and possibly felt a hint of excitement? She walked over to executive row and entered Paul's office. His first words were "I guess you've heard the news by now." Ava didn't want to discuss it. She just wanted to get on with it. Just like her style, five steps ahead of everyone. She wanted Paul to get to the meat of this impromptu meeting. Ava simply nodded her head in affirmation.

Paul began explaining to Ava that two executives from Business Land would be here in a three days to review the inventory operations and processes and as you know, the inventory is the meat of our company. I'd like you to coordinate an impromptu Cycle Count for tomorrow and work with IT to reconcile any differences in inventory. I need you to conduct this without closing down Shipping and Receiving. I'd like to review the printouts and final analysis the following day first thing in the morning. Ava wanted to say, why would you be asking me to perform this overwhelmingly impossible task in an inconsiderate amount of time when you have a Director of Inventory Control sitting in his office twiddling his thumbs? Of course, Ava would never be that confrontational or disrespectful. She immediately laid out the plan to Paul. I'll prepare the Cycle Count paperwork for the most expensive items in inventory and coordinate receipts with Receiving and shipments with Billing. I'll notify IT of our plans. That should give us an accurate picture of where we stand. Paul smiled at Ava and thanked her for her willing spirit and competence.

Ava then called a meeting with the warehouse staff. She prepared the Cycle Count paperwork and sent emails to Shipping and Receiving informing them of what was going to happen the next day. Ava already found herself exhausted. She could foresee that she would not be included in any of the discussions with the

Business Land executives nor would she receive any assistance from the Director of Inventory Control. She just decided to roll with it.

Upon her arrival home, Ava felt deflated and only wanted to do her meditation seeking the solace, comfort and peace it always brought to her. Afterwards she simply went to bed on an empty stomach but found she couldn't sleep. She decided to pick up the Joseph Campbell book she had discarded earlier the other day. She liked randomly opening to whatever page the Universe decided she should read. She happened upon The Art Of Self-Interrogation ***"If the path before you is clear, you're probably on someone else's." Joseph Campbell.*** She laughed to herself. Well, that was quite fitting. She continued.... ***Striking out on our own path is no easy task. It requires ruthlessness and a unique flavor of rebellious courage that most people lack the capacity for. That's why it is "self-inflicted' and not self-discovered or self-empowered. The term "inflicted" has shock-value, just like "interrogation" does. It has a ruthless undertone to it that propels us past our fears. And getting past our fears is the key toward discovering our authentic vocation. The one who has the courage to question everything - self, people, religion, God - this is the one who changes the world. This is the one who discovers their own philosophy.***

Self-interrogation is, in a fundamental sense, a dialectic engagement with our Self about how to lead the best possible life. It is a self-inflicted philosopher's guide through the screwtape of the Truth/Doubt dichotomy. Healthy skepticism is an uncomfortable skill that nonetheless must be honed. We don't hone it by yearning for an answer or settling for answers when they appear." (The Power of Myth, Joseph Campbell copyright 1988.)

Ava felt validated and reassured by this message and began to fall into a deep sleep.

When she awoke she remembered a very strange dream and began recording in her journal:

> "I was in my bedroom looking at a religious statue on the dresser. It began to talk to me. It came to life. I was very frightened by it and got annoyed and yelled at it saying "you are a statue"; you're not supposed to talk." It wouldn't stop so I bit its head off as if it were a rubber doll and flung the pieces in a drawer and felt it could no longer bother me for now."

Ava laughed at the ludicrously of the dream but understood it was representative of her emotional state over the work situation and felt the words she told the statue "you're not supposed to talk, you're a statue" were a direct reflection of how she felt in corporate America. The expectations placed on her and all others for that matter. She believed she was telling herself to be more direct about her feelings and speak up for herself more and it would probably get her further in life. She was still feeling held back by her reservations about revealing too much of her true identity to humankind. Reflecting back on her last read of Joseph Campbell: her abilities must be honed. She did have a healthy skepticism which was an uncomfortable skill nonetheless. She was recognizing herself as a person who questions everything and everyone and that surely it must not be because of her Sanian identity but because it was simply who she was which had elevated her to Sania in the first place. She needed to contemplate the idea once again. The idea that Sania would not be the home she would return to but another even higher dimension. She felt good about that realization and was grateful for who she was. She decided to tackle her day with her usual enthusiasm and vigor.

After the exhilarating but exhausting day, performing the nearly impossible task, Ava decided she was going to leave work early, 6:00 PM. Her Cycle Count and reconciliation had been achieved with the support and respect of her staff and warehouse workers.

She was going home for an evening of meditation and reading and possibly have a discussion with Zachary. This is what she wanted to do. She felt a sense of assertion and accomplishment and almost felt a little high from it.

First things first. She summoned Zachary who immediately came through. Zachary greeted Ava with his typical FANOFU2 greeting. She smiled and asked Zachary if he also was a fan of U2? OF COURSE was his response. Zachary began resonating the word HOMECOMING. "I'm not sure what you mean Zachary," I said. Zachary simply stated, SONG, HOMECOMING.

I immediately stopped the session to look up one of the songbooks I had purchased and indeed it contained the lyrics to the U2 song Zachary brought up:

And you know it's time to go
Through the sleet and driving snow
Across the fields of mourning
Light in the distance

And you hunger for the time
Time to heal, desire, time
And your earth moves beneath
Your own dream landscape

Lyrics by: Adam Clayton, Dave Evans, Larry Mullen, Paul Hewson

My eyes welled up with tears. Not completely sure of the full meaning, I understood that Zachary was aware of what I was going through. My hunger for the time to heal, time for desire, and simply time. The Earth moving beneath my feet was simply my own dreamscape. I was on the borderline of something and Zachary would be there guiding me every step of the way. I was affirmed. I was not alone which understandably brought me a sense of peace and comfort.

I thanked Zachary and had the need to listen to the album which significantly is entitled, "The Unforgettable Fire" and easily related it to the Spirit Guides book about the fire elementals of which I was one, being a Leo astrological sign. I thoroughly enjoyed the album and tried to absorb the messages between the lines but found that their words needed no dissection. They were straight out there in the open to be found by a seeker. I smiled and loved U2.

October was coming to an end and my time as Inventory Control Manager at CE was also. I would be filing for unemployment insurance and had already received a healthy severance package along with a Cobra deal for health insurance. I had not received any responses from the resumes I sent out which was disappointing. I decided I would change my strategy. Instead of marketing myself as an inventory control manager, I would simply define myself as an operations administrator thereby widening the playing field and my chances of securing a job.

Soon, I found myself looking back and leaving the place that was a second home to me. The doors locked shut now and I would never be returning. I cried. I loved working there and felt so accomplished. I kept reminding myself of "that one limiting thought". It was indeed a sad day but I would have to remember that there were good things to come as well. Nostalgia was a difficult emotion to feel and I was going to give it the time and respect it deserved to run its course. I also knew that my best friend Gary would be leaving at the end of November for Colorado. It would be strange not having him close by and doing all the fun things we did together. I headed home with tears in my eyes.

CHAPTER 18

Uncomfortable Metaphysical Surprises

Ava was full of anticipation for the upcoming seminar with Mari Starly they had planned. She packed a copy of her book with the hope that she would get an autograph from the author and headed up to Bergen County to Mari's house.

Still not employed Ava had plenty of time on her hands to explore more books and continue her entries into her journal about her metaphysical experiences and dreams and her sessions with Zachary. Oddly, she did not receive any messages of hope about employment but suspected optimistically that embracing this time of introspection, she knew, as Joseph Campbell stated in his book, The Power of Myth: ***she was not risking this adventure alone; for the heroes of all time have gone before her; the labyrinth is fully known; we have only to follow the thread of the hero-path.***

These introspective thoughts and the books she relished, kept her positive and trusting that the Universe has perfect timing. She had her plans laid out and was working diligently at seeking employment and keeping her networking skills sharpened. She had faith.

Arriving at Mari's she could feel the excitement ahead for their day together. They decided to take public transportation into the City and arrived at the Commodore Hotel in plenty of time for the adventure. As the doors to the auditorium opened, Ava was overwhelmed by the number of seats and wondered how this was going to be a workshop? The set up seemed more fitting for a lecture. Nevertheless she and Mari were directed to third row seats. The stage was very large and not elevated and all the chairs were on the same level. They had set up a ballroom like an auditorium. As participants piled in and took seats, Ava could tell that it was a small gathering of only about two hundred people. This felt quaint and more personal she thought. Within moments, the celebrity, author came out from the curtain and everyone clapped. "How exciting, there she is" she said to Mari! "I can't believe my eyes." This celebrity had been in many movies and performances in Broadway musicals. She looked exactly the same as she did in her films. She was congenial and thanked everyone for their participation and began with a brief outline of what her objectives were for us as a collective group and individually. She explained the reason for the small group was conducive for a more personal experience given that she expected audience participation in all she had planned.

I couldn't imagine how this was going to play out but I was all in for the experience. Shortly we began one of the exercises that would show each of us the power of psychic ability that we all possessed. I laughed at Mari and said, "You already showed me this." A crew came in and took all the folding chairs away and since there was no stage the celebrity was on the same floor level as we were. She had us group ourselves into two but not with anyone we knew. She wanted us to sit on the floor opposite this person and quietly look at them and see if we could know in a vibrational sense anything about them, even to the extent of possibly seeing their aura.

My partner was a young male probably in his early 30s. I did not know him from Adam. After a while the room quieted down and everyone settled into a partnership and began their concentration.

My mind's eye began to develop a picture of a blueish/grey house with white trim surrounded by a plush green lawn and a white fence. I easily allowed myself to relax into the vision and hoped for more but nothing else came through.

After a short while moment, the author asked the group to stop and asked to communicate with our partners about what he had seen. I told my partner of my vision and he said that he just moved into that house with his new spouse about three months ago. He told me that I described it to a "T". I was amazed although I felt I shouldn't be but I really was. I asked him if he had seen anything about me and he said he could not. Nothing came to him. Feeling disappointed that he had nothing to share from the experience, I figured maybe I was truly an empty vessel given my circumstances. Of course, not an empty soul but being that I was reliving a life once lived before under unusual circumstances may have interfered with someone's ability to read me. I just wasn't sure if it was my situation but remembered during my initial meeting with Mari she detected something unique in my energy field.

The author asked us to raise our hands if we had anything to share and I immediately raised mine but was not called upon. It was interesting to here the experiences of others, however. At this point, I had lost Mari in the shuffle and couldn't know if she had any good news to report. The celebrity passed directly in front of me and I was hoping she would feel my energy and ask me something, anything that would single me out. I wasn't sure if it was because of my ego hoping she would recognize my uniqueness and pick up on my frequency as being different from any one in the room or because she could genuinely provide me with insights on how to develop my gifts even further. After all, her book was life changing for her and myself as well. She went through incredible changes and developed her psychic abilities to an unimaginable degree. Sadly, she walked passed me with no special recognition.

Shortly after, the crew returned and set up all the chairs again. We took our seats and listened intently to the author explaining various stages of development and the effects of meditation on our consciousness. I myself understood how transforming meditation was and how it heightened my psychic abilities and allowed for "other worldly" encounters. It had an affect on my happiness and dream states and knew how well it balanced my energy field allowing for unique experiences, such as astral projection to occur. I knew how it elevated my strengths and variants that I wanted to actualize and were already at my disposal because of this practice. It also broadened my perspective on the conscious and unconscious minds and allowed glimpses into probable realities. Meditation, and of course my reading material, brought me to different physical experiences that broadened my perspective and made sense of this reality and helped me cope with the understanding that I was existing in a dual reality.

With her brief discussion of meditation, the author wanted us to do another exercise. By now we were all back in our original seats and Mari was by my side again. I asked her if she had any luck with the previous exercise and she replied that she did not. I said, "I'm sorry. Maybe this just wasn't a good day for you." She just smiled but I knew she felt disappointed.

Our next exercise was prefaced by a deliberate attempt to meditate on the very origin of our existence as male or female but joined to our soul mate in a large tank of birthing fluid as one being. I thought to myself, we have many soul mates. However, maybe she was referring to a special opposite sex mate that we may be seeking in this lifetime. She had us close our eyes as she began to deliver a very picturesque scene of our being splitting into two. One male; one female. We were to step out of this tank using a ladder as the person we are presently. The other half was leaving the tank from another ladder on the opposite site of the tank.

With this visual, we were now to begin a meditation that would allow us to visually see who this other half of us, our soul mate as she described. I immediately went into a meditative state but felt an awful rush of energetic power overcome me. I was stuck in its grip and tried with all my might to stop it. I sunk down deep into my chair. I pried my eyes open to be sure that I was still there and alive. I could feel my heart beating out of my chest. I was panicking but didn't want to cause a scene. I kept fighting the sensation of leaving my body. I was in a room full of strangers and I couldn't cope with their presence not knowing where this was going to take me. I was sweating and breathing heavily. I was hoping that Mari would come to my aid but her eyes were closed and I couldn't imagine that she could not feel my distress. I kept fighting the feeling of lifting straight out of my body and could partially see that I had. From that perspective I saw a tumultuous cloud over to my left side high up in the atmosphere. It had a shape to it that resembled a large face that was not pleasing to look at. I was scared out of my mind. I wanted to scream and cry but I also didn't want to cause a scene.

Soon, the author brought everyone out of their meditation. I was so relieved to hear it was over. I immediately sat up in my chair. My heart rate began to slow and I could control my breathing again. I had not been sweating much to my surprise but I felt like I was drenched. I looked over at Mari and she looked like she just woke from a sleep. I asked her how she was? She said, with a sad look on her face, "OK but nothing happened." I told her she looked like she was sleeping. She asked me with surprise, "Were you looking at me?" I told her I was vibrationally screaming to her for help! She looked very puzzled and asked, "Why?" "I'll tell you later" I said. In the meantime, the author asked for confirmation on anyone's experience and if they could feel that they had an astral projection.

I did not want to call any attention to myself this time. I just wanted to get out of there. The lecture had soon concluded and we all lined up to leave the building. I was exhausted and couldn't wait to talk to Mari. I began to immediately reflect on why I had such an adverse reaction to this exercise and realized, of course, all that energy in that room! The participants as well as their own spirit guides coming through was so overwhelming to me. I'm surprised I didn't go mad! I was ready to explode from it. I should have known better. It confirmed for me in the worse way possible that I was a sensitive and an empath and simply outside my element. I wanted to escape back to my home and center myself again. I needed it so desperately. Mari did show concern and felt I did not enjoy myself. I tried to console her and said, "I loved it except for the last part. It was too difficult for me, try to understand." I knew Mari would not be able to understand. She still wanted to get autographs and I obliged her so we went around the back of the building and waited for the author to appear where her limousine was waiting. We got the autographs. Then we headed to the train for New Jersey. If anything, I could tell that my constitution was stronger than anything I had ever known up to that time. I simply wanted to put this event behind me and continue my practice in a solitary manner. If I gained anything from this experience, it simply was that I didn't need its confirmation that I was psychic, intuitive and could project astrally, which was the whole purpose of the event.

CHAPTER 19

Confirmations From Zachary

When I arrived home I felt complete relief and satisfaction to be in my familiar surroundings again. I was not ready to intermingle with the world as who I presently was. Not that I had the right to tell them who I really was, but it was evident that I barely knew my own potential much less give any attention of it to strangers. I obviously had much work to do in this lifetime and I was simply going to enjoy the pace that was allotted me. I wanted to talk to Zachary.

I summoned him and he immediately appeared. After identifying himself he simply stated the word SORRY. I asked him why he wouldn't have warned me? He said YOU NEED TO KNOW. "I needed to learn this lesson on my own"? YES, he said. "You knew I would be okay though, right?" Again he responded YES. I said, "OK, I think I get it. Some things I have to learn on my own and make my own decisions." Again, Zac said, YES. "Well, it still doesn't make me feel better but I do understand that you cannot interfere with my decisions. You must allow me the freedom of choice whether I make the right choice or not. Zac, "Will I find fulfilling employment soon?" Zachary said YES AND THERE IS MUCH MORE TO COME. LISTEN U2. I wasn't completely sure what that meant and

Zachary could sense my confusion. He said STREETS. To me that was the abbreviation to the "Joshua Tree" album song, "Where The Streets Have No Name".

It made me wonder if I would be going home to Sania where indeed there were no "streets". In my thoughts I wondered if this would be the right time for me to return to Sania. Was my work here done? Zac immediately said an emphatic NO. So, with that I put U2's "Joshua Tree" album on and enjoyed the words and music. When I was done listening, I decided to make a light dinner and then go into a meditation but I will admit, I was scared to do so. Nevertheless, I was home surrounded by my energy field which always proved comforting so I began my meditation. I then simply went to bed and fell asleep.

When I awoke, I remembered a very disturbing dream that was a direct reflection of the events of the day before:

> "Dreaming I was dreaming trying to wake out of the dream screaming but found I could not get a scream out of my mouth or throat. Finally I was able to yell out loud and woke out of the dream but did not remember what I was dreaming. I remember searching my bed for someone with my legs and arms under the covers - stretching my body across the whole bed to feel the presence of someone. I heard someone say, It's okay Ava, I'm here. It's only a dream, you're okay." I felt Zachary's presence, his love and his compassion made me feel safe and secure."

I recorded the dream realizing it was because of the previous day's events and understood that Zachary would be guiding me until a time when I would not need him. I couldn't imagine such a time but I intuitively knew it would come. It would be another example of a changing time, an evolution in my progress, another example of the evolutionary purpose for reliving this lifetime.

I began my day with a shower and my Yoga session. I checked the answering machine and noticed there was a message. It was Paul DeMato. He wanted to talk to me about a job opportunity. How exciting. He left me his number and asked if I would call him at 10:00 a.m. that morning.

I immediately began preparing paperwork for a phone interview and making sure I was equipped with all that would be needed for the interview. I was feeling optimistic. I still had two hours before I needed to call him so I made my breakfast and stared out the window looking at snow capped trees and the grey skies of winter. It would be a good scene if I was on the ski slopes but with my friend Gary gone, who would I ski with now. Mari did not ski but she always wanted me to teach her son Riley. I decided to check my calendar and see if we could make that lesson happen. I'd call Mari later in the day to see if it would work out.

With that thought, I sent an email to Gary telling him how much I missed him and hoped he was doing well. I was certain he was enjoying the powder of the ski slopes in Colorado as opposed to the ice on the slopes of Hunter Mountain and hoped he was enjoying life.

While eating breakfast and waiting for 10:00 a.m. to arrive, I began reading from my Seth book, ***"Which you, which world?" These questions are to be answered in the now, as you understand it, through the realization that your power of action is in the present and not in the past. Your only effective point of changing any aspect of your world lies in that miraculous instant connection of spirit and self. Re-pattern your past from the present.*** (Seth: The Nature of Personal Reality, Jane Roberts copyright 1978)

I felt confused. I wondered which past? Which present? Which present am I to re-pattern? I would concentrate better later in the day after my telephone meeting with Paul. The statements from Seth were stirring up something in me that I felt would interfere with clear, concise thinking during the interview but needed to revisit the Seth passage later knowing it held important insight on how to actualize and combine this existence with my Sanian identity. I always felt discord with my two identities excluding the suspicion that this repeated lifetime was for the purpose of evolution.

I rang Paul promptly at 10:00 AM and he picked up the phone. "Paul?" "Hello Ava," he said. "Hi Paul, how are you?" I replied. "I'm doing well and I wanted to run something past you. I've started up my own inventory distribution company and wondered if you would be interested in the position of Operations Manager"?

"Paul, I'd be very interested in the opportunity. Can you tell more about the company"? Paul said we should meet for lunch tomorrow at his offices. He would order lunch in and we can eat in his private conference room while discussing the opportunity. I agreed and took the address. Ironically, his offices were located in Bergen County near Mari Starly's house.

I told him it would be great to see him again and grateful he thought about me for the opportunity. Paul commented that he couldn't think of anyone else who would be so perfect for this position! We hung up the phone and I started jumping around the living room. Operations Manager! How cool is that, I exclaimed. It would be a startup operation which would allow me to implement my very own processes and systems to be put into place based on the logistics and size of the operation. Oh, I am blessed.

Too excited for any introspection, Ava decided to take the one and a half hour drive up to Hunter Mountain. At least she could get a half day of skiing in. She would fly through those mountains as if she were on wings. Ava was going skiing!

When she arrived at Hunter, she immediately got herself a locker and snapped on her ski boots and skis. She headed for the chairlift that would take her to the intermediate slopes first, giving herself an opportunity to warm up her muscles and get an idea of how strong her body felt on this particular day. Swishing down Eisenhower, a relatively steep slope but with no moguls she found her stride and enjoyed the familiar feeling. She was a fast skier and found herself back at the chairlift rather quickly. Her next ride up she decided to attempt Hell Gate with complicated turns and a narrow skiing field, but she handled it like a pro. She was enjoying the icy air on her cheeks as the wind blew past her sleek form. Her skill of navigating this terrain showed how she owned the mountain. After a few more runs, she decided to try K-27, the steepest slope on the Northeast. It was always a fun challenge for Ava and she loved the idea that it had a double fall line which required a greater, higher level of skill. K-27 also had moguls that reached her height. On her first attempt, she fell. She tried again and this time, she made it. Oh wow! What a thrill, what an achievement, she exclaimed to herself! The sun was beginning to set and Ava decided to call it a blessed day and headed back down to the lodge to her locker. After changing, Ava headed back to New Jersey. The only other thing that could have made this an even greater day would be if Gary had been enjoying this with her but she had to appreciate that a job offer was in the works also and it was in her field of expertise.

On her ride home, Ava considered the possibility that skiing was like living life. Having the expertise to own that mountain with the skill and confidence that eliminates all concerns and just simply enjoy the experience. Life should be like that she thought. She suspected that life could be like that but it wasn't, at least not for the moment. Ava supposed the lessons required in learning how to ski are similar to the lessons in life that one gains to live with skill and enjoyment. This was the path she was on. This was her intent. She flashed back on that confusing paragraph from the Seth material earlier, "***miraculous instant connection of spirit and self***".

She supposed that was her experience on the ski slop and was grateful for her spontaneous decision to ski that afternoon. It made that passage real and it gave her the meaning with hardly any introspective thought.

When Ava returned home she was too tired to enjoy a session with Zachary so she decided to put on some U2 music and prepare dinner. Afterwards, she diligently performed her meditation and before retiring for the evening she double checked her briefcase for all the essentials she would need the following morning for her meeting with Paul.

When Ava awoke, she reached for her dream journal to jot down that she witnessed again in the middle of her sleep, Zachary sitting at a sofa chair at the end of her bed reading to me which that was becoming commonplace by now. The bizarre dream she remembered seemed more important:

> "I was at work and there were people around me. I wasn't familiar with the work environment. Someone started yelling that there was a white rat behind my desk. I saw it scrambling to get away. It was the size of a rabbit. Then I saw a white mouse running quickly behind it. The rat was ripping and tearing into an employee who was laying flat on his stomach bleeding and crying. No one could help. We just stared in horror. I felt anxious and repulsed."

Ava felt quite disturbed by the dream. For now she needed to get ready for her interview with Paul. She had time for her Yoga practice and a light breakfast and began dressing in one of her best professional suits. With briefcase in hand, she left her apartment and headed up to Bergen County periodically checking her handwritten directions.

CHAPTER 20

New Beginnings

Ava arrived at the building one-half hour ahead of schedule which was nothing new for her. She always left ample time for unforeseen emergencies. She parked in the office parking structure and reviewed some of her paperwork. Checking her calendar she remembered she needed to contact Mari to schedule a ski lesson with Riley which she would do upon returning home. She listened to a U2 cassette and enjoyed a couple of songs from "Rattle and Hum" and noticed the time was nearing to meet with Paul.

She took the elevator to the tenth floor and gave the receptionist her name and she had an 11:30 a.m. appointment with Paul DeMato. The receptionist rang his office and Paul came into the lobby with an outstretched hand to greet Ava. They smiled at each other as Paul welcomed her into his office.

Ava could not believe her eyes at the sight of his massive, ornately decorated office. It was the size of a small ballroom! Oriental rugs and gold trimmings abound. Leather couches and Louis XVI chairs surrounding a small conference table by the floor to ceiling windows. Ava was quite surprised by the size of his desk which was French provincial and began to suspect that Paul may have some potential ego issues but who was she to judge. Maybe he liked this sort of set up and his reasons were his. His desk telephone was even the old style lift handle of white and gold. She almost wanted to laugh thinking this was quite the spectacle.

He asked her to take a seat at the desk and he walked around to his massive high back leather studded chair while Ava immediately began to take out her credentials from her briefcase. "Oh stop Ava," Paul said. "I know who you are and I know your capabilities. I don't need to see your resume. Let me fill you in on this operation first. I've got lunch ordered for us to arrive at 11:45 a.m. I'll only be able to spend an hour with you so let's begin."

Paul began describing the reasons for starting up his company and it had a unique twist to it. It would be a computer supplier with no inventory held on site. The distribution center is located in Tempe, Arizona and our clients are located here on the Northeast. All order fulfillment would be handled out of Tempe. The position I want you to manage is Operations Manager. In other words, you would work with Sales here in the Northeast and set up a staff to process these orders through Tempe. The beauty of this operation is that there are no carrying costs for the company to handle inventory, either incoming or outgoing which means no storage costs. I said, "That sounds clever and interesting. Do you have a contract with the warehouse in Tempe"? He said, "Yes, I do and I must guarantee them a minimum two million dollar inventory in-house at any given point in time otherwise my costs for using their facility would be raised."

"Who are your clients?" I asked. He said, "I have some of the biggest clients on the East Coast and most of them are hospitals, commercial industry, computer outlets" but just then he was interrupted since our lunch had arrived.

We adjourned to the conference room which surprisingly was rather conventional in its decor. I joked to myself he probably hadn't had a chance to get his hands on this room yet. As we ate our lunch, Paul continued to fill me in on the Tempe location which I would have to visit to gain knowledge of their systems and how our orders would be received and the turnaround for shipping directly to our clients. I was secretly excited because I knew Tempe, Arizona was where "Rattle and Hum" was filmed during the live concert at Sun Devil Stadium. I was hoping to make a side trip to see the place where U2 had performed.

After more discussion Paul asked me if I wanted the job, and if I did, my salary would be $65,000 annually plus benefits and an annual bonus depending on how well the company did. I wanted to jump out of my chair but of course that would be extremely unprofessional. I accepted without hesitation and we decided on a start date; when I would make my visit to Tempe; as well as when I would begin the hiring process. I asked if I had a HR department to assist with candidates. Paul provided me with a contact list and confirmed that HR had already been on the hunt to fill my staffing needs. He gave me business cards of important contacts within the organization, of which he employed twenty-five people. I thanked him and said I would see him next Monday morning. He mentioned I'd be working on the third floor where he rented office space for Sales and Operations and wanted to take me on a quick tour. We wrapped up lunch and headed to the third floor. Paul had a set of keys in his hand for me to lock and unlock the facility. It was a functional, professional and spacious set up where I would have three assistants processing orders and then a large room equipped for a staff of about six sales managers and then he took me to my office. "Wow, this is huge Paul!" I said. It was nothing of course compared to his but I wouldn't have wanted that. It was nicely decorated but I especially loved the floor to ceiling windows which gave me plenty of light and a view of the outside world. I really felt like I had arrived. I couldn't believe I was someone so important and had such a great boss whom I already knew and who respected me enough to hire me for such an integral position in his company.

As we started to part ways we shook hands. I was so happy but scared. I knew I had my work cut out for me. Challenges that would make me anxious and doubtful of my self-esteem issues again but even more marketable and more experienced. I felt like the sky's the limit with this job as long as I could overcome my doubts. I had to hold on to the belief that I was manifesting this reality for personal growth and overcome the fears that plagued me. I felt tempted to call upon my abilities from Sania but knew I shouldn't. I would fill out my HR paperwork when I got home and fax it immediately. I would then have a session with Zachary and then call Mari with my good news as well as email Gary.

After a long conversation with Mari, my nerves were calmed, and truly could not understand my doubts. Why couldn't I see me for the human I was? Mari could not believe I was apprehensive about my abilities and tried to convince me that I was a natural at this and would succeed beyond my dreams. "Look at how much you have achieved so far Ava" she said. "You not only have the smarts but also the spiritual abilities in your favor." I was still afraid, however. I was not understood by many people, even my closest friends. Of course, I couldn't blame them, after all they did not have a clue about my mission here and how torn I was between two worlds. I was in a juggling act. Trying to be human with the advanced abilities of a Sanian. I needed my meditation to calm my nerves and then I'd have a talk with Zachary.

Zachary immediately identified himself and said DISGUISE. I asked him to be more specific. I could feel his powerful energy coming through with "UNLESS WE PREFER TO BE MADE FOOLS OF BY OUR ILLUSIONS, WE SHALL MEET OURSELVES TIME AND AGAIN IN A THOUSAND DISGUISES ON THE PATH OF LIFE".

"Wow," I said. "That was the most insightful information I believe I have ever received from you. I get it, I should stop imagining the worst possible scenario because this will produce a repetitive behavior manifesting an outcome that would surely prove why I should continue my doubts. Almost like a self-fulfilling prophecy." YES, Zac emphatically stated. "I get it Zac, this is a way for me to stop finding myself everywhere I go. That self-doubting, self prophesying uncertainty. In a sense, blaming myself for every failed outcome and never fully realizing that not everything is in my control and not everything is my fault. Issues arise because I do not necessarily have any control over them. They arise so that I may understand myself better through examining them." Zac emphatically said YES. He continued, AS A HUMAN YOUR BIRTH WILL ALWAYS COME FROM DARKNESS.

"I know that all too well Zachary but I hate the idea. I can only hope that you will remain by my side guiding me. I know to use my own resources such as my reading and keeping my journals and my dreams are a tremendous source of enlightenment but I also need you." Zachary said **YES**. For now I decided I would rely on the seen and unseen forces of Zachary's guidance.

Ava was heading up to her new place of employment on Monday morning. Excited and anticipating a positive aura but not at all happy about the commute. She entertained the idea of moving closer. Of course, that would be a decision to be made later in time.

Ava walked into her new office and plopped her brief case down on her desk and looked out the window. It was winter and as all East Coast winters go, dreary and cold and damp. Well, when the spring comes I would have a great view of the birds and budding trees and above all the sunshine!

She immediately began organizing her desk and setting up the telephone for voicemail. She turned on the computer and began to familiarize herself with some of the programs that were already loaded. She needed IT to set up a password so she could read any email that may have been sent. She contacted IT and left a voicemail message for them for assistance. Well, it was only her first day so she wasn't going to put much pressure on herself. She would need to contact HR to see if any candidates were scheduled for interviews with her. She also wanted to check the operations area to see if they were set up with the equipment she assumed they would need. She looked for a coffee machine and began a fresh pot of coffee.

With not much more to accomplish, Ava enjoyed a cup of coffee and decided how she would like her office to look. She needed to bring some color in, maybe a vase or some inspiring art work. She was waiting for someone to call, hopefully from IT to get her computer started.

As Ava was drinking her coffee, someone entered the facility. It was one of the sales reps. He introduced himself as Mark Simmons and informed her of the accounts he worked on. He was pleasant and welcomed her to the company thanked her for getting the coffee started. Ava smiled and said it was her pleasure. Soon after, another sales rep entered and introduced himself. He was Patrick Murphy who also welcomed her to the company. So far so good, she said to herself. These people seemed professional and probably quite competent.

Then the phone rang. It was the IT guy and that made her happy. He assisted her in setting up the login and password. Now Ava could begin to explore some of the operations of the company. She immediately went to email first. There was an email from HR informing her that a candidate for order entry would be meeting with her at 10:00 a.m. that morning. They had one more lined up for Wednesday and informed her that the third one was already hired and had begun work two weeks ago. That was Sara Helson who was a very pleasant, energetic and organized person. She had already begun the tasks of setting up desks and communicating with IT for assistance on all computers and the ordering of office supplies. I reviewed her HR file and was happy to learn she would be competent and eager at her responsibilities. She had a strong background.

Ava was surprised that Paul had not sent an email to the entire staff introducing her as the Operations Manager and possibly suggesting a meeting to make introductions and review our goals and objectives. Well, maybe that would come later she figured.

Next person to enter her office was Barbara Hanson. She was in her late 30s, attractive and had a very forceful handshake and she didn't seem to know how to walk, she ran. She immediately told Ava that she was in charge of the Sloan Kettering account in New

York City. With that she did her distinctive "run" out of my office to hers. Ava laughed to myself. Oh boy, just a tad tense. Maybe she had a hot deal going on and was under the gun.

As the day progressed Ava became increasingly acclimated to her environment and assignments. She set up meetings of introduction and laid out plans. She thought this would be a good time to contact Paul since she hadn't heard from him. She had already interviewed one of the candidates that HR had sent over for 10:00 a.m. and liked her. She was Kelly Swanson who also had an impressive background and Ava felt she would be a good candidate for the position. She was quiet, professional and spoke of her brief history in operations and logistics and Ava could see a great deal of potential in her. Ava contacted HR and informed them that she liked her and wanted to offer her the position. HR would manage the details from that point onward.

Ava telephoned Paul and he welcomed her aboard. She asked if he wanted to review anything with her from his perspective. He just wanted to know how things were going. She filled him in on her morning, including her decision to hire Kelly Swanson whom she had interviewed earlier. "Good he said, get that place in shape and have us running like a fine tuned machine as quickly as possible."

Ava asked Paul if he would send out email introducing her as the company's new Operations Manager and give a brief history of her background and responsibilities. He suggested she pull something together and shoot it over to him and he'd have his admin send it out. Ava thought to herself, lazy ass. However, in all fairness, maybe he had a lot on his plate and then she felt bad because she called him that. In any event Ava pulled together a two paragraph compilation of an introduction providing a history of her background and what her responsibilities for Paul's Compu Inov company would be. After careful editing and review, she sent it over to him.

Ava decided to lunch with Sara so that she would get a better understanding from her perspective how she perceived her responsibilities and what she had witnessed thus far. They both understood she was still so new to the company and had no real direction from anyone until now but Ava thought it would be a good start. She also wanted to explain to Sara that a trip to Arizona was in the works to familiarize herself with the procedures from their end so that she could develop processes here to comply with contractual obligations as well as assisting her staff with a guided set of assignments and our own internal procedures.

When Ava returned from lunch, she saw that Paul had sent out the email of introduction but noticed a glaring omission. He had not sent it to the folks in Arizona. Ava called him on the phone and asked him if he should have included our direct contacts there. He replied, "Oh, I should have done that! Thanks for bringing it to my attention." Then Ava asked him in order for her to get started in full throttle, she'd need to reach them as soon as possible. After all, the success of her operation hinged upon complying with their set up. He agreed and gave her the contact names in Arizona to begin setting up a date for her to meet them. He also mentioned that she should include the head of Sales Management, Rob Nelson on my trip. Ava mentioned she had not met him yet. Paul said he works over here in my offices and to come to the tenth floor to meet him. Ava contacted his admin to set up a meeting to get some available travel dates from him. His admin was quite compliant and provided her with his schedule. Afterward Ava placed a call to Arizona and left a message for Kathy Larson who would be her main fulfillment contact of their orders.

Well, it was quite a busy day and I felt I had accomplished a great deal but there was still much more to set up to get this ball rolling. First thing in the morning I should have a response from Kathy Larson about dates for a possible visit and then schedule flights and hotel rooms for myself and Rob Nelson or just hand that off to his admin to accomplish. Maybe that was proper protocol. With this being a new company, I suspected that not many ground rules had been laid yet. I'll check with Rob's admin in the morning especially since a corporate credit card would be required to achieve the purchase. I wonder who handles expense reports.

As I drove home in the commuter traffic listening to a musical meditation tape approved for driving, I realized I had not had one single thought today about my first love, spirituality. That made me sad. I hoped that it would change for me soon because spirituality was of the utmost importance to me. After all, all that I had achieved was the result of my practice in this realm and I needed it to survive, literally. Everyone needed it but I was aware of my need. It provided me with a connection to my source and it guided me to an understanding of everything I experienced. It brought meaning to my existence and provided me with the power to actualize and transform. These were the things that were important to me.

I began to wonder if corporate America was truly not the place for me. The reasons I achieved so much there and excelled was because of my very practice in the field of all things metaphysical. I began to suspect that corporate America was simply an ends to a means or was my spiritual practice, a Promethean act where we are audaciously downloading an experience that could be considered "the knowledge of the gods," and then transforming it into mortal power that we can use practically, like succeeding in a high paying corporate job? Yeah, it paid well but would I be sacrificing my spiritual needs, the one thing that meant everything to me. I had to survive, pay rent, buy food, clothing, I needed a car to drive around in. I knew the path of the spiritual warrior is not soft and sweet. It will not falter where directness is essential. Well, for now I didn't want to consider my needs of spiritual practice. I wanted to comfort myself in believing that because this was a new position within a new company, there was only a slight interference with my practice. Things will go back to my normal, when I had achieved the well oiled machine Paul so confidently stated. I needed Zachary tonight and I needed to meditate to bring myself to my center again. I couldn't wait to get home.

I had a brief dinner and I slipped into comfy PJs and the phone rang it was Mari Starly on the other end asking about my first day. "Hi Mari," I said. She asked, "How'd it go?" I told her a lot of ground work needed to done and hopefully once I get things in order I will be confident that this is a dream job. I also didn't consider Paul a big help but, it was only my first day. I thanked her for her call and said I needed a session with Zachary. She understood so I told her I appreciated the consideration and we quickly hung up the phone. I immediately turned off the ringer. I didn't want any interruptions, it was as simple as that.

Zachary immediately appeared. I asked him if I would happy in my new position and if he understood my earlier dilemma? He simply stated, GREEN WARRIOR CARLOS CASTANEDA. I immediately went to my books and looked up what Carlos had to say about the Green Warrior.

"Green warriors are fiercely interdependent and sensitive to interconnected energy. Their Third eyes are wide open to the astonishing synchronicities of life. They fluently speak a language older than words. Their eco-conscious power arises from spiritual contact with the earth and a sense of awe for the cosmos as a miraculous whole. They are all about rebirth, synergism, and interconnectivity. They seek to heal all types of nature deprivation where the human animal has become "autistic" or dissociative in its relationship with the natural world. They understand that this disassociation arises from the apparent psychosomatic split between spirit and flesh. They seek to heal the divide between the microcosm and the macrocosm, by revealing how both are needed to put the whole into holistic. They are eco-warriors, disaster shamans, and the fifth horseman of the apocalypse. Their eco-moralism trumps any and all outdated notions of morality, and so they have moved beyond good and evil. They are light travelers who travel light, and no longer have the need to own things. They understand, as Krishnamurti did, that the "earth is there to be loved, to be cared for, and not to be

divided as yours and mine." (The Teaching of Don Juan, Carlos Castaneda copyright 1968)

Great understanding came to me that I could relate especially to the part about being light travelers who travel light. I also related quite keenly to my desire to heal all types of nature deprivation where the human animal has come "autistic" or dissociative in its relationship with the natural world. It explained to me why I grew impatient with humankind not understanding how they didn't understand who they were or why they were. It always frustrated me. I simply said, "Thank you, thank you, thank you Zachary." I concluded that my job at Compu Inov was simply a stepping stone to something better for me and that something better was not going to be in corporate America. I felt hopeful and validated. I didn't feel that I would shirk any of my responsibilities at CI however, I would continue to give it all my talents as well as develop any latent ones I possessed. It was not my style to be dead wood but I felt assured that it would provide me with more insight into who I am, along with Zachary's assistance of course, but I was not going to be the one to carry all responsibility for the company with the hope of a "big" bonus at the end of a year. That was not my aim nor was it what I would consider a prize. The prize was in furthering my spiritual growth, gaining greater insight into my true human nature and the nature of recognizing what was really going on around me.

After my session with Zachary, I began my Chakra meditation with greater emphasis on my Third Eye Chakra and off to bed I went.

When I awoke in the morning I quickly remembered my dream and began writing in my journal:

> "I was dead but not really dead. I was placed in a coffin and was being sent to the moon. When I arrived on the Moon, I realized it was a beautiful place and I was let out of the coffin. It

had oceans and lakes, mountains and trees, fresh air and sunny warm weather. I felt this wasn't so bad but still had some resentment about having to be there with the feeling of responsibility. I then found out that I could still commute to my old life everyday if I chose to. A long commute to the office about 2 1/2 hours. Nevertheless, I felt better but still resentful because I didn't believe my being there was what I really wanted. I saw a female there who looked very familiar to me but I just couldn't place her."

I completely understood the dream on two very distinct levels. The moon was the job being "dead but not really dead" as represented by the coffin. Perhaps it was also my existential lifestyle? I could have both but was confused that I felt resentful about being "on the moon" if it did represent my spirituality. That really concerned me, unless, of course, my source being was trying to convey that I was not yet ready to return to Sania or wherever I was going to end up. I still had work to do here. That was a possibility for interpreting the resentfulness. The familiar looking woman who I had seen was possibly a spirit guide comforting me and making her kindness known.

I had to quickly shower and prepare for work. I made my breakfast and soon was headed to my car for my second day at Compu Inov. I really didn't like the name of that company, but it was not my concern. Who knows, maybe someday this name would become a household word.

Opening the office, I started the coffee. No one was there yet. I could only make it in at 8:00 a.m. because of the longer commute but I figured it was still an hour earlier than anyone else. I opened my email and Kathy Larson from Arizona had replied. Good I said, she's responsive and that makes my life easier. She provided a list of available dates for our trip there and I immediately forwarded the email to Rob Larson's admin asking what works for him. My schedule was wide open and she need not worry about me, I'd accommodate Rob. Whatever worked for Rob was fine and she should just go ahead and book reservations and let me know my itinerary. I also asked if she reconciled expense reports.

Barbara Hanson barged into my office in her usual running style and demanded where her order for Sloan Kettering was? I was shocked to say the least. I could not believe the behavior of this woman. How can she call herself a professional? I told her that we are not up and running yet and I don't have any orders for Sloan Kettering for input. We are not connected to the warehouse in Arizona yet. She screamed back that she sent the order directly to Kathy Larson via email. I wanted to tell her she should check with Kathy then, why are you asking me? I wouldn't dare be so rude and infantile, however. I told her when Arizona is open, I would contact Kathy to determine the location of your shipment. In the meantime, can you provide me with a copy of the order? She screamed back at me "why don't you have it?" I asked her if she copied me on the email to Kathy?" Valid question of course. She screamed back at me to get on the phone with Kathy and find out where her order was. This is our biggest account and we better not screw it up!

I must admit I was unnerved by Barbara's behavior. How in the world does this woman barge into anyone's office screaming in that manner and make unreasonable demands. I wondered if there was something psychologically wrong with her.

In response to Barbara's inquiry, I emailed Kathy Larson asking about an order that would have been placed by Barbara Hanson of CI for Sloan Kettering. I asked her if she could give me an update on its status. I copied Barbara Hanson on the email.

I checked with Sara Helson to see if she knew anything about the SK order and she did not. She confirmed that our Order Entry system was up and running and no orders were placed through the system. We had not received any fax confirmations from Arizona that anything had shipped either.

Ava began to wonder why Barbara would place an order using the email system when our Order Entry system was in place and in full operation. It was the best and only way to track orders. They would be assigned an order number and could then be tracked with shipments sent using that order number. Oh boy, is this one going to be a problem? Well, that was a dumb question, she already was a problem. In our systems analysis monthly report, we would use the Order Entry data to tabulate everything we had ordered and reconcile against what was shipped. It was also crucial to maintain a $2 million dollar inventory level in Arizona for contractual reasons and with no clear defined order tracking system, we would not know if we were within compliance. There was no way to keep track of inventory if people were going to be sending emails for their orders. I wondered if any other sales managers had placed orders like this.

Ava decided to send a polite and friendly reminder to all sales assistants informing them that orders are to be placed through our Order Entry Department. The Order Entry system was up and running and it was crucial to keep track of our sales and inventory levels copying Paul and Rob on the email.

Ava was waiting for Barbara to come charging like a bull into her office after having read the email. Ava was preparing herself. She was nervous and felt rattled to the core, trying to maintain an outward appearance of calm and steady. Ava was also hoping for a quick response from Kathy in Arizona. Barbara never showed.

Kathy in Arizona promptly called me letting me know that they were working on the Sloan Kettering order and they anticipated shipping today. She asked me if our order entry system was down and I reported that it wasn't. Barbara took it upon herself to place the order via email and I asked Kathy if she could send me a copy of the email. I wanted to record the order in our system but I would flag it as a NO SHIP so that the order would not be duplicated, I simply needed a record for inventory purposes. Kathy agreed and she sent a fax confirming shipment. I thanked her and apologized for Barbara's deliberate attempt to ignore our process. Kathy asked me to tell Barbara going forward, no orders will be processed unless they come through the Order Entry system as originally agreed upon. I told her I would re-enforce the process with her.

I wondered if I should talk to the sales force and let them know about the order entry system even though I just sent an email. I did not hear back from Rob or Paul about the email but I guess that was okay, I was the Operations Manager and this was my area.

Soon I received the email from Kathy for the SK order and after reviewing it, gave it to Sara to enter it into the system. I explained to her to process it as a NO SHP that I have already spoken to Kathy. Sara began the entry process. It was good to have her on board. She was pleasant and didn't need much training.

After reading more email, I learned that Kelly Swanson accepted the position to join our team. This was great news and I was looking forward to have her begin work on Monday. I let Sara know she'd have some company. There was another resume HR wanted me to review for the third order entry position. I thought the resume looked good so I told HR to have her come in this week if she was available.

Soon it was time to go home. I thought about the commute and my driving meditation music and getting back to Zac and my reading and meditation. That made me feel great. I realized another day went by without the awareness of feeling connected to my source but of course it only felt that way. I was always connected to my source, I just didn't have time to think about it. I also missed Gary who would stop by at least once a week when I worked at CE and our luncheons were always consumed with existential discussions. I quickly wrote Gary from my office email letting him know I was thinking about him and was hoping he was doing well. I also told him that I had not had any time for horseback riding but as he knew, I had been skiing.

It was a long and exhausting day but a productive one. I felt I was getting my land legs and maybe this job was going to be okay. We'll see I thought. I was trying to maintain a positive attitude. Barbara seemed to be the thorn in my side and I was hoping she would settle herself down when she realized she could have confidence in me. I sent her a quick email before leaving the office to let her know her shipment was leaving Arizona today.

On my way home I put my usual driving meditation music on and it began to immediately change my auric vibration to one of relaxed and fulfilled. I was looking forward to a session with Zachary, my meditation and a good night's sleep.

I entered my apartment and felt at peace and serene. I immediately changed into comfy clothes and started dinner. I began to think maybe I should purchase a crock pot and have it cook a delicious rewarding dinner while I was at work during the day. Brilliant idea I thought. It would be on my mind all day and the thought of my favorite Greek Chicken for instance, fermenting for me during the day would surely put a smile on my face.

Yes, this weekend I would buy a crock pot. Decision made. After my dinner and clean up, I went to the living room and before I could summon Zachary, the phone rang. It was Mari Starly. Mari wanted to know if this weekend was a good weekend to teach Riley how to ski. I said, "Sure." "It would be so much fun to get out on the slopes again." Mari wanted to go to the Poconos because it was very close by. I said, "I've never skied the Poconos." She said, "It's not a Hunter Mountain but it was a better starter mountain for Riley." I replied, "No problem, I'll have to familiarize myself with its terrane." Mari laughed and said, "There isn't much terrane to get familiar with." We arranged for Saturday and I'd meet her at her house at 8:00 AM and hung up the phone.

Immediately Zachary appeared in his usual spot near the silk fig tree and simply stated FANOFU2. I smiled and said, "Hello Zac, how are you doing this evening?" He demonstrated his feelings by moving his hands to his heart and smiling. He spoke the word

FERMENTATION. I was puzzled. I asked if it had anything to do with my buying a crock pot since I had just mentioned that word? He simply said NO. He continued to speak DARK NIGHT OF SOUL. I remembered I had a book that referenced the different stages of soul transformation and told Zac, "I will look for that book and read about fermentation." He agreed and bid me a good night. I smiled and said, "Good night Zac."

I began to search for the book but couldn't help wondering if my idea to ferment my food was not a subconscious thought revealing this stage of soul evolution. I would put money on the fact that it was. I found the book and read the many stages of Soul Development but sought the Fermentation Stage. I began to read:

Fermentation is the quality we envy in great artists, prophets, and spiritual leaders. Once fermented, a person becomes suddenly alive and irrepressibly hopeful because their attention is diverted from this world to something much greater. This is a time to tune into the full intensity of your thoughts, feelings, and body sensations, since they are offering you a true escape from the mundane world in which you feel yourself trapped. You are undergoing a period of true inspiration during which you should try to keep as grounded as possible. Keep a journal of your thoughts and dreams no matter how strange or irrelevant they may seem, because they may be communicating great insights. (Fractal Enlightenment Newsletter 2015, Gary McGee).

I knew who I was because I had already reached Light Being status yet Zachary seemed to be telling me that I would be evolving within my current human existence. That could only be a good thing. Upon further examination of the paragraph, if I remained connected to this reality, I would see the unseen with more clarity and heightened perception. It made sense in an odd sort of way. I began my Chakra Meditation with emphasis this time on the grounding Chakra hoping it would further solidify the paragraph from The Dark Night of the Soul.

Afterwards, I simply went to bed and fell into a deep, delicious sleep. I awoke the next morning recalling a strange and vivid dream that I began to record in my journal:

> "I was looking at a large rock about 3 feet wide and 1 1/2 feet high cut in a half-moon shape resting on a pedestal. The rock was eye level to me. On the top of the rock were 7 mountains and on top of each mountain were statues. In the center of the rock was a statue of a royal, majestic spiritual figure. At the base of the rock in the forefront at eye level was a brilliant gleaming emerald gem. I knew in the dream there was reverent significance to this but I didn't know the details of that reverence."

After recording the dream I tried to absorb its meaning during my shower. I knew the heart Chakra was green so there must be some significance there but I wasn't going to rule out any other symbolism. I understood that the number seven represented one of the most sacred numbers along with victory and the highest stage of illumination and according to mythology it possibly represented the seven stages during which the sacred mountains of the world arose. I also knew the color green was representative of The Holy Ghost in Catholicism. A lot going on there I thought to myself. Then the thought of the Emerald Tablet occurred to me from 3000 BC, "As Above so Below, As Within so Without"

I had to concentrate on getting myself to work but knew I needed to bring my dream journal with me to keep notes about ideas that would pop into my head during the day enlightening me on the hidden significance of this dream. This was no ordinary dream. I asked the Universe and like they say, ask and you will receive. I received symbols, as most of us do, which I now had to translate. I would ask my guides and Zachary for help here. This was the first time I could not satisfactorily understand my dream. I didn't like the feeling of not knowing. It was not like me at all but I would give it attention with the purpose of clear knowing.

Arriving at work I started the coffee. I was surprised to see Sara Helson there typing away. Good morning Sara I said. Why are you here so early? She said she had a ton of orders to enter. It bothered me because I wondered if these sales managers had been entering orders via email all along and because of my notification, they began to submit them to Order Processing. I couldn't help but wonder what that would do to inventory tracking. Will there be duplicates? Will Arizona go into a tailspin? Well, they obviously had not been given direction before my on-boarding and I wanted to blame Paul. I wanted to give everyone the benefit of the doubt however but I knew if I was right in my assumption. I would be the one left trying to unravel and reconcile at month's end. I told Sara, not to worry, we have Kelly Swanson starting on Monday so it will get easier and after I see what's on my plate for the day, I'll try to help her.

I checked my email and only had one from Rob providing me with his available two-day schedule for our visit to the Arizona facility. Great I thought, let me get his admin on board to schedule flights and hotel.

Shortly, Barbara Hanson came storming into my office without as much as a good morning, glaring at me and demanding if her orders had been entered into the system yet. I jumped out of my skin! I said, "Barbara, we're working on them now. As you can see we only have one order entry person so I will also be helping her get them entered as well. I would greatly appreciate if you could knock on my door before entering and greet me with a hello or good morning in a professional manner. I'm always happy to work with you and answer any of your questions." She simply ignored my polite request and then had the audacity to scream back at me. "Have my orders shipped yet? When will they arrive at Sloan Kettering?" "I'll check" I told her.

Oh this must be that white rat the size of a rabbit in my dream several weeks ago. I was not going to tolerate her insolence and unprofessionalism any longer.

I constructed an email to Paul DeMato asking for a half hour of his time today so that I could get to the bottom of this woman's behavior and attitude. I also sent a quick email to Kathy asking if she could confirm an ETA for the Sloan Kettering order that shipped yesterday. I then proceeded to join Sara at one of the order entry desks and assist her in entering orders for Arizona to fill. Sara was very appreciative. By now, I was shaking. No one should ever be subjected to such behavior I thought. If this could not be resolved, I knew I would not stand for this treatment much longer. I had faith in Paul.

Within an hour and a half, all orders were entered into the system. Sara was extremely grateful and I simply told her that I have no objection to rolling up my sleeves and pitching in. I entered my office and closed the door. It was unusual for me to do this. I believed in an open door policy. I needed to calm my nerves and think. I didn't know what I needed to think about. I just knew I needed a few moments to breath and reflect. I stared out my window at the grey overcast sky and knew the temperature outside was freezing and it all looked so dreary. I tried to visualize the Spring season and what it would look like and that calmed me a bit.

I opened my door and asked Sara for an encapsulated printout of all the orders we entered thus far and that I would like her to keep a daily binder of the same matching the summary with faxes confirming shipments of the order summaries. She jumped to it with delight. I thought to myself, who ever hired her, thank you!

I received an email from Paul saying he was available from 2:30 - 3:00 that afternoon. Good, I said and marked my calendar.

I began to wonder if the order entry system was connected to the sales managers computers where they could click a link to follow the progress of their requested orders. I called IT. Dan said, "Yes," and provided me with a verbal procedure that I wrote down to instruct the sales force. Oh thank God for IT and why haven't I been given the courtesy of this information before? I constructed the email to sales explaining the procedure and if they had any questions they could feel free at any time to ask me or my assistants for help.

I quickly called Sara into my office and asked her to close the door behind her. I wanted to inform her of this procedure as well in case she was getting bombarded with unreasonable demands from the sales force. I showed her the process on my computer and then we walked over to hers to repeat the steps. She smiled and said, good to know! I smiled at her and said, yep... I feel the same way!

After lunch, I headed to the tenth floor to meet with Paul. I entered his office and he showed me to his guest chair. I sat down but he didn't. He remained standing and had papers in his hand that he was reviewing. I began by letting him know the reason for this meeting. He didn't seem at all interested that I had a concern. I spoke frankly about Barbara Hanson's behavior and wondered if he could provide insight into her apparent issues. How did he come to hire her and was he aware of a crass reputation that she might have? He looked at me now giving me his attention. He sort of agreed that she could be difficult but he would have a talk with her. I reiterated that her behavior was extremely unprofessional and disruptive and not conducive to a productive work environment. He just shook his head in agreement and all I wanted to say, but didn't, was "thanks for the warning buddy. Let me walk into a war zone with no knowledge that a war was going on." Instead I simply said, "Thank you I would greatly appreciate any assistance you can provide" and I got up and left his office.

I was hoping for more comments from him but it was apparent he knew about her behavior issues and I suspected he was intimated by her. After all, she had the Sloan Kettering account which I was certain by now was his company's largest grossing customer. I was beginning to lose respect for Paul.

I returned to my office. I was beginning to adjust to this pattern. Mornings are hell and afternoons are normal. I reviewed my emails and called Rob's admin to see how scheduling Arizona was going and if she needed any help. She said, "I just finished up and I'll be down in a moment to give you your Itinerary." I said, "Great, It will be nice to meet you. Thank you."

Nancy was Rob's admin and very professional. Good for her I thought. We reviewed the Itinerary and I knew I'd be in Arizona this upcoming Monday and Tuesday. I didn't mind. It would be a quick fast paced trip and it would get me out of the office for two days. I was very much looking forward to seeing Arizona especially because I knew it would be warm and I had never been there. I informed Sara that I would not be here Monday or Tuesday because of my trip and she would need to acclimate Kelly Swanson who was starting work on Monday. Sara said, "No problem, I'll be happy to welcome her."

The day came to an end and I packed my briefcase and headed for home.

Listening to my driver approved meditation tapes and feeling glad I got through another day, I drove home in peace and a feeling that I didn't need any reading, Zachary or even meditation tonight. I just didn't feel it in me. Tonight I was going to watch some U2 videos and clear my head of any existential thinking.

That evening I began listening intently the song lyrics of U2's "With or Without You" and felt a deep sadness come over me. I related to the words because I felt the cold stone looks in humanities eyes and could feel the twist of my own thorn in my side. I began reminiscing about my life in Sania and how these mundane, confusing, irritating issues were virtually absent from that existence. I especially wondered if my Light Being companions were waiting for me to return after I had accomplished whatever it was I was here to accomplish. I often felt their presence around me and knew I had strong guidance from other sources, but I felt alone and confused here regardless. I wondered if my need to come back was just a twist of fate and it did truly feel like I was on a bed of nails.

I had hoped I would "reach the shore" so to speak but pondered over the prospect of what I would be confronted with before reaching the shore. I knew I could not use my Light Being abilities, telepathically influencing the conditions I was confronted with including altering a person's perception. It would only defeat the entire purpose of my experiencing this lifetime again but I also knew I was extremely frustrated with being human. I could not help but realize how the words "with or without you" were a direct reflection of how I could not be with or without my Light Being self. Quite a conundrum. I wondered what U2 were thinking when they wrote those words. I even wondered if they were living the same experience that I was. I also considered the irony that I was not even experiencing the beauty of lovemaking which was the temptation that brought me here in the first place.

See the stone set in your eyes
See the thorn twist in your side
I wait for you
Sleight of hand and twist of fate
On a bed of nails she makes me wait
And I wait without you
With or without you
Through the storm we reach the shore

Lyrics by: Adam Clayton, Dave Evans, Larry Mullen, Paul Hewson

After listening to the Joshua Tree album as well as the Unforgettable Fire album, Ava began to gain her confidence again. She did understand that she had more gifts and awareness and an understanding than the humanity she was living amongst and felt blessed even though she did not want to be here. She was beginning to understand for the first time that she herself was evolving as a human with the exceptional benefits of her Light Being gifts.

Therein was the wisdom of the Fermentation quote Zachary pointed out to her. What a light bulb moment she had.

She would work on a way to keep in mind the possibility that she would always have a choice. The choice of being or not being effected negatively by the issues presented for the purpose of her human evolution. She felt this was a major breakthrough for her.

The idea gave her a sense of gratitude that there is always a way. She did not have to stay at Paul's company if she chose not to. Of course! We always have choices. Ava began looking at this situation as a test of her human consciousness. We're not always as stuck as we think we are. Ava knew she was fortunate to have special wisdom and attributes that allowed her to think on a higher level in spite of being human. One of her thoughts consisted of the possibility that she could always quit her job. It would be acceptable because it would not appear to be "out of the ordinary" for a person to quit their job. It was certainly not out of the ordinary to seek self-respect and do what your inner voice knew what was right. Yes, she realized, that would be the enlightened human way of accomplishing the best outcome.

As the week drew to a close, Ava was looking forward to a Saturday of skiing with Riley and then off to Arizona on Monday. She could not believe she had only been with Compu Inov for only one week! It felt like a month! Especially since there continued to be uncontrollable bursts of demands from Barbara. Ava wondered if Paul even spoke with her.

Ava began to prepare for her day of skiing Saturday before retiring for the evening. After all was organized for her trip, she had a steaming cup of green tea and began to communicate with Zachary.

Zachary greeted Ava with his usual FANOFU2 greeting and began to speak YOU HAVE COME TO LEARN THE MEANING OF FREEDOM WITHIN SELF TO CHOOSE THAT WHICH YOU CAN ACCEPT WITHOUT DOMINANCE OR FORCE, THAT YOU MAY SPREAD FREELY AMONG OTHERS THIS FEELING OF EQUALITY. THIS IS YOUR PURPOSE. Ava was stunned but not really surprised. Zachary always knew what her concerns were; what was on her mind, and he could simplify her struggles in one full sweep. She smiled and began to prepare for bed and decided to read some poetry. She selected a book by Annie Besant knowing that she was being guided to its contents by other worldly forces, or even perhaps her own inner force.

No soul that aspires can ever fail to rise,
No heart that loves can ever be abandoned
Difficulties exist only that in overcoming them,
we may grow strong
And only they who have suffered, are able to save.

Yep she realized, for sure. This was a reminder for her at this moment in time and that this was coming from her own consciousness. She smiled to herself and thanked the Universe for its divine blessings, grateful for her conscious connection to its gifts. Unable to keep her eyes open any longer, Ava drifted off to sleep.

CHAPTER 21

Detours

Saturday morning had Ava remembering a great dream and she began recording it in her dream journal:

> "I was traveling a familiar route until I came upon a detour sign. I followed the detour sign to several other detour signs. In the end I realized that the detoured route was a lot simpler and quicker than the original route. When I got to my destination I was on the top level landing of a staircase with a gentleman and we talked together."

Ava knew how to interpret her dream. She was heading for a detour in the direction of her human life, with no small thanks to her steadfast studies and introspection. She understood that she would be taking some detours as she was increasingly gaining knowledge of how to navigate the conundrum she was in. She was excited about what was ahead for her. For now, she needed to get ready for a day of skiing.

Of course she could not disappoint Riley, or Mari for that matter. She did commit her time to a ski lesson for Riley and she would fulfill her responsibility. She got up and showered and prepared a good hearty breakfast for the day ahead.

Shortly, she found herself on the Garden State Parkway heading for Mari Starly's house. She began to change her focus on a beautiful sunny day on the ski slopes and felt good about keeping her word. She had plenty of time tomorrow to do her continued soul searching studies.

After greeting Mari, her husband and Riley, Ava positioned herself in the back seat of their car. Since she and Riley sat in the back, Ava thought this would be a good time to talk to Riley about skiing and get an understanding of his level of technique as well as his enthusiasm for the activity. He was very excited and very eager to learn more about how to go faster and make shorter turns. I told him I would like to see his abilities first and then we would go from there. He asked me what kind of skis I used and I told him I had racing Dynamics. His eyes opened wide. "Wow are they really long?" he asked. I said, "Yes, they're taller than I am." He said sadly his skis were very short. I reminded him that when I began skiing, I started on the GLM method (graduated length method). So, if you want to know the proper way to ski well and enjoy your skiing, it is always best to start with a shorter ski and gradually increase the length. If you started on a longer ski, you would hamper your ability to learn the technique properly and you would not have much fun. He shook his head understanding the concept of GLM.

We arrived at the mountain within an hour and I was quite surprised at how few slopes were available. I did not want to discourage anyone from the fun day we planned but I knew this looked like a very boring mountain. I kept that to myself.

We entered the lodge and Riley and I began getting our equipment on and I showed him how to hold his skis like a pro. He smiled and said, "I know." "Oh, good for you" I said and smiled. We headed out and snapped our skis into our boots and began the bird walk up to the bunny slope to the T-bar. I explained to him I wanted to get an idea of how he skied which is why we were doing the bunny slope. He understood. If he showed technique, I'd take him to the beginner. He agreed.

He released the T-bar like a pro with his two poles in one hand. "Well done Riley," I said. We found ourselves at the top of the mild bunny slope and I asked to see his form on his first turn and then just stop. To my surprise he did a snow plow turn. I asked him if he wanted to learn to ski with both skis together. "Yes," he exclaimed. I showed him how to do this. He was a little apprehensive at first, took a couple of falls but he had it mastered before we got to the bottom of the slope. He had the biggest smile on his face. "Well done," I said. "Now let's try the whole bunny slope with skis together." We were quickly at the top again and I reminded him how to initiate the downhill start by bringing both ski tips facing down and to quickly assert more energy on the inside of his right ski would result in a left turn using his poles as a rhythm timer. He was a natural. I could tell he took instruction well and this was going to be an enjoyable a day for him as well as me. It was cold outside and the best way to keep warm was to keep skiing.

After that run, we went over to the beginner slope where Riley could pick up more momentum learning the technique. He did very well and only resorted to the snow plow position a few times. We did the beginner slope again and I felt he was ready for the chair lift to the intermediate slope.

Much to my amazement, probably due to the incline of the slope and his determination to be a great skier, he did quite well. I thoroughly enjoyed the intermediate slope myself because it had no challenge for me. It allowed me to comfortably feel the slicing of my edges into the snow and ice appreciating the command being transferred from my brain to my legs to my skis onto the surface of the mountain. I could often keep my skis facing down hill just to pick up speed. It was an opportunity for me to understand the technique and the skillful design of my skis and my fervent love of control of the terrane. My face was icy cold and I loved the smell of the cold fresh mountain air. Looking around I could see the beautiful snow capped evergreens and blue sky and the smell of wood-burning fireplaces coming from nearby village homes. I could feel my skis slicing through the mountain with accurate precision hearing the chatter of "ice cubes" under their edges. I made giant slalom and slalom turns to my delight. I would swish up the loose snow with the tails of my skis on some turns. It felt like I was dancing to my own tune and this mountain was my partner. We were one and had a mutual appreciation for each other. I wished I had ear phones on with U2 music playing. Forever watchful of Riley, I could tell he was feeling as empowered as myself and secretly wished he could be as fast as me but that wasn't going to be possible. He was doing so well though, it was hard to believe he was a beginner and knew that my graphic technical descriptions for him were absorbed and translated by simply looking at the joy on his face. There is nothing like the feeling of being in command and knowing you have total control over the enjoyment of your experience. A little like life I'm realizing. Technique equals joy. I'm learning that about creating the human life I wish to live, emerging from confusion and darkness into my pure spirit. There seemed to be no limit to human creative powers.

Riley asked me with his rosy cheeks and a sparkle in his eyes, if we could explore another intermediate slope so he could continue practicing. I said, "Sure and by the way, you've done me proud." Without the benefit of a trail map, I suspected that the second chairlift over to the right of our conquered slope would lead us to another intermediate run. We took it to the top and headed down a meandering path surrounded by tall evergreens. We finally came out to a clearing and the blood felt like it left my body but not before turning icy cold! The sign on the trail said Triple Black Diamond. I shouted "Riley, we've made a big mistake." He had a look of excitement on his face. I said, "No, you do not realize, this is a triple black diamond. A slope for expert skiers." It is very narrow and had waist high moguls. "Riley, there is no other way out of here. We are in trouble." Riley insisted we would be okay. I insisted that I would now teach him how to get down the mountain carrying his skis using his ski boots. He insisted that he could do it. I could not believe this child. He had no fear. He had no idea what this was going to be like and I thought of having to tell his parents I killed him! "Dear Riley," I said, "please let me show you how to get down this mountain with your ski boots." He wouldn't hear of it. I decided I'd have to explain to him how to ski moguls. Since his skis were short, he could ski the terrain in between the moguls and if he fell, he should try to aim his body for a mogul, it would stop his fall and subsequent slide into the woods or off a cliff. I, on the other hand with super long skis had no choice but to ski the moguls, which would be dangerous given the incline of this slope. Making it worse, was the slope curved sharply after several yards and I couldn't tell what was ahead. I told him that our strategy would be for him to go first so that if he fell, I would ski to him quickly to help him. So, he was going to have to go first. He obviously couldn't follow me because if he fell behind me, he might take me down with him and we'd both be doomed.

We reviewed our plan and headed down. I must admit, I had never been so scared skiing in my life especially because I felt responsible for the safety of this little boy. I watched Riley ski in between the moguls as I instructed him. He struggled the entire way down this triple black diamond but I could see that he remembered what I said and used the moguls to steady himself when he felt he would lose control. I struggled as well having to keep my eyes on him and the unfamiliar terrane. We made it! In one piece. Riley was ecstatic but I was more than relieved. I told him, "He should never ever attempt that alone." He just smiled at me.

After that experience, we both agreed to call it a day. However, wouldn't you know, the first thing he tells his parents when we met them in the lodge was that he skied a triple black diamond! Mari and her husband looked at me with severe shock in their eyes. I apologized deeply explaining to them that I had no intention of bringing him to an expert slope. We were lost and we had no way out. I'm deeply sorry. I felt awful but secretly grateful that Riley was still in one piece and safe and was going to become a great skier. He had no fear which was a lesson for me as well. The excitement of exploration in our youth should never be lost in adulthood but merely cultivated with sophisticated wisdom and trust. Riley showed me an ever-deepening awareness that no matter what life throws at you, you can get through it. I would have booted down that mountain but still Riley had a good lesson for me.

As Ava returned home Saturday evening exhausted by her exhilarating day of skiing and her gratifying sense of achievement teaching Riley the proper ski technique, she only had slight concerns about the Starlys. She knew they would adjust to the idea that she made a genuine mistake and would eventually accept her apologies. Ava took a hot steaming shower and then into some soft comfy PJs to begin a session with Zachary. Zachary, of course, immediately came through with his sweet familiar greeting.

FANOFU2. I smiled and said. "Hello Zachary. How are you?" He circled his heart round and round. He was giving me a hug. I smiled again. Zachary wanted to begin immediately and began to speak the words SPIRITUAL - GOD WILL SET YOU IN FRONT OF PEOPLE - WRITING BOOKS with a DYNAMIC BLACK COVER VERY SCHOLARLY. COMBINING BOTH WORLDS. I was quite taken back. "Zac," I said, "I cannot imagine me being a writer, much less discussing how to combine my world in Sania and my human existence here. Besides, who would ever believe it?" I began to ponder the thought that maybe it could be believable, maybe even enjoyable. It would have to be written as a fiction of course, and who better to write it but me. Heck, I think Zac might be on to something here. I may contemplate doing this very writing that Zac seemed so adamant about. Zac continued to speak MOVING TO ANOTHER STATE OUT WEST. I was surprised by that comment but felt that part could be true. I had a feeling within me that I was about to make a geographic move and with Zachary's guidance, I began to wonder if I wasn't even going in a different career direction. As I was beginning to feel sleepy, I decided to bid Zac a good evening and end my communication. I still wanted to perform my Chakra meditation and then I would go to sleep knowing that I would have a peaceful restful sleep after my most enjoyable day.

Ava was awakened at 4:00 AM by a disturbing dream. She was frightened and felt uneasy. She immediately began writing in her journal:

> "I was being sent somewhere. A place where I would not have chosen to go voluntarily. I felt captive. There were many people, perhaps hundreds, all ages and both sexes. I was new and everyone knew it. There were masters or instructors who were in charge. They were organizing groups of people into different projects. I was part of one group and I knew this was extremely serious and I would be punished severely if I didn't get it right. I raised my hand and asked my instructor if the project I was assigned to had a list of regulations to guide me or if I was allowed to be as creative as I desired. My instructor informed me I could be as creative as I wanted to be. He looked pleased with my question, both appreciating the fact that I was cognizant of rules and the fact that I felt confidence enough to speak up."

Ava wrote in her journal a clear analysis of its meaning and the significance it held for her. She understood her life here on Earth was of her own choosing and not governed by a Spiritual governing body. This was her choice she had to make in order to make amends for her discretion and was beginning to understand that it was a deliberate act for a deliberate purpose. She actually began to believe it was a natural progression in consciousness in order to possibly be elevated beyond Sania. She was taking a leap of faith in this creative process and she could use her own creative powers as an enlightened human being to form any life she wanted as long as she didn't use any Light Being magic. She did question however if writing a book would accomplish her mission in a clandestine way.

Ava wondered if her discontent with the apparent duality of her life was the result of her believing she had no choice or say in the design of her existence here. Now she realized she had all the power to empower herself to create happily and joyfully as she desired. She had every choice possible, every amount of assistance the Universe provided as long as she allowed it. She had every right to be here and design the life she wanted. She even had a choice to react to any given situation in a manner of her choosing. She felt inspired by her dream even though it was uncomfortable but realized that any leap of faith in unfamiliar territory would be frightening but with trust and belief in oneself, one could see the wisdom in its scenario. She was grateful again for Universal wisdom and guidance and allowing herself to receive whatever blessings may come.

It was now Sunday and Ava decided to do her Yoga and have breakfast. She also wanted to prepare for her trip to Arizona the following day. She reviewed her itinerary and confirmed her car pick up time and flight schedule. It was a peaceful, sunny, brisk winter day, a perfect day for indoor chores. She was feeling content and was looking forward to possibly renting a movie at Blockbuster. After the laundry was done, Ava took a ride to Blockbuster and felt compelled to review the videos in the Foreign Film Section. One caught her eye immediately, "Wings of Desire". On the cover box was a large angel wing with gracefully defined feathers spreading out over half the cover box featuring Peter Falk as Columbo. She thought it looked interesting and it had a certain energy to it that she needed to explore. It was a German language film with English subtitles but Ava could understand and speak any language because of her Light Being status. Ava read the cover box and was immediately struck by the similarity of the character's existence to hers! She read the cover box, "Wings of Desire is set in modern day Berlin and follows Angel Damiel's path from heavenly flight to earthly delight in a manner that's comical, touching and entertaining. Though considered a love story, it also serves as a reminder of just how good it feels to live." The movie was directed by Wim Wender, an acclaimed filmmaker. Ava knew this movie had unforeseen significance and she headed back home to cozy up on her couch and spend the next two hours enjoying every bit of it!

It was brilliantly performed and written and the cinematography was unsurpassed. She easily related to the romantic fantasy about an angel who wishes to be mortal and willing to fall from the sky if it meant a chance to fall in love. Damiel had no reservations about living a human life even though he was consistently warned by his fellow angelic buddies that he was crazy for wanting to do so. Damiel insisted it would be great to taste coffee, feel cold air, and touch the skin of the woman he loved. He was giving up all the powers of his angelic existence for the sake of being with someone he had fallen in love with. Ava could not relate to his decision to sacrifice all his powers to have the human experience of loving this woman. She could see the comparison between herself and Damiel but knew he could not understand how difficult it is being human. Ava understood that her willingness to return was for a different purpose than the angelic character in the movie. She was developing the notion that she was deliberately willing to return to advance higher in her spiritual consciousness. Nevertheless, Ava loved the story and suspected it was a divinely guided choice. She already knew there were guides around all of us, protecting and gently nudging us to a more elevated state of existence.

As Ava frequently did with a movie she enjoyed, she decided to watch it again to be sure she didn't miss a thing. She prepared lunch and cozied up again on the couch to begin again.

Arizona

As morning came, Ava remembered an interesting dream. She was viewing a constellation but didn't recognize it as any known star formation. She quickly wrote it down in her journal and without a suspected interpretation, she looked up the meaning of constellation in a dream book she recently bought. The interpretation read: To see a constellation in your dream, indicates that something in your life is coming together in a complex way. It represents a mental process.

She was satisfied with the interpretation from her Cloud Nine Dream book and suspected that there were going to be many changes for her that she would not fear. She knew from the culmination of all her sessions with Zachary; meditations; dreams; experiences and the Seth books that she was transforming her life and had no doubts or issues about the future.

As Ava's plane was beginning to prepare for lift off, she chuckled to herself remembering how easy it was to travel as a Light Being. You simply thought of where you wanted to go and puff, like magic, you were there. The dense matter of the Earth plane was quite cumbersome and humans literally had to work against the forces of nature to achieve almost anything and that included their very own existence. From her Seth book Ava began reading: **Such a task meant that man must break out of the self-regulating, precise, safe and yet limiting aspects of instinct. The birth of a conscious mind, as you think of it, meant that the species took upon itself free will. Built-in procedures that had beautifully sufficed could now be superseded. They became suggestions instead of rules." (Seth: The Nature of Personal Reality, Jane Roberts copyright 1978)**

Indeed Ava thought, but eventually, this planet would also reach a higher state of consciousness too. It might take a million years but it would still happen.

Ava did not want to be rude to Rob who had accompanied her on her trip to the Arizona facility so she politely closed her book and asked him if he wanted to review anything with her about their upcoming meeting. Rob did open his brief case and wanted to go over some procedures and some of the players they would be meeting. He began intertwining business talk with personal talk and asked Ava about her background and where she came from. Oh joy, she thought. Very mundane but she had to be corporately respectful and gave him a snippet of her background as well as how she knew Paul DeMato. Rob provided some insight into his background as well and I felt so compelled to ask him about Barbara Hanson. I decided I'd take the risk and dig a little into the history of the formation of Compu Inov and wondered how Barbara Hanson fit into the picture. Rob was open to the question and knew that Barb had contacts at Sloan Kettering that guaranteed her a secure place within S/K and Compu Inov. He did not provide me a the connection between Paul and Barbara, however. I didn't want to push it. I really didn't care. I was just making corporate talk. It seemed unconsciously, I had already made up my mind that I would not tolerate her behavior and I suspected I wasn't going to remain there for long. It was a gut feeling with no clear cut plan, really.

As we landed at Phoenix' Sky Harbor Int'l, I immediately felt different. The climate was warm and dry and the air had a different smell to it. You could tell there were no evergreens here and there was no familiar fragrance of the Earth's soil or flowers present. I liked the smell and the feel of the energy of the desert! I could see mountain ranges all around in the far distance which I knew to be the Sierra Nevada's and noticed that most of Arizona was flat. I was stoked! We disembarked the plane and headed for baggage claim where we caught a taxi for the hotel. After double checking our first meeting that afternoon, we agreed to meet in the lobby at 1:00 PM for a brief eleven mile cab ride to the distribution center. I was very much looking forward to seeing the surrounding sites secretly hoping the cab ride would take longer. I wanted to look all around and enjoy the Palm Trees. I felt like a tourist and needed to keep my enthusiasm to a limit so Rob would not think I was here on a pleasure trip instead of a business trip. I brought my camera with me because I wanted to take as many pictures of the desert for my photo album. I wanted to keep this memory alive forever.

We arrived at the distribution center about fifteen minutes before our scheduled appointment with Kathy Larson. I was excited to meet the face behind the voice. I grew to know her as very responsible and reliable. A big plus considering the logistics involved in getting orders placed and shipped.

We were greeted by the receptionist who contacted Kathy and she immediately welcomed us to join her in her office. From the brief walk to Kathy's office, I could tell this was a very well organized, clean, efficient operation. The size of the facility alone was staggering.

We made our brief introductions and Kathy wanted to begin a tour of the facility. She was excited to show it off and her skill at managing the operation. In some cases, because the facility was so large, Kathy had us hop on a golf-cart-like vehicle to get us around. She reviewed the incoming order process equipment showing where our orders were received and processed for picking and shipping. There had to be at least seventeen bay doors. I momentarily flashed back to the Computer Enterprises' facility, which only had two bay doors, one for shipping, one for receiving and wondered how many people it took to manage this facility. Kathy wanted to introduce us to the shipping and receiving managers for the Northeast. There was so much inventory coming and going from this facility it required five managers categorized by geographic region. I was mightily impressed. Kathy continued to introduce us to various managers in charge of our operation whom we spoke briefly but intently with so that we gained a full comprehension of what we were required to do from our offices in New Jersey.

Five o'clock was quickly upon us. The afternoon flew by but in reality, my body clock was still on Eastern time and it knew it was 7:00 PM. I was growing tired. I knew Rob and I still needed to get dinner so I suggested we find a place near Sun Devil Stadium. Rob gave me a sour face and said, "Are you kidding, this is a college town. What kind of food do you think they'll have here?" I said, "I know, but I simply must see Sun Devil Stadium." He obliged me. He didn't seem to mind because he could tell I really wanted to see the place. We ate at a nearby pub which was filled with college students and we sure stuck out like two sore thumbs but it really was quite entertaining for us and the food wasn't bad. Afterward, we walked over to the Stadium.

I knew it would be dark but they did have some of the flood lights on inside the stadium so I could sort of make out the immensity of the venue. I was so knowing that I had been to a place where U2 had performed. I owned the movie where their live concert was filmed right here in this stadium. I felt like a little girl. I tried to see if a nearby Security Manager would allow us into the stadium but he quickly forbid it. "It is not allowed," he said. I was a little disappointed but fully understood the need for security and secretly knew that it wouldn't matter in the end. I was going to see U2 in concert live and I was determined to meet them.

At that point, Rob and I caught a taxi back to the hotel in Phoenix. We had an early flight in the morning which would get us back east two hours later than flying time because of the time difference. I was so happy to have made the trip and very impressed with the desert. I began to wonder what it would feel like standing in the middle of Joshua Tree National Park. I considered making plans to visit on a vacation in the very near future. After all, Zachary said, "This is where it is." Exactly what he meant I wasn't sure but I was being guided there. I supposed it was for a good reason. I certainly knew I felt a different vibration being here in the Mohave Desert. It seemed spiritual and ethereal and I felt a deep connection to something here. I wasn't exactly sure what the connection was and even pondered the thought that I may have been feeling my Light Being identity somehow.

Upon arriving back at the hotel, Ava was looking forward to a hot shower and a cup of tea. She was already missing her books and wondered if she would have an interesting dream that night. Ava, slowly drifted off to sleep.

Indeed, as Ava awoke, she had a clear picture of her dream and took out her journal and began writing:

> "Standing in a room looking at a window. It was completely covered on the outside with snow. I had an instrument in my hand and started to methodically, painstakingly, chip away at the snow which was crusty. I began at the bottom right corner and slowly with great precision began chipping away until the entire window was free of snow and I could view the outside. I noticed that I did not get a single bit of snow inside the room. I looked outside the window and to my delight was a true winter wonderland. It was dawn and just moments before the sun rose. Everything was covered with

pure white snow completely untouched by human or animal. The evergreens were heavily laden with snow and the soft rolling hills shown in the dawn light with pristine glistening snow. I could smell the cool clean air and here nothing at all."

What a cool dream, no pun intended, I thought. It represented how methodical and deliberate I was about all things in my life. I didn't like sloppy or messy. I approached all decisions and actions with exactness and the reward was a view of nature's beauty, inside and out. I was surprised it was a winter scene however, I was secretly hoping for a desert scene. Nevertheless, the dream was a penetrating insight into my approach to life including my intention to self-actualize.

I began to dress and pack for my trip back east knowing, I'd need my heavy winter coat. I phoned Rob's room and told him I'd meet him in the coffee shop in the lobby for breakfast in 20 minutes. He agreed.

I felt an uneasiness about leaving Phoenix. I didn't want to go back home. I wanted to remain in the desert and explore. It was calling for me and I couldn't answer it. Right then I made myself a promise to begin planning a vacation. Our flight departed on time and it was uneventful. Rob and I reviewed our impressions of the meeting with Kathy. I went over some of Compu Inov processes that I wanted to revise to be more compliant with the distribution center to achieve a more unified operation. The thought of returning to that office again dealing with Barbara Hanson was a real downer. I distinctly felt that she had the upper hand here and she would not be disciplined. The wheels began to turn in my brain so to speak. I was going to make a plan. Remembering a session with Zachary, I knew I always had choices. I was going to make a choice here. This was going to be a turning point in my human existence. I was always going to provide for myself what would make me happy. I knew I was standing at that Red Pill crossroads. I was leaving the matrix of Plato's Cave into the cocoon of independence and I would then, enter the Cosmic Commune. It felt so right deep down in my soul, it was a memory of how I became a Light Being!

Arriving at Newark International I peered outside the tiny windows of the cabin and could see snow. The only snow I liked was under my skis. I hated driving in this stuff and everything looked dull and dreary. Very different from the beauty of the Arizona desert with the sun shinning so brightly. It was a happy place. I could not help but notice a sea of grey and black coats in baggage claim. Even the people dress different here of course, the weather influenced fashion. Baggage claim at Phoenix was bright and colorful. I could clearly see there is a definite influence on an individual's energy field dependent on their environment.

Ava bid Rob farewell as their taxis pulled up and both said, see you at the office tomorrow. Ava reflected as the taxi drove through the highways heading for her apartment where all her treasures were and especially the most important ones, her books; videos; meditation spot and of course Zachary. Ava knew she would immediately have a session with Zachary. She missed him. Everything looked so grey here. Of course it was the winter time and things did look more inviting in the spring and summer months, however, there was no winter in the Southwest and if one wanted to ski, well you were so close to the Colorado Rockies there was no deprivation of the best skiing in the U.S.

Upon arriving at her apartment, Ava quickly unpacked her suitcase and began to prepare a light meal. She was eager to hear what Zachary would have to say and to complete a meditation and possibly look forward to some reading. Ava loved the solitude her home provided and reveled in the peace and centering power. Ava didn't realize there was a message on her answering machine.

The message was a song! It was being sung by a band she didn't recognize. It was all that was on the message. She played it over and over because she desperately wanted to write it all down. She thought of her Light Being friends telling her they would communicate from a particular device that she was not familiar with. She could only figure they were showing her an answering machine. The song played out as Ava began writing as fast as she could:

I was only waiting
For a better moment that didn't come
There never could be a better moment
Than this one, this one
This one is gliding above the ocean

Lyrics by: Paul McCartney

Astonished by the song, Ava he could not help but cry. She began to sob. She was deeply moved by these words that touched her soul and realized she was in pain. After rereading the lyrics several times she composed herself and her existential intellect kicked in. She was eternally grateful for the divine guidance but knew she was responsible for its interpretation. She thought a long time about the words and felt they were suggesting that there is a great love here for her and it was near the ocean. She was vaguely familiar with that type of deep love and connection that had brought her to tears, tears of joy. She wondered who it was and where could he be? Was he just around the corner or was he near an ocean? She would ask Zachary for some direction to her questioning and immediately began to summon him.

Zachary began his session as he always did. FANOFU2. I smiled and said, "Hello friend, I missed you." Zachary circled his heart several times conveying a reciprocal response. I began immediately to ask about the song on my answering machine and if my interpretation was an accurate one? Zachary's response was SEEK OZ. I was annoyed. I had no time for riddles I suggested in my vibration to Zachary. I stated that I knew it was coming from my Light Being companions but I wasn't specifically clear about how to interpret the message. Zachary then stated: OZ JOSHUA TREE AND PACIFIC OCEAN. STEP OUT OF THE CAVE. I immediately understood. I thanked him. Zachary was referencing Plato's Cave of codependence that I was giving some thought to earlier. I thanked Zachary immensely and with great passion for his support before bidding him a good evening.

I began to reflect on the words of the song again and looked up in my journal of Fractal Enlightenment verses about the Red Pill referencing Plato's Cave reminding myself I was a lion and not a sheep and this decision was not going to be a walk in the park for me. I had a spirit of adventure and I was going to test the waters. It made me chuckle at the prospect of the waters of the Pacific Ocean. I began to suspect I was moving to California and somewhere there I would find this love I felt so deeply passionate about. I knew no one there but I could gather the determination and logistically make this happen. I reminded myself that the passion was not only the love interest of a man but also the love of my human life coupled with my initiated soul. I was filled with excitement that I would also find a passionate career that would make a difference somehow. In my imagination, there were no "limiting thoughts". I would not be a prisoner in the Cave and I would welcome the Desert of the Real as mentioned in a Fractal Enlightenment snippet.

Ava decided it was time for her Chakra meditation and prepare for bed. She wanted to read some Seth material before retiring and selected a book to place by her bedside along with her dream journal. Before placing the journal down she felt compelled to open it and leaf through it. She began to realize that her notes reflected what was happening to her in reality. She connected a recorded session with Zachary about the HOMECOMING song by U2 reflecting on the lyrics specifically, 'And you hunger for the time, time to heal, desire, time and your earth moves beneath your own dreamscape'. Ava completely understood that all of life is a dream. The referenced song Zachary was pointing out to her was a message that she was and is on the borderline. "And you know it's time to go through the sleet and driving snow; across the fields of mourning Light in the distance." Of course Ava thought. It was all coming to this. She had an immediate urge to look through all the lyrics of the U2 songbooks. There was a definitive connection to her life there that she could not explain but she knew the messages were in those songs.

She also saw what seemed like the first time, a Seth passage she had recorded. It jumped off the page of her journal! **"To rid yourself of annoying restrictions, you re-pattern your past from the present.**" She was so grateful for her journal and knew it was to be referenced frequently going forward. She was not simply to jot things down that were of interest to her. She was understanding that the record keeping exercise of topics and dreams was for her higher good. Its purpose was to elevate her consciousness and make deliberate beneficial decisions toward her goals that she might not even be aware of as of yet. These notes were gold, she said and promised herself she would do more reflection of her journal.

By now it was getting late and Ava did not want to miss her Chakra meditation. She closed her journal knowing what she would plan for her weekend and then began her meditation practice. Afterward, Ava simply went to sleep without any further reading.

The alarm clock went off and Ava woke startled. She remembered she had to go to work but also remembered a significant dream. She began to write it down:

> "I was standing at an alter in a church and a Light Being was walking toward me in the distance. The Being was engulfed in a warm yellowish light originating from above. As he approached me he looked straight into my face and we stood staring at each other for a short while. He then began to walk down the aisle of this church to the front door.

As he opened the door he looked back at me and said, "Follow me". I did not want to follow him."

She was surprised by her decision not to follow this Light Being. It disappointed as well as confused her. She was ready to step outside she thought to herself. She would give more attention to this dream during the day trying to come up with an interpretation. In the meantime, she needed a hot shower and breakfast and get herself to work wondering what the day would be like and remembering there would be a new employee to acclimate into our processes. Her mind now had to shift modes and become grounded for the tasks at hand.

Upon entering her office, she did the usual coffee startup and headed to her office. She immediately needed to check for emails and respond where she was able. There were no messages from Paul she noticed. She felt he could have inquired about the trip but maybe he'd touch base with her later in the day. Ava thought it would be best to write him a synopsis of her meeting as a courtesy and let him know it was very successful. She then noticed HR had copied her on several emails sent to the new employee Kelly Swanson. It was the typical stuff, insurance forms, W-4 paperwork, etc, etc. She then decided to check the order entry program on her computer to see how many orders had been entered in her absence. There were seventy-five orders! Wow, these girls have been busy. She could see that shipments were going out on time and Ava specifically ran a printout of all Sloan Kettering orders knowing that Barbara Hanson would do the wild entrance into her office. Ava wondered if Kelly Swanson witnessed this behavior yet.

Sara entered the office with a cheerful good morning and I asked her "how'd everything go while I was gone"? She said, "Fine, the new girl was very capable of handling things and I made a good choice in hiring her." "Great, so glad to hear that," I said. "Were there any outbursts from you know who?" "No," Sara said. "Oh, I guess she saves that for me." We both laughed. I told her I was going to do a review of our procedures to be more in sync with Arizona's operation and meet with her and Kelly this afternoon to go over them. Nothing major, just a couple of minor changes. "Okay," Sara said and walked over to her desk. "By the way, excellent job on all those orders" I shouted to her. She said, "Thanks, Kelly was a big help."

Barbara Hanson appeared in my office doorway. I looked up at her and said, "Good morning." I was surprised she was not screaming but wondered why she was standing there. She asked if I had reviewed the S/K shipments against the orders in Arizona. I said, "Of course, and all our other orders as well." Then she raised her voice and shouted "yes, but Sloan Kettering is priority." "I understand that very well Barbara, but I reviewed all the company's orders along with more efficient procedures that can be incorporated here." Barbara shouted back and demanded, "You can't change anything with S/K orders!" I told Barbara "Arizona is extremely proficient at their tasks and if she had a specific complaint please state it." Barbara's response was loud and unprofessional, "Don't do any changes to S/K." I looked at her and said, "OK but even if I can incorporate some short cuts to make it even more productive?" She glared at me and swiftly turned around and walked away. I suspected she was going to get Paul on the phone. I didn't care. I was hired to do a job and I was doing it. Let Paul be in the middle I decided, besides he's probably getting his nails buffed at the salon right now and I laughed to myself.

HR replied that Carol Miller was the third candidate that looked good and would be available for an interview Friday at 10:00 a.m. Her resume was attached and I reviewed it. I replied to HR and stated "it's a go," 10:00 AM Friday works for me, she looks good for the position." Great I thought. We'll have this place up and running like a well-oiled machine.

At this point, Ava turned to her dream journal and reviewed the dream she had last night. Still not able to comprehend why she did not follow the Light Being outside, she closed the journal again.

Everything pointed to this venture for her. She was certain she was going to make this move.

As the busy day progressed Ava was preoccupied with the details of her upcoming actions. She began to organize a notebook on how she would make her move to California happen. It seemed complicated when thought about in her mind but once she began to organize her thoughts on paper, it started to take shape and manifest more like a reality. She decided she would contact moving companies for estimates and auto transporters. She would need to contact available apartment dwellings but had to decide where in California she wanted to live. She needed the library to research locations but concluded wherever it would be, it would have to be near Joshua Tree, the low region of the Mohave Desert and a location where she would find formidable employment. She even considered the possibility that Blockbuster would have some videos of the region. She could not believe how daring her dream was but she had to stretch her comfort zone to make this a reality. Indeed she was taking a leap of faith but understood she really wasn't alone in this endeavor. She had faith that any assistance she needed would be provided by her guides, after all, they've been influencing her in this direction all along. She kept repeating to herself "no limiting thoughts" whatsoever. You will make this happen Ava.

Before going home after work, Ava stopped at the local library to secure the books that she needed to help make some of the decisions that would bring her plan to fruition. She kept hearing in her head the words of Michelangelo, ***"The greater danger with most of us is not that our aim is too high and we miss it, but that our aim is too low and we reach it"***. It gave her more fuel to confidently forge ahead.

Upon arriving home, Ava would have to forfeit a session with Zachary tonight as well as her usual existential reading. She would need to research the library books she picked up along with contacting moving firms for quotes. After a couple of hours, Ava had her notebook quite jammed with information. Decisions,

decisions. She decided her finances were in good order but would not be taking her beautiful furniture with her to California. It was more economical to buy new furniture to suit the place she would rent keeping her move expense minimized. The car transport was relatively inexpensive but it would take two weeks to get it cross country. Ava was not that fond of driving and the thought of driving across country herself was totally out of the question. She decided on a firm and needed the help of Mari Starly to house her for about a week between giving up her apartment and belongings while the shipping companies packed and loaded her stuff. Now, the question remains, WHERE to live and WHEN to move.

After researching the books, Ava felt that Orange County would be the best place to secure a job and therefore would look for apartments there. She also knew it was a short plane ride from the Colorado Rockies where her friend Gary was now living. Wouldn't it be great to ski there with my buddy she thought. She jotted down some locations at Laguna Beach in her note book that she would discretely call from work the following day since it was after hours at this point. Besides, it was getting late and did want to do her Chakra meditation before retiring for the evening.

The alarm clock sounded and Ava awoke with a very interesting dream that she could fully understand was the result of her research and decision the night before. She began to write in her journal:

> "I was with Mari and it was nighttime. I was driving my car home and wasn't sure of directions. Mari had her own car and we were going over directions. I headed off into the dark driving in a strange city. I kept repeating my directions out loud, go right, go right. I did and was near water and had to go over a land bridge. I then continued the rest of my journey on foot and

had to walk thru a narrow overgrown pathway. On my left was a chain link fence and on my right were scary, evil looking characters dressed in bizarre costumes. I was scared but confident and I ignored the stares and disruptive tactics of these characters and forged ahead. I made it through the pathway and found the opening to the street. I had to then jump over a large hole in the ground to get to safety. The hole had white painted hand prints and eyes painted around it depicting others who didn't make it. I jumped and got to the other side but could feel my balance almost pulled me backwards. I was okay, I made it. I continued on foot with a sense of well being."

It was an absolutely simple dream to interpret. Yes, there would be complicated logistics to work out but I would make it. Today I would be calling apartment dwellings in the area of Laguna Beach and it would give me an idea of when to begin the process of my cross-country move. I showered and dressed and ate a fortifying breakfast. Soon I was on my way to work in a cold, damp, drizzly, sleet-like gloom but even my Z-28 knew it wouldn't be for long. There was an excitement in my persona today. I had a feeling of hope and an uplifted spirit with the desert and the ocean on my mind. Again I reflected on the great masters whom I suspected I may have known. Christian Larson popped into my mind. ***"That a man can change himself... and master his own destiny is the conclusion of every mind who is wide-awake to the power of right thought."*** What a beautiful sentiment and so eloquently stated. I wondered how much of humanity was wide awake and aware of their power to forge their own destiny. Some might say there are always obstacles but in reality What You Focus On Expands! If you focus on your inherent right to create, you will find yourself in the situation of your own creation. Everything you have created that you are looking at, is simply a reflection of your inner being. I was so deep in thought I had arrived at the office complex without consciously knowing I was even driving there. I'd better pay more attention but I guess it's what they call "auto pilot." The part of your brain that is conditioned to perform repetitive tasks without your conscious awareness of it.

I tried to shift my mind into corporate mode but was having difficulty. I was more interested in my upcoming plans and was full of excitement. Once I contacted the apartment dwellings in my notebook, I would have a better idea of when I would be giving my notice to Compu Inov. Nevertheless, I had a responsibility to uphold and I was not a slacker. Upon entering my office I could feel the transition take place. Yes, I was now corporate and would fulfill my duties as well as secure my shield of armor for when Barbara entered the office. I laughed to myself but also realized how sad it was that Barbara felt the need to behave with such distain. She must have some serious deep rooted problems to overcome. I wondered if there was a way to connect with her without compromising my principles. Oh well, possibly but it was not a necessary goal of mine at this time. I suppose no matter where I go, there would be people such as Barbara that would be placed in my path to rise above. Maybe she was one of those grotesque characters in my dream last night. I wouldn't doubt it.

The office was humming with data entry and fax confirmations of shipments. It sounded good to my ears. I did good I said to myself. This is how it should be. The only things missing were the sun, ocean, desert and palm trees. Ava laughed to herself.

She began making calls to California and hit upon a location in Laguna Niguel that would be available in six weeks. The realtor sounded very cooperative and knowledgeable and sent an email showing the layout of the apartment which looked spacious and appealing. It had a fireplace which surprised me however it was a romantic fixture in the living room. There was a balcony and the complex included a swimming pool and recreation center for billiards and exercise equipment. The rent was very doable and I completed the application papers and emailed them back to her. I mailed her a deposit check to secure the apartment. Oh my! I did it. I was so looking forward to the next couple of months! Wow. That was fast. With that I contacted the movers and confirmed a date of pick up and an address to deliver my belongings and the car transport as well. I needed to call Mari but I would do that later this evening. The timing of my current lease expiring was right in line with my move date. I love the Universe!

I quickly sent an email to Gary in Colorado and told him excitedly about my plans. He would be amazed and surprised but after some thought, I figured he wouldn't. He knew the kind of person I was. He probably would say something like, "What took you so long?" With that, I got up from my desk and walked over to the floor to ceiling windows and stared out into the grey, misty, dreary cold. In my moment of reflection I simply thanked the Universe for its support as well as my Light Being companions, guides, Seth and Zachary and thanked my own soul. I was so overcome with joy my eyes began to fill with tears. After a while I went back to my desk and began admiring the layout of my new home projecting where I would put her treasures.

When Ava returned home that evening, she called Mari and told her the news. Mari was happy for her but sad that she would be loosing such a good friend. Ava told Mari she would miss her terribly and the fun they have with Riley. Mari decided that I should consider getting Prodigy, a simple email computer system that would allow us to keep in touch with our dreams; spiritual growth; and any books or newsletters that we both knew were of immense interest to us. I told her it was a great idea. Please know you always have a place to stay in California when you visit I told her. We cried a little. I knew I would miss her but we both agreed that this was meant to be.

Afterwards I contacted the building management to let them know I would not be renewing my lease and gave them my move date. I also needed to search corporations in the neighboring cities of Laguna Niguel and submit resumes. I had time for that however, it was still too soon to schedule interviews. I was moving in six weeks. I began constructing my resignation letter to Paul DeMato that I would keep highly professional and thank him for the opportunity he provided however it was in my best interest to make this geographic move. I decided I would give Paul three weeks notice which meant in three weeks, I'd submit the letter.

CHAPTER 23

California Life

My plane landed at John Wayne Airport but not after flying over the Rockies, the Mojave Desert and a portion of the Pacific Ocean. As my eyes soaked in the paradise below, I kept singing in my head "this one glides above the ocean." It was the song left on my answering machine by my companions. I smiled. Indeed I do, I said to myself.

John Wayne Airport flew directly into Orange County which was a short taxi ride from my new apartment. I couldn't wait to see it. I had as may suitcases with me that I could reasonably manage. The rest of my belongings were somewhere across the country on an 18-wheeler which was due to arrive in about two days. The realtor said she would meet me in the office at the complex to provide me with keys and direct me to the apartment as well and familiarize me with the grounds. The pool was immense and there were some sunbathers enjoying the sunshine. I loved the recreation room. It too was immense. I loved the smell of the air. I wanted so much to go exploring around the neighboring Laguna Hills and see the Pacific Ocean but I didn't have a car yet. The best I could do right now was call a local supermarket and have food delivered so that I could eat. I also knew, with the help of the realtor, that Sleepy's would deliver a bed within the day and she provided me with their phone number. Sure enough, by 7:00 PM that evening, I had a brand new bed to sleep on. I only had two days left before I would have the rest of my things here. More important was my car. I needed to shop for furniture! I also needed to look around the area. I wanted to soak it all in before I'd be stuck behind a desk simply looking out the window at the sunshine.

I stepped out onto my balcony to smell the air. It was delicious. It was a warm evening with a slight breeze. I watched some cars go buy and I admired the Laguna Hills. Everything was so exciting and clean and the architecture was mostly Mediterranean. It was so very different from the East Coast. I loved it!

I began to unpack my suitcases and organize my clothes in my very large walk in closet. Thank God for that. I didn't have a dresser yet but I would make do. I decided to contact Zachary. FANOFU2 I smiled. "Hello Zachary. How do you like California so far I asked?" ENJOY YOUR PERIOD OF REFLECTION YOU HAVE ACHIEVED WELL. "I am, Zachary, I am so very full of joy to be here. I look forward to my awakening so to speak." Zachary, said YOU ARE ALWAYS AWAKENING THAT IS GOOD. YOU HAVE TRAINED YOURSELF WELL. I thought about that for a moment and realized Zachary was right. I initially thought I was capable of receiving guidance but only through the assistance of guides. I realized it was my source being that enabled the recognition of these guides. With that Zachary said YES. SEE U2. I was not sure what he meant. "you see me too or I should see the band U2." Zachary responded WE GO TOGETHER. I smiled and said, "Okay Zachary, we'll go to a concert together. I must prepare something to eat now so I will bid you a good evening. Hope to see you in my sleep Zachary." Zac smiled and began to fade from this reality.

Preparing dinner was a challenge in an ill-equipped kitchen but I made due eating a tuna sandwich on a paper plate. I had plenty of green tea and I drank two glasses. I was beginning to consider a rental car because I just couldn't stand not being able to explore my surroundings. I went out to the balcony again to watch the stars in the night sky. Everything was built low because of earthquake code so there was no obstruction to viewing the wide open sky. Oh I love this place. I love the air and the sense of energy exuded by this geography. I'm home I thought. Well, closer to home. I understood where my true home was but then again, I had realized that I may be going beyond Sania and that was okay with me too.

I prepared for bed with a hot shower and soft comfy PJs. I was clever enough to bring some sheets and a blanket with me so I could sleep well. Sleep well I did. I awoke in the middle of the night in that familiar bubble of protection to find Zachary sitting in a sofa chair at the end of my bed reading to me again. I simply laid myself back down and fell back into a deep sleep.

In the morning the bright sunshine was peering through the windows and woke me up. Wow! It almost blinded me. The sunrise was early here being further south than New Jersey. I got out of bed knowing I had no recall of a dream last night but remembered Zachary reading to me and I quickly jotted the event in my journal. Wish I knew what he was reading to me. I went to the living room and stepped out onto the balcony. The air was a bit chilly but I knew the sun would warm it up soon. I also knew the telephone company was due to arrive today to connect the phone. First things first. I needed breakfast. I was living no where within walking distance of a diner so I made some oatmeal in the microwave oven and fried some eggs. I was very hungry. There was no toaster yet so I simply had bread with my eggs.

I got dressed and decided to review my paperwork for job hunting. I had a map and gave myself a radius of 20 miles. As I stared at the map, I saw Joshua Tree. Oh, when my car arrives that is exactly where I'm going first! It might also be a good time to invest in a decent camera.

As I was staring at the map, a thought struck me. I might want to consider getting a low level job rather than a management position. Of course, the money would not be as good but I felt a compelling need to leave myself out of the pressures and demands of top level management. I wondered why I felt this way. I was a proven executive and had made good money. The thought made no sense to me but it felt right. Why not give it a chance Ava, I said to myself. I was hungry for something else. After all, I knew I had to be here and this is where I would find my passions in life. I believed that. I may be able to free up some of my time and energies if I wasn't under the pressures of a high level operations position. I never believed that I should dismiss thoughts that bubbled up from my intuition. I was going to work on reconfiguring another set of resumes. I would not resist the instinct to try it this way. Zachary told me last night that I trained myself well and I will attract the way. Period, I would end the self-questioning.

Since I would have to wait for the phone company, it was the perfect time to redo my resume seeking a position within operations but at a lower level, knowing I was giving up certain privileges but similarly gaining greater freedom which would allow me time and energy to pursue something of greater value. I was already whizzing through my third version of my resume and the doorbell rang. I laughed. Oh my first visitor, even though it was only the phone company. I liked the sound of the doorbell though. I greeted Pacific Bell and showed him where to connect the phone. I wanted it in my bedroom for late night conversations with Mari Starly for which I knew there would be plenty. I was excited over the possibility of having a phone so I could contact the Auto Transporters and learn the location of my car and an approximate ETA! I couldn't wait to see that beauty again and knew driving it here in California would be a spectacular experience. It was made for this region of the country. I could also call the movers and learn of the location of my belongings. I needed my kitchen supplies and vacuum cleaner and my MTV and stereo equipment. I was clearly missing my things. I wanted to be done with the tasks of setting up my home so that I could enjoy the experience of California but first things first. I could feel the excitement building up inside of me but I would have to exercise good judgment and take care of the basic necessities in life first. With that thought, I remembered my conversation with Gary about the theorist, Kurt Goldstein's pyramid theory. I guess there is truth to the pyramid theory if one is living a human life. Cable had not arrived yet so I couldn't email him using Prodigy but I had a phone and I could call him to let him know I'd made it and was extremely excited. I got his answering machine. Of course I thought, he'd be at work. Not everyone was enjoying the luxury of being home on a week day. I left him a detailed message also letting him know that I should be up and running on Prodigy soon and we could stay in touch via email. How exciting! Next call was to Mari Starly. She was home and extremely excited to hear from me. It was so good to hear her voice. I told her that I was already in love with California and the vibration here. I was still without a car and household belongings but I was patiently managing.

My next calls were to locate my car and belongings. I was elated to learn my car was due to arrive at my location in a couple of hours. Wonderful, I thought. I'd have time to explore Laguna Beach if nothing else on this day. It would be wonderful to get out and see where I was living. However, the next call immediately preempted those plans. My belongings would also be arriving that afternoon as well. Silly of me to be disappointed but it was truly a blessing that everything was arriving on the same day. I would organize my belongings and tomorrow I would be free to go exploring! Things would be humming along and I patiently waited for the cable folks to arrive and conduct the hook ups which I would have ready for my electronic equipment. I intermittently soaked up the view and the sunshine on my balcony while waiting and preparing for each delivery. I could have experienced annoyance that I was trapped in the apartment in this beautiful State without the benefit of exploring it, however, I knew that would be a waste of my energy and would interfere with my good vibrations. I was just an excited little girl waiting for Santa to arrive on Christmas. I began to perform a mild breathing meditation to center my energy and remain calm and relaxed. A deep meditation would damage the centering effects of the exercise so I opted for a lighter practice.

Here it was, my car arrived first. It was so good to see it again. I was delighted to drive it into my assigned parking spot. It felt like an old friend! Of course I was tempted to take it for a spin but I would be running the risk of missing my household items being delivered. I turned off the engine and closed the door, saying, see you later baby, I'm going to take you places you never thought existed! I laughed to myself.

Within the hour, the Van Lines truck pulled up! My stuff! The movers were delightful souls and happy I didn't really have much to bring to the top level, second floor apartment. It was an easy delivery. My books; electronics; kitchen supplies; music collection; clothes; bedding; toiletries; and household basics. No furniture. I gladly tipped the guys and closed the door. I looked at all the boxes! Wow. I had work ahead of me. I'd organize my closet first and then the kitchen. I remembered that I needed to do furniture shopping as well but that was going to wait. I could rough it for a while. Besides, who knew what stores I would come across during my explorations of the land. What fun this was going to be.

Dusk began to fall over the Laguna Hills and I was done with unpacking what I could. Many items had to be stored in open boxes in their respective rooms but at least I had my wardrobe set up as well as the bathroom and kitchen and my TV, VCR and stereo. I took a quick peek off the balcony to watch the sunset and I smiled. I couldn't stop smiling. The grin on my face was from ear to ear. I was happy and content and felt well accomplished.

I had time for a hot shower and a decent dinner. I got into a pair of comfy PJs and decided I would have a session with Zachary. Zac immediately greeted me in his usual way, FANOFU2. "Hi Zac, how are you doing? Are you liking California so far?" Zachary replied OF COURSE. WELL DONE. I smiled and asked him, "What books is he reading to me at night." YOUR BOOK was his reply. "What,"

I asked, "My book? What do you mean?" Zachary replied, YOUR BOOK YOU ARE WRITING. My response was simply, "I am not writing a book, I write in my journal" quite surprised he didn't know that. He replied, I KNOW, SOON BOOK. "Oh," I said, "we've had this discussion before. I remember being surprised by your session with me about writing a book and that God will set me in front of people and something about combining both worlds. I resisted your statement but the idea sparked the thought of who better to write it than me." Zachary commented YES. "So, you're telling me you are reading me a book I will write that comes from my journal entries?" YES was Zac's response. I felt overwhelmed by the task and said, "I trust what you are saying Zachary but right now all I want to do is continue to explore my experience as a human and delight in all the possibilities that are open to me." Zachary responded, YES, YOU WILL. "Okay dear friend," I commented, "we'll see how this unfolds but for now, I will behave as an undisciplined child and just seek the fun of it all. If the time comes that I feel compelled to transcribe my journal into a book, you'll be the first to know." Zachary replied, I ALREADY KNOW DEAR. I laughed. Of course, he did. Zachary said SEE U2 and then he vanished. I was quite sure what he meant. He was suggesting I see a U2 concert.

Since Zachary vanished, I began my Chakra meditation now that my electronic equipment was set up and I could view the video. My meditation was calming and centering and I looked forward to a restful, peaceful night's sleep with the hope of inspiring dreams.

CHAPTER 24

Joshua Tree

As Ava awoke the following morning, her third day in California, with a smile on her face. She remembered her dream and began recording it in her journal, but not before realizing that the sun was so bright here, she needed to buy thicker window coverings. She began writing in her journal:

> "I found myself communicating with someone - it was a giant of a man but not deformed - just a larger form of a perfect specimen of a man. He was taking me through caves within the mind. He was explaining the function of each level of consciousness and when he brought me to a third level below..... He smiled and made a theatrical gesture with his right arm and said, 'AND THIS IS WHERE THE MAGIC IS'."

Ava was mesmerized by the dream. She tried to determine what the third level was referencing. The third day in California, the third eye, the third level of dimensional realities? She supposed it could mean all of the above. Then laughed to herself over the written words, "all of the above" feeling that all humans reference "above" as the place of Heavenly bliss. She understood we are only living in a dimension defined by our ideas and rightly so for our evolution. The reality of all dimensions is really all one - all at once - there is no division other than to evolve. One can see one dimension and its compartmentalized realities that serve their own purpose until all can be seen and known at once. Ava thought this was gold!

Ava was now shifting her mental focus on the glorious day ahead. She ate a hearty breakfast, and packed some treats and plenty of water bottles because she knew exactly where she was headed. She turned on the weather channel to get an idea of how hot it would be in the Mojave because Joshua Tree National Park was her destination! She packed some of her U2 cassette tapes for the ride making sure that as she entered the park she would be blasting "Where The Streets Have No Name". She knew this moment held profound significance for her. She also took her journal with her. Of course, Ava brought her map not wanting to waste time being "lost".

It was exciting to drive my Z-28 again. I missed her as much as I knew she missed me. I could tell as I smiled. Driving towards the 5 freeway and then connecting to the 91 freeway, I found the 10 freeway. That was the main freeway that would take me towards Joshua Tree National Park. With each mile achieved, my excitement grew. I was so impressed with the surrounding mountains and landscape and the overall beauty of Southern California. It was simply gorgeous and I couldn't imagine why anyone would live anywhere else. The Palm trees and unique flowers that bloomed here were astonishing. Everything was just so beautiful. As I drove further and further east, I began to feel the temperature grow hotter. Yes, of course I thought. I'm heading away from the cool ocean breezes that keep the temperature more bearable. I just couldn't stop thinking of all the places I would explore. As I neared the National Park I found the 62 notably called 29 Palms Highway which would take me directly into the place of my dreams and the songs that inspired me. I noticed these large windmills on top of the surrounding hills and realized they produced electric power for the surrounding region. Clever I thought, but it must be windy here because those windmills were spinning.

There it was, the West Entrance Station. I began to see Joshua Trees all over the landscape. Quite an overwhelming sight. I really couldn't believe I was finally here. I turned on the U2 song on the highest volume I could manage, "Where The Streets Have No Name". Smiling and filled with joy I approached the Guard Station to pay my entrance fee and received a map specific to the Park along with an entry ticket to be placed on the dashboard. After entering I pulled over and started snapping pictures of the entrance. These photos were going to have an album dedicated specifically for The Desert and I flashed back to one of my Fractal Enlightenment papers on The Desert of the Real. I wonder what I'll find here. I studied the map given to me at the guard station and realized with sincere gratitude that without it, I could so easily get lost in this 825,000 acre preserve. I wanted to get lost so to speak but I also wanted to be found. Using the map, I decided to go as deep into the Park as I could without feeling "lost". As I drove towards Hidden Valley I began to feel a haunting sensation. The deeper I drove into the valley, the stronger the haunting sensation grew along with the feeling I wouldn't find my way out even though I had a map. Something was taking hold of my vibration and it made me feel odd. I didn't feel in control. I wondered what this vibration here was about. Was it meant to take over you to generate greater understanding? The deeper I entered the more of a grip this place had on me. I did not want to reverse my journey, however. I wanted to know the Mojave's secret, even if it wasn't going to be as pleasant as I had anticipated.

I began to question my spiritual journey, my beliefs and how I was becoming increasingly integrated into this physical world while still enjoying an advanced level of consciousness. What the heck is happening here? I began to feel a disorder as if particles within me where being readjusted into more suitable positioning and I didn't care for the feeling. The best way I could describe it was comparing it to a rubber glove being turned inside out. I could hear the sound of the pull of the rubber. I started to wonder if this was a good idea after all. I had to keep going not knowing what the cost would be. Having faith, I continued deeper into the Valley. I wondered if my own existential reality was causing me to pick up on these different sensations but wondered if others had felt this way after experiencing the desert. I thought about Jesus spending forty days in the desert. Now I knew why! It was a place of transformation. Its energy reconstructed you. I was now not afraid and my haunting sensations began to subside. As I drove further into the Park, I began to see what humans define as mirages. I began to play with the images and was getting a kick out of how the brain, through sight, can project a vision that was constructed purely from what it was familiar with without realizing what it was doing. I had fun with that. After finding the most secluded area I could, I parked my car onto the side of the road. I gathered some of my things and began walking to a place where nothing remotely connected to the human experience other than the desert itself, could be seen.

As I circled myself around the panoramic view was bewildering! Nothing but desert with hills and mountains hundreds of miles away surrounding the valley. It was a sight that prompted me to think that I could have been on the moon itself. Indeed it was a sight to behold. I then began to realize that there was no sound. Nothing made noise here. There was a deafening silence. The animals in the heat of the day were all underground. There were no insects flying. The stillness and quiet were eery. Everything all around me was the same. I began to experience what air sounds like. There was no wind yet I could hear air. What an amazing sensation. I continued to look around and realized being here was similar to sensory deprivation save for vision. I could make a connection to my transforming from a Light Being into a human and my first experience with the sensation of air on my skin and gravity on my body. I was completely and truly alone.

I began to faintly hear drums in the distance. I wondered where could they be coming from? There was nothing here. I was compelled to look above into the sky and wondered if clouds produce a soft melodic drum beat. It would not surprise me. Suddenly I suspected someone was behind me and so I swiftly turned, but nothing was there. I kept feeling the sensation that there were many beings all around but each time I looked no one was there. Finally I began to think possibly there were spirits from the desert who were trying to communicate with me or perhaps as a society so conditioned to so much activity around, it was simply natural to be distracted thinking something was going on. Quickly dismissing my second thought, I decided there were probably spirits trying to communicate with me. I didn't want to find out and so I quickly went back to the car. I drank a bottle of water and sat for a while with the air conditioner on. I had wanted to meditate but realized with my abilities it could possibly be detrimental here. I didn't want to take a chance. I was not ready for any encounter of that nature. If Zachary appeared that would be totally different and acceptable besides, I knew he was here with me in spirit.

As I drove out toward the main entrance I began to reflect on my initial feelings when entering the Park. Time would tell what my seemingly transformational experience was all about. I was eager to look at the pictures I had taken as well as see what might have been captured besides the beauty of the Mojave. If some photos proved extra special, I would consider having them blown up and framed. I thought about U2 and wished I could speak with them to ask if they had similar experiences here. After all, they named a complete and powerful album after this place. I'm certain those boys have a spiritual foundation that they continue to build upon. There's something about that band that is hauntingly palpable.

It took Ava an hour and a half to return home but it didn't matter. She enjoyed soaking up the views and driving her sports car again. She was noticing she was getting stares from nearby cars driving along the freeways. She wondered if they were looking at the car or looking at her, or perhaps both. Well, she was beginning to realize that she was quite the looker for the first time in her human existence. I suppose the car was as well, she laughed to herself. She was tempted to see how fast she could go in the wide open spaces of these freeways but didn't want to risk a moving violation. She always considered safety and the law. She didn't accept breaking the rules and didn't want anything negative on her record. With that thought, she decided she would go home and work on her resumes and seek employment agencies in the surrounding area that she would sign with. She had a few hours left in the day before her dinner, meditation, a session with Zachary and some reading. She thought about the beach but decided that tomorrow would be a beach day. She also knew she needed to buy furniture to make her new home comfortable and as inviting as her home in New Jersey. She especially wanted the serenity and calm and began thinking of color schemes that would be conducive to that energy. Well, there certainly was a lot on her plate but knew it would all unfold as it should. Ava understood that she could simply put an image into her mind and make sure the time, conditions, and probable changes in her life were very clear. Once she firmly had the image set in her mind, she would have it. It didn't matter if it was a particular job, furnishings or a man. She knew what she wanted and she knew what she didn't want which helps clear one's mind of junk and keeps you from sabotaging what you wish to manifest. In this process, she was exercising a law of attraction without violating the rules of her existence here.

As Ava was nearing her home, she could sense a smile beginning to form on her face. She loved the fact that she lived here now and knew she would create a beautiful life and would find what she most needed to expand her horizons and evolve. She entered her apartment and while preparing dinner, she occasionally stepped out onto her balcony to watch the sunset over the Laguna Hills.

She almost couldn't believe that this was her new home. When comparing the aesthetics of her new surroundings with that of her former home, she understood how one's environment effected their whole perspective on life as well as their vibrational frequency. Here the weather was conducive to outdoor appreciation year round. She continued back inside but not before realizing that with patio furniture she could dine outdoors. What a lovely thought. Instead she began to eat her dinner while cross legged on the living room floor, picnic style, watching MTV.

When her chores were completed, Ava decided to begin a session with Zachary. Propped up against her living room wall, cross legged on the floor, Ava summoned Zachary. He came through as always with his typical greeting FANOFU2. "Hello Zachary, did you have fun today?" Ava asked. Zachary circled his heart region round and round and said YES. He continued to take over the session before Ava could ask anything else. GOD'S COUNTRY. Ava chuckled and said, "That is a U2 song. Shall I write the words in my journal?" YES So with that I reached for one of the U2 song books containing the words to "In God's Country". As I read them I felt like crying. Not fully sure why, but it seemed to sum up my deepest emotions felt at Joshua Tree.

Desert sky, dream beneath the desert sky.
The rivers run but soon run dry.
We need new dreams tonight.
Desert rose, dreamed I saw a desert rose
Dress torn in ribbons and bows
Like a siren she calls (to me).
Sleep comes like a drug in God's country
Sad eyes, crooked crosses, in God's country

Lyrics by: Adam Clayton, Dave Evans, Larry Mullen, Paul Hewson

Ava had felt more connected to Zachary than ever before. He was truly a special guide for her and understood her deepest human emotions for which she needed overwhelming support. She thanked the Universe for Zachary and was happy she was open to receiving from this divine dimension. He knew how to guide her without interfering with her decisions and mission. She was connected to him and he was selected to provide her with divine guidance in her dual reality but more so because of her century's old lost memory of how to be human.

Zachary continued the session, GO MEDITATE. REST WELL. Ava was compliant albeit she wanted to find the video of U2 performing the song "IN GOD'S COUNTRY" first. She searched her collection but decided that she would get too distracted from her disciplined evening regiment that she found so centering and of utmost importance to her happiness. Instead she would check out the video the following morning.

After performing her Chakra meditation exercise, Ava decided to write notes in her journal. She was not interested in reading tonight. She wanted to record the events of the day and what they meant to her. As she wrote about Joshua Tree, she gained a better sense of its meaning for her. It was indeed a sacred environment where she could connect to the higher source within herself. She was positive the sensations she experienced were simply the human aspect transforming, breaking open and allowing the vibrations there to enter and provide a deeper connection to all that is unseen. The human condition is quite a challenging one she concluded. It was simply not enough that she had the wisdom of a Light Being, that was a separate reality. She realized she was human and had to evolve as such in spite of her preowned wisdom and abilities. Knowledge alone of these inner domains does nothing to change your relationship with them, other than help make intellectually clear which of these two kingdoms should be the object of your soul's affection. She was feeling a hint of being on the right path in her thinking. It was almost contradictory but her thoughts were beginning to emerge with greater clarity along with the division of her existence. This could only be a good thing. She felt fearless. It was a breakthrough for a happier human life which she didn't even consider a possibility. Her mission was becoming more refined and better defined. She was finding the means of not only dealing with the complexities of humanity but she would possibly enjoy it and supposed that was the whole point besides the suspected one of evolving beyond Sania. Sounds like a revelation to me, Ava thought. Now feeling tired and exhausted, Ava decided to put her journal away and went to sleep.

When she awoke the following morning again blinded by the bright sunlight peering through her bedroom windows, Ava remembered her dream and began to quickly record it in her dream journal:

> "She was bringing a couple of people she did not know with her to a place to show them something most incredible. She drove up to a graveled parking lot and could see a railroad tie which defined where the car should be stopped before entering a valley on foot. In the center of the valley was a brilliant ball of yellow light. I waved my arm to the two people pointing in the direction of the Light and said, look what I found. When I saw the light I realized I was at Joshua Tree. The glowing yellow ball of light began to expand from its center with rays of light circling its circumference. As we watched the ball it grew larger and larger until it encompassed the entire valley. She told them that she had found her sun."

Ava was overjoyed by her dream and knew that this indeed was an amazing place and that her conclusions last night written in her journal were quite accurate. She understood that she would be visiting Joshua Tree on a regular basis now because it held special significance for her. Ava was not much of a camper but fantasized what the expansive night sky would look like completely full of stars. What a sight that must be she thought.

Right now Ava needed to focus on the tasks at hand. She made her breakfast and showered. She really needed to contact employment agencies and submit her "dumbed" down resumes as well as get herself some furniture before starting employment. She especially needed some heavier window coverings. She would find stores close to the beach so that she could get to see the Pacific.

She was making progress contacting agencies and now needed to fax her resumes over and visualize the manifestation of the job she desired. As lunch time approached, Ava ate her tuna fish salad sandwich and iced green tea picnic style, she watched the U2 video she promised herself. She smiled all the way through it and developed a secret crush on Bono. Laughing to herself, I think I will meet these guys, at least she was hoping to but certainly she would see them in concert, that was a given.

Ava started sifting through the yellow pages for furniture stores. She wanted to be particular and frugal but she also wanted to get to the beach. Deciding that even if the beach had to wait, it was important that her furniture was of paramount importance. The furniture would be part of her energy field so she would take the time making deliberate choices. Collecting her hand written notes of shops, Ava headed to her car with map in hand. She was just a tad frustrated not knowing the lay of the land but was not complaining. She knew it was simply too gorgeous here to complain.

She loved the surrounding area and was taken by its beauty. She went into a couple of stores and made some decisions based on price and time of delivery. Apparently California is a transient State and delivery times were rather quick which served her well. She supposed many people wanted to live here and for whatever reason could not manage. It had become a reality for her, however.

Ava selected a beautiful "L" shaped couch for the living room. It was huge and all white. Certainly large enough for any sleep over friends. In the same store she found a glass top rectangular dining table with a black lacquer pedestal and 4 matching chairs. She loved it. It had a high price tag but she really loved it and would be perfect for the dining area. Not seeing anything else she fancied, she decided to move on to another store on her list. There she found a black lacquer captain's desk with gold Asian designs that would be perfect for her computer and files. It would fit in a corner of her living room. She began to grow concerned that she was attracted to black which was exactly the opposite of her ivory colored furniture back east. However, she considered it was a balance. East Coast needed to lighten up and the West Coast needed grounding. What better color choice could there be. It made sense to her. She would accessorize with aqua blues and sea foam greens to add balance to the room. With this color pallet she could throw in a little purple for interest. It was beginning to take form in her mind and she was excited to see it all come together. She also chose a rectangular glass top coffee table with a black lacquer pedestal base, perfectly matching the dining room table. These were very hard surfaces but the overstuffed, oversized couch would off set any harshness to the room as well as the splashes of soft seaside colors.

Ava was growing tired and realized that she would need artwork and an entertainment unit and bedroom furniture as well. She didn't have the energy to accomplish all this and it would be impractical to think this could happen in one day. She decided to shop elsewhere for the desperately needed window coverings and call it a day.

The window coverings she selected would be a chore to install but decided to pay extra for the store to do the task. Since it was beginning to approach dinner time, Ava decided to drive to the beach a mere five minutes away and possibly find a place to eat. What a lovely and perfect way to dine she thought. As she drove through

Laguna Canyon she was filled with childlike anticipation seeing the Pacific Ocean coming into view! There it was! Ava approached the main street running parallel to the Ocean and her excitement grew.

Sure wish I could put my toes in it she said to herself. She was not prepared to enter a restaurant with wet feet, however. She found a cozy fish shack right on the beach. It was perfect and she sat outside and had her dinner. The ocean looked rough but the sound of the surf was so calming and peaceful it could easily put her into a trance. She enjoyed watching the surfers perfect their technique but wondered why they were wearing wet suits. It was so warm here. The breeze was soft and the smell of the salty air made her even hungrier. She could almost feel the sensation of being elevated by each wave before it crashed onto the store. Mother Nature is truly magnificent she thought. What a great and beautiful planet Earth is. She reflected on her Higher World in this setting and agreed this was a place of harmony, a peaceful kingdom. She wondered if the people scattered around were at all affected and aware of the existence of two worlds at the same time? The world below knows nothing of the world above, while the world above understands everything that dwells below. Being in such a harmonious place, surely one must have glimpses into other realities.

Ava said a temporary good bye to the Pacific and headed back home, fulfilled and happy about the entire day. There were messages on her answer machine when she arrived home. One of the employment agencies wanted to know if she had interest in a computer manufacturing firm that was looking for a Product Supply Coordinator. She would contact them first thing in the morning and set up an interview. They were located in Irvine and after checking her map, discovered it was located a couple of towns over from Laguna Niguel, perfectly within her twenty mile radius grid. She could also see the best commute would be traveling through Laguna Canyon along the PCH directly looking at the Ocean every morning and every night on her way to and from work. That's the way to do it Ava, she exclaimed to herself.

Now tired from the day and all the fresh air, she decided to simply do her Chakra Meditation, some reading and then go to bed. Zachary would understand. She popped in her meditation video and smiled as she envisioned her new furniture layout knowing it would get more comfortable in a few days.

She could not keep her eyes open after meditation so decided to skip reading and just went to sleep.

When she awoke the next morning, the U2 song "In God's Country" was playing in her head. "We need new dreams tonight" was of particular resonance. She smiled and wondered if it had special significance or if she was just enjoying the song from the day before. She was grateful for having purchased the window coverings that would be installed that day but couldn't resist heading to the balcony to feel the sunshine on her skin and smell the warm air. "I definitely have to find some patio furniture today" she said.

After breakfast, Ava made her call to the employment agency and was scheduled to interview with the computer manufacturer, Orion for the following Monday. She felt confident she would secure the position. Ava was delighted to learn the name of the company. Orion being a constellation was a good sign. It is a prominent constellation located on the celestial equator and visible throughout the world. It is one of the most conspicuous and recognizable constellations in the night sky. It was named after Orion, a hunter in Greek mythology. Orion was a gigantic, supernaturally strong hunter of ancient times, and because of her knowledge she wondered if the Giant man in her dream who was telling her "this is where the magic is" had some precognitive significance. In any event, she was looking forward to her interview and potential employment at the company named Orion.

She prepared a schedule for her upcoming day and decided she would continue furniture shopping and then head to the beach. She checked the weather channel which became a useless task. California weather seemed to always be the same, she laughed to herself and knew that was not such a bad thing.

She bought her patio furniture and a tall silk fig tree. Ava did not have a green thumb and the silk green fig leaves would add a nice touch to the living room. Her knowledge of the fig leaf made the decision easy because she knew in certain cultures it was revered as sacred and symbolized life-giving, nurturing abundance. Her goal was to significantly add an aura of positive energy to her surroundings. She then needed to rush back home since the window installation men would soon arrive. She was eager to get to the beach again and wander through art galleries along the main street for some pieces for the apartment. There was so much exploring to be done and it was all so exciting and exhilarating. She was thinking of how much fun this would be with Mari Starly, wishing she was here. However, Ava knew she would gradually develop friendships adding that dimension to her life. She also wondered about a boyfriend.

With the window coverings installed and looking even better than she imagined, especially the cornices adding an elegance to the rooms yet still casual looking, Ava was now free to head to the beach. This was so much fun but she knew there wouldn't be as much time once she began working.

Walking into one of the art galleries, Ava was overcome with a sense of dreaminess. Soft melodic music was playing overhead that created a relaxed and meditative mood. She recognized the song "Somewhere in Time" and wondered if there was significance to her being at this particular gallery with this song playing. She herself was somewhere in time, a time she lived centuries earlier. Ava was always aware and observed everything in her surroundings, oddly though not the attention she lured from men but that was beginning to change. It was possibly because her focus was far beyond that of a normal human and not wanting to be distracted from her true course, she just didn't notice how men found her so attractive.

Ava enjoyed perusing the paintings delighting in their beauty and envisioning them in different locations in her apartment. There was one in particular that caught her attention for the wide space over her white "L" shaped sofa in the living room. It was an abstract depicting the circular movement of universal energy, at least that was Ava's interpretation and she knew more than the uninitiated mind could see. It contained the colors of the sea with its sea foam greens and blues reflecting the skies circulating the energy of all that is. Ava smiled to herself and thought about how she could visually play with the painting's movement and create for herself different formations with a simple thought. She knew it would be fun to have besides it being a powerful depiction of what she knew to be true. She was also impressed by the simple almost invisible frame used to contain the painting believing the work itself was the statement and an elaborate frame was not needed to enhance it. She wondered if the artist had extraordinary insight into the reason for creating it but it was always possible he was being influenced by a higher vibration to paint it. She decided this one had to be her first art purchase for her sanctuary.

Ava placed the painting into the trunk of her car and headed home to hang it. She did not want to disturb the delicate piece by sidetracking to any other location while it was being stored in the hot trunk of her car. Upon arriving home, she began to visualize where it would hang and began the project of displaying it just right, the whole time humming the melody of "Somewhere in Time". She thought about the synchronicity of walking into that particular gallery with that particular song playing. She owned the movie and wondered if she would watch it that evening. It was such a lovely movie.

She considered if one day she would give her heart to someone here who would hold it tight as if it was their own. Would she wake up and have someone besides herself to live for. Would it allow her to go to bed at night without a worry in the world. Would she ever meet someone here that would realize how beautiful she truly was because of the gifts she possessed. Ava was surprised by these thoughts that entered her heart and mind. She was unfamiliar with this type of need. She was self sufficient and could not reveal herself to any normal human. She wondered if the painting and the melody began to open a portal to a future potential event. She had trust in her powers of connection and would never dismiss thoughts or feelings that bubbled up from these realms although she didn't necessarily have an immediate understanding of them. She allowed the Universe to do its thing and would be receptive to its vibrations however subtle. She most definitely would seek the advice of Zachary tonight.

After making herself a wholesome lunch, Ava realized she had a message on the answering machine. It was another personnel agency about a job interview. She decided to respond and set up an appointment for the following Tuesday. She was excited about getting responses to her inquiries and was confident that gainful employment was just around the corner. After making meticulous recordings in her calendar, she continued to select a book from her vast library and head to the beach for some relaxing reading.

Because of her fascination on the subject of the Holy Grail, she had amassed a large collection of books on the topic. It cemented one of her great delights about her last name being St. Claire, seemingly related to the Merovingians and the descendants of Jesus Christ. She loved this story and was quite mesmerized by the possibilities. For Ava, this was light reading not to mention it contained paintings and history of the great artists Poussin and Teniers and her love of Medieval Architecture. She selected Henry Lincoln's, "The Holy Place - The Mystery of Rennes-le-Chateau". She was ready for her afternoon at the Pacific.

Upon settling into a comfortable spot, Ava wanted to take a dip in the Ocean. When the waves splashed up onto her feet, she quickly ran backwards realizing it was icy cold. She now knew why the surfers wore wet suits. The water is freezing and quite rough and wondered why ever did they name it The Pacific? There was nothing passive about this ocean whatsoever. She tried to take a dip but it was clearly too cold and rough for her. She headed to her blanket and began snacking on grapes and began her reading. Ava could sense there were stares coming her way from some good looking men who were too young for her age of thirty-nine. She began to feel uncomfortable. Was her presence there being received as a sign of availability?

Her purpose was to enjoy the ocean surf and the freedom of the wide open sky, the strong sun, the massive body of water and the melodic sounds of the seagulls while immersing herself in the straightforward geometric and arithmetic subdivisions of the rectangle that the Poussin work, "Shepherds of Arcadia" provided for any art master. She supposed she should expect attention but it still made her feel uncomfortable. She reflected back on her earlier thoughts about finding a boyfriend but was conflicted about this being the way. Ava decided she would exude an aura of disinterest so she could enjoy her intention.

Ava left Laguna Beach after two hours. The sun and fresh air were making her drowsy. She wanted to take a shower and enjoy her nearly furnished living room and make some calls to her old friends. She also felt she should prep herself for her interview Monday at Orion. In addition, she needed to research how to register her vehicle with the California DMV and obtain a new driver's license and plates. She thought of getting personalized plates that read FANOFU2. She laughed to herself and thought it would be brilliant!

As evening approached Ava was fulfilled and content having spoken to Gary and Mari and catching up on all the news from everyone's lives. She was grateful for her friendships and the balance and love she received from them. They were an important part of her life.

She prepared a light dinner and decided to summon Zachary. He immediately appeared with his usual greeting FANOFU2. "Hello Zachary," she said. "Were you at the beach with me today?" Zachary respond, OF COURSE. I asked him if he enjoyed it and he said TIME SPENT WITH YOU IS ALWAYS ENJOYABLE. I smiled and asked how he liked my new art purchase today? Zac replied, VERY APPROPRIATE YOU ARE EXACT ABOUT ITS REPRESENTATION. I was pleased that Zachary confirmed what I already knew. I asked him if the artist knew what he was painting and Zac replied, IT WAS GIVEN FROM ANOTHER REALM. I also suspected that as well. The artist was compelled to paint it without conscious knowledge but with certainty that he needed to create it. I told Zachary that the beach today left me tired and drained and if he knew why? Zachary replied, THE SENSATION IS NEW TO YOU.... LESS INTERFERENCE.... MORE CALMING..... MORE INTROSPECTION. YOU NEED LESS OF THIS VIBRATION. HINDERING. I was quite surprised by his response. "Truly Zachary?" AVA, YOU ARE ALREADY THERE. IT IS LESS GROUNDING FOR YOU. "Oh, I see. I don't need to subject myself for too long in that environment. Well, then, what about Joshua Tree?" Zachary immediately shot back to me YES, THERE IS MORE THERE FOR YOU. "Okay Zachary, I will keep that in mind. I shall plan a trip back there soon." Zachary confirmed that I had received his message clearly and he was vibrationally, affectionately hugging me.

With the end of her session, Ava began her Chakra meditation video and immediately upon finishing, went to sleep.

When she awoke she remembered having an odd dream. She somehow felt it related to another dream she had had some years ago about the perfectly formed giant man showing her the caves of consciousness who brought her to a third level below telling her "this is where the magic is". She also remembered he told her there were many other levels as well. In last night's dream, Ava decided to take the plunge to the final level where she knew she was going to end this human existence. She did not mind. She looked forward to it. She was excited because she knew it was the final hurdle, the end of the struggle, OZ so to speak:

> "I was at a large outdoor celebration and everyone there was congratulating me on my decision to reach the last level. I could see the entrance of the cave that would take me there. A little

blonde boy about two years old, cute as a button, would make the final decision for me to enter the cave. Only he could take me there. We had a telepathic communication with each other and this is how I understood that without him, I could not go. After much celebrating, I was ready and the boy looked at me and shook his head no. I knew he had changed his mind. I was devastated! I also knew I could do nothing about his decision. I would obey. I turned from the beautiful little boy as the celebration was still going on and saw a man waiting for me with his arm stretched out ready to walk away with me. I obeyed as if I was a robot."

Ava found the dream fascinating and complex. She could not imagine who this little boy was or why the change of mind. She knew why she wanted to end her human existence believing that the last level would be what her purpose of reliving this life culminated into. Why the change of mind and who was this darling little boy? He never identified himself to her. She wondered who the man waiting for her was and how could he foretell what decision was made concerning her destiny. He was ready to lead her away from the cave but to where? Ava knew important information was contained in the dream and she would need time to understand its meaning.

CHAPTER 25

The Mall Angel

After recording the dream in her journal, Ava planned on an excursion to explore her surrounding neighborhood. She needed to get more familiar with this lovely part of Southern California that was now her home. Her wardrobe represented the Eastern part of the country rather than the geographic location she now lived in and would shop for cloths more in style with the vibration here. She headed to the Laguna Hills Mall.

The mall was a short trip away and on her drive, she saw many roller bladders. That looks like so much fun, she thought to herself. I wonder if I could try that? What a great form of exercise. Do they sell those things in the mall? Ava was excited to try the sport where she could experience the beautiful outdoor weather and surrounding scenery. Sounds a lot better than falling into a haze laying on the beach, as beautiful as it was, she thought to herself.

Arriving at the Laguna Hills Mall, Ava had no idea where to start. She was impressed with how lovely it was designed and liked the idea of Palm Trees scattered through the center surrounded by park benches for resting. She decided to begin walking and began people watching. She felt many eyes on her which began to feel uncomfortable. She didn't like that old familiar feeling of self-consciousness and wondered when she would get over it. She felt as if she stood out like a sore thumb.

A couple of chic boutiques caught Ava's attention and she was able to find some very casual as well as dressy outfits. T-shirts and light colored jeans and shorts seemed to be the uniform of the area and was sure to stock up on plenty of them. Everyone seemed to be casually dressed here and she supposed it definitely had to do with the weather and the laid back vibration likely due to the hot sun. At least she was hoping that was the reason. She wondered if they had a sense of responsibility and purpose because it sure didn't seem to be reflected in their style of clothing. Ava didn't like the idea she was being critical of people she didn't know. It was beneath her.

With several packages in hand, Ava was now beginning to feel quite hungry. It had been hours since breakfast so she wandered into the center of the mall looking for somewhere to have lunch. She spotted a pizza place and her mouth began to water. It was cumbersome juggling her packages, purse and water bottle, careful not to drop her pizza. Ava looked back into the mall area for an empty bench to enjoy her lunch. She looked around but the benches were occupied except for one where a very little older woman was sitting at its very edge.

She quietly walked over trying not to infringe on the woman's personal space and sat herself on the very opposite end of the bench. She squeezed her packages as near to her body as possible keeping her purse on her lap juggling her pizza and water. Suddenly the woman said, "You don't need to squash yourself and your packages, there's plenty of room for both of us." I acknowledged her and told her I was okay. As I was eating she said, "You are eating the best food possible while busy shopping. Pizza is very good food when you're on the go." She then asked me, "Where did I get the Pizza?" I thought that was strange since we were right in front of the pizza place but I answered her anyway and pointed to the shop. She continued to tell me, "I only eat one meal a day these days. It controls her weight."

I liked this woman. I felt very comfortable hearing her voice. She was pleasant and intriguing and I wanted to continue hearing her speak. She then said, "You are wise beyond your years." I didn't understand how or why she would say this to me. She continued on, "These are overwhelming times we live in and you have a great deal of wisdom for your years." I was now beginning to wonder if she knew who I was and more so, who the heck she was!

I felt the need to tell her I was not as young as I looked. I thought it would be a dumb thing to say but I said it anyway. "I'm thirty-nine years old." She simply responded, "Well then you DO have it all." I was not sure what she meant.

She was careful not to let me say very much. She knew I was not married nor had a boyfriend or children and I didn't know how she knew. She began to speak as if she knew my inner thoughts. "The reasons for relationships today are not the right reasons for having relationships. Trust is not valued as it should be and women should not be fooled thinking that they have to obey men, it's a ridiculous notion." I secretly laughed in agreement.

She then told me, "You have learned many lessons early and you are very direct in relating to others." These were my thoughts that were echoing in my mind but how did she know them? I decided by now I was going to let her speak and not interrupt her with questions she clearly wasn't answering. As she spoke I noticed how incredibly blue and soft her eyes were and her skin was creamy white. Her hair was a soft brown and she wore it in a bob fashion. She was quite old yet she appeared ageless. As I studied her I realized the music being piped into the mall speaker system was playing "Somewhere Out There," a Linda Rhonstadt song. As I recognized the song, chills ran through my body.

She continued speaking. "There is somebody here for you, you should know this, it is true if you want it." I said, "Yes, I do." She then said, "Then don't give up. You will meet someone exact for you."

Now I was completely captivated by this woman and suspected

she was not human. Maybe she was an angel appearing just to me and passersby were wondering who is this nut talking to? My curiosity was getting the best of me and I asked her how she knew these things. Her reply was simple, "You give off a different energy than anyone else here," as she gestured toward the people shopping in the mall.

Her answers only led to even more questions but she was on a mission and was not about to let me interrupt her. She always looked straight ahead even though we sat side-by-side. I thought this was strange but I didn't push the issue.

I was now determined to get my questions asked and I aggressively said, "Who are you and how do you know these things?" She quickly replied, "Ford, Dorothy Ford."

I then asked her where she lived and her response brought a picture to my mind. She said, "In the Tower." I found that to be a very mysterious answer to say the least.

I asked her how she got to the mall and if she was with anyone and planning to do any shopping? She said, "People like green, I give money for gifts and besides it's difficult carrying packages around." She admitted to being alone and said she came by bus. It didn't make sense to me. Why was she here if she wasn't shopping? Was it just to be out and about to see people I wondered?

I asked if she gave money as gifts, why would she be in the mall now? Her response was once again mysterious. "I need to be here," she said. I asked why and she simply smiled.

I asked if she would like to have lunch sometime and she repeated her statement from earlier, "I only eat once a day." I wanted to spend more time with her but instead I stood up and positioned myself directly in front of her now determined to have her look me directly in the eyes. I extended my hand and said, "I'm delighted to meet you." I know I surprised her and it was my deliberate intent. However she quickly returned to a state of calm and control. As she shook my hand, she said, "You will be fine."

I exited the mall, never finishing my shopping. I felt I was floating on air encased in a bubble. I think my car drove itself home because I remained in that bubble and could still feel I was floating when I entered my apartment. I became overwhelmingly aware that I had just experienced an angel. At that moment I could feel the bubble pop and I was back in reality again. I was stunned to say the least. This was new territory for me. After all, my first experience with Zachary was quite similar. Now I simply wanted to sit and allow the Universe to provide me with insight and not think on any conscious level or analyze the experience. Happily, I went out to my patio and reflected on the event with a sense of peace and wonder. I would not make any deliberate attempt to understand. I just wanted to close her eyes and cherish the experience.

I enjoyed the solitude and took great comfort in the smell of the air and the slight breezes that would move past the patio. I enjoyed the serene sound of wind chimes in the distance as the breezes came and went. I was not thinking. I was simply being. Occasionally, I would see a mental picture of the angel in my mind and just admired the beauty of her eyes and skin.

After an hour of absorbing the universal vibration this visitation bestowed on me, I felt the need to write the experience in my journal. It was becoming slightly chilly on the patio so I cozied up on the couch and began writing. I began to connect the words of the angel to my dream last night, remembering the little blonde boy disallowing my entrance into the cave's final level ending my human existence. I had turned around to see a man standing there with his arm stretched out for me to walk away with him.

I wrote her words down about someone being here for me. Was my dream a premonition of sorts? I was confident all would be revealed to me when it was time for me to know. I treasured my journal and was so happy I kept it. It provided a source of experiences enabling me to connect the dots in this human life. It reaffirmed how far I had come.

Now I needed to prepare for my interview the next day and began to select an outfit and collect all necessary documents. I set the alarm clock and began to make a light meal for dinner. I was still feeling somewhat mesmerized by the day's event, but with it came a feeling of elation. I felt privileged to have had such an amazing experience. Of course I had seen Zachary many times but this was different. This happened in the middle of a mall with shoppers all around.

After dinner, I began a session with Zachary. I was curious to hear what he would have to say about the angel. Zachary appeared immediately. I smiled and said, "Hi Zachary. Did you see what happened today?" Zachary said **YES**. "She was an angel wasn't she?" Zachary stated **YES THEY OFTEN VISIT YOU**. "Oh, I was never aware of their presence. This one had much to say to me." Zachary answered **ALL TRUE**. "Thank you Zac" I replied. "How do you think my interview will go tomorrow?" Zachary replied, **WELL DONE**. I took that as a good omen and said goodnight to Zachary. I wanted to get my meditation in and get a good night's sleep.

I gently laid my head on the pillow and began to think of the dream the night before and the angelic visit of the day. I was tired but felt happy and looked forward to a great future here in California.

Waking to the alarm, I appreciated my window coverings that worked so well. I had an interesting yet simple dream of a rainbow. I quickly jotted it down but needed to shower and prepare for my interview. After a good breakfast I headed to my car looking forward to the drive into Irvine knowing I would be driving through Laguna Canyon and seeing the Ocean as the sun was rising over the expansive Pacific. What a privilege to have such a view while going to work.

I arrived at Orion fifteen minutes ahead of schedule and sat in the car reviewing my paperwork one more time. It was a lovely building, three stories high completely covered in glass. It looked relatively new and it had a spacious parking lot. Everything always seems so new in California. I suppose it has a lot to do with the weather not beating things apart. I'll bet they never get pot holes here either and the landscaping is always green with the prettiest of flowers all year long too.

Ava entered the reception area and introduced herself and stated she had an appointment with Len Mason at 10:00 AM. She was asked to take a seat and soon the admin for the Operations Director came to collect her. She was led to a small conference room where the interview would take place. Ava felt only slightly nervous but was very much looking forward to getting the job here. Indeed, it was a job, not a career. She understood what she was doing was a result of an intuitive feeling that she needed more time and energy to pursue other passions. This job paid well enough to provide for her so it would work out well. She knew the pressures of corporate executives were so intense that it left little time to pursue other fields of study or recreational activities that might lead to a fuller more balanced lifestyle. She needed to explore more. She just knew it. She was going with her instincts.

Len Mason arrived at the conference room within a few minutes and Ava stood up and they shook hands. He was immediately interested in talking about the East Coast. Ava would oblige him since he revealed he was from Ohio and apparently missed the weather. How could one miss those brutal winters and dreary grey skies? Oh well, I can't imagine that being my experience.

They began the interview eventually and the job sounded fine to Ava. She certainly had the qualifications and understood the manufacturing side of computers as well as the logistics and value added ingredients that went into their operation. As Product Supply Coordinator, Ava would be responsible for vetting the software and distribution for these massive machines shipping to the Eastern Seaboard of all places. Ava felt the interview went very smoothly and they both stood up and shook hands. She liked Len and thought he would make a decent fellow to work with.

As she left the office complex, Ava smiled and was pleased with how she conducted herself and almost chuckled at the idea that Len should only know she had just come off the heels of his position. It didn't matter. Ava knew what she was doing and was now looking forward to the ride back home passing the Pacific and then through

Laguna Canyon. Maybe she would stop at the beach and grab a bite of lunch. What a lovely idea she thought. She also considered stopping in one of the art galleries to enjoy some more art work.

On the drive home, she noticed a marquee on a small neighborhood movie theatre. The title of the movie was "Far Away So Close". The title intrigued her and she thought she'd stop at the theatre to inquire. Much to Ava's amazement with synchronistic undertones, she discovered the movie was a sequel to one of her all-time favorites, "Wings of Desire"! She couldn't believe it! She was excited and decided to purchase a ticket to see it. She desperately wanted to find out what a sequel to this classic would contain. After all, it was about angels visiting Earth and she herself had just had her very own angelic visitation along with "Wings" being her favorite all time movie. Ava did not believe in coincidences, she knew she was being divinely guided!

As the movie begins Ava sees that Cassiel and Raphaella, two angels, are observing the lives of the people in Berlin. Cassiel has been following his friend Damiel, the former angel who took the plunge, to be with the woman he loved, Marion, a trapeze artist whom he married. Ava was enthralled and delighted and could relate first hand to the experiences of the people and angels on the screen. As the film's background music was playing, she recognized the distinctive voice of Bono from U2 singing "Stay (Far Away So Close)"! Ava smiled at the synchronistic nature of these events! She questioned, how is it possible? Of course it's possible she thought. She knew these guys were exceptional! Their souls knew the true meaning of being spiritual existing in a human body. Their identity was contained in all the lyrics of their songs which spoke to her soul. Concert tickets needed to be secured.

Ava knew there were many delightful things for her to experience being Earthbound. She began to laugh at the transformation that had taken place within her. She was surprisingly feeling excitement about being human. The dual conflict had lost its grip on her and she was excited to experience what Earth had to offer. Especially in the realm of the subtle spiritual influences that came through to humans who were aware and who had an understanding that all that is seen is not all that is. She giggled to herself. If only everyone could see that everything around us and within us is of our own creation. Humans are that powerful and that gifted. She began to think that her influence could make a difference, at least in some people's lives.

Heading for home now, Ava appreciated the rewards of her very fortunate day. She was confident about her job interview and happy to have had another glimpse into the art world, lunch on the beach and a wonderfully meaningful movie. There were so many things piling up on her list of fun things to do.

When Ava arrived home there was a telephone message. She retrieved it and recognized the voice of Len Mason from Orion. Len wanted to make a job offer! Oh wow she said to herself! Could this day get any better? In one day, I received a job offer? She began to prepare a light dinner. Heading out to her patio she reflected on the day's event while staring into the dusk that was beginning to blanket the star-filled skies over the Laguna Hills. She smiled and gave a wink to the Universe. She had her dinner and made a list of her plans for the next day including getting to the DMV.

Later she turned on MTV hoping to get information on U2's new song and possible upcoming concert dates. After a few videos, U2 appeared with their new video for the song "Stay (Far Away So Close)". She laughed with delight realizing that the entire video was a depiction of the movie, "Wings of Desire". The boys were posing as the unseen angels and assisting struggling musicians with perfecting their craft. Oh how brilliant she thought. These guys are the greatest!

Ava knew she needed to do her meditation practice and get ready for bed and turned off the TV not knowing when an upcoming concert was coming to California. In due time, she thought. She knew she was divinely guided and wouldn't miss a beat.

As she lay in bed she began recording in her journal the events of her day. She realized that she had not written an explanation about the rainbow dream from the night before and so reached for one of her Native American Indian books knowing that the Hopi Indian Tribe had prophecies about Rainbow warriors. She began to read:

"Rainbow warriors see the big picture through the accumulation of all the different warrior perspectives. With a question mark in their heart and a teacher in their soul, they are walking, talking, breathing Meditations. They have merged their consciousness with cosmic consciousness and they are able to bring forth sacred knowledge. They have moved beyond the lower vibrations of survival and fear to the higher vibrations of forgiveness and love. They are chameleon warriors, able to assume and subsume most masks and channel most forms of energy. They are calm in the storm. When the rest of the world is falling apart, they are busy falling into place, in order to be the one who can put things back together again."

Ava now fully understood what the rainbow in her dream represented. She was no longer in conflict with her dual identity and was becoming happy being human. It was a sure sign that her dream was telling her the transformation had taken place. Pleased with the Hopi Indian description and the joy of the day, Ava fell into a delicious sleep.

Ava woke the next morning peacefully and well rested realizing that she had not had a dream, or at least not one she remembered. She knew her plans for the day would include a call back to Len Mason to discuss the details of the job offer. She decided on a 10:00 AM call back and afterwards would make a trip to the DMV. She also wanted to locate a concert ticket office to see what U2 concerts were on the horizon. It was imperative that she get to see at least one but secretly knew one would not be enough.

Len Mason picked up the phone when Ava dialed. She was surprised to hear his voice rather than his admin but maybe she was out sick. She introduced herself and he sounded happy to hear from her. He was offering her the position of Product Supply Coordinator and went over the details of the offer including the company's benefits. Ava was especially pleased to hear that tuition reimbursement for a final grade of B or better was also included along with the usual benefits. She considered the possibility of returning to school to begin a different course of study other than business administration. This was another exciting opportunity she thought. They both agreed on a Monday start date with her hours being 8:00 AM to 3:30 PM. She realized with that schedule, she would have the whole afternoon to herself. She liked how her human life was coming together. She was to report to HR on her arrival to complete the necessary paperwork before meeting up with Len. She was feeling butterflies in her stomach. She was certain it was a natural part of being human.

Ava turned on the news to see what was happening in the outside world and catch a glimpse of California's non-weather report. She dressed and headed out to fulfill her plans for the day. The experience at the DMV proved to be, as she suspected, bureaucratic, but followed the maze of infinite lines obediently. After about an hour and a half, her Z-28 was officially a California vehicle sporting FANOFU2 license plates and she had a California driver's license. Now off to the concert ticket office.

Ava found a ticket office and the clerk was helpful and informed. She learned that U2 were performing a series of three concerts on the West Coast in the next two months. She bought two tickets to each concert - only Front Row would do, spending quite a bit of money but it didn't matter. She would not sit anywhere else. She needed to be upfront and center to experience their energy secretly hoping they would experience hers. The thought occurred to her to remove one of her license plates from the car and wave it to the band during the concert. What fun she thought!

Now she wanted to head to the beach for lunch. She began to think of what Zachary said about Joshua Tree and knew she needed to pay a visit the next day. It was time. She was missing the energy there and imagined its sensation and was curious if she would have the same experience of apprehension she felt during her first visit. She would find out soon enough.

After lunch, Ava walked along the beach in her bare feet even though the water was freezing. She had her "California" laid back clothing on, a pretty yellow pair of jeans and a white loose fitting shirt. She was beginning to fit in a little more with the surrounding population. She still felt eyes on her, but she tried not to feel uncomfortable. Maybe she was ready to meet someone after all. Maybe it was time. She was thirty-nine years old and most of the stares were coming from younger men because Ava realized that she did not look her age. She started to feel flattered and giggled to herself. This was a compliment and she shouldn't feel self-conscious about it at all. She would just let it be and if someone approached her she would be receptive and pleasant. An indication to her that she was continually changing.

After heading back home she decided to search for horseback riding academies. She missed riding and maybe there were some places along the beach she could ride. She found some places but none along the beach. Flipping through the phone book for more things of interest, she found some universities. She was drawn to return to school and in particular explore the human brain and its anatomical function. She was fascinated by her experience of being human again and living among them brought a deep desire to understand the human condition.

Most of her afternoon was about searching and planning for her future. To be able to experience everything possible and not waste a minute of her gift. Look at that shift, she thought to herself. She went from defining her situation as a punishment to a gift. How interesting. These were the types of thoughts and revelations that Ava wanted to understand with greater insight. She thought about exploring the field of psychology and if any possible metaphysical courses were offered.

CHAPTER 26

Joshua Tree Again

On her way to visit Joshua Tree National Park, Ava was full of anticipation wondering if her experience would be different now because of her accelerated integration within her human condition. She was full of questions but decided she would not think, she would just experience the joy of the drive while listening to U2. As she grew closer to the familiar windmills on the hills near the entrance of the park, she began to feel butterflies in her stomach. She indeed felt wonderful here. Her level of inspiration began to intensify and she could feel a sense of extraordinary grace and "flow" as her physical body began to raise in perfection. She almost felt high. Her vibrational field was electrifying. She realized Zachary was right about this place.

After entering the park she took the same path she previously did without any reservations. She did not experience the loss of control and apprehension that she did on her first trip several weeks ago. Instead she felt like she owned this place as if she was coming back to visit an old friend. What an odd thought that was. Ava enjoyed the wide open scenery and again played with the mirages that formed tricking the brain. It was quite a bit of fun really. She couldn't wait to find the location where she had stopped previously and walk among the Joshua trees and enjoy the desert's own unique foliage. She pulled the car over to the side of the road and stepped out with her supply of snacks and bottled water. She began walking. Again it was completely silent and the sun was beginning to heat up. She could feel it burning her skin. She stopped in her tracks and circled around 180 degrees. It was as if she were on another planet. Standing still and placing her lunch bag down she took in the smell of the air and tried to listen for the drum music she had heard the last time. She could not believe how quiet it was.

Suddenly, Ava saw a reality distortion field manipulating the vapors in the heated air molecules. She had to blink her eyes to be sure what she was witnessing. Before her appeared her angel from the mall smiling gently and serenely at her. Ava smiled back but couldn't be sure if the angel was really there. She had to believe it. This was not a mirage. That beautiful gracious woman was standing right there about twenty-five feet away from her. When she began to find her voice to speak, the angel was gone once again. Ava wasn't even sure if she had been breathing the whole time the event took place. She was giddy with excitement and felt completely safe and at peace. What an experience and how blessed she was. It confirmed for her how the human brain is the seat of perceptions and is a creative force and how by growing our consciousness the universe comes more and more into being.

Ava confirmed this was going to be her new course of study. She had the added advantage of her wisdom from her Light Being existence and with further human study, who knows where this would lead. Her mind was racing now and she almost wanted to speed up time to see where all this was going to take her. After another hour passed, she left the park not wanting the hot sun to burn her skin. She remembered the U2 song about the desert and stopped in the Park's gift shop to see if she could pick up a desert rose as mentioned in their song! Wouldn't that be a wonderful memento to bring home representing my desert angel visitation as well.

Ava bought a desert rose and was captivated by its composition. It is the colloquial name given to rose-like formations of crystal clusters of gypsum which include abundant sand grains. The petals are crystal flattened sand grains fanning open in radiating crystal clusters. How beautiful she thought.

Ava headed out of the gate and into the town of Joshua Tree itself. She deliberately drove slowly to observe the town. It appeared to be an older town with nice restaurants and typical stores and businesses. She was most interested in seeing what the "natives" were like, wondering if they were any different than the people in Orange County. Deliberately stopping at a small convenience store under the pretense of buying a pack of gum, she wanted to get a feel of the energy of the folks inside. She also stopped and got some gas for the car, again trying to determine if the people who lived and worked here behaved with a higher or different level of energy. Ava could only detect their slower pace and nonchalant behavior but was not able to contribute it to any special energy level other than possibly the sun being so strong and hot. The town of Joshua Tree seemed a bit run down which surprised her. You would think this would be a major tourist attraction bringing in good money allowing the town to build hotels and vacation homes. She decided that it took an elevated consciousness to recognize Joshua Tree as an amazing treasure. As for herself, she would continue to visit as often as she could.

Now she needed to head home and prepare for her first day of work at Orion. She began to anticipate what the people would be like and if she would make any new friends. She also wondered how well she could pull off the pretense of not having as much knowledge as she truly possessed and began to think back on her first day of being human. Her thoughts rushed back to the insecurities and self-doubts on that first day at CE when she worried how she would be received. She felt plagued by her behavior changing from when she arrived at CE but then concluded that to heal her inner turmoil she could only be who she was.

This situation was different now. These people had never known her at this moment in time. It was all new to everyone. She was not stopping in on a Monday after leaving work on a Friday. She just needed to maintain an aura of less knowledge and acknowledge that it was her responsibility to recondition her condition. If she could hold on to that, she would be responsible for her power, knowing she was deliberately concealing it.

When Ava arrived home, she began preparing some of her new California clothes for work and realized her purchases were a good idea. She would bring less attention to herself if she blended in with the fashion of her counterparts. She would definitely not bring a brief case. That would look conspicuous for sure.

During dinner, she flicked on the television because she enjoyed the sound while she was cooking and afterwards, watched it while sitting at her dining table. She began to reflect on the angel telling her that she only ate one meal a day to watch her weight. Ava laughed knowing, angels don't need to control their weight. She had just been making small talk while I was eating my pizza. Ava turned the TV off and took out her journal to begin recording the events of her day at Joshua Tree. What an exciting experience it was seeing the angel appear again. Ava was sure to capture every moment of her day in every detail. She was looking forward to a session with Zachary and then her Yoga and meditation and would prepare for bed.

As Ava began to relax she summoned Zachary who immediately came through with FANOFU2. "Hi Zac, did you have fun today at Joshua Tree?" Zac replied, MOST INTERESTING. I laughed and commented, "You saw her too?" Zac said, SHE CARES ABOUT YOUR WELFARE. I smiled and said, "I know. She is sweet and it was gracious of her to make an appearance." Zac, said, GET YOUR REST NOW. I said, "Sure thing. It is getting late and I want to be fresh for my first day of work tomorrow." Zachary began vibrating hugs and vanished into thin air.

I began my Yoga session and then prepared for bed so that my last event of the day would be my meditation practice. I always felt it was best to meditate just before retiring for the evening.

CHAPTER 27

At Orion

Ava left her house in the morning and the sun was already rising in the sky. She drove down Laguna Canyon and then along the Pacific Coast Highway smiling at the ocean with the sun glistening on its surface. What a beautiful day, she thought to herself. Even if she was a little nervous, this sure was a great way to start one's day. Arriving, she parked her car and was smiling with anticipation, knowing it was so lovely here. She can no longer reflect back on the dreary, grey, cold and snowy skies of the East Coast. She suspected she was now home.

Ava settled into her assigned cubicle and was given a tour of the facility as well as introductions to some of the key players that she would be working with and would be crucial to her success. Everyone seemed pleasant enough but when introduced to a girl named Sheila she just gave Ava a snare. I guess this ought to be interesting Ava thought. She wondered what that was all about. For a brief moment, she thought Sheila was jealous. Another type of human frailty. Well, Sheila will learn that she need not waste her rudimental emotions on me. I am not the least bit interested in controversy, after all, I converse with the angels. I am a Light Being that has lived eons beyond pettiness and elevated to a level that Sheila will no doubt achieve as well.

Ava began to familiarize herself with the computer systems and some of the ongoing tasks. She wanted to set up some meetings with key players to gauge where they were at with specific production orders but she knew it would appear managerial, so she decided to allow her boss to take the reigns. Len sent an email out to the team inviting them all to lunch to welcome her. She thought that was very congenial and it would be a great way to get to know everyone in a more personal setting. As the morning progressed, Ava began working with the computer systems monitoring orders and configurations of software as well as the shipping schedules. It was really quite a simplistic job and she knew it was the perfect one for her end goals.

Lunch time arrived and they all piled into several cars and headed to a Mexican restaurant. She liked Mexican food as long as it was not too spicy. They sat at a large booth and everyone seemed happy and friendly. Sheila appeared right in Ava's face and flatly stated "I'm used to being the prettiest one in the group." At first it took Ava by surprise, but she simply replied, "You still are." Sheila had nothing to worry about. She was a tall, attractive, blue-eyed blonde. I'm sure she had her fair share of boyfriends. Too bad she didn't understand her self worth.

Lunch was delicious and Ava observed how laid back and relaxed everyone was. The group was relatively young and most were not married yet. They were having fun and not yet ready to settle down. She, on the other hand, had her mission and dedicated attitude and understood how easy this was going to be for her. This lovely group of people could never grasp her identity or understand her persevering nature. This was going to be a walk in the park. Ava knew she made the right choice. Again, grateful for the divine intervention. She was led by her higher consciousness and wonderful support system from beyond.

As the next five weeks rolled by, she became fully acclimated to her role at Orion. She could see that the timing was right for her to branch into more diverse interests. After careful research, Ava decided to enroll at Pepperdine University at the Graduate School of Education and Psychology with its campus in Irvine which meant she could be at the first class by 4:00 PM. The sun would be setting without her along the Pacific but she had her goals to achieve. The school's syllabus allowed her to explore the field of psychology to its fullest. Entrance exams were a breeze and she would begin afternoon and evening classes in a week. She looked forward to being successful and had the distinct vision that this was leading her to a field of study where dreams are a beautiful reminder of the vastness of our sensory perception.

Dreams were conceptualized to exist independent of the "waking" world as an alternate reality to our bodily selves. Dreams have a truly greater purpose and potential. Ava had come to realize dreams are deeper realizations of the unconscious represented through the eye of our mind. The soul's intention is to tap into these heightened states of awareness and remain conscious to the underplay of the unconscious as it unfolds its grasp. Indeed her life was changing but she was being reminded of the importance of not expecting gratification or dissatisfaction but to embark on a journey for the journey's sake and not the destination. She was following her soul's purpose. It was following the path she envisioned and allowed it to happen. With that realization her daily routine would need adjusting because her evenings and some weekends would be dedicated to studying and preparing papers. She would not give up her meditation sessions, however. "To everything there is a purpose under Heaven."

CHAPTER 28

School Begins

As I arrived in my classroom for my first evening class, I looked around and realized I was probably the oldest student in the room. It did not bother me, however. I knew I looked young for my age and besides many folks return to school to explore a different path in life. At least the lucky ones do. I was one of the "lucky" one but I knew this was all destined anyhow.

I truly enjoyed the introduction to psychology which began with embryogenesis but knowing how the spiritual cellular integration was part of this miracle formation. Naturally, this aspect of integration was not being discussed in a scientific forum yet but I had the distinct advantage of having this knowledge. It was the beginning of human consciousness and it was certainly not my intention to bring this to anyone's attention. I had a clear understanding of how the spirit enters the embryo integrating its cellular consciousness into human cellular formation. My purpose was to understand the human aspect of this development fully and how through the various stages of physical development, a human's behavior as well as physical characteristics evolve. I was enthralled with the education and particularly found fascination with the brain's function or dysfunction resulting in an inevitable outcome.

I also discovered how social behavior and interaction with one's environment was a significant part of one's behavior as a human. The pressures of society had a profound affect on a human's beliefs and value system and most of what I discovered came from a genetic generational source. What my professor and classmates did not either understand or know or chose not to discuss, was the impact of energy fields in the shaping of genes and behavior outside of the obvious anatomical reasoning. Again, I needed to keep that information to myself. This is why I needed to find metaphysical classes conjoined with my study of psychology.

In due time, I suggested to myself. I would find a way to combine both worlds. Oh, I just said the very words Zachary had told me years ago about writing a book combining both worlds. I was quite amazed and felt a sense of communion with the Universe. I smiled and felt tingly because I was receiving an affirmation from a source of truth, from awareness of all that is, knowing that I would find an institution that would provide me with the knowledge and understanding that would combine both fields of study. I looked up and gave the Universe a wink and then smiled with gratitude.

I progressed in my studies and achieved A's in all my grades, much to the dismay of my classmates since we were all being graded on a curve. My professor decided in all fairness to the rest of the class, my scores would not be equated in the curve. I was clearly more advanced and I knew it was only because of my true identity and purpose and I didn't want to make enemies. Thinking about that made me realize that that too was a study in human behavior itself. I laughed. I could probably write a paper on that but I didn't want to appear antagonistic.

Now most of my time was spent working; attending classes; and my evenings were spent with research papers and studying, but never forgetting my meditation practice. I continued to write in my journal and by this stage, I was up to my fifth journal to record all my thoughts and inspirations and dreams.

Life was good and I even managed to attend a U2 concert with of all people, Sheila! Who would have guessed that she and I had so much in common. We loved rock and roll and loved U2. There was a spiritual side to her that I was surprised to uncover. We didn't become best pals but that was okay. We just enjoyed similar interests and had some very cool discussions. She was as surprised as I was and I secretly hoped she would realize that she should never feel threatened by another human being. Her focus should be on her inner development and her human experience should not be fraught with unexpected challenges of her own creation. Challenges that seem to come at us from out of the apparent "blue" are for our benefit. I never had any really deep existential discussions with her but I did frequently send her white healing energy.

Sheila and I even bought roller blades and on my free Saturdays began roller blading through Laguna Canyon straight to the Pacific Ocean. We had fun and would lunch at the beach often. She spoke frankly about how confusing my aptitude and inner peace unnerved her. She could not understand my confidence or my lack of interdependence with society. She felt a girl like me would have tons of boyfriends and I would or should be having the time of my life. I simply told her that I was having the time of my life. It is all a matter of perspective. The things that interest me that I have the good fortune to explore and delve into with all my heart and soul IS having the time of my life. She looked at me puzzled but I could see her wheels were spinning. Sheila, I said, "I simply am who I am and have a different set of priorities. There is no right or wrong to behavior unless you sense a gnawing feeling that there is something more. If that is the case, go within and find out what it is." She smiled and again I could see the wheels spinning in her head.

During lunch we began to discuss the upcoming U2 concert that was at the San Diego Arena and made our plans. We were determined to meet them this time! Sheila suggested that I take one of the license plates from my car and bring it to the concert with me. I smiled and told her "I thought the same thing." We laughed like two little school girls. Sheila was as excited as I was to meet the guys. We began to devise a daring plan to arrive early and go around to the back entrance of the Arena where the buses would pull up and the road crew would be unloading the band's gear and hopefully coerce one of them to let us in. After all, these guys wouldn't be able to resist two good looking girls! We were excited at the possibility of getting to meet U2 but, more than anything I wanted to pick their brains about their experiences at Joshua Tree. I needed to feel that connection with them face-to-face as opposed to the obvious connection I felt listening to their music.

CHAPTER 29

Institute of Noetic Sciences

One Saturday, Ava was doing research on a particular area of study at the school library for a paper on one of her advanced psychology classes. Because of her profound interest and curiosity in the area of brain dysfunction, she wanted to write about the symptoms and diagnosis of Autism. Clearly there was much focus about the disorder and Ava felt a need to explore it further. Ava knew that the Autism spectrum disorder (ASD) and Autism are both general terms for a group of complex disorders of brain development. These disorders are characterized, in varying degrees, by difficulties in social interaction, verbal and nonverbal communication and repetitive behaviors.

With that knowledge she felt compelled and driven to dissect what she considered a phenomena. She was drawn to the possibility that this could be a new stage in human evolution rather than a "brain disorder," almost like a new way of the development of human consciousness. She realized that this was way out in left field for mainstream medical thinking, but she still wanted to consider the possibility and make a research project of it.

During her research, she came upon an organization by the name of IONS which stood for the Institute of Noetic Sciences.

Something struck a chord within Ava. She became fascinated with their research and studies.

The Institute's primary program areas are consciousness and healing, extended human capacities, and emerging world views. The specific work included application findings in educational products and trainings; original research; and publications in journals. She couldn't believe her eyes when she read from their reference manual "because limitations in our human consciousness underlie many of the problems we face as a global community, research at IONS focuses on exploring the fundamental nature of consciousness, investigating how it interacts with the physical world, and studying how consciousness can dramatically transform in beneficial ways".

There it is, Ava squealed silently to herself! That is exactly what I was looking for! My source for combining both worlds. She started to think of a million things at once and had to center her energy. She had tons of questions for IONS and wondered if they had ever heard of The Indigo Children. Ava secretly suspected that Autism was the gradual evolution of human consciousness into the next stage of human development. She suspected that The Indigo Child is here to bring us closer to our true essence.

"We think our minds are separate because of our bodies. These children know differently. A true Indigo travels comfortably between worlds usually at night when we think they're asleep.

Our thoughts and feelings are not our own. The truth is, we have forgotten who we are and how our minds are connected to each other. Indigos remember and have an inner knowing that far exceeds our psychic abilities.

The intricate inner workings of our DNA are changing, brain-wave relationships are spontaneously moving into higher vibrational patterning as electromagnetic fields within our DNA. Because of this, our brains are working together as cohesive units of consciousness. That means humanity is becoming more aware and moving toward becoming sentient beings – aware of everything all at once all of the time." (Excerpt from: Conversations with the Children of Now, Meg Blackburn Losey)

Ava rushed home and constructed a letter of introduction to the Institute asking to become a member and providing them with her credentials thus far in her studies. Her letter of introduction was created in a way that would certainly impress them and included the idea to incorporate some of their findings in a paper she was creating in her advanced studies course explaining her desire to express consciousness above all scientific findings. She wondered if her professor would have additional clout but she would resort to his recommendations later if she felt she needed them.

Ava continued to work on her project, made lunch and ate on her patio. She just couldn't think of anything else. She was filled with excitement for her future and could sense the vibration she was heading in was the most perfect direction to fulfill the purpose of her return to humanity. Afterwards, she put her books and papers away and relished peacefully with eyes closed in her lounge chair allowing the Universe to do its thing. She was soaking in the profundity of her experience.

CHAPTER 30

Meeting U2

Ava and Sheila had their day planned out perfectly. They took Ava's Z-28 since Sheila loved her car and wanted the T-Tops off to enjoy the sun and wind and the stares from men as they drove down to San Diego. Ava felt light and free and was excited about the possibility of meeting the band. She knew their plan would work out.

As they arrived at the Arena, there weren't many cars parked in the massive lot. They both looked at each other and smiled. They drove to the nearest spot at the back entrance and could see chain link gates clearly forming a drive through pattern for the buses. They looked at each other again and squealed! With the car parked, they began to remove the front license plate from the Z giggling again like school girls. They were ready and now all they needed to do was wait. Knowing that the buses would have to arrive early to set up as well as perform a sound check, their wait would not be long. Some fans started to arrive who had the same idea as they did but it wasn't a major crowd that would ruin their plan.

Soon the first bus arrived and drove down the entrance between the chain link fences. Ava began to feel butterflies! The second bus was not far behind. Then surprisingly, a guy on a motorcycle drove up next. Oh, I'll bet that's Larry Mullen, the drummer. He loves motorcycles. You couldn't really tell it was him since his helmet was a great disguise. We figured the boys must have been on one of the buses. That third bus stopped and out came BONO! He walked up to the fence with his shades on and was just looking at all of us. There were maybe 20 fans hoping for interaction. Bono kept a safe distance but I felt brave and walked straight up to him. No one stopped me. Bono wouldn't let them. He appreciated his fans and clearly got off the bus to greet us anyway. I extended my hand to him and introduced myself. He asked what I had in my hand and I showed him laughing my license plate. He smiled an ingenuous smile and then I introduced him to Sheila. Sheila seemed a little apprehensive, almost like she couldn't believe her eyes. I told her, "Loosen up Sheila, we've been dreaming about this. They're only human." Bono liked that. He asked if we had tickets to the show and I happily said, "Yes, front row center." He then asked if we would like to be present for the sound check! I couldn't believe it. It was real. It was happening.

He took us down the ramp and brought us through a maze of tunnels and then to our seats. We talked a little small talk but I desperately wanted to ask about Joshua Tree. He was in a rush to get to his dressing room and review the playlist with his band members but asked if we wanted to join them backstage after the show. "Of course, we'd love to!" I was bursting at the seams with excitement. I grabbed Sheila's arm until it turned red. We were both going insane. Sheila wondered suspiciously what would happen to us and I told her we will simply be blessed to have met the greatest band in the world. "Have some faith Sheila, cruise lightly I told her. These guys are very good souls and possess a spiritual reality." That seemed to comfort her.

After the most incredible concert ever, Sheila and I were ushered off into the maze of tunnels by Security. We were brought to a comfortable living room type setting and Adam, the bass player was already comfortably relaxing in a chair enjoying an Irish cigarette.

He smiled and I walked up to him and introduced myself. I sat next to him. He mentioned that Bono had spoke about two lovely women coming back stage that wanted to meet us. I smiled and said, "Here we are." He asked what I was holding and I showed him my license plate. He laughed and said, "I saw you in the audience but with the lights I could not make out what it was." He spoke with a lovely brogue and asked us if we wanted something to drink. I asked for a cup of coffee and he made sure one was provided. I then asked for his autograph and he politely and eagerly accommodated.

The rest of the Band piled into the comfortable living room setting as well as other people whom I didn't know and concluded they were roadies or agents. We were having a great time. I wanted to get over to Bono and ask about Joshua Tree but Adam kept me fully occupied with tons of questions about America. "What is it like living here?" "What do we do for entertainment?" "How many places have we been to?" I could barely get a question in. I realized that they had a natural curiosity about our country as we might about theirs had we been visiting. He was clearly sweet, polite and considerate. After some time, Bono came over and asked if we were having a good chat. I smiled and said, "Most definitely. I'd like to ask about Joshua" but before I could finish my sentence, their manager said, "OK boys, the buses are ready, time to hit the road." I was saddened. I wondered if I would ever know the answer to my question. I suppose it would be a long philosophical discussion and there just wasn't much time. I thanked Bono profusely for the invitation and expressed my appreciation of their work. Their words have inspired me. Bono winked at me and I felt like I would faint. I leaned close to him and kissed him on the cheek. He smiled innocently and off they went.

Sheila and I were then ushered through the maze and were led out to the parking lot. We both wanted to scream! Was it real? Did it really happen? We kept laughing and laughing. The ride home seemed like a dream. We couldn't stop talking about the entire experience. "Wait until we tell people at work! They'll never believe it!" We just kept laughing. It felt good to laugh and feel joy and happiness. After dropping Sheila at her apartment, I headed home still wearing a grin on my face from ear to ear. I needed to talk to Zachary. I needed to hear from him and know he enjoyed himself as much as I did. I would not be able to meditate tonight. There was too much adrenaline rushing through me.

Zachary came through as usual with FANOFU2. I asked, "Did you see what happened? Did you enjoy the concert?" Zachary energetically responded YES YES YES YES. I laughed. "I guess you feel as giddy as I do." Zachary responded again with YES YES YES. I simply laughed. He then said DO MEDITATE, NEED "OK, Zachary. I suppose it would balance my energy field. I'm on an exceptionally high frequency right now and I do have a need to center myself. I will meditate and then get a good night's rest."

Surprisingly, my meditation went very well. I felt peaceful and fulfilled, centered and balanced. It was the right thing to do before going to sleep. I would be assured of a proper rest with no interference from sparks of energy bolting through my physical body. I thanked the Universe for its blessings today as always and fell into a deep sleep.

CHAPTER 31

Meeting John

Upon awakening the next morning, Ava recalled an odd dream and began recording it:

> "I found myself traveling to a classroom in the sky and was being given what appeared to be a physics lesson by a small boy around the age of seven years. I was the only student in the classroom. After the lesson the little boy took me by the hand and brought me to the door and opened it. We stepped out and travelled into the skies. We went from location to location all appearing the same..... We were in the clouds. Suddenly, I then found myself alone. I looked around circling 360 degrees not finding anyone with me. Suddenly from a distance appearing from a far away cloud I recognized

Zachary who began floating towards me with the little boy from the classroom. There was no communication between them, only smiles."

Ava quickly contacted Zachary who came through with **FANOFU2**. "Hi Zachary. That was quite a dream last night. What was going on?" Zachary replied, **YOU WILL KNOW SOON**. "Oh come now Zachary, you can do better than that" she replied. Zachary said IN DUE TIME. "Well, I understand what you mean Zachary but astral projection is not a new thing for me and why was I in a classroom being instructed by a little boy?" Zachary simply responded, **THERE ARE GREATER THINGS IN HEAVEN AND EARTH THAN CAN BE DREAMT IN YOUR PHILOSOPHIES.** Ava was quite surprised by his comment. It was one she often quoted from Shakespeare herself and now he was putting her in this process of thought and it frustrated her. "Oh well, I guess I'm not going to get an answer just yet but I trust the dream's meaning will come and unfold as it should when the time is right." Zachary began to fade from Ava's living room.

Ava took out her research papers for school and began pouring over material for her studies that she had spread over her dining table in organized piles.

With some difficulty focusing because of her dream, she began with her project on Autism as defined in standard psychology realms as a mental disorder but introducing some of its symptoms as potential Indigo Child characteristics. Oh boy, my professor is going to think I've flipped. She had never introduced metaphysics into any of her scholastic research papers before but Ava was very committed about presenting this viewpoint as a potential way of looking at what is defined as a disorder with a new vision - a gift not yet understood by humanity and the halls of current science.

Ava was making progress and realized with the excitement of the previous day she had forgotten to check her mail box. She grabbed her keys and went to collect her mail getting a blast of that hot California heat hitting her as she opened her front door. Wow! I almost forgot where I was. My central air conditioning certainly kept things comfortable within my home. Next to her keys were her sunglasses which she quickly placed on her face. She was anticipating a reply from the Institute of Noetic Sciences and reached the mailbox with great hope. With a twist of the key she had reached in and retrieved some bills and there it was! The envelope with a return address The Institute of Noetic Sciences.

She opened the letter before her trek back to the apartment. They were responding positively and wanted to meet with her to discuss a panel she might find of interest to her school research. Oh my, she thought, does it get any better than this? Well, of course it does she answered herself. It gets better and better as long as you remain on a positive trajectory with your vibration and understand the Universe is here to provide what you desire. The secret was to always remain calm and expectant with no doubt or nonsensical mental chatter about reasons why or why not. It really was simply a matter of physics. Humanity had been conditioned but had the responsibility of reconditioning that condition. She had the advantage of her wisdom and it was becoming clear to her that her course of study and her future desires would aid in making a difference. She felt the privilege of the responsibility as well as the excitement that accompanied it. She began to suspect that the little boy in her dream was going to be part of this magic. She smiled and could feel Zachary's smile as well.

Returning to school the next evening, Ava was bursting with excitement to submit her research paper. She wondered if this would be her first failing grade since she was veering off the standard medical course and moving toward exploring the effects of other dimensional realities - that being the potential reasoning for what she considered, a conflicted and stodgy diagnosis of Autism.

Before Ava's next class she had a half hour to kill and decided to get herself some dinner in the university's cafeteria. She wondered if the food was good but even if it wasn't, she needed nourishment. She was still feeling uplifted from the research she uncovered preparing her paper and was still on a high from IONS accepting her proposal to join a panel specifically on the evolution of human consciousness.

She grabbed a tray and headed to the line for what appeared to be mashed potatoes and meatloaf hoping it would not poison her. As she paid for her meal she turned around looking for an empty table. There were none. She slowly walked through the crowded tables and found one with a single person occupying it. She wondered if he would mind if she shared his table but before she could ask him, he lifted his head up from his papers and said, "If you'd like to join me, you are welcome to do so." Ava smiled and thanked him for his kindness. She immediately noticed his beautiful blue eyes that seemed so soft and kind. He was a distinguished gentlemen about ten years her senior and she wondered who he was. He extended his hand and introduced himself as Professor John Young from the University. "Hello," Ava replied, "I'm Ava St. Claire a student here." He was well dressed in the typical professor tweed jacket and trousers with a standard nondescript shirt and tie but was extremely handsome. He had chiseled features and beautiful wavy white hair. They both began to speak at the same time, asking what the other's field of interest was. They laughed. He politely said, "OK, you first." Ava smiling back said, "I'm a student of psychology, okay, your turn." John, still smiling said, "I'm a Professor of Renaissance Art here at the University." "I love Renaissance Art," Ava exclaimed. "Well, you should take one of my classes" John said. "I have already been through college back east and took several courses already. I am now returning for a degree in Psychology." "Are you a professional student?" he asked. They both laughed and she said, "No John, I've had a career in business for many years and simply wish to change my future." John replied, "Interesting choice of words, changing your future. I like that Ava. It takes courage and insight to achieve such a lofty goal at such a young age. Are you planning on becoming a psychologist or a psychiatrist?" Ava replied, "I do have a different calling now and I'm quite certain it is something I need to do. I'm not necessarily interested in becoming a psychologist or a psychiatrist but something that might branch from those fields exploring human consciousness." "Good for you Ava. It sounds exploratory and very interesting. By the way, you have a lovely name." Ava began to suspect John was being a little flirtatious with her but she didn't mind. She was fascinated by his handsomeness and she noticed he wasn't wearing a wedding band. She was also excited about his niche being Renaissance Art and could picture the two of them in and out of art museums enjoying the beauty of these magnificent works. She also liked the way he looked at her. She could tell he was interested and wondered who would break the ice first. She didn't want to finish her dinner too quickly but she knew she had a class coming up.

She asked him when his next class was and he said, "Unfortunately I'll have to leave your gracious beauty in about seven minutes." Ava smiled and said, "Me as well. I mean, my next class is in about seven minutes, but I'm taking my gracious beauty with me." They both laughed at her humorous comment and Ava could feel herself blush a bit. John asked her if they might have coffee or lunch some time. Ava was delighted. "Yes," she replied, "I would love that." As was becoming the social custom, John handed Ava one of his business cards and wrote his private number on it for her to call him when she was available. She took it and placed it in her purse and smiled back at him.

She had a hard time taking the grin off her face and wondered how she would concentrate on her next class knowing that handsome man was about to receive a call from her the following day. She could see that he couldn't take his eyes off her either and he had a very warm smile for her. She thought, we make a very good looking couple. She could feel the magnetism between them and it felt better than good. As they packed up their belongings to prepare for their next class, Ava felt sad to leave him but optimistic over the possibility that her road to interdependence was about to be transformed as well.

Ava could only focus on John during her next class. She wondered if he liked poetry, what types of books he liked, what type of movies he enjoyed, if he was a skier or a tennis player. Did he like to dance, did he like U2? She even fantasized a bit of what it would be like to kiss him. She really needed to stay focused. This was an important class and she should not be distracted. Her thoughts kept coming back to John, however. Well, I'm gonna have to do extra reading to know what this class was about she concluded.

When she arrived home, she placed her books and papers in an organized fashion on her dining room table. It was late and she needed to rest for work the next day. At least she didn't have any classes but she did have studying to conquer. Ava began her meditation and before retiring for the evening, she began writing in her journal about her meeting with John. She immediately remembered a past dream she had where she was being sanctified in some sort of religious ceremony and kept hearing angelic voices calling out the name John; John; John. She wondered if there was a connection. She fell into dreamland with pen and journal in hand.

Ava awoke laughing because she realized her journal was still in bed with her but had to search for the pen to begin recording another odd dream:

> "I found herself in the same cloud dimension I had been in recently with Zachary and that little boy. This time I was alone. I looked around and around and there wasn't a soul there. I was quite mesmerized by the experience even as I record it here."

Ava could only perceive the dream as an analogy of a frame to a painting symbolizing her spiritual progression that had not yet come to fruition. She surmised that the little boy who had appeared in the previous dream was going to help her paint that picture which would evolve her to her suspected purpose, and of course, Zachary would forever be present guiding her in her creation. She headed for the shower and then made herself breakfast. She had a day of work ahead but it would be a breeze and she could do classwork at her desk. That was a bonus. She would have a few chapters to read from her class the evening before since her focus was more on John then on the task at hand. She would call John that evening and hopefully they would make plans to meet for that coffee he suggested.

Ava managed to get her work done that day along with a substantial amount of classwork. She was pleased with her progress. During lunch with Sheila, they gabbed about John. Sheila's response was, "Well, it's about time Ava." Ava told Sheila that they simply were interested in each other and that she didn't know where it would lead. After all, they hadn't even been on a date yet. Sheila was overjoyed that I was making a potentially romantic connection. I had to laugh at the human condition that felt the need to categorize behavior and make everyone the same. Otherwise you were looked upon as weird, strange or had hidden motives. They could not understand that our world is full of all kinds of diversity which ultimately leads to power and inner strength and unimaginable progress. Ava played along with the giddiness of Sheila's hope that she had finally "found" someone to share her life with that would give her an identity and fulfill a dream.

Ava knew she would not resist the idea of developing a relationship with John and would allow the idea to gain momentum naturally. Ava understood that the desire, any desire is born within you because without it, there could be no new desire born. She would allow the Universe to take its course. There was nothing further for her to do. There was no contraction to the momentum of the Universe, IF she didn't provide it with one.

Upon returning home, Ava picked up the phone to dial John's private number. She wondered what his schedule was. Would he be working late classes tonight? She really had no way of knowing. To her delight, John picked up the phone. He sounded happy that she called. "Hello John, I wasn't sure if you had classes to teach tonight." John, said, "No, I only teach two night classes on Mondays. The rest of the time I'm on a day schedule at the University. I'm so happy you called Ava. What is your class schedule like?"

I responded telling him "I take 4:00 PM classes Mondays, Wednesdays and Thursdays. I have another Monday class at 6:00 PM so I'm doubled up on Mondays." "It sounds like you are carrying a full load," he said. "Do you have time to have dinner with me on Friday night?" "Of course John, I'd love to." My school and work schedules are manageable and I look forward to dinner with you on Friday.

John asked me if I liked Mediterranean and if I had ever heard of Adonis Restaurant in Laguna Beach. I told him I hadn't but I'm close to Laguna Beach and that I loved Mediterranean food, it was one of my favorites. He said, "Why don't we meet there at 8:00 PM Friday." I said "great! I'm very much looking forward to it." "Me too," he said. We continued talking a little more about our day getting slightly more familiar with each other. I loved the sound of his voice. It was melodic and gentle. My mind began to wander during our conversation and I had to force myself to keep on track with the topic of discussion. His voice was so soothing I kept imagining him whispering in my ear and what it would feel like to kiss him. Oh dear, I was feeling giddy. We wrapped up our conversation with excitement about our date for Friday. I really liked his style and manner and especially looked forward to dining at the beach which was one of my favorite places. I began to anticipate what we would talk about and found myself imagining the date. This was new territory for me but in reality I'd been here before but not having a specific memory of this lifetime I had no way of understanding the nature of our relationship however, I suspected it was a highly exciting one. I had a feeling this was going to be very interesting and provide me with even greater insights into my human nature.

As the week progressed with my typical work and school schedule, I secretly hoped to run into John l but I never did. After all, we had different schedules and I had no art classes which would take me to his area of the university. I was happily planning my outfit for the date and very much to my surprise learned I received a 'B' on my paper which combined the parochial box potentially shifting the paradigm into a higher consciousness perspective. I was pleased with the grade albeit the only 'B' I ever received. I had concerns that I would fail presenting an approach that flies in the face of everything psychology believed. My professor wrote a note on my paper, "I had an interesting approach but should stay within the confines of the classwork presented."

Of course, I couldn't have expected him to praise my idea. After all he was a seasoned psychology professor with a Ph.D. and I sincerely doubted he ever dabbled in existentialism at any given point in his career. I was still satisfied though and knew of one organization that would appreciate my approach, IONS. I still smiled that I had achieved a 'B' grade and applauded him for being somewhat open minded.

I was feeling the need to touch base with Zachary and decided that evening I would summon him. First, my Yoga and meditation but not before finishing my studies for school. Zachary greeted me in his usual way, FANOFU2. I greeted him with a warm and welcoming hello. He began stating ALCHEMY PAULO COELHO. I asked what the significance was. I loved Paulo Coelho's books and collected all of them. They were intriguing and insightful. Paulo had a delightful way of unfolding hidden truths in what appeared to be fictional. However, any wise reader knew Paulo was camouflaging existentialism using fiction. It gave me an idea. Maybe that book Zachary confirmed I should write would be just the way for me to get my insights across combining both worlds. Oh, but what a task. I certainly didn't have the time for that just now. I asked Zachary to wait until I found Paulo's book on Alchemy. I began to read briefly and found an interesting quote:

"This is why alchemy exists. The alchemists will search and find it, and then want to be better than he was in his former life. Lead will play its role until the world has no further need for lead; and then lead will have to turn itself into gold. That's what alchemists do. They show that, when we strive to become better than we are, everything around us becomes better, too" (Excerpt from: Paulo Coehlo, The Alchemist cc 1988).

Zachary was in full agreement expressing YES YES YES. "I need to give this some thought Zachary. I feel it is a very important message about my mission as a human. If I'm not mistaken, my thought processes about my paper expressing my perspective on Autism being characteristics of an Indigo Child and not that of a brain damaged child has something to do with this. Is it possible the lead thinking of the established parochial world will no longer be needed because it will transform into gold. The gold of realizing Autism is the evolution of human consciousness?" Zachary continued to reply YES YES YES. "Wow! I guess I must really be on to something here. Well, I accept your premise and would like to switch gears and ask some questions about John Young. "You know I have a date with him on Friday night."

Zachary complied and responded with **YES**. "What do you think of John, Zachary?" **FINE FELLOW AND LOTS OF FUN FOR YOU**. Oh, that is good to hear. Zachary continued... **INTELLECTUALLY COMPATIBLE ON FUNDAMENTAL SUBJECTS**. "Well, I get that Zachary. You are basically saying he is not much of an out-of-the-box thinker."

Zachary said YES. "Well, that's fine" I said. "He still would make a wonderful boyfriend I'm sure." And once again, Zachary replied with the word **YES**. I smiled and proceeded to bid Zac a good night and on with my ritualistic evening disciplines.

CHAPTER 32

Dining with John

Friday finally arrived. I was so looking forward to having dinner with John. As I showered and dressed my mind was on him. I selected a blue chiffon ruffled dress and as I slipped it over my heard I was brought back to my first day as a human. The memory of feeling the soft fabric on my human body was sensual and exciting. I liked the way it made me feel.

John seemed very kind and intellectually advanced and I just had a very good vibration about his energy. He was upbeat and charming and enjoyed laughing. I had high hopes for our evening. The telephone rang and it was John confirming our time and place for dinner. I thought that was very gracious and forthright of him. This was a man with manners and consideration.

I pulled my car up to the parking lot of the Adonis Restaurant and allowed the valet to park my car. I didn't want to walk across the parking lot feeling a little self-conscious if he was in the restaurant and saw me walking to the front door. In spite of not having a good reason why I felt this way, it felt special having the valet park my car. I walked into the restaurant at about 7:55 PM and immediately caught John's eye sitting at a table near the window overlooking the

Pacific Ocean. Oh how lovely. And he looked good too. He was sporting a navy blazer and a white pull over light weight sweater. He looked smart but casual and quite classy. I was grateful not to see that tweed jacket. Walking toward the table I enjoyed the way my body felt in the chiffon dress. I wore white accessories and as I approached the table, I said to him, "We match. Great minds think alike," and we both laughed. John stood up and pulled my chair out as I sat down. I thought that was quite chivalrous of him and hoped it was not just to make a good first impression. I appreciated a man with refined manners even though I was an independent woman capable of managing my life. It was still a classy thing to have a man pull your chair out while you sat. He immediately asked me if I would like a cocktail and I asked for a bottled lemon water. John had asked for a Martini. We began to discuss our week and catch up on the events between our first meeting on Monday. He had a lovely smile on his face and clearly looked pleased to be with me.

After reviewing the menu, we both placed our orders. John's back was to the ocean which was another chivalrous thing to do but I wanted him to have as much of a view as I did so I suggested that we reorganize our seats so we could both enjoy the natural beauty of the ocean. John told me his view was the only view he needed which was facing me. I smiled and was quite charmed by his attention and quick wit. He spoke of my gracious beauty again and I began to blush. I wondered if all of this attention and flattery was going to distract me from getting to know John the person. But I quickly dismissed the thought believing that his attention toward me was who he was. Indeed, an elegant gentleman with sincere compliments who was not afraid to express them. Even his choice of restaurant was elegant with candlelight and soft music from the Mediterranean Isles filling the air with sensuality and peace. I was quite pleased to have met him.

As we enjoyed our meals, I was pleased that John only began dinner with one Martini and quickly changed to water. I had a quick flash back about Robert picking up a six pack for the ride home in his Ford pick up.

John was quite taken with my ambitious workload between school and job and expressed concern that he would not have much time with me. I assured him that I managed quite easily and specifically took a dumbed down job in order to focus on the things that were more important to my direction in life and politely added, and maybe that includes you too John.

I came to learn that John enjoyed tennis and we agreed to play together on Sunday. He began rattling off the things he wanted us to do together, such as art museums, theatre, music, architectural exhibits, Blue Angels Air shows, sharing favorite books and enjoying the beach together. I was overwhelmed but in agreement knowing that all will unfold as it should. We were in agreement with our compatibility and I was happy to have such a polished, well educated man to share these ventures with. I learned that John had been widowed five years and lost his wife to cancer. It was a difficult time for him and I understood he was now ready to begin living again and considered himself lucky to have found such a lovely person as myself. I was excited for the relationship and for the first time since transforming into a human I felt a sincere connection to a love interest. I could never reveal my true identity but it didn't matter. It never really matters. As long as I was experiencing what it was like to be human in all facets of the word. That was of paramount importance. If John couldn't stretch his mental capacity into the existential world I knew, that too, was a human experience that I would grow through and learn from as well.

When our dinner was finished, we enjoyed coffee and dessert, neither of us wanted the evening to end. John asked me if I would like to take a walk along the beach. "I would love to John," I replied. We gathered our things and headed to the back patio of the restaurant and down the stairs to the sand. I removed my shoes and walked barefoot and the feeling of the cool sand on my feet was exciting. John smiled at me and placed his hand in mine. We walked and talked and stared at the ocean and the wide span of sky showing off its stars. I began to quote from Robert Frost "Choose something like a star to stay our minds on and be staid." John smiled at me recognizing the poem and squeezed my hand. "You are so beautiful" he told me and I replied by squeezing his hand back smiling. We walked along the shoreline listening to the surf as it made its presence known, a soothing and rhythmic consistent sway and appreciated the coolness of the California air brushing along our bodies. I recalled the song that played on my answering machine "this one glides above the ocean" as I looked up into the night sky, I smiled and winked at the stars.

John stopped walking and turned to me and in an apologetic way almost bashfully stating that it was not in his nature and realizing it was only their first date he said that he really wanted to kiss me. I looked up at John and smiled as I placed my right hand around the back of his head and moved his face towards mine. I was intoxicated by the evening's pleasure and decided to kiss him. I felt his warm face on me and enjoyed his sweet full lips that expressed a sincere desire for me. He wrapped his strong arms around my slender body and held me close to him. I felt a distant memory of joy and a caring sensation. I savored every moment of our embrace and allowed my mind to be set free and experience the pleasure of this moment. I could not tell how long we were connected but knew there would be more times in the future with John and knew he felt the same specialness towards me. He was a delightful soul with a magnetism that I could not resist.

As we began to walk back to our cars hand in hand, smiling and chatting, I felt like I was walking on a cloud moving more gracefully than usual. "Parting is such sweet sorrow" John spoke, and I replied, "That I shall say good night till it be morrow". We both smiled and kissed each other good night. I got into my car and drove home in a dreamy state of mind feeling lifted from all the burdens of the human world. My drive home seemed different this time. The Laguna Hills seemed more vibrant as if they had known the elevation in my awareness and sensed my greater appreciation of life. I felt the command of my power parting the canyon road to my journey home and the hills were bowing and issuing me through because of the difference in my vibration. I thought to myself, I could get used to this very easily.

When Ava returned home she wanted to speak with Zachary but it was late. She suspected they would commune in a dream tonight about this evening's event so she simply washed up for bed and did her Chakra meditation. She was still too elated to even write in her journal of her evening with John. She decided because tomorrow was Saturday, she would write her thoughts and emotions down then. Ava slipped into dreamland with a Mona Lisa smile on her face.

Ava awoke the following morning well rested and eager to record her interesting dream:

> "I was entering a crowded restaurant that was ornately decorated with lots of wood carvings. There was much hustle and bustle and a long line of patrons waiting to be seated. I and an unknown date along with other patrons were being ushered to the top level of the restaurant where more dining tables were set up. As we climbed the angular stairs, we stopped on a landing. I was admiring the wood carving on the stair ballasts and touched one. It broke off so easily and dropped. I was aghast and so worried if anyone below would be hurt and what the cost would be to fix it."

It disturbed Ava and in her infinite wisdom understood the rise on the staircase represented her elated feelings from the evening and the potential for an elevated human experience with John. She could not imagine however being responsible for breaking such a unique piece of artwork and having it come crashing down onto a patron below the stairs. She could not accept the dream as a possibility of her future but knew that the Universe provides what we seek through our vibrations whether we are aware of them or not.

Ava readied herself for the chores of a typical Saturday as well as some school work for the week. She also needed to complete a questionnaire for the IONS panel she would participate on and call Sheila who was certainly anxious for a review of last night's date. Ava was also excited about playing tennis with John the next day and was grateful that as she was approaching her 40th birthday, she was still in excellent shape because of her Yoga practice.

Ava mailed her completed questionnaire to IONS submitting her report on UCLA's experiments on a gene called Rbfox1 which regulates how the cell makes proteins linking mutations to an increased risk for Autism based on earlier studies by Daniel Geschwind. Ava was particularly interested in the medical approach and all its findings thus far but was keen to integrate within this research the evolution of human cellular development leading to the evolution of human consciousness. And once again, perceiving this mutation as a natural course of evolution as opposed to a defect in our existing DNA. She was excited to be accepted for this panel and anticipated a start date to work on the IONS project.

Now I need to connect with Zachary. Zachary of course greeted me with his usual FANOFU2. "Hi Zachary. How are you doing today?" TIME ALWAYS PRESENT. "OK, I understand. There is no today, tomorrow, or yesterday. Let me restate my question. How are you now?" Zachary chuckled showing appreciation of my humor. "What did you think of my date with John?" ENJOYABLE. "Well, I would have thought it was more than enjoyable but okay, I accept your response. Zachary, tell me, what was the message in my dream last night. What was my unconscious revealing to me?" Zachary replied: **YOUR REASON FOR BEING HERE IS TO GAIN**

NEW INFORMATION AND DATA TO MOVE YOUR LIFE FORWARD FOR FINE TUNING YOUR UNDERSTANDING WHICH WILL UPLIFT ALL. YOU HAVE CHOSEN TO DEVOTE YOUR ENERGY TO BUILDING DEEP ROOTS OF SPIRITUAL ESSENCES OF THE ELEMENTS AROUND YOU. "Quite true Zachary but I also look forward to enjoying my human experience with John and know it will not negate my purpose and mission. More than likely, it will add to it." Zachary replied. **EYE OF THE TIGER**. "Yes, Zachary, I will provide myself with human pleasures but my eye will always remain fixed on the eye of the tiger. I have come to observe how the human experience is fraught with unexpected challenges and hardships. I understand that there isn't a single person in the world that can become his best without the assistance of others. I am grateful for yours and I look forward to observing the reflection of myself through John. Thank you Zachary." Zachary smiled as he vanished.

Ava began her Yoga and then into her meditation practice. Before retiring she recorded her session with Zachary in her journal with greater understanding of her dream and how dreams have a way of reminding us of the vastness of our sensory perception.

She knew dreams have a truly greater purpose. She was also looking forward to any human sexual contact and was confident that would become available now that she had this brief encounter of a sexual nature with John.

Tennis With John

Sunday was here and Ava woke with a happy feeling for her 10:00 AM tennis match with John. She could not recall having a dream and instead began to prepare for her day. Dressed in her tennis gear she headed out to meet John. She remembered that John told her to bring a bathing suit since there was a pool they could take a dip in afterwards. She decided to wear her hair in a french braid since she needed to keep it out of her eyes and face. She realized she looked even younger with her hair pulled up and back and decided she should wear it this way more often.

John had a membership to a Recreation Club in the nearby town of Dana Point. It was a distance away but not too far. They would lunch at the Ritz Carlton overlooking a cliff which overlooked the Pacific Ocean. It was a beautiful drive to Dana Point along the Pacific Coast Highway. She enjoyed the scenery as well as the cleanliness of the freeways and flower draped hillsides and of course the glistening sunshine on the Pacific Ocean dancing as if covered in glitter. She began to sing in her head, "This one glides above the ocean." She felt happy and gratified. She very much looked forward to being in the company of John again.

As she pulled into the parking lot near the front entrance, John, being the proverbial gentleman that he was, was waiting for her at the front entrance. He understood she was unfamiliar with many places in California and did not want her to feel uncomfortable arriving at a new location. He walked up to her car and assisted with her tennis gear, asking if she wanted something to eat or drink first before they began their match. Ava was appreciative of the offer but said she was fine. He brought her to the lockers where she could place her personal items and then off they headed to the courts.

Ava had not played tennis since being in California and was happy to begin with a rally to warm up. John agreed believing they should get an idea of each other's style and strength first. They began to play. John was a commendable opponent for Ava and they enjoyed their rally, including some of the blunders which they laughed hysterically over. He was a patient player and clearly was enjoying himself. He had a much better serve than Ava and consequently could win easily. Ava gave him a run for his money, however. She was no slouch on the tennis court. They truly were compatible players and genuinely enjoyed themselves. After their match they headed to the showers to change into their clothes and enjoy a lovely meal at the Ritz overlooking the cliff with a view of the Ocean. They laughed and talked and joked about some of the crazy strokes and maneuvers they performed on the court. John had brought his camera along and they took some photos on and off the court. He wanted to take Ava down to the beach so they could enjoy the surf. Ava said it would be fine but she would not go swimming since the Pacific was so cold.

John agreed so they headed to the lockers to change into their bathing suits for the pool. They headed to the beautiful crystal blue waters of the massive pool and splashed around. On several occasions John held Ava by her arms playfully as they joked pretending to dunk each other. John clearly was stronger but he was considerate of his strength and sometimes pretended Ava had him beat. In the midst of their laughter and fun John looked at Ava in a way she could sense he wanted to kiss her. She would not stop him even though it was a public display of affection with several people around. John was polite with his kisses not like the ones he gave her Friday night. She was relieved. She didn't necessarily care for public make-outs, that was not her style. He rested his back along the side of the pool with legs bent as if he was sitting a chair. He pulled Ava up onto his legs and held her by her tiny waist as she sat on his lap. She liked the feeling of his thighs on the backs of hers and she suspected he liked the feeling of her thighs on his. She held onto him with one arm wrapped around his shoulders and neck.

Anyone witnessing their movements and interaction could clearly tell that these two were genuinely in love with each other.

After their fun, they headed to their poolside chairs to towel off and lay in the sun. John asked Ava if she would like anything to drink. She could go for some bottled water and John ushered the waiter for two bottled waters. They sat in the warmth of the California sun holding hands and talking. Ava started to tell John about her upcoming panel work with The Institute of Noetic Sciences. He was impressed. He wanted to know more. She began to explain to him how it coincided with her research work in her psychology classes specifically focusing on consciousness and Autism. "Wow," he said, "that is mighty impressive work. How is someone so beautiful, so smart?" he asked. Ava smiled and said "thank you John but what about you? You are quite handsome and quite accomplished yourself. How do you do it?" He understood her sarcasm and appreciated it. He laughed out loud and apologetically said, "I didn't mean to offend you, I simply am amazed at your abilities. And even more than that how kind and sweet you are. How do you remain so focused and so much fun and seem so together about things?" I looked at him and all I could think of saying was, "John, there are greater things in Heaven and Earth that can be dreamt in our philosophies." He laughed and appreciated what he considered a "joke." I knew better of course. I felt confident that I would be able to have deep discussions with John without revealing a hint of my true identity. And if anything accidentally slipped out, I could easily make a joke of it.

The sun was beginning to set and it was beginning to get late. John asked me if I would like to get together next weekend for a trip to The Orange County Museum of Art in Newport Beach. It contained modern and contemporary works but he was curious to see their new exhibit. "I would love to, John." I replied. "I've never been to Newport Beach. I hear it is an interesting place." "Yes," he said, "and since you've never been there, why don't we make a day of it. We can plan a Noon entrance to the museum followed by lunch and then I can take you to the harbor. We might take in some shopping and then have dinner along the pier." I said, "it sounds wonderful." John immediately said, "I don't want you doing all that driving. Why don't I pick you up at your house and we'll take my car." I told him that was considerate of him. John reminded me we both had finals this upcoming week. I taking them and he was giving them. He was considerate in allowing us to take the week to study and prepare and would only call me on Wednesday to check in to see how I was doing but he also wanted to here my voice. I smiled at him and complimented him on his foresight and consideration. Secretly, I was ecstatic over the possibility of having such a potentially wonderful boyfriend and happy this was progressing along nicely. He will get to see where I live and we'll have the whole day together. I was full of joy. As our fun day alas came to an end we did a little snuggling and kissing in the parking lot and then I headed home filled with contentment and pleasure and very much looking forward to next weekend. I really liked John in so many ways. I could envision a perfectly wonderful relationship with him.

My week at work was uneventful and most of my time there was spent brushing up on my studies. My evenings were crammed with assignments for school along with my usual Zachary sessions, Yoga practice and meditations. I found myself falling asleep earlier than usual since I was working on so many research papers. Zachary appeared almost every night reading books to me. I could never figure out what books he was reading, however. I suspected it was to assist me in my studies.

CHAPTER 34

The Book

One night I decided to have a session with Zachary to ask about the books. I summoned him in my usual way and in his most comfortable corner of my living room where the silk fig tree stood, Zachary appeared with his predictable greeting of **FANOFU2**. I immediately said, "Hello Zachary. How have you been?" He said, **I AM**. I smiled at him and agreed, "Yes you are." I asked him what books he was reading to me during my sleep. His reply astonished me. **YOURS**, he said. "I raised my eyebrows in disbelief. Zachary, I have not written a book." He replied, **BUT YOU HAVE**. "OK, I'm not quite sure exactly what you mean but we have had discussions about this before and I considered the possibility that my journals would be turned into a book one day based on those discussions. Is this what you are reading back to me?" **YES**. "I'm quite amazed over the possibility and I do trust in your guidance. I suppose my journals would make for some interesting reading but as you can see, I have very little time for that now. I also have an additional research project coming up for the summer months with IONS. I cannot imagine how I would find the time. I am also developing a relationship with John whom I wish to spend a great deal of time with as you know." Zachary replied, **I KNOW. HE IS ANOTHER DIMENSION TO YOUR GROWTH AND UNDERSTANDING OF HUMANITY**. "Yes," I replied, "he is that indeed." Zachary interjected with Y**OU WILL KNOW WHEN THE TIME IS RIGHT FOR YOUR BOOK.** "Thank you Zachary. I appreciate your insight and your devotion to my experience here in the Earth plane. Is there any possibility that you might give me a glimpse into what the finished book contains?" **I WILL SHOW YOU IN YOUR DREAM IF YOU ASK**. "Okay, thank you Zachary. I will make that request."

I concluded my day with Yoga and meditation and fell into a deep sleep but not after writing about my session with Zachary. During my sleep I began to experience a Lucid dream:

> "A book was dangling in midair but it was too far away for her to read any of the words. I asked if the book could be brought closer and on my request, the book began to move in midair closer to me. I once again requested, closer please, and the book continued to move closer until I could read the words.... I got as far as the words 'with FISH' and with the excitement of the reality of the lucidity of the dream and my ability to read it, I immediately snapped out of the dream!"

Ava was so disappointed that she was unable to maintain her vibrational energy which allowed the dream to end, she awoke with sadness and frustration. But quickly realized with great excitement that she had had this very same dream years ago! She searched through her journals for it and eventually found it. It was exactly the same dream. There had to be some significance to it being repeated especially in light of her request of Zachary to show her the book she was to write.

She thought and wondered what in the world does "with FISH" mean? There had to be a correlation to the dream being repeated especially after asking Zachary to show her the book. Well, it was still the middle of the night and Ava was tired and fell back into a deep sleep.

As Wednesday arrived, Ava submitted her final papers for her classes and was pleased with their contents. She felt confident with the material and look forward to receiving all A's. She was fascinated by the study of genetics knowing that every cell in your body is multi-dimensional but the human awareness is only trained to live within the limitations and restrictions of the three-dimensional matrix. She had sourced this material from Aurora Ray whose book on the topic was truly insightful and had Ava wondering if Aurora herself might have been a Light Being possessing this multi-dimensional knowledge.

The experience of different dimensions is one that goes hand in hand with the shift in consciousness that many people, in Ava's opinion, were beginning to experience but possessed some apprehension about still. Ava was confident that her work at IONS would nourish these concepts and hoped that IONS was able to secure the author Eileen Seiler who understood that science is now moving closer to documenting the effects of other dimensional realities. Ava would covertly and ably suggest these existential theories from her very own gifted reality. She knew with IONS the exploration of consciousness transformation would be an exciting research field leading to the gradual but steady human evolution without such things as "good" and "bad" or "right" or "wrong".

The phone rang and as Ava answered, John's sweet cheerful greeting made her smile. "Hi John. I'm so glad you called. How is your week going so far?" She could hear the happiness in his voice. He was glad that she had her work submitted and he could tell that she was excited about its contents. He wondered since the pressure was gone from her school work, if she would like to get together for an early, light dinner so he could hear all about the material. Ava was pleased about the suggestion and they agreed to meet at a nearby bistro in the Laguna Hills.

She selected casual yellow slacks and a white short sleeved ribbed cotton pull over with the cutest pair of yellow ballet slip ons to wear. She wanted to wear the very stylish silk scarf she recently bought that matched her slacks perfectly. It made the outfit complete. Throwing a light coverup over her shoulders in case it got breezy, she was off to meet John. She liked the feeling of being with him. He was so handsome and fun and easy to be around.

There was no valet service at the bistro and Ava felt more than comfortable now walking across the parking lot to meet her man. At least she was hoping their relationship would develop to that status. John was not yet at the bistro so Ava secured them a quiet table in the corner and only had to wait about five minutes before a very handsome, casually dressed John walked in and immediately saw her. They both smiled at each other as John sat down and began talking about their finals. John was tired from all the grading and reading but he always had time and attention for Ava. He felt rejuvenated when he was with her. He was fascinated by her energy and the aura she presented but Ava knew it was her essence from her Light Being status that drew him in. It was not something they would ever discuss. It simply was not possible. The higher state of vibration is nothing that can be explained but only felt.

John began discussing some of the antics his students had written in their papers almost in a critical manner but Ava did appreciate the humor. "What a shame she said" to John. "Sometimes humans miss the point but they, nevertheless have their perspective and views from their level of consciousness." John was surprised by Ava's use of the word "human". He joked with her and said, "You sound like you're from another planet Ava" and started laughing. Ava simply said, "No, no, John, I mean people, you know. People all exist within different levels of knowledge and are always valued for their perspective." John laughed and said, "I quite understand that you are heavily into your research and are probably still in scholastic mode. It is okay honey. I understand." She smiled at the sound of him calling her honey and was grateful for his insight. She needed to be careful using that word "human" as if she were not one. For the most part, she was half and half.

She continued to tell him about her research papers and John was simply out of his league on this subject matter. As brilliant as he was from a creative and academic perspective, he could not quite grasp the existential ideas that fascinated Ava. It didn't bother her. John was an intelligent, seasoned man who could converse on many topics with her but the world of existentialism was a far reaching concept for most humans to relate to.

After dinner, John asked Ava to sit with him in his car for a bit before they headed home. John wanted to hold Ava in his arms; he wanted to be close to her; he wanted to smell her; he wanted to caress her face and give her long passionate kisses on her mouth and neck. Ava had no objections. She became extremely aroused and allowed the feelings to move her through the vibration of passion and heated sexual excitement. Her mind kept wandering as if they were in bed together and imagined what it would feel like. She felt like a school girl being kissed for the first time. Ava and John clearly had a deep passion for each other and she knew it would not be long before they would experience their full sexual desires for one another.

They began to revise their plans for this upcoming Saturday and John wanted to make a simple change to their day. He admitted his feelings for Ava and asked if she would mind if they shortened their day and planned a return to his house for the explicit purpose of a romantic evening together in front of the fireplace. Ava told him that it would be more wonderful than anything she could imagine. She was in full agreement so to speak that they would consummate their relationship. She was only upset that she would have so long to wait.

When she arrived home that evening, the phone rang. Ava answered and it was John. He told her that he could not stop thinking about her. She smiled and said she had the same wonderful thoughts about him. He was looking forward to having the summer off allowing him to have more time with her. They would go sailing; swimming; and maybe head up to Napa Valley for a weekend. Ava was a little taken off guard and told John that she didn't have Summers off. She would still be working at her office job as well as on the IONS project. "I hope that does not disappoint you, John." He said, "Oh that's right. Well, we'll be fine nevertheless. I respect your work and I will remain forever hopeful that you will have time for me." "Of course I will John." "I will have more time because I am not taking summer classes because of IONS."

"Do you know what specific project you will be working on at IONS?" he asked. "Well, I know that it will be in the development of consciousness and human evolution but other than that I do not know the specifics. Tonight coming home, I just received a letter from IONS asking me to meet with them this Monday at 3:00 PM to discuss the project and my area of focus. I'll have to leave work a little early. I'm rather excited about the meeting." John simply stated "you never cease to amaze me Ava, there are so many levels to you and I admire your enthusiasm and thirst for knowledge. I sure do hope I continue to excite you." "Oh John, do not ever say that. You are very dear to me and I have a great appreciation for you." John replied, "I hope so Ava, I've become quite fond of you and I have high hopes for us." Ava smiled over his comment and in return reassured him that she felt the same towards him. She was excited about their future. "My mind races about the possibilities of our experiences together John. I look forward to a mutually gratifying experience with you." "Well, I'm so very pleased to hear that Ava, it puts my mind to rest. I'm never sure what you will explore next that will take you even further from exploring a life with me." "John, there is no reason you should be concerned about that. You will only project that into your reality. Fear is detrimental to one's soul. You would not want to manifest that possibility, please for both our sakes." John could only reply "Ava your are like a puzzle within an enigma." "Not really John, Ava told him. "I am a very conscious being who understands the laws of physics and how in that understanding, we create our reality". With that said, Ava was forbidden to reveal any more of what she knew for fear of disclosing her true identity. Again finding herself juggling her dual reality but this time in an intimate relationship which posed its own set of challenges.

John replied telling Ava that she was a deep thinker and he could benefit from her way of looking at life albeit, he wasn't sure it would make a difference to him now. Now that he was set in his ways and the only imagined enthusiasm for his future was enjoying the grace and beauty of Ava in his life. Ava told John that we never stop growing, we never stop changing, we are continually evolving from our experiences and we possess the power to make any change in our lives that we wish to make. John felt injected with hope after hearing her words. More than ever he was assured that she was extremely crucial to his happiness and without even experiencing physical intimacy, was beginning to fall in love with her.

Ava and John ended their phone conversation with excitement about their upcoming date this Saturday both knowing it would be a turning point in their relationship. Ava hung up the phone smiling and imagining how wonderful Saturday would be. She continued on with her evening routine of Yoga and meditation and looked forward to a night of sweet dreams. As she fell into the first stages of twilight sleep, she could hear a U2 song playing in her mind. "I have climbed highest mountains..... I have spoke with a ton of angels..... but I still haven't found what I'm looking for". She didn't question it, she just enjoyed the sound of it and drifted off into dreamland.

Ava awoke the next morning with a smile on her face and thoughts on her mind from a Fractal Enlightenment paper she had recently read:

"What I'm going to feel is what I have to decide. Manifestations come on the heels of what you've conjured in thought". Ava understood the nuances of daily human existence. Inspiration comes in many forms whether it be from another's words; dreams; melodies; books; visions, art. Inspiration is all around and she was grateful for her astute wisdom and divine guidance, knowing she was once one who did the inspiring and quickly realized that she was still actually inspiring humans only now in human form herself. She chuckled at the circular communion of all levels of being. If only humanity could come to this awakening they could understand that truly we are simply all ONE.

As Ava drove to her job at Orion, she turned on her car radio and much to her realization of unseen forces, she heard, for the first time, U2's newest song, "ONE". She was filled with a sense of her character of truth. Her eyes began to well up with tears from the soulful words being sung confirming her recent thoughts in addition to affirming that U2 were indeed an extremely exceptional source of spirituality brought to humanity for its growth.

Inspired by the words, Ava began to understand the meaning of her life. She had once, of course, ascended to what she considered the peak of her spiritual level to only turn around and descend back to Earth for a greater purpose. That purpose being to raise humanity to the gifts that awaited them.

Ava found it difficult to focus on her mundane chores at work. She wanted to continue writing in her journal exploring the meaning behind the recent events of her week and wanted to speak to Zachary. She had John on her mind and was full of anticipation about Saturday night as well as her meeting with IONS Monday afternoon. These events were the true meaning of becoming an evolved human being otherwise her own evolution of purpose would be left incomplete.

In spite of her preoccupation with more gratifying creative thoughts, Ava made it through her day and was now eager to drop by the university to receive her final grades. She also needed to formulate some notes for her meeting with IONS that upcoming Monday. Most of her thoughts however were on John and what pleasures her day with him would bring.

Ava came to learn that she received a final grade point average of 4.0. She was pleased and look forward to signing up for additional classes next fall and completed a successful outline of how her contributions to society would benefit both herself and humanity for the IONS meeting. Daily life sure can get in the way of successful development in the areas that matter most she thought, unless of course your daily work life is your passion and purpose. With that thought she secretly wondered if a switch in paths was potentially signaling to her that she would no longer be using the corporate world as a means to enjoy her passions, but rather making her passions her means of supporting herself. She smiled at the prospect and it gave her insight into how important IONS was going to be for her to complete her mission. She would sail on the expanse of her mind and provide the winds of change for those who chose to follow.

Ava felt the need to summon Zachary upon arriving home. He appeared near the silk fig tree with a smile and a greeting of FANOFU2. “Well, Zachary, what do you think? Do you believe my interpretation of my thoughts earlier today was spot on?” Zachary beamed with acknowledgement and replied WELL DONE. YOU ARE FINDING EASE INCORPORATING YOUR HUMANITY WITH YOUR SPIRITUALITY AND WILL FIND LESS NEED FOR ME. “Oh no, Zachary!” Ava exclaimed. “I will always need you. Please don’t ever leave me.” Zachary replied, I AM FOREVER YOURS. Ava sighed with relief. “Thank you Zachary. I feel like a baby learning to walk” Ava told him. Zachary acknowledge her statement and added SOON YOU WILL FLY.

Ava smiled as Zachary dematerialized. She was grateful to have such a wonderful source of comfort and camaraderie in Zachary and knew he always had her back. He would always be ready to assist whenever she needed him.

CHAPTER 35

The Melding of Two Souls

Ava's Saturday with John had finally arrived and since they would be heading to Newport Beach for a relaxing museum visit and some shopping, she decided to wear a light weight sun dress and matching ballet shoes. She loved fashion and took great pride in the clothes she chose to wear never loosing sight of the fact that she had a great looking body that wore them well. She also packed a very special neglige for their romantic evening in front of the fireplace.

John rang her doorbell exactly at Noon. He was casually dressed and looked quite dashing. They smiled at each other and embraced with a gentle kiss on the lips. Ava was proud to show him her apartment which impressed him and found her decorating style completely in line with her personality. He said he wasn't all that surprised at how lovely everything looked. After all, it was her home and only the best would do for such an elegant lady. Ava blushed a little and before long, they headed to his car for their drive to Newport Beach. It was a lovely sunny day and they enjoyed the scenery as they listened to U2's music that Ava brought along. John liked U2 and considered them quite a force to be reckoned with. This took Ava by surprise but she was happy he felt that way. She talked about the concerts she had attended and how she was able to meet them. John was surprised but on second thought said that Ava could do anything. She was not afraid of being forthright and achieving anything she set her mind to.

Ava asked John if he had ever been to Joshua Tree in the Mojave Desert. He had not. Ava wanted them to go together. It will be a wonderful experience John and I would love to take more pictures there especially with you in them. He smiled and agreed. They quickly decided that the following weekend they would go. Ava did not feel John would be receptive, at least not at this stage, to the experiences she had there and it wasn't important. What was important was that they were there together. They talked about school being finished and John was very pleased that Ava received a 4.0 average for her work and dedication.

Arriving at Newport Beach, Ava was enthralled by the city which was an upscale community, well kept with many fun amenities to offer. Initially, they had lunch at an outdoor cafe along the Pier. They watched the sailboats and yachts drifting lazily along the Harbor and they even saw a wedding reception taking place on one of those yachts. What a lovely idea Ava thought. After lunch they walked arm in arm and headed to the museum to enjoy the exhibit called "ExplorOcean" which was an interactive experience designed to teach visitors about the seven principals of ocean literacy and the maritime history of the area. Ava loved it and was taking pictures for her scrapbook. She was quite impressed that the museum also had an Arts Commission that offered outdoor performances of Shakespeare by the Sea. She told John that they must definitely attend some of them. John agreed and loved that Ava and he had so many interests in common. He very much looked forward to attending some of these performances with her.

They held hands often and stole a few kisses in between their excursion and by 4:00 PM were ready to head back to Laguna Hills for their special evening together. It was a refreshing delightful day and it would be recorded in Ava's journal as quite memorable.

Arriving at John's house, Ava could appreciate how beautiful the grounds were kept and how lovely his home was. It was definitely sleek and comfortable. "John, she asked, do you have a maid to clean this very large house"? John said, "Oh yes. It is really too big for me and I've considered downsizing. I don't know what possessed me to buy it in the first place. I guess after my wife passed away and not wanting to live surrounded by all the memories, I jumped on the first house I liked. Now I realize it's too big and I need a maid and a gardener and a pool maintenance firm. It is out of hand at this point". Ava said, "You have a pool?" "Yes, it is great exercise and would be even more fun with a lovely lady to share it with." And he smiled.

John led me to the guest room with its own bathroom for me to shower and change and said he too would also like to freshen up. He had some Champaign on ice and some finger foods if we got hungry for snacks. He continued to light the gas fireplace and I shouted out to him if he could put Beethoven on the stereo. He complied. I was so nervous. I had to take deep breaths. I kept imagining this for weeks and now it was finally here. I felt like a bundle of nerves but I knew I wanted him with all my body. What a feeling of anticipation and wonder. I guessed that he was feeling the same way. I had to keep taking deep breaths to center my energy.

Finally, I walked out into the living room which was dimly lit with soft Beethoven playing on the stereo. The fireplace was sensual and inviting and John was sitting on the floor in front of it with a look of love on his face. He had Champagne with two glasses already filled and I quickly decided to sit close to him and snuggle up under his arm and chest. I asked him if he was nervous and he said yes but he wasn't going to let that spoil his wanting me. We smiled at each other and embraced in a long passionate kiss. He placed his strong arm behind my head and back and gently laid me down on the pillows. He began to caress my shoulders and ribs and waist. He was strong and filled with a fire that ignited the flames within me.

He kissed my neck and shoulders and pretended to bite them.

He softly told me "I had sensual shoulders and he loved them". He brushed my hair back from my face and kissed every inch of it. He held me tight and was breathing heavy from the anticipation of penetrating me. I wrapped my legs around his waist as I opened his robe and realized that he was completely naked. I touched his chest and back and brought my hands down to his hips. We thrusted back and forth in complete boiling passion for each other yet not actually having begun the act of physical sex. We were exploring each other's bodies and energy and grew more and more aroused by the thoughts of our eventual consummation. John was very hard and beginning to moan for gratification and the pleasure of penetrating me. He cradled me in his arms and lifted me up and walked to his bedroom. As he placed me on his bed I could tell he had an exciting physique that I wanted to consume me. He laid himself on top of me and with one hand opened my thigh to ready himself for penetration all the while moaning for the gratification of my steaming, wet source of pleasure. As he drove himself into me, I could feel my entire body charge with an exciting energy. We kissed deeply and held each other tightly. He held the small of my back with each penetration and squeezed my buttocks as if it were putty. I screamed with an orgasm that took my breath away as John released his desire and passion into me. I could feel my entire body flow with a tingling vibration like a wave of morphine running through it. We gave each other sweet satisfying kisses and held each other tightly as we began to regain our senses. I rested the side of my face on his chest as he cradled me in his arms. What joy, what pleasure, what great sexual energy I thought to myself. This man is magnetic and I could do this over and over again. I loved the heights of ecstasy he brought me to and I loved how my body and mind felt completely out of my control because of this magnificent lover. John spoke first and said, "That was amazing. I could eat you up." He hadn't ever experienced such sexual gratification and pleasure like that in his entire life he admitted wanting me so badly from the day I first sat across from him in the school cafeteria.

As we continued to talk he caressed my breasts and began to kiss them. He loved how plump and firm they were and it aroused a very sensual sensation that began my desires for him again. We kissed and explored each part of each other's bodies gently messaging and touching. He rolled me on my stomach and caressed my sensual back licking it all the way down to the small part below my waist providing a sensation much like an erogenous zone. Our rhythmic playful exploration grew into another heated passionate need that could not be controlled or contained. John thrust himself into me again and we began to reach heights of explosive ecstasy one more time.

After some refreshments and a playful shower together, John knew that Ava was not prepared to stay the night. He understood that was not in their plans and would not infringe upon her work and study program even though it was really what he wanted. He gave her the option however and Ava did let him know that she needed to get back home even though she really did want to stay.

John drove Ava back home and they said goodnight to each other after many long kisses. He waited for her to enter her front door and drove away. Ava was completely and totally mesmerized by their experience together. She could not stop thinking of the moments in each other's embrace. She knew she needed to perform her meditation to gain a sense of balance but it was going to be difficult to concentrate. Nevertheless, she initiated her meditation and much to her surprise it was better than ever. It made her realize that being human was also about being present in all its experiences and fulfilling all the needs of a human, sex being part of that. And now, she had John to fulfill that aspect, both emotionally, intellectually, and physically. How fortunate she was indeed.

Ava drifted off to sleep, much too sleepy to record the experience in her journal. Instead she chose to savor the day's joy into what she imagined would be a splendidly content night's sleep.

Upon awakening Ava did not recall any dreams. She smiled with thoughts of John on her mind and she planned for her day's activities. There were of course the usual chores but somehow they all seemed trivial and easy to accomplish now.

She called Sheila who she knew would be pantingly waiting to hear about last evening. They talked about Ava's day and how wonderful the evening turned out. Sheila squealed with glee and started chanting, "Ava has a boyfriend, Ava has a boyfriend." Ava just laughed and accepted Sheila's giddy albeit immature behavior. After all, Sheila was a good friend and only wanted the best for Ava. They decided to get together for a roller blading session through Laguna Canyon in an hour and have some lunch out by the beach.

Ava wanted to be in her best form for her meeting with IONS on Monday and so decided to take a personal day off from work. She hadn't missed a day yet and thought it would be okay to do. Decision made. She missed John and decided to call him to see how he was. John answered the phone and said "Hello honey!" Ava loved that. She wanted to hear his voice and know how he was doing. "I have not been able to take my mind off of you Ava. I had such a wonderful day and evening with you. I hope we have many more in our future." Ava reassured John that she had every intention of a repeat performance and they both laughed. He was heading out to play golf at the country club with some buddies and wouldn't be able to spend much time on the phone with her now but wanted to know if it was okay if he called her later that evening. She understood and was looking forward to hearing back from him.

Ava and Sheila had a wonderful time rollerblading through the canyon and stopped along the PCH for a bite to eat. They were both starved. Ava asked Sheila if she knew of any nice boutiques along the PCH so she could pick up some alluring evening lounge wear. Sheila squealed and said, "Yes, I know a great little shop just up the way." They headed to the boutique with roller blades swung over their shoulders and for the first time Ava felt like a real Californian. Sheila helped her pick out some alluring evening wear but tasteful and classy, just the way Ava liked it. She couldn't wait to wear them for John and wondered when they would be together again. Sheila and Ava headed back through the canyon on their roller blades again until they reached her house. Sheila got into her car and smiled and winked at Ava and said "have a good time"! Ava giggled.

It was getting dark and as Ava entered her apartment the phone was ringing. She ran to reach it and it was John. "Hi sweetheart." "Oh, I've graduated from honey to sweetheart I see." John told her he could not stop thinking of her all day and his buddies wondered what he was so preoccupied about. It was his worse golf score ever. They laughed and she apologized. He asked her if she was hungry and would be in the mood for a pizza and a movie at her house. She was excited to hear his words and agreed almost immediately. She told John she had been roller blading and needed time to shower and get ready. He asked if he could come by in an hour and she agreed. Ava could only think of the sweetness of being near his skin again and having him touching her in only a way he knew how. She couldn't wait to wear one of her new lounging yet tantalizing outfits for him.

An hour passed and the doorbell rang. Ava answered it and John was standing there holding a pizza and a bottle of wine. He said "did you order a pizza Miss?" She laughed and grabbed him by his waist and coerced him into the apartment saying I ordered more than that! As they laughed they entered the living room where Ava had a fire going in the fireplace and the coffee table was set up for their meal. They kissed passionately as if they had not seen each other in weeks. He complimented Ava on her pretty negligee and commented that she looked way better than the pizza for dinner. Laughing they prepared to sit and dine while they watched their movie. Before the movie barely got started, John began to massage Ava's neck and shoulders and she reciprocated likewise. They clearly could not keep their hands off of each other and their mounting passion brought them quickly to the bedroom where they made passionate, exciting love igniting all the sensuality they could individually and collectively feel in their act of lovemaking. John whispered in Ava's ear, "Would it be okay if I spent the night?" Ava smiled and told him it would be wonderful to fall asleep wrapped in his arms. She told him she was not planning on working the next day so that she could be fresh and energetic for her meeting at 3:00 PM with IONS. John told Ava that "she was glowing. You look so young and almost not human, Ava. I hope I always bring this beauty out in you." Ava smiled almost naughtily knowing she must look radiant because of this human sexual experience this Light Being was enjoying.

They realized the movie had ended hours ago and they never even watched it. The pizza was cold by now but it didn't matter. They cleaned up and prepared for a shower together where they enjoyed each other yet one more time. They walked over to her bed and cuddled under the blankets holding each other tightly until they drifted off to sleep.

When morning came John got up first to make coffee and breakfast. Ava woke to the smell of fresh coffee and bacon and stretched and yawned and smiled. What a wonderful man. She searched for her bathrobe to join him in the kitchen but could not find it. Throwing on a sweat shirt and tights she walked into the kitchen to find John wearing her bathrobe. She laughed and laughed. "My you do wear some strange clothes for such a virile lover." "I hope you don't mind Ava, I couldn't think of anything else to put on other than wrapping a towel and that would be tacky." "I agree, she said, "remind me to sign you up for best dressed category." As they ate their breakfast they discussed the day ahead.

Ava was a little nervous but was well prepared. She went over some of her notes with John at the breakfast table explaining how she wished to be part of this panel that would invoke a different approach to viewing Autism suggesting that it potentially could be a natural progression of human evolution. John didn't understand the concept but had full confidence in Ava's understanding and abilities to grab attention in this new line of thinking. Some of what she said made him consider this as a possibility but without the proper background training he could not relate completely to why this would be viewed as a natural course in our evolution. He wanted to hear from her as soon as her meeting was over. He would be waiting with bated breath.

John was going to do some grocery shopping and some reading during his day but mostly wondering how Ava was doing. He knew they would be talking on the phone later that evening about her meeting and was anxious for her that it would go just the way she planned. After cleaning up the breakfast dishes and the living room, John left for his day of chores and relaxation and kissed Ava passionately as he left.

As Ava showered she began a mental review of all the various aspects of her presentation over and over. She was not nervous, she was excited and had a very hopeful almost instinctual feeling that this road was the one she would find most rewarding and fulfilling. She selected her outfit and carefully put her briefcase together with all the materials she would need.

She began to reflect back on her life as a human, how it began, how she had transformed and by now it felt like it was a distant memory. She had gained the confidence, direction and happiness through her guidance in dreams, through Zachary, through her belief in being who she was in spite of the fact that she was existing in a dual reality. She had kept it together through her wisdom and grace as well as an appreciation for her divine guidance and her desire to KNOW.

CHAPTER 36

Meeting IONS

Ava walked up to the receptionist in this very futuristic looking building feeling as if she entered a different world. The heightened level of energy was palpable. Immediately she felt like she was floating and remembered the sensation she felt when she first met her mall angel. Interesting, there must be some very enlightened souls here. I think I have found a home. She introduced herself and informed the young woman behind the desk that she was here for a 3:00 PM appointment with Dr. Grace Lynch. "Oh yes Miss St. Claire, we are expecting you. Won't you please sign in and have a seat. I'll let Dr. Lynch know you are here." "Thank you," Ava said.

Dr. Lynch arrived in the reception area and greeted Ava with a warm smile and friendly handshake. She led Ava to a conference room where two other doctors were in attendance. After introductions, Dr. Lynch began to explain to Ava the purpose of their meeting expressing deep interest in Ava's school research papers on psychology and human consciousness. Ava was told that she had a very unique and unconventional view of integrating sources of knowledge of the human anatomy, spiritualism and consciousness and thought she could assist in making great contributions to a specific research project IONS was developing. Dr. Lynch had mentioned that the project involved the subject of Autism and was very impressed on Ava's paper suggesting the possibility that this diagnosis was not one of a disability but instead one of heightened abilities instead.

Their receptivity to her ideas brought Ava a sense of inner strength and knowing and she anticipated a powerful and transformational contribution to the project. What Ava didn't realize was that Dr. Lynch wanted her to head the research spearheading her ideas after submitting an outline of approach. Ava wanted to ask for more details, but Dr. Lynch obviously had great confidence in her and continued by asking Ava's schedule and availability to join the team. Dr. Lynch felt it was imperative that Ava spend as much time as she could afford on the project. She was actually offering Ava a job at the Institute! Ava couldn't believe it. Dr. Lynch added that her schooling would need to continue in order to receive her doctorate degree and she would be provided with tuition reimbursement. Ava would be saying goodbye to Orion. She knew it was simply a carry over position anyway until the real passion would enter her life and now, on both fronts - a job that would allow her to develop her theories on the next stage in human evolution and finding the love of her life in John. Does it get any better than this she wondered?

Ava expressed willingness and excitement being selected for this groundbreaking work. She was indeed willing to provide input for an outline to incorporate all facets of the experiment and felt a surge of energy flood her body which only she could understand was an acknowledgment of universal cellular knowing. She had found her purpose and was going to make a difference.

Dr. Grace Lynch reviewed more of the details of the project and laid out a timetable to guide Ava for when her input would be evaluated. Ava suggested a plan of approach for the project and Dr. Lynch happily provided Ava with the on-boarding paperwork for IONS welcoming her to the organization. They discussed the date for their next meeting which would be in one week. After exchanging pleasantries, they stood up and shook hands. Ava tried to remain fixed to the floor because she felt like she wanted to fly.

On her way to her car believing her feet were not even touching the ground, she couldn't wait to call John and tell him the outcome of her meeting/interview. It was so wonderful to share these experiences with him because he was truly happy for her and excited about her goals.

Ava understood that she was not playing this human game for power but rather with the power of her gift of the human condition in unison with her awareness of enlightened knowledge. If humans play for power their game will eventually end but if you play with your powers the games continue and therein lies the evolution of humanity to its fullest potential. Humanities' horizons were without limit if they could know their experience as spiritual beings. Her work with IONS would lead to humanities embarking on an immortality project and become a part of something that would last forever, beyond death.

Immediately upon arriving home, Ava ran to the phone and called John. Ava was talking so excitedly and so fast, John had to slow her down. "Wait, wait, Ava. I can't understand what you're saying. Honey, slow down. You mean they offered you a job?" he asked. "Yes, they did", replied Ava. "I will be working on Autism incorporating my theories into their research. I cannot believe how marvelous this feels. They will reimburse my tuition as I continue to my doctorate. Can you believe it John? I'm going to be working for IONS." John laughed and said, "Honey, they'll be working for you soon enough." And they both laughed. "Oh John, this is going to be groundbreaking work and open doors to new possibilities in the realm of human consciousness."

John said, "I think this calls for a celebration Ava. I know you have to report to work tomorrow but how about I come over with a nice dinner and we celebrate?" Ava immediately agreed. She wanted to share every moment of her success with John whom she knew understood how truly fulfilling it was for her. He knew the hard work she put into this and was genuinely happy for her and what better way to celebrate than embraced in the arms of the man she loved.

Ava tried to calm her nerves. She took a hot shower and prepared for her man. She set up the coffee table in the living room in front of the fireplace and selected some very sexy music by Enigma for the stereo. They both loved chamber music and Gregorian chant and this would sooth both their energy fields while enhancing their already heightened sexual passion for each other. Oh what a wonderful day and evening this is she thought to herself. It's good to be human.

John and Ava had a most incredible evening enjoying a wonderful meal and great wine sitting in front of the fireplace enjoying each other's sexuality and desires for each other. As time clicked by, John knew to respect Ava's alarm clock in the morning and was sad to have to say goodnight and not have her wrapped in his arms while they slept. He did have to respect her schedule. Ava asked that he call her when he arrived home so she would be able to say goodnight one more time. He agreed and said this weekend they would dine out at the restaurant of their first date in honor of her success. She smiled, she liked that idea. They said goodnight to each other and embraced in a long passionate kiss and John told her the words that she wanted to hear, "I love you Ava, you are my angel". Ava told John she loved him too.

Even though Ava was quite exhausted from her exciting day, she still wanted to summon Zachary to share with him her good fortune. Zachary appeared at the fig tree in the corner of her living room. He greeted Ava as always, FANOFU2. For the first time Ava questioned Zachary about his greeting wondering if he was a fan of the rock group or a fan of her? He smiled and said, **WORDS HAVE MANY MEANINGS AVA, IN THIS CASE IT IS AN EXPRESSION OF BOTH THOUGHTS AND PERCEPTION.** Ava smiled at him in satisfaction. "Zachary, I am curious about what I have created in this present human existence and I know my question to you may sound like one of doubt, but I am not in doubt. I am simply examining the reality that I am currently experiencing as one which I truly created in this time centuries ago or is it indeed one I am creating now because of my Light Being experiences?" Zachary responded **YOUR CONTINUED PRACTICE OF YOGA AND MEDITATION KEEPS YOU ON TRACK AND IN TUNE WITH AWARENESS OF YOUR DUAL REALITIES. YOU COULD NOT HAVE EXPERIENCED THIS EVENT CENTURIES AGO BECAUSE THERE WAS NO AWARENESS OF THE CONSCIOUSNESS OF INDIGO CHILDREN AND AUTISM, OTHERWISE YOU WOULD NOT HAVE BEEN BROUGHT BACK NOW FOR THIS MISSION.**

Ava's eyes opened wide. She did understand Zachary's words. In a sense she was receiving confirmation that indeed her coming back as a human was for a mighty specific consciousness altering purpose and proudly yet secretly wore her badge of honor. She felt empowered by Zachary's words and felt a shift in her own abilities and the future of humanity. She could also feel the weight and responsibility of her mission but was honored to make this contribution.

Ava decided she mentally could not handle more. Her head was spinning and so she thanked Zachary and bid him a good evening. She did require a meditation process before retiring but could not find the energy to write in her journal. She decided she would do so at work the next day. She then prepared for bed and fell quickly into a peaceful sleep.

When Ava awoke, she was mesmerized by her dream. She promptly began recording her it in her journal:

> "That little boy whom appeared in my dream several weeks ago instructing me in the classroom and then taking me on a journey has appeared again in my dream. I was with him in the clouds and reached for a section of a complex metal object that I could not define. I

dislodged a portion of it and handed it to the boy with an understanding that this was going to help him immensely along with others of like nature."

Ava was puzzled by this object. She could only sense it was part of the matrix of life. She had never seen anything like it and wondered what purpose it served. It wasn't often that Ava was confounded. No time to focus on this now. She needed to get to work.

CHAPTER 37

Leaving Orion

Ava resigned from Orion as soon as she arrived and explained about the awesome opportunity that had come her way for a position at IONS. Everyone was happy for her but Sheila was shocked. Sheila could not believe that Ava had not confided in her about her plans. She explained to Sheila that her studies and research had led her on this course without her even realizing it. She did not know IONS was preparing to offer her a position. Sheila was happy for Ava but disappointed that she would not pal around with Ava at Orion any longer. Ava suggested to Sheila that she herself might want to consider another career for herself.

Sheila was so very interested in animals and had such an empathetic nature toward them that she might want to consider that course of study. "The world is yours for the taking" she told Sheila. Sheila's eyes brightened and you could tell she had begun to consider the possibility. "After all," Sheila said, "if you could do it, why couldn't I." "That's the spirit Sheila, we'll always be friends and share our adventures together." Sheila wanted to take Ava to lunch that day to celebrate and talk about her new job. Ava agreed but knew she wanted to write in her journal and do some research.

But did not want to be inconsiderate of Sheila's offer after she had just gone through the shock of her news. Ava agreed to lunch and thanked her for the offer.

Ava was happy to be leaving Orion to work on her passion and reflected on what Zachary's comments were the night before. She began to realize the reason for her dream with that little boy. Zachary was revealing that her own consciousness was firmly focused in her human experience and that the dream state focus was a separate consciousness altogether, hence the phasing in and out without being aware of it and being sure to keep track of it.

Ava began to suspect her dream states were connecting her to a multitude of realities and could be used as an insightful source of knowledge enhancing her effectiveness within the reality she lived daily. She suspected the little boy in her dream would play a significant role in her work at IONS. She may have been giving him the "key" to a DNA sequence that may alter his abilities or possibly even the other way round and with that thought, she laughed. Yes, her initial suspicions were coming full circle about Autism - altering humanities perception, not as a misfortunate act of birth but the evolution of humanity to a completely higher level of consciousness - that of The Indigo Children.

Ava was writing so fast in her journal she could hardly keep up with her thoughts. She was ecstatic about her revelations and couldn't contain her excitement about her work at IONS. Her first day just couldn't get here fast enough. She decided to hit the library for some research on DNA sequencing.

First, she wanted to call John to check to see how he was doing but he sounded a little off. She wondered if he was not feeling well. He told her he was fine and that she should go ahead with her plans. "Are you sure John, because this can wait if you need me." John said sweetly, "Honey, I'm fine. Maybe just feeling a little tired." "OK," Ava reluctantly said. "I will call you later to be sure you don't need anything." "Thank you", he said. "I always want to hear from you. I love you Ava. You are the light of my life". Ava smiled but still felt there was an underlying tone of worry in his voice. She hung up after telling him she loved him and would talk later and then headed out to the library to research DNA material.

Ava delved into the world of genetics and its relation to the diagnosing of Autism as if her life depended on it. She came across a particular study that sent her energy soaring. ***In a genetics laboratory FISH is used on samples of blood, chorionic villi or other material containing cells. FISH enables scientists to visualize the location of particular genes or DNA sequence to check for a variety of chromosomal abnormalities which may cause a genetic condition.***

If Ava hadn't been in the library she would have screamed out loud. She couldn't believe the synchronicity of her lucid dream from years ago and again very recently reading the words "with Fish" and the discovery of a genetics test called FISH. Zachary was so right on so many different levels, from the pairing of multiple worlds of consciousness to the book he was reading her telling her it was her book! After calming herself again, she read more and took notes. By now, hours had passed and she wanted to head home to call John again. She was hoping he was okay and was looking forward to a wonderfully pleasant evening with him even if it meant she would care for him if he was coming down with a cold.

Maybe they could snuggle and watch a movie and she would make him some chicken soup. How truly lucky she had been to have met him and develop a warm, loving, respectful relationship with him. They each added new dimension to each other's worlds. She smiled as she drove home thinking of their relationship.

When Ava arrived home, she plopped her research materials down and ran to the phone to call John. He answered with a happy tone and they agreed on a time he would pick her up for their celebration dinner. She was happy to hear that he sounded better but could sense there was something different in his tone of voice. She pretended to ignore it and was hoping to have a better feeling when they were together in a short while.

When John did come by to pick Ava up he put on a very happy face and they kissed passionately. They were both excited to be together and headed to the restaurant where they had their first date. An awful feeling came over Ava which she couldn't understand. This is the first place of our first date and it will be our last. How horrifying! Why would she think such a thing? Ava knew better because of her abilities but didn't want to admit to herself there was a reason she was sensing such a negative thought. She knew she was deliberately denying the reality that this potentially could be their last date. She became angry with herself and it began to show. John asked her if she was okay. He was beginning to detect her agitation and took her hand in his and kept it there as he drove. She tried to free her mind of the negative thoughts but understood the energy she was picking up was really John's energy. Something was up and she would have to be quite the actor to get through this evening. Ava smiled as he held her hand and asked if he would like to listen to some music. He said, "No honey, right now I just want to hear you talk to me in your sweetest voice and feel your energy." So she began to tell John about her day at the library. "I was working on DNA testing and found a wealth of information that will contribute to my job at IONS." He smiled and said, "I'm happy for you. Want to tell me more?" She continued on and realized it must be boring to him so she tried to make it as interesting but as short as possible. She could not let on about any of the synchronicities she encountered and realized that this was really only turning into small talk and wanted instead to get to the heart of what was troubling him.

Ava just came right out with it. "John, I'm sensing you have a problem that you wish to talk to me about." John, looked sad but as they were arriving at the restaurant, he said, "I'm okay Ava, let's talk inside." They walked into the restaurant and took the same table as they did on their first date. This time, Ava wasn't smiling. What is going on and why have I not been given a heads up about this shift in our energy from Zachary. Ava realized that Zachary was not permitted to provide future predictions but only to support and guide and Ava would have to do the work of connecting the dots. She was playing that old futile game of seeking blame and she could never disrespect Zachary with such pedestrian, childish behavior.

Ava decided to redirect her energy in a more positive light suspecting that maybe John was nervous about possibly asking her to marry her! Wow, wouldn't that be amazing she said to herself. Now that's a better way of looking at things, but I hadn't ever thought about marriage. I wonder if I would need time to think. Heck, if it were me asking, I'd be preoccupied as well.

They each ordered their meals and John took out a brochure from his inside pocket and told Ava he would like them to attend Shakespeare by the Sea at the Newport Pier in two weeks. They are performing "A Midsummer Night's Dream". Ava was delighted. She immediately agreed and told herself, silly girl, this is not your last date! Nevertheless she knew John was keeping something from her and was a little disappointed that he didn't realize he could talk to her about anything, even marriage. John seemed to relax a bit after his Martini and they continued to have a delightful dinner. John asked if they could walk along the beach together like they did on their first date. Ava smiled and said, "I was hoping you would ask, only this time we don't have to go home in separate cars to separate homes. We will spend the night together wrapped in each other's arms." John smiled and said, "how things have changed".

They walked along the beach and John was extremely passionate, hardly ever letting go of Ava. He kissed her over and over again and they talked about the stars and the sound of the surf. He decided that he would take his shoes and socks off and put his feet in the freezing water. Ava dared him and called him a reckless crazy man as they laughed and giggled. John playfully tried to push Ava into the water and she playfully fought back. Memories of their fun together flooded Ava's mind and she couldn't understand why she had any doubts of their relationship. She kept wondering if he was going to propose marriage right here on the beach but he never did. It was okay with Ava. All good things come to those who wait she said to herself. She had not ever given marriage a thought. For Ava, it was never a priority but if John wanted that, she would have no objection. She felt they were extremely compatible and could foresee a beautiful future together. At this moment she had no worries and John was back to his usual delicious self.

They went back to his house and had a passionate night of lovemaking and a peaceful night's rest holding each other tightly as if nothing else in the world existed or even mattered.

Nevertheless, Ava knew something was up. John was wrestling with something on his mind and he simply could not find the courage yet to talk to her about it. Ava would cut him some slack. She knew the human condition could be quite fragile at times which made it difficult to face reality. John would communicate with Ava when John was ready. She was going to let it go for now.

As the week passed, Ava continued with more voluntary research in the field of diagnosing Autism and learned of another diagnosis that is found in some Autistic children called Fragile X Syndrome which was considered to be an inherited condition characterized by an X chromosome that is abnormally susceptible to damage, especially by folic acid deficiency. Affected individuals tend to be mentally handicapped and resemble mental characteristics of Autism. She had never heard of this condition and it was just now in the beginning stages of discovery. Understanding this mutation provided her with more genetic DNA research and a greater sense of how she would approach her upcoming future at IONS. She was grateful for every opportunity that would enhance her communications with individuals possessing these conditions always keeping in mind, the genetic sequencing could potentially be a natural human evolutionary process of our DNA.

CHAPTER 38

First Days At IONS

Ava was more than excited to begin her new adventure. She could hardly contain her enthusiasm but understood she had plenty to grasp and get accustomed to. This was the big league now and she had humanity's future at stake. Well, at least their evolved vision at this stage of their evolution.

She was immediately greeted by Dr. Grace Lynch who had a magnetic smile for her and a warm and welcoming handshake. Dr. Lynch said, "Finally, you're here. We are so looking forward to have you join our team. I'd like you to once again meet in the conference room with the doctors you met at the interview and then I'd like to get you settled into your office space."

Ava enjoyed the surroundings and decor that IONS chose and again felt very much at home in this environment almost as if she belonged here. She supposed it was written in the stars.

Ava presented her recent genetic findings with all three doctors in the conference room. They were quite impressed and Dr. Lynch was delighted to have found this brilliant student. She knew there was something about Ava that was ethereal and could bring a fresh insightful perspective to their research. Several hours had passed and everyone was beginning to get hungry. Dr. Lynch directed Ava to her office to put her papers down and asked her to join her in the cafeteria for some lunch. She promised her there would be no shop talk to give their minds a rest. The rest of the afternoon, Ava would simply settle in and get acclimated to her new surroundings.

After lunch Ava decided to call John from her private office and let him know how things were going. John was very excited for her. "Oh John, this is the greatest place in the world! I am so thrilled to be involved in this research and tomorrow I get to meet my first patient, and guess what his name is? You'll never believe it! James Bond." John laughed and joked that maybe she was really working for the CIA under the guise of IONS. She laughed at his humor and then at the humor of his parents obviously being fans of Ian Fleming's books on James Bond and named their son after him.

Nevertheless, he is a complex case. "He is only seven years old and has many difficulties that smack of the research I've been doing." John listened intently and told Ava, "If he can be reached by anyone Ava, it will be you my sweet." Ava appreciated John's confidence in her and it felt good that he was so proud of her. "Will I see you tonight?" Ava asked John. He hesitated and said, "I think you need your rest after the first day on your new job Ava." Ava was disappointed and could hear the tone in John's voice that he was thinking about something very intently and was eager to speak to her about it but was still not ready. "Okay," she said. "I will miss you." John said, "I will miss you too honey. Starting a new job of your nature requires good sound rest and your meditation." "Well, you do have a point John. I'll be sure to get some rest. I miss you and I look forward to Shakespeare by the Sea this weekend." "Me too" he said. "I'll see you on Thursday night if that's okay with you." "Yes," said Ava. "That would be fine. My place or yours?" "Why don't we have dinner at Laguna Beach and then we'll head back to your house," he said. I smiled and said, "Sounds wonderful."

Ava could not shake the idea that things were different. There was a certain tone in his voice that was foretelling but she tried so hard to keep herself thinking positively. She thought about having a session with Zachary that night. It might provide her with guidance and then realized she had never had a dream about John and thought that was strange. She had concerns about being distracted at this point in her life. She couldn't pretend that things were great, however. Ava decided to call upon some of her alchemical powers to invoke a vision that might lead to the reasoning behind John's shift in energy.

She first went into a Chakra meditation to clear her own energy fields and then put herself in a trancelike state. Upon opening her eyes she could see a large white projector screen and from the corner of the screen John entered holding a piece of mail. The screen began to populate with the details of his den. John looked puzzled as he opened the letter and then he looked shocked. Ava zoomed in on the letter and could see it was addressed to him from the National Gallery of Art in London. With further concentration she could see that he was receiving congratulatory news of his application for the curator and was being offered the position at this most prestigious institution. She could see the anguish on John's face. He looked torn apart and confused.

Ava was stunned and with the energy of sheer disappointment and anguish, the vision popped out of view. Her heart sank to her feet.

She was completely devastated and felt a sensation of mental and emotional shock. She sat on her living room floor for what felt like hours. She didn't want to live without John yet she would never consider standing in the way of what could potentially be his dream. Tears began to roll down her face. She wanted to scream. She felt anger. Ava had not yet experienced this type human emotional toil that comes with Earthbound realities, however, she was experiencing it now.

Why hadn't John communicated this to her? Why did he look so disappointed in the vision? She was confused and almost felt remorse about conducting the alchemy exercise. She was grateful to know that her detection of his energy shift was accurate and began to pull the pieces together. She clearly saw the angst on John's face as he read the acceptance letter and realized that his news must have felt like a double-edged sword to him. The sword of Excalibur, would he draw it from the Stone or would he leave it there. What a predicament he has found himself in. Why had he not told Ava of his plans in the first place? Ava felt a sense of betrayal but did not want to make a hasty judgment. After all, sometimes we may see or know information but it does not always convey the full picture of a situation. Ava would ask John about his emotional shift without telling him of her vision. She would give him the benefit of the doubt and allow him to reveal his intentions in his time. Ava was comforted by the memory of something Zachary quoted to her from the book Dan Millman wrote "The way of the Peaceful Warrior". **"All along I've shown you by example that a warrior's life is not about imagined perfection or victory, it is about love. Love is a warrior's sword; where it cuts, it gives life, not death."** She had to allow John the freedom and time to make his decision regardless of her emotional response to it. It was the loving thing to do. Besides, her own abilities and identity were being hidden from him in spite of the agenda forced upon her in a sacred, solemn assertion for the sake of humanity which she accepted from the depth of her soul.

She and John were to meet again on Thursday evening but she decided that she would tell him she'd rather they have a quiet dinner at home rather than go to a restaurant as he had suggested. She would try to persuade him to talk about what she knew to be a shift in his energy, one of preoccupation and would try to coerce a discussion about it with as little pressure on him as possible. Now Ava needed to get some sleep for her day at IONS tomorrow and her first time meeting James Bond.

Ava began her day at IONS meeting her first patient, James. She was given background medical and psychological screening information and found him to be a complex personality. James rarely spoke and when he did, it would be in one or two words only. He was seven years old and was diagnosed with Fragile X Syndrome and Autism. He did not exhibit much interest in social interaction and experienced seizures and sleepless nights. By all accounts, on paper at least, he appeared to be a complex confusing case. However, Ava knew better. She needed to come face-to-face with little Mr. Bond and get to know him in a spiritual capacity more so than the picture painted on a medical report.

Ava entered the conference room equipped with a double-panel view window so that Dr. Lynch and the others could witness their interaction. An aid knocked on the door before entering with James at her side. Ava and James locked eyes and both greeted each other with big smiles. Dr. Lynch, viewing from the other side of the panel was quite shocked by James' smile. He, for the most part was expressionless especially when meeting people for the first time. He extended his hand to Ava for a handshake. Everyone on the other side of the panel were quite surprised. Ava introduced herself to James and they both seated themselves at the table.

James kept smiling at Ava and stared into her eyes, occasionally looking away but then stared back into her eyes again, then looked away and once again back to staring at her eyes again. Ava could not help but smile at him. Ava asked him, "James are you happy today?" James simply responded by showing Ava his tie. He uttered the word "tie." Ava acknowledged that it was a very handsome tie and he was well dressed. This delighted James who could not stop grinning. He pointed to Ava's dress and said, "pretty." Everyone was in an excited mode and in disbelief at how quickly and easily James had taken to Ava.

Ava asked James if he would like to play a game or draw or listen to music. James responded with "yes." Ava chuckled to herself and said, "Well which would you like to do?" James responded by saying, "All three." Ava was now quite surprised. This little boy was counting the activities and wanted to do all three activities with Ava. What a delight! She asked him what he would like to start doing first? James said, "Paper." Ava pulled a blank piece of paper from her pad and handed James several color pencils. James immediately went for the red one and in a complete sentence said, "This is my favorite color."

Ava was confused. She distinctly remembered from his report that he could only speak one or two words and never put a whole sentence together. She continued on with her session asking James why red was his favorite color. He could not give Ava an answer. He just kept scribbling on the paper in the red pencil. Ava wanted to know if James could write his name. James began to write the letter J and then began scribbling. "James," Ava asked, "Do you know how to write the rest of the letters of your name?" James did not respond to that question. He continued to write the letter J over and over. Ava acknowledged that James was doing an excellent job. She then realized that writing his name was not drawing and asked him to draw something instead of writing. With that recognition of wording in James' mind which was one of Ava's initial three requests, James began to draw a heart still using the red pencil.

Ava began to suspect that she was not dealing with a non-communicative human. It was the humans' asking the questions of him that were off track. Ava was developing a process of entering into his mind which she began to suspect was indeed quite responsive after all.

Ava wanted to know what James wished to do next? He clearly said, "Math." Ava was quite surprised he knew what math was and that he verbalized it. She asked James, "What is math?" James took a green pencil and turned the paper over and began to write mathematical equations for Ava. James looked at Ava and called her silly for not knowing what math was. Ava laughed and so did James. He went on to say, "Easy, 1+1=2; hard E=mc2." Ava's eyes opened wide and asked James if he knew what that meant. James looked at Ava with a surprised look on his face and said, "Of course".

Ava felt silly. This little boy was actually making her feel foolish. She laughed to herself. Ava's suspicions felt validated that the institute may have approached his capabilities from a level of a standard Autistic aptitude approach as opposed to challenging those standards.

Suddenly, James looked up at the corner of the room and said the name Zachary. Ava was shocked! "James, who is Zachary?" "You know Ava," was his response. "Do you see Zachary James?" "Yes, he is over there." Ava was beginning to feel a tinge of panic knowing that he was really seeing Zachary and wondering what the folks on the other side of the panel must be thinking. She quickly changed the subject and persuaded James to write more math. James accommodated and began to write out long division. She wanted to know how he knew long division but James did not answer her.

Suddenly James told Ava, "Zachary in dream." Ava could feel a surge of energy run through her and realized this was the little boy in several of her dreams, one of which contained Zachary. She needed to sort out a few things and wanted to know if James was now tired and wanted to end their time together. James responded by saying, "If you need to." Ava felt like the student. This little seven year old boy was putting her in a precarious position mostly because they were being observed. She wanted alone time, one-on-one with him so that they could share their secrets. She knew he was a highly evolved being and recognized Ava for her true identity. Ava suggested that they end their session only because it was necessary to understand why he was so communicative with her and not others and why he exhibited math skills only to her and not others. James looked at Ava and smiled and said, "Because you are Ava". Ava reciprocated with a smile and a gleam in her eye. She tapped little Mr. James Bond on his nose and said, "That's right and we are going to be great friends." James beamed a huge smile and stood up to shake her hand but instead he wrapped his arms around her and said, "Good bye Ava. See you tomorrow." "Yes you will James. I so look forward to it." And off he went escorted by the aid who brought him in.

The doctors entered the room after James left buzzing about the encounter. No one could believe it. "How in the world is this possible Ava?" they asked. "What in the world?" Ava responded with amazement herself but explained that her conclusion may have been based on the approach to his assumed disability. "Yes, he does have communication issues, however, if he is approached as a "normal" seven year old, he can pick up on that energy and respond likewise. He doesn't see himself as disabled in anyway. If anything, he does not express himself to those examining him because he considers them disabled and therefore withdraws because he surmises that there is no ability to communicate with those who are not like-minded as himself.

Of course, we will conduct more sessions and delve further into his responses and capabilities. I think James had a very positive reaction to me because of my own belief that these are not necessarily "disabled" children and because I'm willing to explore the idea that they are simply on a different wavelength than what is considered "normal". Ava added, "you know, an alteration of DNA should not necessarily be looked upon as an abnormality. Just because we can identify a change in someone's DNA doesn't mean they are not "right". It could simply mean, there is an evolution taking place."

Secretly, Ava really knew that James knew who she was and was hoping he would not give away her identity. She probably had nothing to worry about, after all, this whole event was already written in the stars.

John's Decision

Ava called John when she arrived home. She was eager to hear his voice and to tell him about her day. There was not much change in his tone and he was willing to switch their plans and have dinner at Ava's house and spend the evening. She was delighted. Maybe this was a good sign and she would be able to have a discussion with him if he was willing to open up.

Ava made spaghetti and meatballs which she knew John enjoyed and he would be over in time to start the salad. She asked him to stop off and bring the Italian bread and he suggested some red wine as well. She was excited to be with him again and missed him dearly. She was hoping for an enlightening evening and an open honest discussion.

John was on time as always. She loved that about him, heck she loved everything about him. They kissed at the front door and John was smiling. He was happy to see her. They entered the kitchen together and began preparing their meal with smiles on their faces and a couple of kisses and playful body rubs during the process. Ava felt hopeful but she knew it wasn't necessarily the answer to her concerns. They were just a very sexual couple who took great delight in each other's bodies.

As they prepared the dining room table lit with romantic candles and crystal wine glasses, John asked her about her meeting with James. Ava was happy to report it had gone extremely well. She suggested that her research and suspicions were indeed encouraging and she was on a new path of working with Autistic souls. "I'm so glad to hear that Ava" he replied. "I knew, even though I did not have the background knowledge, that you were onto some breakthrough discovery. I had full confidence in you." "Thank you sweetie" I said to him. "That is very kind of you to say."

John continued to talk about Ava and how she had a sense of knowing that was extremely unique and insightful, "It's almost as if you can see through people. You are a very special lady." Ava commented, "Are you the Ava St. Claire Fan Club President speaking?" They laughed. "No honey, I'm serious. You are a remarkable person, unlike anyone else I have ever met." "John, you sound like a man in love. You know I have my faults too" said Ava. John immediately said he had not found any yet.

Ava thought this was the perfect segue to bring up her detection in the change of his energy so she took the opportunity. "Well John, would you agree that my observation of a shift in your energy as of late is accurate?" John looked at her with soulful eyes as if he was not at all surprised she detected the change. He asked if they could clear the table and load the dishwasher because he wanted to sit on the couch and talk to her about something that she might be able to help him with. "Sure," Ava said. But her heart was pounding, wondering what direction he was going in. Would he pull Excalibur's sword or was he going to leave it in the stone?

They completed their chores and sat on the couch listening to Mozart softly on the stereo with a peaceful fire lit in the fireplace. John began talking. "Long before I met you, I had submitted an application to The National Gallery in London for an open position as curator. I hadn't heard back from them so I never mentioned it.

I assumed they passed me up. I hadn't given it any further thought. Then you came into my life and I have fallen madly in love with you. I think of you constantly and I want to be with you constantly. I'm fascinated by your loving ways, and your openness, your fun-loving nature and insatiable thirst for knowledge and how sweetly and gregariously we make love. You are the best thing in my life Ava. You have brought new life to me. However, I received a letter from the Gallery in the mail last week and they accepted my application and offered me the position. I was amazed that it took so long and quite shocked that I was selected. It is a brilliant position and it would cap off my career in the arts with great flourish and honors. I could go down in history. I would be hobnobbing with the greats in the art world. There would be magazine articles about me and I would be connected to all the art museums around the world. I find myself in a conundrum that feels like a cruel twist of fate. I want my cake and I want to eat it too.

I love you Ava, but I don't know what to do? I would love for you to join me and continue your work in London but I feel terribly selfish asking you to do that. I've checked and IONS does not have a campus in London. I am perplexed and feel awful about something that should be such wonderful news."

Ava rubbed John's neck and shoulder with great concern. She was looking at a man who truly was in pain over having to make this decision. She tried to find words to comfort him and yet with all her foresight she had none. She began to cry and it surprised her. She empathized with John saying, "If I had to make that type of choice it would tear me apart too. We want our cake and we want to eat it to. I suppose when faced with a decision like this, one needs to consider what is most important, bringing ourselves to the bare tacks and envision life without one of the two and experience what that feels like. John, I don't want to lose you. You have made my life complete. I love you and it would hurt very very deeply if I had to say good bye.

You complete me but I would never be able to live with myself if

I did not allow you the opportunity to advance and blossom in what you love. I wouldn't dream of holding you back from anything that might make you happy and add to your growth. I could never live with myself knowing that I've hampered an opportunity for you to be happy even if it meant crushing my heart to pieces."

"See that's what I mean about you Ava, you'd be willing to accept your own heartache rather than see another lose out on their own happiness. Ava, I believe this decision is mine to make. I felt responsible to communicate this in all fairness to you but it is my decision. It is a difficult one and I'm torn to pieces at the thought of not having you in my life. As you would not hold me back, I cannot expect you to drop your achievements and potential and move to London with me for the sake of my happiness. Ava, let me go home now and search for my answer. I'm sorry to cut the evening so short but I do have a bit of soul searching to do and unfortunately not much time since I've got to give them an answer in a week." Ava told him she understood as her heart jumped into her throat and held back sobs of tears. She told him "remember John, the freedom of choice, you always have a choice. Which feels better? When you think of one decision how does it feel, and then think of the opposite decision and feel how that feels. Whichever feels lightest, is the right one. Your thoughts will project your future."

They rose from the couch and John put on his jacket. Ava walked him to the front door and he held her tightly and kissed her passionately. Ava wondered if this kiss was their last. He left with a look of sadness on his face that broke Ava's heart. She wanted so much to make it easy for him but knew she had nothing to do with this decision. It was John's to make. It was his path to follow. She could not interfere even though her heart was breaking both for herself as well as for him. Ava felt ill-equipped for this emotional sensation of being human.

She fell back onto the couch in human despair and before she could begin crying, Zachary appeared. She smiled at him and said, "Hello Zachary. You knew I needed to talk." Zachary responded, **OF**

COURSE AVA, I'M HERE FOR YOU ALWAYS. I AM YOUR GUIDE AND SOURCE OF WISDOM.

Zachary, "I will not use any of my mystical powers to interfere with John's future. It would be a discretion that I would and must, by the laws of the Universe, make amends for as I am here and now. I will exhibit the secret of grace and abide by the absolute decree of my own supreme power. Infallibly it will come to pass that which is John's divine right to his life as he chooses."

Zachary interjected **"GOD HAS ENLIGHTENED THE HUMAN MIND IN ANY WAY HE PLEASES. BUT HE HIMSELF MAY SPEAK TO THE PROPHET AND ILLUMINATE HIS MIND.**

"Zachary, do you believe the God within John is asking me to illuminate his mind?" **AGAIN, THE SUPERNATURAL LIGHT OF PROPHECY MAY BE CONVEYED TO THE INTELLECT OR THROUGH THE SENSES OR THE IMAGINATION. YOU HAVE ALREADY PLANTED THE SEED AVA.**

"We fell in love Zachary. There was no foreknowledge on my part that a love as deep as ours would be formed." Zachary continued explaining **YOUR MAGNETISM AND ENERGY FIELD MANIFESTED THIS LOVE AVA. IF NOT JOHN, IT WOULD HAVE BEEN SOMEONE SIMILAR TO JOHN. HIS ENERGY FIELD COALESCED WELL WITH YOURS AND HENCE A GENUINE JOINING OF SOULS WAS THE RESULT. YOU MUST NOT LOOK UPON THIS EVENT AS SOMETHING IN ERROR OR DIABOLICAL ON YOUR PART. YOUR DESIRE TO NOT INTERFERE WITH JOHN'S DECISION IS FUTILE. YOU HAVE ALREADY DONE SO. HE PROFESSES HIS LOVE FOR YOU WHICH MAKES HIS DECISION DIFFICULT. THE SECRET OF PREDESTINATION HAS BEEN REVEALED ONLY IN EXCEPTIONAL CASES, BUT THAT OF REPROBATION HAS NEVER BEEN REVEALED BECAUSE SO LONG AS THE SOUL IS IN THIS LIFE, ITS SALVATION IS POSSIBLE. IF YOU CHOOSE TO KNOW THE**

OUTCOME, YOU MAY UTILIZE ALCHEMY OR YOU MAY ALLOW YOURSELF NO INTERFERENCE WHATSOEVER. YOU, OF COURSE, MAY NOT DELIBERATELY ALTER HIS FUTURE. IT IS YOUR CHOICE AVA, YOU ALWAYS HAVE A CHOICE. VIEWING YOUR FUTURE IS NOT AGAINST THE RULES. UNFAIRLY INFLUENCING ANOTHER'S DECISION FOR YOUR GAIN IS INDEED AGAINST THE RULES. AGAIN, IT IS YOUR CHOICE AVA.

Ava thanked Zachary for his guidance and reminders of the rules of this game of life. She felt a greater sense of peace and harmony even within the midst of her human emotional conflict. She would remain true to her convictions to not know what the future held. She would allow the Universe its freedom and not hold onto any forced outcomes or stress over what those outcomes might be. She would remain in faith with whatever the result might be, shelving her emotional needs which would only interfere with attracting the best possible result for all concerned.

After meditation, Ava went to bed peacefully falling into a sleep pretending she was being held in the arms of John.

When Ava awoke the following morning, she was mesmerized by the dream she had recalled and began writing in her journal:

> "I found myself again in the sky among the clouds. At first no one else was there. Suddenly a man unfamiliar to me appeared. He began to speak "I chose you and appointed you to go forth and create everlasting change." I began to show this man my white blouse and said that the shoulders of the blouse did not fit, they were too big. He replied, "Those are for the wings that you are growing. Soon you will know that they fit perfectly." Suddenly I saw a little

> boy in the far distance and figured he could only be James. He never approached me. Afterward, I began to fly with the wings the man said I would grow into and found myself gliding over the Pacific Ocean. I landed on the lifeguard station and folded my wings which then disappeared. Sheila came by and said, "Look at my ring! I'm engaged!" I looked at her ring and said it was marvelous and congratulated her. Then John walked up to me and said, "Your's is quite beautiful too Ava." I was puzzled and looked down at my hand. I had a beautiful diamond ring on it."

Ava realized that even beyond her knowing and Zachary's guidance, she was predestined to live this life with her clear knowing. She was the one gliding above the ocean providing lifeguard protection to those who would come into her circle of energy. Her waking conviction to not know the future was even more futile than ever since within her dream state she would allow certainty to come to her situation providing she trusted her interpretation as accurate. Then she realized Zachary's words from a while back, **SOON YOU WILL FLY AVA!**

It did not matter if the ring on her finger was from John or from the Universe, she was engaged in her efforts of transformation within herself and within the world she was living in. For the first time she realized she dreamt of John. John was guiding her in the dream. Imagine that! He was, in a sense, telling her that she was engaged as well, however, not necessarily to him but to humanity. She knew John was as committed to her work as much as she was.

It seemed like a good indication of the decision John would make but only time would tell.

She now needed to start her day of work and was anxious to see James again and wondered what their session would reveal.

At work, Ava began reviewing her paperwork and emails and had a cheerful morning greeting for everyone she met. Her schedule showed she had a 10:00 AM session with James. She was hoping it would take them to lunchtime. She was grateful that the previous day's events were not stuck in her energy field for James' sake. She wondered if James knew about her dream last night and if he had any awareness of being in it.

Ava asked Dr. Lynch if her session with James could be arranged in a more relaxed, playful setting rather than the conference room. She felt a young child's classroom set up would be more fun and add a curious dimension to her sessions with James. Dr. Lynch was in full agreement and made the arrangements. "We do have one in particular that also supplies a two way panel for observation purposes as well. Let me show you where it is." She headed to the classroom and was delighted to see smaller chairs and tables and a colorful pallet of pictures and books surrounding the room albeit, minimal. Dr. Lynch explained that sensory issues could interfere with an Autistic child's ability to focus and gain centering. Ava understood the thinking but knew that James would not be concerned about these details. James was beyond these issues when Ava was with him. He was more about exploring the consciousness of her Light Being identity and knew, because of that, he was free to be exactly who he was.

James entered the room with his aid. He greeted Ava with a great big smile and looked happily around. He was so excited they were there together. He was familiar with this particular room and wanted to show Ava everything! He walked up to certain books and pointing to them would tell her in a single word, what the book was. He walked up to pictures and squealed with delight telling her what the picture meant to him. Ava couldn't help but smile. She asked

James what his favorite color was. James happily replied, "Pink." Ava asked him if he could point out something pink in the room and he did so. She asked him with the intention to discover if James saw letters as colors. She asked James, "What letter is the color pink?". The doctors behind the panel looked puzzled and wondered where Ava was going with this. They wondered why would a letter be represented as a color? James immediately responded, "O is pink."

Ava understood that synesthesia is an involuntary joining in which the real information of one sense is accompanied by a perception in another sense. Synesthesia is in violation of conventional perception and this would fit in perfectly with how James viewed the world. She asked James to come sit at the table next to her and write out each letter of the alphabet in the color he saw it as. James did so without hesitation. The doctors again were quite amazed. Ava on the other hand, understood perfectly that James' perceptions were misunderstood by almost everyone and she could develop a trust and communication with James beyond conventional principles. Ava understood that our spirit and every cell of our body is multidimensional and that only our conscious awareness is trained to lie in the limitations and restrictions of the three-dimensional matrix. James was unable to live in the three dimensional matrix and with guidance and assistance could be shown how to do so without effecting his brilliant gifts sourced from a multidimensional Universe.

She then wanted James to decide what he wished to explore next. James quickly said, "Italy and Japan." Ava looked around the room and found a very fundamental book on Italy. She figured it would do for now but knew James would be able to comprehend and explore more than this room had to offer. James looked at the book and spoke the word "Boring." Ava laughed and said, "I know James. Tomorrow I will bring you a more elaborate book that you will relate to with more depth and enjoyment." James said, "Good." They began to look at the book together and James could recite for Ava, verbatim what every picture was. Ava was surprised but then again not really. She asked James if he had ever been to Italy and he immediately responded, "Yes." Ava had no doubt that he had probably traveled the world astrally in his dream states. The doctors behind the panel were thinking that James was lying when he said yes.

Ava then asked James if he had a dream last night. James looked at her with a special grin and said, "Yes." "Do you know what the dream was about James?" His response was an emphatic "You, Ava." They smiled at each other and James lifted his tiny hand and brushed it against Ava's face and told her, "Hang in there." Ava wanted to cry but wouldn't allow herself to do so. She filled with emotion because she understood this little boy knew exactly what her underlying concerns were and indeed was present with her in the dream, or rather, "their" dream.

The doctors behind the panel were now completely baffled by these two and how they interacted with each other. They had no clear reasoning for their connection but were witnessing it first hand. They couldn't wait to sit with Ava after the session to have her explain what in the world is going on between you two?

Ava asked James if he spoke another language besides English. James said, "Of course." She asked him if he could speak to her in another language. James immediately spoke the words, "wata shi no namea wa James des." Ava said, "Yo Ko Deki Masta! You told me your name is James in Japanese. Do you like the Japanese language?" James' response was yes and then continued to say in Japanese, "Tsu ka re ta." "OK James, I understand. You are tired. It has been a good visit and you need some rest. Tomorrow I will try to gain permission to bring you a special book on countries of the world that we can explore, okay?" James looked at Ava with a smile and said, "Yes, Arigato," meaning thank you. He rose from his chair and hugged Ava and said good bye.

In all honesty, Ava was tired as well but she still had analyzing to do and especially explaining to the other doctors on the panel what her approach had been and why it led to James' sudden transformation. She knew James didn't suddenly transform. She was approaching him as she knew him to be, an enlightened soul. She began to feel the conflict of John's decision affect her again and decided she and Dr. Lynch should lunch together while discussing the progress made in her session with James thereby nourishing herself and equalizing her energy field at the same time. She reflected on James touching her face and telling her to hang in there. How perceptive he was but that was no real surprise. James understood the exact frequency currents going on around him and only had interest for what recognized his field of energy and respected that. He had no interest in anything that did not reflect his vibration however, integrating that would become important to at least ground him to this plane just a little. After all, his probable future would have a transformative and powerful effect on humanity.

As the day ended, Ava began to feel the human pain of her predicament with John. She didn't want to go home but she was too mentally drained to remain at work any longer. She gathered her briefcase with pertinent papers and took off for home knowing how empty it would feel and everything around it would only remind her of the possibility of losing John. She needed to shake this feeling. It was not of any benefit to her. She could do her Yoga and meditate to raise her frequency and maintain a focus of allowing the Universe the freedom to act in everyone's best interest.

Ava felt in dire need of sleep and wanted to forego her usual rituals of exercise and meditation but knew it would be detrimental to her well-being. Suddenly, she had a thought that in a strange way, lifted her spirits. I think I will put my ruffled blue dress on, the one that I wore on my first date with John and head to the beach. It will feel so rejuvenating to see the sunset while standing on the cliff bridge looking up into the night sky as the glittering stars began to perform. Somehow that thought made Ava feel refreshed and hopeful.

As she drove herself to the beach, tears started to run down her face listening to U2's song, "One" on her radio. Memories of her and

John listening to it that day driving to Newport flooded her mind with sweetness and desire that she wasn't sure she would have with him again. Ava arrived at the cliff bridge and parked her car. She decided to leave her shoes and walk barefoot. She really didn't know why. Maybe it had something to do with feeling more grounded to Mother Nature, nothing to separate the two of them.

She indeed watched a glorious sunset manifest and it reminded her of her dream of Joshua Tree. She realized that she had an enriched life beyond what most people could feel even though there still existed the possibility that John would not be a part of it. As the golden liquid of the sun poured into the waters of the ocean, the night sky came into focus in all its dazzling, mysterious beauty. Ava soaked it in as if she were the ocean receiving the day's sunset looking up into the night sky. Sania seemed like a distant memory by now and she reflected on her existence there and felt very far away from that life now. She wondered when she would return and if indeed she would be heading back there or to another dimension of even greater magical experiences.

Suddenly, she heard her name being called. Startled from her dreamy thoughts she wondered if Zachary were here. It would be the first time he would have shown himself in public. Maybe it is time for me to go she wondered. She heard her name again. As she turned around she was ecstatic to see John walking toward her! John called out to her again and Ava rushed up to him in total amazement and surprise. He wrapped his arms around her so tightly she could hardly breath. She hugged him and said, "John, John, tell me what are you doing here?"

John told Ava that he could not live without her. There was no way he would give up on the love they shared. He held her tightly close to him and kissed her with a magic that resembled the melding of two souls. When Ava could catch her breath she asked John, "Are you sure, John, this is the dream job of a lifetime?" John said to Ava while still holding her tightly, "Ava, what is more important, the job of a lifetime or the soul of a lifetime?" Ava began to well up with tears and they kissed again with tears streaming down both their faces blending into one majestic waterfall. Finally, with great exuberance Ava jumped onto John's hips and shouted out to the Universe "Thank You!"

They both laughed and turned to the parking lot holding hands and talking. John spoke first and said to Ava, "I think I'm going to open an art gallery right here in Laguna Beach." Ava smiled with delight and said, "What a perfect idea." She then looked up at John smiling with a twinkle in her eye and said, "Honey, I think I'm going to write a book."

##

Printed in the United States
By Bookmasters